Penguin Books
Flamingo Feather

Laurens van der Post was born in Africa in 1906.
Most of his adult life has been spent with one foot
there and one in England. His professions of writer
and farmer were interrupted by ten years of
soldiering – behind enemy lines in Abyssinia, and
also in the Western Desert and the Far East, where
he was taken prisoner by the Japanese while
commanding a small guerrilla unit. He went
straight from prison back to active service in Java,
served on Lord Mountbatten's staff and, when
the British forces withdrew from Java, remained
behind as Military Attaché to the British Minister.
Since 1949 he has undertaken several official
missions exploring little-known parts of Africa.
His independent expedition to the Kalahari
Desert in search of the Bushmen was the subject
of his famous documentary film and of *The Lost
World of the Kalahari*. His other books include
Venture to the Interior (1952), *The Face Beside the
Fire* (1953), *The Dark Eye in Africa* (1955), *The
Heart of the Hunter* (1963), *Journey into Russia*
(1964), *The Hunter and the Whale* (1967), *A Portrait
of Japan* (1968), *A Story Like the Wind* (1972), *A
Far-Off Place* (1974), *A Mantis Carol* (1975),
Jung and the Story of Our Time (1976) and *First
Catch Your Eland: a taste of Africa* (1977). His
latest book is *Yet Being Someone Other*. Colonel
van der Post, who is married, was awarded the
C.B.E. for his services in the field, and was
knighted in 1981.

Laurens van der Post

Flamingo Feather

A STORY OF AFRICA

Le rêve est le vrai dieu des Primitifs
LEVY-BRUHL

Penguin Books
in association with The Hogarth Press

Penguin Books Ltd, Harmondsworth, Middlesex, England
Penguin Books, 40 West 23rd Street, New York, New York 10010, U.S.A.
Penguin Books Australia Ltd, Ringwood, Victoria, Australia
Penguin Books Canada Ltd, 2801 John Street, Markham, Ontario, Canada L3R 1B4
Penguin Books (N.Z.) Ltd, 182–190 Wairau Road, Auckland 10, New Zealand

First published by The Hogarth Press 1955
Published in Penguin Books 1965
Reprinted 1973, 1977, 1978, 1983, 1984

Made and printed in Singapore by
Richard Clay (S.E. Asia) Pte Ltd
Set in Linotype Times

To Maria Magdalena van der Post, my mother,
and the many good and dear people of all colours
who made the fast vanishing Africa of my
vanished boyhood

Contents

I owe more than I can say to my wife,
Ingaret Giffard, for preparing my manuscript
for publication and for keeping the
desire to write alive in me

Chapter 1

Feather at Nightfall

My story has its manifest beginning in that moment when I came out on the stoep of my house in the turbulent twilight and heard on the steep slope below me the sound of desperate running, followed almost immediately by the exultant war-cry of the Amangtakwena: 'Mattalahta Buka!' 'At last we kill!'

The year was 1948, the day 12 July, the hour 5.30 in the afternoon and the place my own home, which stands high on a slope of the grey mountains behind the village of St Joseph's in the peninsula of the Cape of Good Hope. On a clear day I have a superb view north over the blue waters of the Bay to where the far purple Hottentots-Holland Mountains push the incredible Cape Hangklip so determinedly into the sea that, as its name 'Hanging Rock' implies, it leans heavily over its own base to stare sombrely into the waters of the Indian Ocean snorting wearily far below. But that evening as I came out on the stoep there was no view at all except smoking village lights. Not only was the day nearly over but also the fierce storm had suppressed what little glimmer of light was normally left at that hour. I slammed the front door quickly behind me because of the gale. The cry that had gone up and the sound of those desperate feet was still clearly in my ears despite the wind's moaning.

It was the last sort of cry I would have expected at that time and in that place. Though there are many 'Takwena * working in the Peninsula, they do not go roaring and plundering through the suburbs over week-ends as a number of other tribesmen do. Yet I did not doubt my senses for one second. I know the 'Takwena well. They are my favourite African people. I had in fact, only a few minutes before stopped writing in the midst of the nineteenth chapter of my work, *The Mind and Myth of the Amangtakwena*. So, as I heard those voices come ringing with

* The Amangtakwena are popularly called that.

9

a dark, archaic will straight out of authentic 'Takwena hearts and throats, I found myself spurred unhesitatingly into action.

On either side of the front door of my house are two very beautiful Somali shields which I once brought back with me from the north-west frontier of Kenya. Each is flanked with an heraldic cluster of the most decorative and deadly Masai throwing spears. So great was the feeling of urgency released in me by that cry, and so instinctive my acceptance of the fact that somehow I was there in a relation of special responsibility towards it, that I wasted no time on going back into the house to fetch a gun but jumped towards the right-hand cluster of spears. Doing so, I saw the face of Umtumwa, my personal servant, my old batman and friend in war and peace, appear at the drawing-room window hard by. His massive, distinguished 'Takwena face, nose flat and ridiculously wrinkled, was pressed tightly against the glass, as it was each evening for a last brief look-out before he drew the curtains on the dying day.

'Umtumwa, follow me quick!' I shouted at the top of my voice, while wrenching a spear out of the socket with such force that the whole lot clattered to the ground.

A look I'd often seen on his face in the war in Burma possessed Umtumwa's features. Instantly he vanished from the amber window and I knew he'd not only heard my cry but understood its urgent nature.

I've never moved faster in my life as I went down the twenty-one steps leading from the stoep to the drive which led into the garden. But Umtumwa came faster still, for I heard his heavy naked feet thud on the ground not far behind me. Yet alas! we were neither of us fast enough.

I came out on the dim, winding roadway leading up from the village to my house to hear first another: 'Buka edabuka! Kill! and kill!', then three heavy thuds and with each thud a heavy involuntary grunt, the meaning of which was unmistakable.

The light of the nearest lamp-post was made dimmer by the storm but it was just good enough to show me a tall dark figure go down before a group of seven prancing black shapes.

'Stop that and stand, Fingani* dogs,' I shouted at them in their own tongue.

---

* Finganis are a sub-tribe of the Amangtakwena, to this day infamous for their betrayal of a great chief two hundred years ago.

'Litter of bitches, miscarried children of hyenas,' Umtumwa roared behind me. 'Do as you're told for Umtumwa of Amantazuma comes.'

Polite, dignified, and self-controlled in ordinary life, Umtumwa in action was a great and fertile swearer.

Immediately the prancing figures became still with the shock of their surprise at being so boldly challenged on such a night and in so unlikely a place. For a brief moment they seemed paralysed with apprehension and then six of them broke and ran. The seventh, obviously the leader, took one more jump towards a dark shape on the ground, whirled a hunting-stick above his shoulders and brought it down with a crack like the smack of a bullet on the prostrate head before he, too, turned and ran.

'Stand or I'll shoot,' I shouted, so enraged by the meanness of the blow that I forgot I'd only a spear and no gun with me. The fellow took no notice and merely went down the hill in long, effortless strides. Realizing the futility of giving chase I stopped short by the fallen man, just as Umtumwa caught up with me, moaning to himself in a storm of rage: 'Oh, what an evil blow! Oh, what evil men!' Then without waiting for permission he snatched the spear out of my hand.

The last of the seven men was fast nearing a steep bend in the road and there was no time to waste. Umtumwa, in a flash, had the spear poised above his shoulder and aimed. For a brief moment he twirled and vibrated the slender shaft so vigorously and expertly that it sounded almost like a tuning-fork in the air, and then he launched it after the fleeing man. I caught my breath with suspense and so, it seemed, did the storm, for the wind dropped into a lull. I heard the spear take to the air with a silky swish, and far below us the sea hissed like a brood of angry mambas on the foaming beaches. It was, so it appeared to me, a great and deadly throw, for I distinctly saw the point of the spear as it flashed underneath the lamp-light making straight for the fatal join of neck and shoulders in the back of the running man. But at the critical moment he stumbled on the steep slope, went down on hands and four feet * like a cheetah, and as he went down the spear just scraped the top of his head and removed some kind of cap he was

* Literal translation of Afrikaans idiom for a person on all fours.

wearing. Almost simultaneously he righted himself with incredible agility and without bothering about his head-gear vanished round the bend. I heard a heart-rending moan from Umtumwa. Then the fanatical wind broke loose again.

'No! Umtumwa, no!' I ordered him, for he was about to resume the chase. 'Leave him to the police. We've more urgent work to do here. Run up to the house. Call the rest of the household and come back as fast as you can with blankets!'

He was off at once. I knelt down and lifted a great black head as gently as I could on to my hands from the shingled road, saying again and again in staccato Sindakwena:* 'Friends! Help. All right now. All over.'

He did not answer but only moaned to himself, as I've so often heard the deeply-hurt African do, without complaining but as if trying to relieve an agony by making rough music of the pain. I'd time barely to establish that he was stabbed deep in several places and bleeding fast, when Umtumwa came back with my cook, gardener, houseboy, *umfaan*† and two rugs. We laid the wounded man on a rug. Even in that dim light I could not but notice how quickly a stain of blood spread like a sunset shadow in the soft wool. We covered him over with the other rug, lifted him gently between us and soon had him in my big, warm kitchen on the floor by the fire which was burning brightly in a large open old Dutch hearth, with two of my softest cushions under his battered head. As the kitchen door shut behind us, I heard fresh forces for the gale coming, like a pack of wolves, down the mountain-side.

'Umtumwa, you know as well as I how to dress wounds, get the field dressings from my study quick, while I telephone for the doctor.'

I was put through quickly to my own doctor, who fortunately lived only a few miles away. He, good fellow, although Sunday evening was almost the only night he ever had alone with his family, just said: 'I'm coming at once,' and rang off before I could even say thank you.

I came back into the kitchen to find my five servants forming a tense half-circle round the wounded man. Umtumwa had already clapped field dressings to all the worst stabs. There

* The language of the Amangtakwena.

† *umfaan:* 'Takwena youth.

12

were four of those as well as numerous minor cuts, two in the side of his chest, one in the thigh and one in the pit of the stomach. When I saw the crimson stain in the purple of his stomach my heart sank, for I realized then not only how slender were his chances of recovery but also how great his pain.

'Get me the morphia quick, Umtumwa,' I told him while I knelt by the man's side.

I'm afraid I didn't even bother to sterilize the hypodermic needle for I knew somehow that all I could do was merely to drug and not cure this man's pain. I put the needle into his arm. As I did so, he suddenly opened his eyes wide and looked into mine. I shall never forget that look. It is a look proper not only to man but to all deeply-hurt and dying animal matter. I've seen it in the eyes of my askaris, dying in the slimy green of Burmese jungles, far from their trembling purple and buff African uplands. Africans can endure the most amazing physical suffering provided the causes of it are concrete and visible. But when this look of which I speak comes up on dark, valedictory waves of the outgoing tide of their blood, I know that the answer of life is finally and irrevocably in the negative.

Kneeling there I found myself instantly and profoundly moved by it. I've seen many people die in many different ways but I never get used to dying and death. I always feel when I meet it as if it comes for the first time, and I uncover all my mind and heart humbly before such uncomprehended royalty. This man was an utter stranger to me, but in that look he was suddenly very close, was almost part of me, if only because we are in life all near to one another in our common nearness to this end which ultimately makes us one.

As his eyes opened with this great impersonal tide of light, he seemed to have just enough of his receding self left to distinguish my white face close to his black one and to read the compassion in my eyes. Then the most amazing thing happened. A slow, fluttering smile moved over his thick, firm lips and he said quite distinctly: 'It is you, Bwana: It is you I see: Ekenonya! Ekenonya!'

I wish I could translate the meaning of 'Ekenonya' adequately but, alas, there is no English equivalent and it must be experienced and lived to be fully appreciated. I can only say that it is a kind of ecstatic 'thank you', an expression of the most profound gratitude of which the Amangtakwena are capable. It is a 'thank you' addressed not merely to another person nor even to a God, but to all life and all the great shimmering African totality of things. And as he said 'Thank you' thus, he died.

'Auck! My bwana! Auck! Auck!' Umtumwa exclaimed in Sindakwena. 'He goes the long way to the great sleep. But he saw you, Bwana! He saw you!'

So Umtumwa, too, had not failed to notice the recognition implicit in that last moment. Yet I had never seen this man before. Africans don't all look alike to me as they do to so many of the townsmen in my country. To me their faces are all sharply individual and distinct. Moreover, I have as good a memory for faces as for names and I was convinced this man and I had never met before. So I shook my head sadly and said: 'Yes, Umtumwa, he thought he knew me – but I don't know him. Have you any idea who he could be?'

'None, Bwana, except this!' he answered, sinking to his knees by the dead man's side and pointing a long finger at two thin black lines tattooed lightly on each cheek.

I caught my breath in surprise for those marks were tattooed only on the faces of 'Takwena royalty and their immediate descendants; two for a man and three for a woman. They helped to account at once for the tense look I'd noticed on the servants' faces when I first came back from the telephone. I was about to speak again when the bell for the front door overhead rang in our ears with such violent and sudden hysteria that my *umfaan* Tickie, absorbed in the tragedy, gave a startled gasp.

'That will be the doctor, Umtumwa,' I told him. 'Show him in here. Then take a torch, go and retrieve my spear, and have a good look round the place to see if those devils have left anything behind that will help us to trace them.'

When my poor old doctor joined me, wet and breathless from the speed with which he'd come, he gave the dead man one look and said simply: 'I'm sorry, Pierre, I came as fast as I could but obviously not fast enough.'

'You've been wonderfully quick,' I replied, looking at the grey, old-fashioned head bowed over the body. 'But I don't

14

think you could have saved him even if you'd been here when it happened.'

'Looks like it,' he agreed, throwing the rug clear of the body. I, too, looked closer and noticed all sorts of details I had no time or mind to notice before. The dead man was dressed like a sailor. His feet were bare but he wore a pair of sky-blue merchant seaman's jeans. The jeans were unbuttoned and the dark blue jersey above them was still as Umtumwa had left it, tucked firmly under his armpits and chin. A leather belt, undone, was lying underneath him with the empty sheath of an able-seaman's knife attached to it, a knife drawn probably in defence. But a 'Takwena *sailor*? I thought, that's curious.

'You're right, Pierre,' the doctor said, standing up with a sigh. 'He'd no chance whatsoever. How did it happen?'

I took the doctor into my study, gave him a large whisky and soda and started telling him. Half-way through I heard the front door open and shut and Umtumwa's barefoot tread in the passage. To my surprise the feet stopped at the door, and suddenly Umtumwa stood in the entrance with an eager, portentous face. But some instinct made me sign to him not to come in.

However, the front door had hardly shut on the doctor's 'Good night, Pierre. I'll report to the police myself in the morning,' when Umtumwa stood beside me.

'Please, Bwana! Please come quickly to the kitchen!' he pleaded earnestly.

I followed him readily and found the rest of my staff, their backs to the dead man, standing with solemn, anxious faces by the kitchen table. They raised their eyes, the light of apprehensive drama in them silently begging for some kind of reassurance, then dropped them again to focus on a strange assortment of objects on the table, presumably those Umtumwa had collected outside. To this day the memory of that odd assortment, lying on the white surface of the clean scrubbed kitchen table like a *nature morte* by a surrealiste of genius is enough to provoke, with unbelievable freshness, the emotions let loose in me by the events of that evening.

First of all there was my spear, and neatly impaled on it a cloth cap such as stokers and trimmers used to wear ashore. Beside the spear lay what looked like a cheap yellow envelope,

15

official foolscap size, torn, muddy, stained with blood and yet with writing on it. Then a pink and white bird's feather so light that, as we looked, the draught from the far end of the room to the fire tilted it on its side. I glanced up at Umtumwa and he, reading my thoughts, confirmed my fear with a low: 'I looked everywhere, Bwana, but that was all I could find.'

The spear, the cap, a torn and seemingly empty envelope, one slight feather and a dead, silent body, with the mark of Bantu royalty on it, were all we had from which to read the meaning of this tragic evening.

Yet my servants now all looked up at me as if they thought I would read it at a glance.

I walked to the head of the table, picked up the spear, removed the cap, saying: 'You threw well, Umtumwa. It's not your fault that the spear didn't find its mark.'

That brought him briefly out of his anxious solemnity. A smile of great delicacy appeared on his broad features, a smile of such shy and sensitive pleasure that he instantly raised his long hands to his face to cover and protect it.

I turned the cap round my fingers. Though I have no special knowledge of such things, I knew at once it was not of British or American make. It was pre-eminently the continental idea of a sailor's cap. There was no maker's or ship's tag inside it.

Next I picked up the feather and as I did so I immediately felt the atmosphere between me and my servants change. The tension I'd observed in them ever since we spotted the mark of royalty on the dead man, rose swiftly to a steep, new pitch. I looked from one to the other but they did not see my look: their eyes were only for that feather.

'Feather of a flamingo, flamingo's feather,' I exclaimed, holding it up to the light, and five pairs of 'Takwena eyes followed the movement of my hand but not one of them spoke. 'Where did you find it?' I asked Umtumwa as casually as I could, because for some unknown reason my heart suddenly began to beat faster as if it already knew something my mind did not.

'In his hand,' he said pointing to the dead man.

'What d'you think it is?' I now asked softly, but clearly determined to get an answer.

He did not reply but suddenly bowed his head, troubled and

ashamed. The other heads followed his example. So there it was beyond doubt: more than anything else this feather was the cause of the tension between us.

'What is it, Umtumwa? Why don't you answer when I ask?' I remonstrated.

'Forgive me, Bwana,' Utumwa said at last, a conflict of loyalties so keen in his eyes that he looked as young and helpless as did his kinsman Tickie the day I came on him with his mouth full of forbidden kitchen sugar. 'Forgive me, but it is forbidden to speak of this. It is only Amangtakwena "business"!'

I nearly smiled at the way he popped the English word 'business' into his formal Sindakwena sentence. The others simultaneously finding their courage uttered a deep 'Aye. This is Amangtakwena "business".'

Disappointed, but knowing of old the utmost importance of patience in all dealings with 'Takwena, even 'Takwena who knew and loved me as these did, I said no more, put the feather beside the cap, and picked up the envelope.

Then I got the shock of the evening, designed for me in particular. The letter was clearly addressed to:

'Pierre de Beauvilliers, Esq., D.S.O.,
Petit France,
St Joseph's,
Cape Peninsula,'

and it was written in a hand I knew as well as my own.

'D'you remember Colonel Sandysse, Umtumwa?' I asked, my throat suddenly dry.

'How could I not remember him,' he answered almost reproachfully. 'Did not I share blankets with him and you many a night in Burma?'

'Well, this writing,' I said, 'is Colonel Sandysse's* writing.'

'Auck! Bwana!' he exclaimed, unbelief clearly marked on his face. 'How can that be when the Colonel as we all know is dead.'

'Indeed he is *thought* to be long dead as you say. But how can that be when this writing is clearly his, and the ink not so very old?'

* Pronounced 'Sands'.

17

'Auck, Bwana, there is powerful Tagat* mighty medicine, in all this,' he said, giving the facts grudging and awesome acceptance at last.

'Is there anything you know about this feather that might help to explain this letter?' I pressed him quickly while he was exposed in his surprise.

He drew back at once, hung his head obstinately and reiterated: 'No. There's nothing to tell! The feather is only Amangtakwena business.'

'Listen!' And this time I addressed them all. 'Listen . . . carefully . . . Have you not told me I am like a brother to you all?'

'Aye! Bwana. Aye!' They responded at once without reserve. 'You are truly a brother and father to us.'

'Then listen. In a few minutes I must pick up the Efoena-Indabakulu† and call the police to this house. They will look at all these things and ask many questions. One thing they are certain to do is to pick up this feather.' I took it up and held it in front of their hypnotized eyes. 'And ask each of you, "What does this mean?"'

'Oh, no, Bwana,' they cried in dismay. 'The police must not see it. You will surely not let them!'

'Why not?' I countered quickly.

'It would be very wrong,' Umtumwa said lamely; the rest feeling trapped, stayed silent.

'How can I judge whether it would be wrong or not when you will not tell me?' I told him sternly. 'What strange good reasons are there that you should have to hide their goodness from a brother?'

The look of misery on their faces was so great that I realized the battle might yet be won. So I pressed on quickly. 'Tell me what it is that troubles you, and if it's as you say, we will not show the feather to the police, and will speak of it only among ourselves.'

At this, significant glances passed swiftly from one to the other of them. Then somewhere within themselves without a word being spoken, their individual meanings became one. Tickie's fresh young eyes suddenly shone with relief and

* Sindakwena for magic.

† Literally 'Who desires speech with who', the Sindakwena for telephone.

Umtumwa lifted up his glance to meet mine, saying: 'Bwana, it is the sign for all the Amangtakwena that a great dream has been dreamt again.'

'What great dream, Umtumwa?' I asked, my heart and mind going black with apprehension, for did I not know something about the Amangtakwena and their great dreams?

'I do not know that yet,' he answered sombrely, and pointing to the dead man added, 'Even he who carried the feather would not have known. All we know is that when such a feather is passed among us by such a one as he, it is a sign that a great dream has been dreamt. Then no matter how far from Umangoni,* one man from each group of us must hasten to be home in the spring in order to be told of the dream and its meaning, so that at the end of the summer, when the fields are harvested and the corn is in the bins, the dream can be lived out. . . . But I have done wrong to speak so much, for it is forbidden to talk of this to anyone except ourselves.'

He finished in such distress that I put my hand on his shoulder and said: 'Shame, Umtumwa, shame. Am I not like one of you? Have I been a friend of your people for nothing? You have done right to tell me. I give you my word that we shall speak of this only among ourselves. Here . . . I give you back your feather!'

He held out two great hands cupped gratefully together as if they were about to be filled with gold, and I dropped the feather into them, like a flake of light on a shadowy pool, before continuing: 'All I ask is that this envelope with the Colonel's writing on it is spoken of only among ourselves. It, too, is only our business!'

At that they cheered up greatly and with obvious approval watched me pick up the envelope and put it away in my wallet. I was certain they felt reassured by my last request because it made us equal, united us firmly in a reciprocal rôle of keepers of one another's secrets, and I knew more than ever I could rely on them.

'And this spear, Umtumwa,' I went on. 'It had better go back to its place on the wall. Only this cap, we'll leave that for the police to see.'

He took the spear as if it tingled between his fingers and

* The Land of the Amangtakwena.

19

exclaimed with totally unexpected anger, 'This spear, Bwana: he is "no damn good".'

'No good, Umtumwa!' I asked. 'What do you mean?'

'He would not fly true. He is bad, bad, bad,' and he shook it as a mongoose does a snake it has just killed.

I didn't agree with him, of course, but I've learnt from long experience what harm is done daily to the African by denying him the symbolic gesture of the meaning which he cannot express in words. He's continually experiencing new meaning for which his capacity for abstract expression is not great enough. He's forced, therefore, to act it openly, or covertly, before he consciously thinks or speaks it.

So I told Umtumwa, not without regret, for I like my spears and love the associations they help to maintain in my mind: 'Then do what you think is necessary with it, Umtumwa.'

He gave me a grateful look, put the spear over his knee snapped it in several places, separated the wood from the head which he kept, and threw all the rest into the fire, while I went to telephone for the police.

But, I confess, no sooner was I out of the warm kitchen and alone in that long familiar passage of my home, than I was filled with a profound nameless fear and wordless apprehension. I felt as if Umtumwa's gesture of punishment of the spear was a kind of intuitive warning that the approach symbolized by spears was no good in the problem that had been thrust on us, and that we would have to do much better than that if we were to solve it in time. That 'in time' tolled out in my mind like a mediæval bell at nightfall, and I heard again Umtumwa's sombre, reluctant voice explaining that one of them would have to 'hasten to be home in the spring to hear the dream so that at the end of summer it could be lived by all.' Our spring in this Southern Cape was only three months; and the end of summer only six months away. Yet the heart of Umangoni, where the great dreams of that great people are dreamt and told, was several thousands of miles away: difficult miles, made more dangerous, my intuitions warned me, by our inability to understand the situation. Unconsciously I quickened my pace and found myself taking up the telephone and summoning the police in a voice made unusually authoritative by a sense of the need for haste.

Chapter 2

The Great Togethernesses

The police came and behaved very much as police do the world over on these occasions, except perhaps that they were less interested in this murder than they would have been had the victim been white. However, they were conscientious enough and asked me all the prescribed questions. Much to my relief they appeared so satisfied with my answers that they hardly questioned my servants at all, the young Inspector in charge finally shutting his leather notebook impatiently in its clasp and saying: 'Ag! Meneer. I'm sure it was just another of those faction fights. We have dozens of them every week-end. Once these creatures get some illicit brandy in them there's no knowing what they'll do.'

I then drew his attention to the stoker's cap on the table. Like me, he did not believe in the possibility of the dead man and his assailants being genuine sailors, saying: 'Ag: Meneer: these fellows don't go to sea. They wear any uniform they can get hold of. He probably got this secondhand from a Greek pawnbroker. All the same, I'll get the water police cracking on it at once.'

Soon after that the police left, taking the dead body, no longer black but now purple in its ancient, royal cold. I went alone to my room, eager to come to terms with the emotions and wild speculation let loose in me by the events of the evening. But I didn't find it easy. I went and stood at the window, parting the curtains and looking out. A bright light was shining in the window of Umtumwa's room in the servants' quarters, and between us the storm charged ceaselessly streaming so fast with long phantom hair of elongated mist, torn and tattered cloud, that Umtumwa's window looked like the glow of the cab of a great Northern Express drawing its darkened coaches through the night with proud dispatch. The storm, indeed, seemed to have achieved its climax. It sounded as if the world outside had suddenly emptied itself of substance and gone as hollow as a plundered tomb with the great wind of time itself howling around inside it. The house was shaking like the deck of a windjammer, and in the rare lulls I heard the wind on the fringes of a weird pocket of calm fly deeper into the night like a salvo of shells out towards an ocean target. Yet I did not mind it. It seemed curiously appropriate to the moment. I got into bed and turned out the light.

I'd have liked to fit the situation and the day's events into a nice, neat explanation, designed with clear, two-dimensional logic in mind. But I couldn't. I even failed utterly to focus the events of the evening in the order wherein they'd occurred, for at each twist and turn in my reasoning I found the flow blocked, with seeming incongruity, by the vision of a young Chinese General who had shared a cell with John Sandysse, Serge Bolenkov, and myself in a grim Japanese prison outside Harbin. I hadn't thought of him for years, but now there was in my mind his slight, maidenish figure and high-pitched, sing-song, girlish voice, insisting that I should relive my associations with him.

I remembered him lecturing to us one cold day in prison. 'You Europeans,' he said, 'have a tendency to select from life only the facts that suit your immediate, practical purpose and to despise the rest. You're a great people for setting up partial systems and partial investigations and persuading yourselves in the process that they can be elevated to totalities. You ignore that life itself has a purpose and totality overriding yours, and often in direct opposition to it. We Chinese make many mistakes, but not that particular one. We are obsessed with the totality of things. That is why we often fail in the specific and practical. We see cause and effect as but two of several aspects of the paramount drive and purpose of life. Cause and effect to us are really by-products of the ultimate purpose which causes and effects all. Chance or what you call 'luck' is another manifestation of the same thing, not just an accidental occurrence unrelated to the general order of events, but also part of a fundamental law of whose workings you are either painfully ignorant or arrogantly contemptuous. We, however, have profound respect for it and are continually studying it and devising methods for divining the nature of this law. We do it instinctively. You see, it is precisely the togetherness of things in time, not their apparent unrelatedness in the concrete world, which interests us Chinese. Our scientists have actually invented a system for devising the typical and abiding "togetherness" of chance, time, and circumstance for each individual. It is not perfect, of course, but it is amazing how it works. Would you like to try it?'

At first we three had declined this offer, politely. It sounded to us no better really than a suggestion that we should consult a gipsy crystal. Besides, at this time, John, Serge, and I were completely absorbed in a long, patient plan for escape from prison. Serge Bolenkov was a White Russian, liked and admired by both John and me, who spoke several Central Asian tongues and was convinced he could make his way safely back into Russia. The gallant Russian resistance against the Germans had revived his pride in his people to such an extent that his bitterness over the 1917 Revolution had vanished and made him determined to return to Russia.

But we were, after all, all three of us completely cut off from the outside world and under suspended sentence of death, and it's amazing how such a combination of circumstances stimulates the irrational perceptions in human nature. Once the escape plan was completed the little General's offer became more and more attractive, until finally we decided unanimously it could do no harm to ask him to divine the great togetherness of chance, circumstance, and time for the success of our scheme.

So the three of us went together to the little General for advice by divination. The result of it was he'd told John and Serge to try to make good their escape in five days' time at two in the morning, on the night of the new moon. That shook our faith in him at first, because it was mid-December 1944 with the snow ice, and long-maned winds of a desperate winter driving from Siberia with fast accelerating speed across the wide, featureless Manchurian plains. But he insisted that the 'togetherness' of things favoured escape for John and Serge only at that moment.

Then he looked at me compassionately and said, sadly, that I was not part of the pattern he'd just read. When I asked 'Why?' he smiled, a whimsical, introverted smile and told me gently there never was a 'why' in 'the great togethernesses', only a 'thus', and my 'thus' was 'so'.

I believe we'd have rejected the whole thing as nonsense if, on the very next day a friendly, Christian Korean guard had not come to warn me that I was once more to be taken away by the secret police for interrogation and he greatly feared I would not come back alive. So I made John and Serge promise that if I were not back by the night of the new moon, they would pool my supplies and money and make their break without me, according to the little General's estimate of 'togethernesses'.

I was duly fetched by the secret police and I did not come back into the general prison again until two days after the bomb was dropped on Hiroshima. I myself was then almost dead but was able to discover that John and Serge had escaped on that night of the new moon in December and had not been recaptured. But the general opinion in prison was that they could never have survived the dreadful winter outside. As for the 'little General', he too was gone, tortured to death for heroically refusing to let one word about our plans cross his lips.

In the months and years that followed, John and Serge appeared to have vanished for ever, and after two and a half years search was abandoned. They were officially presumed dead, and accepted as such by all except John's mother, Lady Sandysse, and his youngest sister, Joan. I myself did not know what to think. It was not that I believed in their being alive so much as that I couldn't accept the fact of their death. Somehow or other my uncertainty had been sustained – as I now realized with the letters in John's own hand on a blood-stained envelope dancing like a crackle of flame in the dark before my eyes – by a submerged faith in the timing of their escape according to the General's reading of their 'togethernesses'.

Then, suddenly, as I lay there with brittle eyes wide-open, unable to sleep, it was no longer the General's face, but Joan Sandysse's face which occupied the forefront of my memory, for, after all, it had all begun with Joan. My own private and personal beginning in the affair was not there and then but years back. It began for me, to be precise, at three o'clock in the afternoon of 17 June 1937, in the Grootekerk, the first church ever built in Southern Africa. I was sitting in our pew, my heart black with misery and my mind full of a thousand resentments, Oom Pieter le Roux, my dead mother's brother and only surviving kinsman, beside me. My father was dead and we were there for his funeral service. The church was crowded out with people, for my father, by the time he died, had become a legendary figure in Africa.

In 1899 at the age of twenty-one, when the war broke out between Britain and the Republics up north, he'd at once decided to leave Petit France, his rich and comfortable wine estate in the Cape and to hasten north to join the Free State Commandos. He was a superb horseman and shot, a fearless and passionately self-reliant person, and soon made a unique military reputation for himself as a leader of an independent and daring band of scouts. He could hardly credit the news of the surrender of Vereeniging in 1902, and resolved that he personally would never accept so unfair a defeat. So disbanding his scouts, he quickly made his way north and one cold, grey morning in July 1902, slipped quietly over the Portuguese border to start a new life in a foreign country at the age of twenty-four as a professional hunter. Even the great and generous Act of Union failed to break through the ice formed in his heart by the Boer War and finally his friends at the Cape one by one stopped urging him to return and even ceased writing to him. It was at this stage with his bitterness and disillusionment at their deepest, that he met my mother in romantic circumstances in Tanganyika. They were married a month later and except for six months before and six months after my birth, were never again parted. Even my birth in 1917 was not allowed to make much difference and when it was clear after six months that I was as strong and sturdy a male animal as had ever been born in East Africa, my mother packed up at once in the town to which she had been sent and went off to rejoin her husband who, together with her brother, Oom Pieter, was hunting elephant on the Abyssinian frontier. From then on the four of us were inseparable as we wandered and hunted from one end of Africa to another. I was not sent to school; my mother taught me to read and write, my father to shoot; Oom Pieter to ride and a host of other hunter's crafts. From our servants and black hunters I learned the languages and rich, instinctive lore of Africa. We rarely went near the towns except to sell our ivory and skins and to replenish our supplies. So I grew up contained in ancient Africa as few white people could ever have been.

Then one day in 1934 my mother fell ill. All our proved and trusted remedies failed to cure her. Panicking for the first time in our lives, we forgot all our prejudices against travelling by train, flagged the Southern Express at a sun-bleached siding in the far northern bushveld, and took her to the little hospital in Fort Beaufort. But already we were too late. Within a fortnight she died. Yet before she died she made my father promise that he would go back to his home in the Cape. I suspect that when she saw our three faces bending anxiously over her she read them, in the light of her own illness, in a way they'd not been read before. Behind our features burnt black by the implacable sun of the interior I believe she saw submerged something too great for mere flesh and blood to endure. I suspect she realized we stood there not as three free men but as prisoners of my father's iron resentment over a war fought far back at the beginning of the century. Drawing my father's head to her for the last time she'd said: 'Promise to go back: promise to accept the past: not to judge but to accept. And homeward, please; home, my dear love.' And without an instant's reservation or hesitation, my father had said simply: 'I promise.'

So once my mother was buried we hastened north again to sell our wagons and equipment, and to pay off our loyal old servants and bearers. That done we turned south.

In the Cape my father's return caused a great and long-sustained sensation, for, the last of the self-exiled Boer leaders, he was, as I said earlier on, a legendary figure. But the labour of reintegration for so stricken a spirit was too great, and I fear neither Oom Pieter nor I helped him much. I could not take calmly to my first orthodox schooling. I felt trapped in this new civilized situation and seethed with rebellion. Then poor Oom Pieter found tending neat, algebraic vineyards so little to his taste that after six months of it he announced regretfully that he was going back to his old life. My father did not try to stop him, but watched him go with such a fierce flame of longing and envy in his eyes that I was for a moment appalled by the power of the aboriginal nomad in the three of us. Then in May 1937 came an invitation for me to join Oom Pieter on an expedition into the Congo. It was selfish to inflict another separation on my father at that moment but I couldn't help myself. Yet if my going was a defeat for myself, his consenting to it was a victory for him, and I shall never forget the tender look in his eyes when I said goodbye to him. I never saw him again. Oom Pieter and I were about to set off into the blue when an urgent telegram summoned us back to the Cape. But my father died some hours before we could arrive.

So there I sat at the funeral service, staring in front of me with such a fierce pain of misery in my heart that no tears could come. I hardly heard the sombre words of the service but longed passionately to have done with it all, so that I could get on my horse and ride alone with my unhappiness far out into the hills. Then suddenly an odd thing happened. I found my eyes slowly drawn upwards and my vision pulled subtly and yet surely out of its inner focus. I had, to the best of my belief, no conscious rôle in this reorientation of my senses. I was as sealed-off from the people and the world about me by my misery as a silkworm in its cocoon. Yet there I was slowly but unmistakably being forced back into cognizance of my surroundings. The movement continued until my eyes came to rest on the back of the Governor's pew on the other side of the aisle, three rows in front of ours, and I found myself looking at a young girl who'd deliberately turned her head to look at me. As our eyes met she made no effort to turn away. I had time to notice that her eyes were calm and wide, and intensely blue. In that light, under a big, black straw hat she wore pushed back slightly from a brow rather broad for a girl, but white and unbelievably calm, her eyes were almost purple. Two long plaits of black hair fell over her shoulders and this contrast of blackness and blueness, of the white of her skin and the black of her hair, this counterpoint of fair and dark in her, of weight in her brow and hair and imponderable in the line of the lovely features made it the most disturbing face I'd ever seen. It looked as enchanted as it was enchanting and the magic of that moment lives with me still. I don't know how long I'd have gone on looking at her if I hadn't seen the expression in her eyes change suddenly from one of profound recognition to such living compassion and understanding that I felt as if a flash of lightning had joined us in the selfsame current of being, and I had to turn my head away not to be completely unmanned. But from then on, all through the service, I was conscious of her and the knowledge sustained me to the end.

That night I crept into bed exhausted by recent lack of sleep and by the emotions of the day, yet I lay awake until suddenly I remembered again that girl's face in the church and the compassion in her eyes. At once the ice in me broke and I wept for the first time in years. When I woke at my usual hour the next day I felt better. Quickly saddling my favourite horse Diamond, I rode through the old gate at the far end of the property which now was mine, just as the dawn broke.

It was a crisp, cold dawn of mid-winter, but bright without stain of wind or flicker of cloud. It was intensely still and almost the only sound was that of the sea going over the sands like a leisurely wind from one end of the great Bay to the other. Instantly I put Diamond into a fast gallop and rode straight for the shining beaches, and as I rode along the level sands close to the curled edges of the sea I saw in the wet, shining surface Diamond and the whole of the freshly-lit sky so clearly reflected that it was as if we had yet another sky below us and I was mounted on a Pegasus of my own and flying fast between two heavens on some errand of the gods. And as I rode I realized that here was also a reality and a beauty which my first love of the vast Northern Interior need neither despise nor exclude. I turned back only when that realization was at last complete. By then the sun was well up in the sky and the blue of the mountains going pearly with the rising light of the day.

Half an hour later I saw a mile away three riders coming towards me at a leisurely canter. As they came nearer I recognized one of the Governor's A.D.C.'s whom I'd met several times, another man whom I didn't know, and the young girl I'd seen in church.

'Hullo, Pierre,' the A.D.C. called out to me in a tone of easy assurance, 'do you mind if we ride some way with you, these two here are anxious to meet you!' And so, formally, I met Joan and John Sandysse, her brother.

Joan, at the time, was barely thirteen, John twenty-three and I was just nineteen. No three people could have led more different lives, but by the time we'd reached the gates of my home we were friends and I insisted on giving them all breakfast. Oom Pieter, surprised but secretly delighted to see me return, almost cheerful, with young people, rose to the occasion.

Over breakfast I learnt that John and Joan were the eldest and youngest of four children of Lady and Lord Meldmourne, at that time Governor-General of British Central Africa, and were staying for three weeks, with our Governor at the Cape who was a friend of their father's. John was there to see Joan safely into the ship which was taking her back to school in England in three weeks' time, but he himself was returning to Central Africa to see more of it before settling down to a diplomatic career. That was one of the reasons why he'd been so interested in the story of our lives published in the papers on the day my father died; and why he attached himself so firmly to Oom Pieter.

For the next three weeks John, Oom Pieter, Joan, and I were seldom out of one another's company. John quickly heard from Oom Pieter of our plan to resume our interrupted expedition to the Congo and Upper Loando as soon as we'd settled the more urgent affairs arising out of my father's death, and he asked at once if he could join us. To my joy and amazement Oom Pieter agreed readily.

So while John and Oom Pieter talked Africa, Joan rode with me, went scrambling round my favourite peaks in the purple Hottentots-Holland, or lay side by side with me in the sun on warm and sheltered sands, the sound of the sea joining in our own hungry conversations. Though I was a good six years older than she there were no conscious barriers between us. She had a clear, urgent spirit and her upbringing appeared merely to have stimulated in her an unusual zest for what lived beyond the normal horizon of people of her kind. She seemed to me to live close to the centre where her life bubbled-up like the source of a mountain stream flashing immediately into sunshine and sunlight. She threw no backward, regretful glances over her shoulder to the garden of a receding childhood wherein so many of the hurt, unrealized lives of our desperate time seek shelter. Though still a child she was contained utterly in an instinctive trust of her own vivid sense of life; was as immersed in the present, and eager for the future, as she was content in the past. Her zest for living was matched only by her appetite for knowledge of any world she didn't know. She was indefatigable in asking me questions about my life. And as I tried to tell her all she asked, another curious thing happened to me. I began to recapture memories which either had been forgotten or profoundly overlaid by the outward events of my life. I rediscovered feelings I'd never suspected I'd possessed. In fact in telling Joan the story of my life, I relived it more completely than I'd been able to live it in its first crude experience; and what is more I relived it in the companionship of this eager young girl. As a result by the time I'd finished I felt there'd never been a moment in my life when I hadn't known her and when the time came for parting it was like a surgeon's knife cutting me in two. When the last siren shook the funnels of her ship, and the gongs in the saloons, and bells in the engine-room were all set ringing to warn the last visitors that they must leave forthwith, I could hardly control myself.

Fortunately, Joan was too young to know what time and distance between them can do to even the most loyal and loving hearts. Holding up her face spontaneously to me to be kissed, just as she did for John, she put her arms round my neck and said confidently: 'Promise you'll always write to me; promise!' Then she handed me a flat square cardboard parcel, tied in red string. When I undid it some hours later, I found an enlargement of a photograph John had taken of the two of us a fortnight before. It shows Joan and me on our horses side by side. The ample white lace of the great velvet cloak of a still afternoon sea is spread out with warm, inviting elegance around us. Behind and above a dazzling head of cloud is bowed gravely over the mountains. The sun flashes on the white and blue of the sea. Across the right-hand corner was written: 'With all my love: Joan.'

I kept my promise. But I never saw her again. The war came and we were all swept away in various directions on the unpredictable current of events far beyond our control.

Meanwhile John, Oom Pieter, and I became the closest of friends. Our expedition to the Congo was such a success that

30

John insisted on repeating it, and finally stayed with us till the War broke out. Then he was asked by the War Office to raise a special African force, and he in his turn asked Oom Pieter and me to help him. We both did so; but when John and I were eventually ordered to Burma Oom Pieter, because of his knowledge of Africa and the Africans, was left at base in Africa. It was a sad farewell. To this day I see him standing on the quay at Mombassa, hat in hand, his little yellow, greying, Napoleon beard, pointed accusingly at the sea, while silent and immovable, he watched us out of sight.

So John and I went to the war in Burma and made ourselves so troublesome and notorious to the enemy that, taken prisoner, we were lucky to escape with our lives. Then came John's and Serge's escape; and finally, on the Japanese surrender, I emerged from solitary confinement in our prison outside Harbin.

But by then I was more dead than alive. In fact, at that moment of release, with John and Serge both presumed dead, I really did not care whether I lived or not. Only a faint flicker of individual desire still lit the darkness of wartime negation in me: I had a longing to see the Africa of my childhood again. In the hospital ship on the long voyage home I believe this alone kept me alive: this and the fact that Oom Pieter came to fetch me home at Kilindini. From the moment I saw his slight, tall, patient figure on the quay I began to feel better, better still when he said with that almost maternal understanding he always had of me: 'We are not going South just yet. You are coming up with me into the highlands on a good long safari first.'

Yet although my body recoverd soon enough on that leisurely journey over a favourite route, my mind and heart did not mend nearly as fast. I found myself more and more reluctant to bring the journey to a close; to take up the pre-war threads of my life and face up to my grown-up, civilized responsibilities. The truth was I had been driven by the war back into the era before my mother died and seemed bent on repeating my father's pattern. Even an appeal from Joan in her great need and distress over John's unexplained disappearance failed to move me as it should have done. She and her mother begged me to come to England and help in their search. I promised to do so if all other expedients failed but I always found some excuse for not carrying out my promise. For instance, our safari at last over, I found cause to go to Umangoni, the land of the Amangtakwena. Most of my father's bearers were 'Takwena; I had had a 'Takwena nurse and I spoke Sindakwena before I spoke Afrikaans or English. From the age of six one of the 'Takwena headmen had attached his youngest son, Umtumwa, also six, to me as my permanent companion. He was with me constantly until my mother died. When the war came and I decided to form a special 'Takwena Company I had sent for him at once, and at once he came. I had been told that several of this Company, including Umtumwa, had come back alive and felt I must go to them. No sooner had I done so, and mingled freely with a natural people who had known me all my life, than a great burden seemed to fall from me. The grip of the war on my mind loosened. Other claims, other memories long suppressed, rose to the surface. One day I came to, profoundly displeased with myself, thinking: 'There you sit in the sun, Pierre de Beauvilliers, day after day, as if you did not have grown-up work to do and others to think of besides yourself.' Soon after I was back at St. Joseph's in the Cape and wrote to Joan that I was eager and ready at last to help. I do not know whether she had lost patience or heart with me. All I know is my letter was still unanswered. So conscientiously I resumed the task of tending my ample vineyard, and in an effort to appease my submerged longing for the interior of my childhood, which was like an acute physical pain within me where there was no specific work to do, I devoted all my leisure to a book on *The Mind and Myth of the Amangtakwena* until 5.30 in the evening of 12 July 1948. I was interrupted by the ringing war-cry of the 'Takwena there, just outside my very stoep, and all else which flowed swiftly from that moment in the storm.

Chapter 3

The Amangtakwena and their Dreams

Africa has always walked in my mind proudly upright, an African giant among the other continents, toes well dug into the final ocean of one hemisphere, rising to its full height in the greying skies of the other; head and shoulders broad, square and enduring, making light of the bagful of blue Mediterranean slung over its back as it marches patiently through time. But here on the night of 12 July 1948, thinking of it in terms of my past and what might now be before me, for the first time the reassuring image failed me. Try as I would the giant would not come alive, the resolute, self-reliant male character was gone in the darkness of the storm and of my own mind. Clearly, the other main reason for this disturbance was the flamingo feather and Umtumwa's 'Bwana, it is the sign that a great dream has been dreamt again.'

I've mentioned already that the 'Takwena are my favourite African people and have said enough of my past to make it plain that my connexions with them have been of long standing. As a boy I sat many a time with Umtumwa round the fire at night in the hut of his grandfather – one of the great Indunas* of his day – and heard him tell of the great dreams of his nation and the rôle they'd played in his people's history. When working on my book *The Mind and Myth of the Amangtakwena* I'd been most struck by the brief and brittle patterns of most African peoples. Few African tribes have maintained their identity for long, few known specific continuity. But the 'Takwena are one of the great exceptions to this rule. They have preserved their national identity and character longer than any African people. They take their history very seriously and are the only African people I know who have a well-organized institution for keeping their own history alive.

* Headman and Adviser of his Chief.

They have official 'Keepers of the Nation's Memory'. It is one of the most respected offices among them and its holders are always drawn from the same families. There is no unit of the nation, however small, which has not a family in its midst where the future keeper of its memory, from the time he is born, breathes, hears and talks little else than this business of the nation's history. The traditional 'Takwena version of their origin, as told once in my presence by the principal keeper of the people's memory and the witch-doctor in chief of the Nation, the dreaded Umbombulimo, was this: 'Sixty generations ago in the day of our great father Xilixowe, the 'Takwena left their first home in the north. Far, far, beyond the land of the thousand valleys, hard by the black split in the earth on the other side of the mountains of the moon where the long yellow river falls from the water serpent's own cloud and coils round the feet of the assegai peaks that throw fire and smoke in the sky, our people left their home and came south. Yes, they left their home where they were prosperous and came south because Xilixowe dreamt a great dream.' And there you have it, at the beginning of all a dream and because of the dream – great change. So it goes on and on, all through 'Takwena history. At the beginning of each new convulsion, like the special star which precedes the dawn, intimation of change comes first through a dream. Only once in their history did it appear as if this dream mechanism had failed the 'Takwena. And that occasion, because it has a significant bearing on my story, I am forced to refer to at greater length.

Nearly a hundred years ago the 'Takwena had reached a point of grave crisis in their history. Their march south, begun nearly two thousand years before, appeared to be finally halted. Early in the eighteenth century their first advance guards had brushed up against Europeans advancing from the Cape. In the far north and to the east 'Takwena territory was being increasingly harassed by well-organized bands of Arab slave traders equipped with modern firearms; while to the west the Portuguese had recently sent a military expedition to claim one of the most fertile of their grazing and breeding grounds. Some of the most experienced of the King's Indunas, there-fore, wanted him to call in all the outposts of his people, regroup them around him in Umangoni proper and there make

34

a stand, for Umangoni was not only by far the richest land the 'Takwena had come across in their long and bloody march through the centuries down the middle of Africa, but also easy to defend. Even an enemy armed with the most modern weapons would be appalled by the task of entering it since its wide valleys, broad, shining rivers, and dense pearly rain-forests* all lay securely tucked away behind range upon range of iron-clad mountains. The argument of the King's Indunas was formidable and the King (alas! who can deny it now?) might well have taken their advice if one of his subjects had not dreamt a dream.

One night in early June 1848 a young girl, daughter of a poor cattle-herder in an outpost on the great crocodile river, far, far south of Umangoni, dreamt the dream in question, and so compelling was the dream that she went and woke her father, an unheard of thing for a 'Takwena young girl. He was so impressed by the dream that as soon as daylight came, he took her to the nearest witch-doctor, and the local Keeper of the People's Memory. This man listened, obviously impressed, but sent father and daughter back to their huts without telling them what he thought about it. The following night the girl dreamt exactly the same dream again and the same procedure was followed. But on the third night Xilixowe's mother, with a terrifying expression in her face and eyes, appeared in the dream ordering the girl to take her dream immediately to the King himself. This time the witch-doctor did not hesitate. He knew from the lore of his profession that one ignored dreams repeated with such insistence at one's own, as well as one's nation's, peril. He set off with the girl and her father to consult his elders and betters at the sub-chief's kraal, while the girl, who seemed to be in a kind of trance, with the dead voice of Xilixowe's mother, a queen who died nearly two thousand years before, still ringing like a live person's in her ears, was cross-examined and questioned for days and nights on end. But her account never varied: 'Xilixowe had come to her in a dream and told her plainly to go to her Chief and tell him to tell the King to order his people to kill and eat all their animals one by one until there was none left alive in the land.

* Rain-forests: African name for dense wood found in wettest altitudes of Tropics.

If the 'Takwena did that, Xilixowe had said, then at dawn on the morning after the last head was eaten, all the animals that the 'Takwena had ever eaten would come alive, more, all the 'Takwena that had ever died in battle would come alive, healed of their wounds, refreshed and fully armed, Yes, Xilixowe himself would be there in that dawn to lead them forth into the last great battle against the white invaders and drive them back in to the sea out of which they came.'

Much as they believed in dreams, the most fanatic among the royal specialists on the matter shrank from the course of action which this girl's dream demanded of the nation. What if the cattle and dead animals did not come alive again on the appointed day? The answer to this was too horrible to contemplate, for it was obvious that the whole nation would starve to death. For days, as a result, it looked as if the dream might be declared false and the girl and her whole family put to death. But at last the senior witch-doctor, the Umbombulimo, smiling a superior smile and with a great show of assurance, had taken the girl alone into his cave. Few expected to see her come out alive and those who did were convinced she could only emerge transformed into a lizard or a hyæna. Nor did any of them know precisely what happened in the cave, but the version left to posterity was unanimous: the witch-doctor, once alone in the cave, had examined the girl in great detail about Xilixowe's physical appearance in the dream, and to his satisfaction. Four hours later the girl emerged not only in her own shape but also with a resolved expression shining on her face, while the witch-doctor, more serious than they had ever seen him before, had cried in a great bass voice. 'A great dream has been dreamt again. Go forth and gather your harvest as swiftly as you can and in three moons from now come back to this place to hear how the dream is to be lived.'

It is typical of the quality of this primitive African people that once the dream was told them by their witch-doctor they lived it out to the utmost spirit and smallest syllable of its context. With one honourable exception they lived it out in such a way that there came a day in the middle of January when there was not a domestic animal of any kind left in Umangoni or any part of Africa under 'Takwena control. As the sun went down that evening all along their farthest southern frontiers, the fires of the greatest army ever massed in Umangoni hung like a long necklace of rubies round the dark throat of the African night, as the warriors cooked their last meal before battle and revelation. The air was charged with the excitement of a nation of millions united in one unanimous, electric expectation. Umtumwa's grandfather, who was a boy at the time, told me that all night long, by their large leaping fires, the *Impis* ecstatically danced the greatest war dance Africa had ever seen. They danced until the earth shook with the shock of hundreds of thousands of feet all stamping down on it as if with one and the same foot. The tallest peaks resounded with this thunder of human feet, the old man said, and the stars themselves from horizon to horizon went by shivering and trembling with fear. And then the dawn came.

I can still hear the life go out of the old man's voice, and see the despair of a long-vanished moment flicker at the back of his antique eyes, as he said to me: 'But my great little Bwana, my big, small master, when the dawn came it was but an ordinary dawn.'

At first no one would believe it, everyone fought with a desperate courage against the evidence of their eyes. Wild rumour leapt into being and sped from one regiment, from one extended flank of the great army to another. 'Xilixowe is with the Impi of the Black Elephant,' one regiment would signal another. 'No, he is not with us,' a sweaty and exhausted runner would come back with the answer: 'Is he not with them of the Lion?' And so back and forth the whole day long. And then the final question presented itself. Even if Xilixowe were there, where were all the great warriors of the past who were to rise up out of the earth with the coming of the sun? Where were all the resurrected cattle? No, as the sun rose higher the last hope faded fast, and when it went down that night it set on a nation in terrible despair, a nation which knew that for the first time in its long history a great dream had failed it.

I need not go into the detail of what followed, for from here all the history books have taken up the story and the great famine is recorded in them all. No statistics are available, but it is thought that two-thirds of the nation perished in that famine. Indeed, only one thing saved the 'Takwena from being overrun and exterminated. I have already mentioned that there was one honourable exception who did not live out the dream as the rest of his countrymen did. Just before the news of the dream was broken to the nation, the King's eldest son, 'Nkulixowe, had come of age. In accordance with national custom all the young men of the same age were immediately summoned to the capital, formed into a regiment under his command, and the King then despatched them, together with his own guards, to make war against the Arab slave traders in the north. It was an astonishing expedition and I regret I cannot tell the whole story here. 'Nkulixowe from the start showed himself to be a most remarkable and gifted leader He struck at the Arab traders and followed their fleeing remnants a thousand miles down to the bases on the coast, which he plundered empty, and fired. From there he turned back to the interior, fanning out towards the north-west, raiding and collecting rich booty on the way. When his father's messenger finally reached him, he turned back at once with his army and vast herds of cattle collected on his raids, arriving to find his homeland in the grip of famine, his father dead by his own hand, the senior witch-doctor and Keepers of Memory killed, the people dying of hunger and a broken heart and all their bitterest enemies closing in fast. Again the story of how the young 'Nkulixowe took over from his father, manned the narrow passes into Umangoni with his few thousand and held them against all attacks while he nursed his people back to health, is recorded in the history of my country. Under his wise rule the 'Takwena once more became a powerful and prosperous people. When the danger of European penetration during the great scramble for Africa was at its height, 'Nkulixowe asked Britain for a treaty of alliance and protection which was readily granted, and to this day the terms of 'Nkulixowe's special treaty govern the relations between Umangoni and Britain.

The result has been that the life of the 'Takwena has appeared to change little. Indeed, they would have been content, I believe, to stay behind their own frontiers and keep clear of us Europeans if the rapid growth of their population had not begun to make Umangoni, great as it is, too small for them and forced the men more and more to look for work in the world outside. In Southern Africa they are now everywhere, in the police, the mines, on the railways, farms, in garages and hotels – where they are welcome, for they are an honest, reliable, and disciplined people; but they seldom stay anywhere long, for they find the strain of being with Europeans, away from their own people and out of the ancient rhythm of their primitive life too great, and every year or so return to the tribal life in to which they were born, re-emerging again only when necessity compels them.

But despite appearances, one great change really has come over the 'Takwena since 'Nkulixowe saved them in their desperate plight. Their dreams have left them.

I remember so well asking Umtumwa's grandfather if there had been any great dreams since that fatal June in 1848. I can see him shake that grey old head of his, with the thick metal ring he wore as crown and badge of his high Induna office, and say sadly, 'our dreams have been taken from us and no one knows if they will ever come back. ... Some say that the white people have taken them from us and now do all the dreaming ... But whatever the reason there are no dreams now among the people.'

'But, old father,' I asked anxiously, for it seemed so wrong to me that one monster dream should end the glorious line of great 'Takwena dreams, 'surely they will come again, these dreams?'

'Who knows, my little old master,' he answered, smiling affectionately over the obvious anxiety in my voice. 'I know only what I know. There are those who believe that 'Nkulixowe before he died said he was going to prepare a true great dream for his people, a great dream that one day will bring all our scattered people once more together.' But there he paused, shook his head at himself and stressed again: 'But I know only what I know.'

There then, for the moment, I must leave the 'Takwena, their history and their dreams, and hasten to pick up the threads of my own immediate story where I left them, in the dark of the storm pouring over my house in St Joseph's.

Chapter 4

Zwong-Indaba Goes North

The storm, as these peninsular storms often do, blew itself out in the night. I woke up to find the morning hanging like honey in a comb at my window and to hear a warlike 'Takwena chant going up in the garden. In view of what had happened the night before, I jumped out of bed in some alarm, but one glance from the window reassured me. It was Tickie, making melodrama out of his task of clearing up the little of the storm in the garden. With a sack held like a fabulous shield over one arm, a rake like a spear in his right hand, he was stalking a wheelbarrow piled up with dead leaves and broken twigs. As he did so, he taunted the enemy it represented: 'You thought you would get away, you son of a hyena bitch, but little did you know that Tickie of the leopard, Tickie of the royal night watch was on your spoor. Take that, and that, you father of a dog,' and with each 'that' he leapt forward and stabbed the wheelbarrow violently with the handle of the rake.

The sight made me feel better. Tickie had been with me a year now, brought to me one day unbidden by Umtumwa who by way of explanation merely said: 'Bwana, this is Tickie, the son of my sister. His father has sent him to work for you.' I didn't really need him at the time, but I knew that he would not be there unless Umtumwa's family needed the little money he could earn, and took him in at once. He was a fine boy, with an eager, fearless light in his eyes, and such a sensitive expression on his face that when I asked Umtumwa why he was called Tickie, he'd hung his head at the laughter which my question provoked among the other servants.

'But surely, Bwana, it is obvious!' Umtumwa had said.

'Not to me,' I told him.

'But what, Bwana, is the smallest coin struck in the land? Is it not indeed a tickie?' he'd asked, archly rhetorical.

He made a gesture of mock despair at my slowness and, raising his hands to cover the laugh that was surely coming, said: 'Tickie is the smallest coin struck in his father's hut!'

So Tickie had become a member of the household and was by no means the dullest.

As I watched him now going deftly and with a sure instinct through all the motions of a full-blooded 'Takwena warrior in action, the pleasure his graceful movements gave me was tinged suddenly with sadness. He looked so young and innocent and the pattern of life which prescribed these movements was so old, so experienced and exacting, that I felt frightened for him and again had the conviction of danger of the most pressing kind.

Then I saw two sticks leaning against the whitewashed wall of the servants' quarters, next to the door of my cook, Zwong-Indaba,* and beside them two little bundles of clothing, one in scarlet, the other in deeep green calico, both vivid in the morning sun. I knew by that that Zwong-Indaba was ready for a long journey, and clearly was the one chosen by the others to go to Umangoni for news of the dream. I suppose the choice was inevitable. He was the oldest and, therefore, of greater tribal prestige than the others; but I would have preferred Umtumwa to have gone. The whole tempo of the older man's character was so much slower than Umtumwa's. I knew, however, that I couldn't interfere in such a matter, so I called Umtumwa to me, heard him announce the decision and accepted it with good grace, merely saying: 'There's an express train north today at 10.30. Tell Zwong-Indaba I'll get him a ticket to Fort Herald and will drive him to the station myself immediately after breakfast. And Umtumwa, hasn't it occurred to you that these people who came last night might come back?'

'It has, Bwana!' he said at once.

'Well, then, keep a good watch while I'm out and let everyone stay close to the house today.'

I bathed and shaved in a hurry. Before sitting down to a light breakfast I wrote a letter to the Provincial Commissioner at Fort Herald, who was an old acquaintance of mine. I begged him to help Zwong-Indaba to get to the frontier as quickly as possible as he was travelling on an urgent errand on my behalf.

* Literally: 'Hear – the news'.

41

Fort Herald was nearly two thousand twisting, turning miles away. The fastest train there took five days and five nights. From there Zwong-Indaba normally would have walked the remaining thousand miles to Umangoni, along one of those footpaths that unobtrusively link one extremity of Africa to the other. But I knew that government jeeps carrying police supplies go some hundreds of miles towards the frontier and I hoped Zwong-Indaba could be given a lift in one of them. I didn't, of course, know at the time, but I might as well never have written the letter. In fact, as things turned out, it would have been better if I hadn't; and it was as well that I said nothing in it to explain the urgency of my request. I finished the letter with a postscript asking the Commissioner to be good enough to telegraph me how long he expected Zwong-Indaba to take to get to the frontier.

As I finished writing, I heard a sad little moaning whine behind me from my copper ridge-backed dog, Slim, called so after my commander-in-chief in Burma, and also because 'slim' in my native Afrikaans means 'clever'. On the day of the storm he'd taken shelter with the horses in the stables, but now he was standing in the doorway, head on one side, looking at me with a sad, intent expression on his face. I called him over and he came slowly, without zest, never taking his eyes off my face. I put my hand out to comfort him, but Slim merely put his chin on my knee and continued to look me in the face with troubled, hazel eyes. Even the ridge on his back, with its shining copper hair arranged around the nerves of his eager young spine like iron filings in a magnetic field, seemed less electric than usual. I could only imagine that a sense of disastrous change just around the corner of our lives had invaded him too.

Later, driving Zwong-Indaba to the station I noticed a brown commercial van parked close against the kerb at the corner of the lane where the fleeing murderer had lost his cap. The bonnet of the van was well up, and a black driver and white man had their heads deep inside it as if examining the engine for a fault. They didn't look up when I passed, and with their heads well down stood so that I couldn't see what they looked like. All I did notice was that the white man was large, fat, rather knock-kneed and had on a pair of black trousers almost green with age and shining with wear. The van itself had painted all over it in large golden letters, "Lindelbaum and Co.: Wine and Spirit Importers, Exporters and Wholesalers, 359, Keerom Street'. I remember thinking it rather unusual that such a vehicle should be thirty miles out from its headquarters so early on a Monday morning, but Lindelbaum's had a reputation for being a very enterprising concern and I gave the matter no further thought.

A crisp, sunny winter's morning in this part of Africa is close to my idea of perfection. The dark blue mountains rising in clear outline to the mother-of-pearl air of the early morning, the blue sky purified and refreshed in the waters of a great storm, the shining sea, still breathing deep and fast from its exertions of the night before, and far away to the north a fall of snow, like the brush of an albatross wing on the purple Hottentots-Holland ranges.

On this particular morning on the way to the great harbour city I thought a great deal of Joan and John, but mostly of her. Once I'd tried to write a poem for her. Significantly, it had begun with a 'but':

> But sometimes still a dream like flame
> Burns through my country calm
> And desires without shape or name
> Haunt me with vision of jungle and palm: —
> Across the long savannah and starlit plain,
> In purple woods, by jungle's feathered rim,
> With oxen black I tread my dark land again.

And so on, ending finally—

> Africa was but the glass wherein darkly I learnt to find,
> Vision of your face and reflect of your mind.

I'd never sent the poem, yet never had those lines applied more than this morning. I saw her face in my heart as I'd first seen it that sad day in church, twelve years before. It was like a vision at night in the final fever of life and the feeling it called forth in me was one hopeless hunger. Would I ever see her again? Had I left my offer of help too late? How unforgivable my first negative response must have seemed to her. Would she ever understand the cause of it – that strange paralysis left by six years of war? More immediately still, how best could I now break the news to her that she and Lady Sandysse were right after all, that John had been alive all the time and might still be alive today?

One of the two main reasons why I had not shown John's envelope to the police was because I knew for certain that if I did so they'd have tried to trace him by enlisting the help of newspapers and national radio. The last thing I wanted was to see sensational public speculation about John's fate suddenly inflicted on Joan and her mother, who had already suffered so much from deadful uncertainty. Also it seemed obvious from the way in which John had tried to communicate with me, and from the killing of his unfortunate messenger, that if still alive, he must be in a great and complex danger, too. A public hue-and-cry could only make his danger greater still. But Joan I would have to tell at once. I was still drafting a cable to her in my mind when we came to the railway station.

We were in good time. I found a berth for Zwong-Indaba and his bright calico bundles and hunting sticks in a third-class carriage in the Northern Express.

Ah! those bundles and those sticks. So often in my life I have seen Africans all over the continent tie up all they possess into light bundles, pick up two sticks just like these, and then with a free heart and the blind trust of a child take the first quick step of a journey a thousand miles into the unknown. There is heraldry in those brave bundles and gallant ivory sticks, yet Zwong-Indaba was not going into the unknown but going home, so there was no need to be so fanciful on his behalf, I told myself. All the same, I fear, our parting was a solemn one. There was nothing abnormal in the scene about us. The people in the coaches were happy, laughing, good-natured Africans who never fail to enjoy a train journey as much as does any average, healthy European child. I saw no evil on any of the faces, nor intimation of further tragedy anywhere there in the station. But I could not help saying to my servant: 'Remember one person has already been killed in this business of the feather and the empty envelope . . . even though we don't know why. Remember and be very careful. Beware of strangers and hasten, Zwong-Indaba, hasten to your home. Do what you have to do and then hasten back to us. There is no time to spare.'

'Aye, Bwana, aye.' The loyal soul promised willingly enough. 'I shall not linger on the road but hasten as you say.'

Then I left him standing by the train, for I thought I would attract too much attention if I lingered too long with him on the busy platform. When I came to the exit, however, I looked back over my shoulder and saw him still standing there staring after me, very silent and rather forlorn. Instinctively, and most incongruously in my civilian clothes, I turned right about and gave him a military salute. Immediately he raised his hand high above his head and gave me the salute the 'Takwena reserve for their royalty. The thought of my gesture comforts me to this day.

As I walked out of the station to my car, I was just in time to see a dark brown commercial van drive quickly away. I could not see who was inside it but the golden legend: 'Lindelbaum and Co., Wine and Spirit Importers, Exporters and Wholesalers' was unmistakable. During my life I've acquired an immense respect for coincidences of any kind. I don't believe them to be meaningless. That a chocolate-coloured Lindelbaum van should feature at both ends of my journey to the railway station seemed to me, to use my little general's favourite concept again, a fact of 'togethernesses' which I was determined to note and investigate; but first I drove to the main post office nearby to send my cable. I didn't send it to Joan direct, but to a friend of mine and of Joan's family whom I knew had just gone to the War Office:

Please see Joan immediately stop tell her I have just encountered important possibly not unhopeful clue about John stop beg her not to break the news to her mother until letter containing full details airmailed today reaches her
de Beauvilliers.

That done I send this long telegram to the Provincial Commissioner at Fort Herald:

Most grateful if you would send runner after Pieter le Roux with message to rejoin me as quickly as possible for most urgent repeat most urgent reasons stop believe he intended leaving your district two days ago for Upper Wuandarorie stop please telegraph how long you expect runner will take recall him stop assure you my need most pressing or would not bother you regards
Pierre de Beauvilliers.

From the post office I quickly went to the main police station near by. The inspector who'd been out to St Joseph's the night before was at home and asleep, but he'd been as good as his word and left a message for me saying he'd fully briefed the Water Police and ordered them to give first priority to the murder case of the day before. After reading through a type-script version of my statement, making a few minor alterations and signing it, I was free to go.

It was still early. I noticed as I drove past the station that the railway clock showed it to be only just after ten-fifteen. I realized that the Northern Express would still be standing in the station and for a moment my general anxiety tempted me to go and have another reassuring glimpse of Zwong-Indaba. However, I rejected the impulse, warning myself to be careful not to let my uneasiness get out of its natural proportions. So I drove straight on, past the statute of Jan van Riebeeck which once had stood close to the waters of the great Bay, his head delicately cocked to one side as if he were trying to gauge a subtle whisper of the sea which, three hundred years before, had brought his three gallant ships over the last silver coil of the South Atlantic horizon. Today, however, vast harbour extensions have driven the Bay far back from him and he stands with light fastidious poise in all his bronze and seventeenth-century frippery, incongruous and forlorn among the urgent press of traffic about him, his elegant back turned determinedly on the smoking ships of a new day.

Once past Van Riebeeck's statue I turned for the entrance to the old harbour. A Customs officer cheerfully took my word that I'd nothing to declare, let me into the harbour and directed me to the Water Police. A constable told me that though the officer I wanted was out, he was soon expected back from the inquiries he had been making since early morning among ships in the old harbour. Would I care to wait? Saying I'd come back in half-an-hour, I left my car parked outside the police station and went to look at the ships in the harbour.

The sea on this side of the peninsula was still and shining, with hardly a ripple on it. The harbour was full of shipping and the air clanging and clamorous. Ships and the sea have always possessed a kind of magic for me, perhaps because my own life had been so landlocked, and to this day they still retain to some extent a childhood element of dream material. As I strolled along for a while among them, I almost forgot what had brought me to the harbour. As I walked down the long line of ships I played the game of trying, from afar, to determine to what companies the ships belonged, judging purely from the colour of their paint and the markings on their funnels. I had eleven companies to my credit and only two wrong when a ship that I knew at once I'd never seen before swung into view.

The moment was vivid. I happened to be standing in the gap between the bows of a ship of the Clan MacGillivray and the stern of a Harrison freighter called the *The Statesman*; I remember thinking what a good master *The Statesman* must have for she looked as smart as if she had just been done-up for her first deep-sea wedding. There was not a speck of rust to be seen on her anywhere, a new Blue Peter fluttered briskly from a slender beige mast, while a gull, flashing like a mirror in the keen winter sun, sailed swiftly overhead. The ship was obviously loaded and ready for sea, and the air there so still that I heard above me the great hawsers which moored her to the quay groaning faintly with the strain of keeping her from the ocean. As my ears acknowledged the sound I looked down between the two ships to see what swing there could be to such tranquil water in so well-locked a harbour, and saw a dirty, indeterminate, uncommitted, greeny-grey bow poking out the tip of an undistinguished nose from behind the Clan MacGillivray. After the nose, equally unbeautiful, came the rest of the ship. Her decks were piled high with a cargo of timber which I admit did look golden and warm in the sun, but the vessel herself was colourless, drearily functional and without any lift or fancy of imaginative line. She lay extremely low in the water. I couldn't even tell who owned her, for her flag in the still air clung surlily to the stern-post and refused to unfurl. Two cheeky, snappy, harbour tugboats, their bulldog noses in the air, came yapping at her heels, so I hastened to the harbour mouth thinking it would be fun to see such spurious baggage bundled out of this beautiful tranquil bay.

I got there just in time to see the ship, about two hundred yards away, take the first slight tremor of the sea: but the light and shadows on it were still against my being able to read the name. I have good eyes and I could see the head and shoulders of the pilot pacing up and down the bridge and the crew in the bows and stern busily stowing away their mooring chains and tow-ropes, but I could pick out neither features nor faces at that distance. Yet, as I stared, I did see distinctly two heads suddenly pop out of portholes in the central deck-house. They were instantly withdrawn, as if someone behind had forcibly pulled them back, but brief as their appearance was, they were, I could have sworn it on the Bible, authentic Bantu heads!

So astonished was I that I could only stand there staring after the departing ship. And then suddenly I heard someone who'd come up behind me let out an amazed:

'Well, I'll be damned!'

I swung round, startled. 'Good heavens, Bill!' I said not without relief: 'What on earth are you doing here?'

'Good heavens, Pierre!' he answered, repeating my own question, an attractive smile going up like a light on his dark face. 'What on earth are *you* doing here?'

Bill Wyndham was a great friend of mine. He had a gallant war record and had lost his right leg as a result of it, but that didn't prevent him from being one of the most able and respected journalists in Africa. He'd have had his own paper long since if it had not been that he hated administrative work, loved the open air, and possessed a passion for reporting unusual events in his own unique and vivid manner. In particular, he loved the sea, and sailed his own boat up and down the coasts of Africa, in and out of every bay, nook, cranny, lagoon, and river mouth. He knew the East Coast of Southern Africa as no one else did, and for years now he'd made it the one condition of employment in his profession that he was allowed three months' leave every year for sailing. He never talked about the war, and, except for the limp, it seemed to have left no scars. But there was a look far back behind those warm, generous black eyes of his that I knew only too well. War, like any other school, has a special tie for its graduates, cut not out of silk or cotton but out of feelings and thoughts that walk cat-footed in the silences of the human heart, and this old school colour is easily recognized by all those who've worn it. That is why I say that, when Bill Wyndham smiled

48

at me it was like a light going up in a dark place in more ways than one. There was no one I would rather have met than Bill at that moment. Quickly I told him why I was there.

'And you, Bill? Why are you here?'

'Because of that ship,' he answered, shaking his stick at it with a mock disillusioned air. 'For that ship's no honest, decent ocean lady. . . . Here, let's sit on these stones and rest my leg for a minute, and I'll explain, if you really want to know, why the sight of that baggage enrages me.'

We found ourselves a seat on a large concrete boulder at the end of the breakwater and while Bill spoke I kept my eyes on the ship, which was beginning now to pick up the gentle swell and occasionally going just far enough over on her side to swill a glitter of sunlight round a porthole like the first sparkle of champagne poured into a crystal goblet. But I saw no more black heads come unexpectedly out of her side and soon, alas, she was too far from me to see any detail at all.

Yes, Bill told me, he was interested in that ship. As I surely knew, quite apart from loving the harbour for itself, he liked prowling around the place for stories for his newspapers, and from time to time he picked up some extremely good and unusual ones. For eighteen months now he'd been trying to go on board one of the vessels of the Line to which that ship belonged. For one thing the Line was a new one and that was news in itself. For another those ships had some unusual features about them, and moreover they were the subject of an odd rumour, but God knew where the rumour came from. This rumour had it that the ships were built in Russia; were, in fact, the Russians' idea of liberty shipbuilding. Whether they were Russian-owned, however, was another matter. The company's name translated into plain English was 'The Baltic and Gulf of Finland Trading Co.' and appeared to be registered in Helsinki. But the owners apparently had something odd about them, too, for try as he might, the agents of that Line did not seem to want him on board. They were always extremely polite and had the best of excuses for heading him off, always promising they'd invite him on board next time. But next time never came, although regularly, once a month, they had a ship in port. What is more, when in port, the ship kept herself to herself in a way no normal ship would do. As a rule nobody except the master and his purser, not even the first-officer, came ashore. They set about the task of getting their cargo landed and took fresh supplies in quickly, for, he had to admit, they were efficient beggars. At first he'd accepted their excuses, telling himself that they were foreigners and, perhaps, understandably nervous of newspapers. But it'd gone on too long; a month ago he'd visited the agents and warned them that unless they cooperated forthwith he would write a 'negative' story about the ships, under some such headline as 'Baltic Mystery Ships in Table Bay'. That had thoroughly alarmed them and they'd promised faithfully to invite him aboard the very next time. On Saturday morning he'd received a written invitation to lunch on the ship on that very day, Monday. Now here was Monday, here was he . . . and there was the ship.

'Yes,' he said, 'there she goes not only with my hopes but with my vodka and caviare or schnapps and smorgesbrod, or whatever it is they eat. However, I'll have revenge with my pen.'

He spoke with mock bitterness, but I knew enough of newspapers to see that he already possessed material for a first-class negative story and my instinct at once was to plead with him to hold his hand.

I asked first: 'What's she called?'

He smiled and shrugged his shoulders in a quite un-South-African way; he could do it more elegantly than anyone I knew.

'She's called the *Star of Truth*. They're all stars of some kind: Star of the East, of the Morning, of The Pole, of the Evening, and so on, but *that's* the *Star of Truth*, believe it or not!'

'But, Bill,' I interrupted, ' what sort of cargo does she carry, and what sort of crew?'

'Mostly timber and newsprint, I believe,' he answered. 'As for crew I can only guess, but I imagine a Baltic mixture.'

'She wouldn't carry any black Africans as well, would she?' I put the question as casually as I could.

'What?' Bill exclaimed, looking at me with such outright amazement that I knew he couldn't have seen what I'd seen. 'Don't be an ass, Pierre. I know you're a bit of a dreamer but you know what the rules are in this country against that kind of thing. We use black Africans on our own tugboats, coasters, fishing vessels, and official harbour craft, but we'd never let foreigners use them.' He shook his head. 'Of course, she might have picked up one or two black sailors further along the coast. But I don t believe even that. Causes too many complications on board. But why d'you ask?'

'Just wondering,' I replied casually, 'because as I told you, that chap who was killed at St. Joseph's last night was dressed like a sailor; judging by the cap Umtumwa speared, so were his killers.'

'But I thought you said he was a 'Takwena,' he remarked at once, curiosity obviously satisfied.

'So I did.'

'Out of the question then. 'Takwena don't sail willingly. You know better than I what they feel about the sea! Zulus, Basuto, 'Xosa, Fingo, Shangaan, Ovambu, even Herero, yes. But 'Takwena never . . . "

'I know—and yet I can't help wondering . . .' But again my instinct to keep my trouble as confined as possible held me off. So instead I asked: 'Where do these ships go, what cargo do they take from here? And you mentioned their agents: who are they?'

He stood up before he answered and I with him, and we both looked out to sea. 'They don't pick up much cargo,' he said slowly. 'A little tinned crayfish, some wine, and so on. Their biggest cargo they pick up in Port Natal. That's where they go from here, Port Natal to put down timber and load wool, bags and bags of it. Then from Port Natal to Sofala, Mozambique, and so on up the coast, through the Suez Canal, on, on back to their back Baltic sea. And their agents, of course, are Lindelbaum and Company in Keerom Street.'

So startled was I at this last piece of intelligence that before I could stop myself I said the loudest 'Oh, Lord!' of my life.

Bill looked down at me with renewed concentration and asked calmly: 'Why should you be so astonished at that?'

'Because I thought Lindelbaum's were wine and spirit merchants,' I covered up quickly. 'Not shipping agents.'

'So they are,' Bill said. 'But they're a lot of other things as well. For instance, they own a small crayfish factory here. But I can't pretend to know much about them.'

'Who are the Lindelbaums? Do they really exist or is it merely a trade-name come down from the past?' I asked.

'Old man Lindelbaum who founded the business is still alive, but that's almost all I know about him. I've heard he came out here penniless as a boy somewhere from the eastern part of Germany, and is today one of our richest men. But that's all. I've never met him. His manager at the end of the telephone is enough for me, and . . .' Bill stopped abruptly and added: 'Look! She's dropped the pilot and is hard about for the open sea.' He paused. 'You know, Pierre, that lady has something on her mind – and so have you.'

I smiled at him and pretended to take his last remark as a joke. Then I said: 'Bill, to be very serious a moment, will you do something for me?'

'Of course.'

'Then please don't write that negative story of yours about "Baltic Mystery Ships in Van Riebeeck's Bay" . . . and don't ask me why.'

For a second the expression on his face hardened, so I hastened on. 'What is more, please be very nice to the agents. Accept their excuses, whatever they are, with a good grace. Do everything you possibly can not to scare them. I'm certain you're right. There's something very, very odd going on. And I believe it's all got to do not only with the murder outside Petit France last night but also perhaps with other far more serious things; issues perhaps of life and death for whole peoples and countries. Every instinct I've got warns me you can't go carefully enough about this matter.'

I spoke earnestly from the start and when I'd finished Bill suddenly put both hands on my shoulders, looked me straight in the eyes and said irrelevantly:

'D'you know, Pierre, I don't believe you've changed a bit since the day I first saw you!"

My relief at the warm tone of his voice was intense, and with a light heart I asked: 'Why?'

He dropped his hands from my shoulders and resumed his watch on the sea. The receding *Star of Truth* was coming round now towards Signal Point and the Lion's Rump, to lay a course parallel to the Twelve Apostles. Port Natal, obviously, was her destination. As she did so, she wrapped a shawl of black cashmere smoke around her shoulders against the cold of the keen South Atlantic air.

Then Bill asked me if I remembered he'd been the first newspaper man to interview us the day my father returned to Petit France fifteen years ago? Well, he went on, he'd never forgot how, from the moment he heard of my father's return he had felt there was a symbol of contemporary history come alive, a symbol of history about to be carried into the future. If a man with such a history as my father could return like that, walk out of an iron resentment like someone out of a torn and tattered garment, then he believed millions of others could do the same. So he had come out to Petit France in great excitement to meet us. He had not been disappointed. But even at that time he'd realized it was I who'd got to live the future, since my father, obviously, had not long to live. And quite honestly he'd feared for me, I'd looked so like a young hunter bred and reared on the veld and brought straight away, without any preliminary training, to go through complicated paces in the crowded circus of civilization. And how and what was I to hunt among the neat vineyards of Petit France? Yet he needn't have worried, he now said with a smile of rare affection. He might have known I would learn to hunt in other dimensions. After all, what was I doing here on this ancient waterfront? It was no good thinking I'd fooled him. He'd known half-way through our conversation that I was here on the prowl after some strange new game, big game: perhaps some Arctic wolf or polar bear: who could tell? But that it was more than a 'Takwena murder trail that had brought me there he was as certain as certain could be. So he'd do all I asked. He'd be as sweet as a woman to Lindelbaum's manager. Moreover, he'd do it gladly and readily. No need to stress to me how hatred of one race for another was creeping over Africa. Ever since the war, he'd been aware of this dark breath of evil and negation like the imponderable contagion of a new black death in the shimmering air of Africa. But so long as the moment of rebirth which François de Beauvilliers's return had symbolized to him still lived in flesh and blood as he believed it did in me, then he'd continue to hope.

'So don't worry, Pierre,' he ended relapsing into his normal gay tone. 'My story can go to hell. You go after your beast, *and go to kill,* and I'll set about getting another host for lunch.'

He looked affectionately at me. I was so moved by the manner in which he'd spoken and the living concern in his point of view, that I couldn't meet his eyes but said: 'Thanks, Bill. I think you've got me and my rôle out of proportion . . . you always were an over-generous friend. But it's done me good to be taken so completely on trust by someone like you . . . Look, I can't ask you to lunch for I've a lot to do today. But what about coming out to Petit France for dinner and spending the night with me and I'll explain myself as fully as I can to you?'

'I'd like to very much,' he accepted at once.

'Well, that's settled then: we dine and talk tonight. . . . But meanwhile d'you think you could find out, very discreetly, if there were any black sailors in the *Star of Truth,* and if so how many?'

'Of course. But I warn you it's a waste of time.'

'No, it's not, Bill,' I said, and feeling that it was no longer fair to withhold the fact from him, I added: 'Keep it to yourself: but just before you came up behind me here I saw two black heads pop out of two deck-house portholes of the *Star of Truth.* No! I promise you I'm not mistaken; my eyes are too good for that and the ship was too near.'

'If you say so, of course I accept it,' Bill replied. 'But it's most unusual – so unusual that it wants most carefully looking into. I tell you what: our regular shipping correspondent knows all the pilots in port. I'll ask him to have a word with the pilot who took the *Star of Truth* out. . . . Phew, look at her, hull down already. Obviously fast in more ways than one, the hussy. D'you know, I think we'd better hurry. D'you think you could give me a lift back to town?'

Yes, he was right. I'd no time to spare. The sun stood as high as it could in the sky at this time of year. The grey old mountain behind the town had hardly a shadow left on its face and a breeze was beginning to rise from the sea. The lap of the water along the sea-front was quickening, the gulls overhead sounded sad and impatient, and across the harbour came the sound of an engine's imperious whistle and the huff and puff of a heavy goods train setting out on its long climb to the country north. One last look at the vanishing *Star of Truth* and we hurried to the Water Police. The officer I wanted was there, but he'd no news for me. He was still going on with his inquiries, but held out no hopes. He obviously agreed with his colleague's deduction that the dead man and his assailants were just a drunken lot of hooligans dressed in sailors' clothes bought from a Greek pawnbroker. I was careful not to mention the *Star of Truth* to him now and glad to leave after the shortest of interviews.

'D'you mind, Bill,' I said as we got into my car, 'if I drive to your office by way of Keerom Street and you show me Lindelbaum's?'

'Not at all,' he replied, and ten minutes later we were driving up Burghers Street in order to come down Keerom Street, when Bill said: 'Look! That's the back of Lindelbaum's.'

I saw a huge grey-storied building designed in the featureless soap-box manner which has taken both warmth of heart and charm of character out of the aspiring line of Van Riebeeck's city. In the courtyard stood a squadron of about twenty-five vans exactly like the one I'd seen parked at St Joseph's and the station. Had I been too hasty to look for extra-territorial meaning in that early-morning coincidence? The question answered itself a minute later for, when I drove slowly past the main entrance of the building, a big American car, luxuriously wide, drew up in front of it. A large, fat man, with a round sallow face, odd Mongolian head and dark sunglasses, got out and went up the wide steps with a marked agility strange in so large a person. Quick as he was, the moment his back was turned on me I recognized the black trousers green and shiny with age and wear.

'Bill! Quick! Who's that going into Lindelbaum's?'

'That, little old brother,' Bill said, 'is Hermann Harkov himself. Lindelbaum's shipping manager. Would you like to meet him?'

'On the contrary,' I said, as I put my foot hard on the accelerator. 'I would hate him to see us together just now. What's he like, Bill? What's his story? He looks like a kind of eunuch.'

'Really, Pierre, you're incredible,' Bill laughed, 'so he is; so he is if rumour is correct. Was made so by a splinter from one of Botha's shells in the German south-west campaign. I don't know much about him except that he's an old South-West hand and very efficient. Don't let his bulk ever deceive you though; it's a disguise. He's lean and sleepless inside. Why d'you ask?'

'I'll tell you tonight. But whatever you do when you speak to him later, don't tell him that you've been with me today.'

With that warning I left him and hastened back to Petit France to write, at last, to Joan.

Chapter 5

I Fly to Port Natal

My letter to Joan was written and ready for the late afternoon air-mail to the north. I drove back into town to the main post office where I myself sealed and registered it.

'How soon will this get to London?' I asked the clerk behind the counter.

He calculated quickly. 'Palmietfontein on the Reef at nine-thirty tonight; London-bound plane at 12.45 a.m. tomorrow, and Heathrow at 10 a.m. on the next morning. Your lady friend ought to have it by Wednesday afternoon at the latest.' His knowing smile suggested that only an affair of the heart could explain such expense and urgency, for the letter was both long and heavy.

I confess I hadn't found it an easy letter to write. Just to tell Joan the facts was not difficult, for they were straightforward enough. What was difficult was to interpret the facts, and after their interpretation to indicate what course we should follow. I didn't try to ignore or evade any of the difficulties. I admitted at once how wrong I'd been in not accepting sooner her clear intuition that John was still alive. The moment I was restored to health I should have started with all my energies to search for traces of John and Serge. I did not tell her about the paralysis of war I have mentioned because my own feelings now seemed to me unimportant. What did matter was that Joan and her mother had felt all along that John was alive, and had maintained their faith against the most painful circumstances without active help from me. I could now only tell her how grateful and glad I was they'd been proved right. I then added that, slight as the available facts were, I could not believe that John was dead: the ink on the envelope was too fresh and the hand-writing too steady for that. So henceforth I was assuming that John was alive, and was going at once to

57

set about discovering where. The only problem was how best and quickest to do it. I'd decided for the moment that my duty was to follow all local clues. I didn't complicate the picture for her by going into the 'Takwena aspect of the matter. Indeed I couldn't have done so without betraying the confidence of my servants. But I told her that I'd sent for Oom Pieter and was myself flying in the morning to Port Natal to see what light the *Star of Truth* could throw on the matter. Once Oom Pieter joined me, I concluded, I would quickly evolve a definite plan of campaign and let her know. Above all, I begged her to keep to herself what I'd told her, saying I was convinced that official investigation into John's fate could only imperil him at this stage. With that I signed it, 'Always, Pierre'. As I did so I wanted to say: 'Always yours, Pierre,' but wouldn't allow myself to do it. Again as I blotted the page, I wanted to add: 'Your photograph is still beside me, still where I put it twelve years ago on my writing table.' But some impediment forbade this addition too.

With the letter written and safely in the post I felt better. I returned to Petit France with the same sort of warm excitement mounting in my blood as I used to feel whenever my father and Oom Pieter announced a fresh *safari*. I felt as a becalmed sailor feels when he sees a Persian paw of wind darken a silver sea and the look-out in the human heart cries: 'The wind at last: the Spirit moves.' Perhaps Bill was right and some blessed alchemy of mind and being of which I was unaware had sublimated the primitive hunter in me. Anyway, whatever it was, it sent me to my tea with a zest.

After tea I saw to the business of my estate which I'd neglected all day. For defensive reasons, the first François de Beauvilliers had built his lovely Petit France unusually high up on the slope of the mountains which overlook the present-day village of St Joseph's. He was the first settler there, miles from any neighbour in a country full of wild game, roving Hottentots, and bow and poison-arrow bushmen. The vine-yards start immediately behind the house, round a broad spur of the mountains, and run on far into the sheltered plains be-yond. The farm buildings, wine presses, stills, cellars, and fer-menting vats are all at the far end of this cultivated area. A brisk walk took me there in ten minutes and I was glad to find my manager in the cellars with all the coloured foremen assembled about him planning the next day's work. Soon I'd given them a programme guaranteed to keep them all occupied for many months, and was about to say good-bye, when suddenly I saw old Arrie, the oldest among them, born and bred on Petit France, wipe some tears with the back of his hand out of dim but oddly blue eyes.

'Why, Arrie, what's the matter?'

'Ou Seur,'* he said in the spontaneous way of our coloured people, which is one of many qualities that so endears them to me. 'You talk as if you are going away for a long time again and that is not good for Petit France. Here you are talking to us again just as you did the night before the war took you. Why must you always be going to places where your eyes cannot see us and our words cannot reach you?' He finished unashamedly in tears.

'No, Arrie,' I reassured him, putting a hand on his shoulder, 'I'm going, so far as I know, only for a day or so. But I've a lot of new business to attend to and may not see you all as often as I'd wish for a while.'

But I fear old Arrie was not really comforted. Just shaking his grey head, he muttered tearfully to himself.

Then I left them. Already it was dark and cold. The stars were out and very clear with a crisp crackling silvery winter shiver in their light. I went quickly down the long line of the vineyards. The heavy cropped winter heads of the vines showing up as a deeper dark on the night around me, seemed charged with New Testament meaning. Down the western shore of the great False Bay, past the Naval Base just clear of a faint mountain line, the Southern Cross was sinking to the sea like Arthur's sword returning to the waters of Avalon. I thought that perhaps Bartholomew Diaz who first rounded this stormy Cape, or Vasco da Gama who found it full of great Good Hope, and all of the stalwart band who followed them, from Albuquerque to Francisco D'Almeida, must have seen it, too, on nights such as this, and corrected their urgent courses

* *Ou* – old, but used continually in Afrikaans as an endearment, or sign of respect or both. *Seur* – Originally the French 'Seigneur' introduced by my Huguenot forebears and used by all the older coloured people in preference to Meneer.

thereby. Behind me the planet Venus, softly locking the great door of the day on the sun's departure, was so large and bright that it seemed to throw a faint shadow of myself in the road before me.

Soon I was out of the vineyards, and for convenience entering Petit France by the back door. The kitchen was empty but on the table stood my tray still with cake and uneaten toast on it, reminding me I had lately been neglectful of my horse Diamond, who, in his eighteenth year, was handsomer than ever because of the grey rising and spreading out like a mist at night in the hair around his sensitive black muzzle and smooth cheek. He expected me, whenever I was at home, to visit him after tea with buttered toast which he loves and which in his old age I gladly give him, though I am warned I shall ruin his teeth. So I took four large slices, buttered them quickly and went out again. Diamond knew my step as well as any human being. Before I got to him, he heard me and neighed with pleasure. I know no lovelier sound. Out there in the dark, in the clear Antarctic air of our winter, the sound went up like a scatter of silver sparks on the night. Then I entered, gave him his toast and stood there with my hand in his great mane, listening to him crunching contentedly in the dark, for that, too, is one of my favourite sounds.

I got back to the house just as Bill turned up, and I talked with him until late by the fire in the old drawing-room of Petit France. I told him all about John and Joan whom he remembered, about Serge, my little General, and the escape from the grim prison outside Harbin. I told him everything about the night before – except, of course, about the feather and its meaning. I did tell him, though, about the tattoo marks on the dead man's face and their significance.

He listened to me with growing excitement, and when I reached this point his emotion heaved him out of his chair so violently that I think his artificial leg hurt the living stump, for he made a slight grimace, before exclaiming, 'My God, Pierre, what a reflection on our prevailing attitude to the black people of Africa, and our appalling ignorance of their minds and customs. . . . A member of an ancient royal house, a prince among people of millions, is murdered in our midst – and only you recognize the assassination for what it is.'

'Must be fair, Bill. You can't expect the people here to know the 'Takwena as I do.'

'No. But we – and I include myself – should know more than we do for we employ enough of them,' he returned with emphasis. 'Listen! I've combed all the papers for news of your murder and all I've found is a tiny paragraph used to fill an awkward column at the foot of the page to this effect: "Over the weekend fifteen cases of stabbing among natives, two of them fatal, were reported to the police in the Peninsula and are being investigated." Just that and no more. . . . For what do we care? That's what we always do; lump them together in our minds and our hearts, lump them together in life and death, never see them as individuals with their own unique imaginations and needs, but just go on lumping them together as in this report.' He paused. 'But to return to first things first. Did you recognize your assassinated prince? Did your servants? What's his name?'

I shook my head and told him we none of us knew, but that I had that morning put Zwong-Indaba on the Northern Express to Fort Herald and Umangoni, and hoped he'd bring back some sort of an answer, though I was careful not to indicate what else I expected from Zwong-Indaba on his return.

'Have you thought of the next step?' Bill asked me then with a grave look in his warm eyes. Between his question and my answer, in the winter stillness of Petit France, a log suddenly hissed like a salamander in the fire and ran a small blue-peter of flame up the chimney.

'Yes,' I told him. 'I can't go to the police yet. Too dangerous for John . . . if he's alive. I must begin by investigating it by myself with my own people, and out of my own resources. I've wired to Fort Herald to bring Oom Pieter back as fast as possible. Meanwhile I propose flying to Port Natal tomorrow to have another look at the *Star of Truth*. How long will she take to get there, Bill?'

'Three days and a bit, perhaps. Today's Monday: so Monday, Tuesday, Wednesday – Thursday afternoon by the latest, I should say. But Pierre, you mustn't talk as if you're alone in this. Won't you let me help?'

I thanked him warmly and said that the kind of help I needed might not satisfy his adventurous soul. What I needed most at the moment was someone, wise and trustworthy, to stay at Petit France and hold it as a base for me; someone who'd open all the letters and telegrams that came and communicate anything relevant to me; someone who'd watch over my servants as if they were his own. I knew of no one who could do it except him. Would he be prepared therefore in the morning to move in from the City and take over Petit France for me?

'Of course,' he agreed at once. 'I see that it's important, though I'd much rather have come with you. I can't, however, move in until the evening, for I've to lunch with your eunuch tomorrow.'

'What, Harkov?' I exclaimed.

'Yes. He telephoned to me just as I got back, full of apologies. Said he'd had a telephone call from Port Natal on Sunday evening ordering the *Star of Truth* to report there as soon as possible for an extremely profitable charter up the coast. He'd had no option but to order the ship to sea first thing on Monday morning, and direct it to transfer its local cargo to a Lindelbaum coaster at Port Natal. I was as sweet to him as I promised you I'd be, and he was so relieved that he asked me to lunch. I'm looking forward to it more than I can say and I'll let you know at once how it went. But how shall I get hold of you?'

'I was going to ask you to arrange a fixed telephone call to me at the Port Natal Club every alternate night at nine. I shall reciprocate with a call to you here on the nights in between.'

By the time we'd talked out our subject, I confess I was more than ready for bed. The night before I'd hardly slept, and now the sight of the sheets turned back over my warm Dassie-Kaross* looked to me like the haven of peace. But before turning in, the night being so fine. I flung the curtains apart and the windows wide. The last thing I remember was seeing the night standing quietly to attention at my window like a tall pine in the Black Forest. Yet hardly had I fallen asleep when I heard Slim whimpering rather as he does in camp when there are lion about. I was awake at once and feeling for my gun, which on safari is always beside me, before I realized I was lying in a solid, Dutch double-bed and that the noise had

* A rug made of the skins, of *Dassie*, a furry African rock-rabbit.

ceased. I listened carefully for a while but heard no sound except that of the sea swishing its skirt like a *sari* of Indian silk along the sandy beaches of False Bay below. I thought I must have been dreaming, and was instantly asleep again.

At seven Umtumwa called me with a large cup of hot coffee and I went to stand at the window to watch the dawn sailing like a ship of flame into the sky. Then I heard a loud wail from Tickie and saw him dragging something heavy from behind the border of my sky-blue hydrangeas.

'What is it, Tickie?' I called out.

'Auck, Bwana, Auck,' he cried with fierce despair. 'Slim . . . he is dead.'

Though the 'Takwena will use the term 'dog' as an insult, they themselves, unlike many other African races, are very fond of dogs. Tickie from the start had taken to Slim and Slim to him, and his grief now was as great as mine.

I hastened down and looked at the dog. He was stretched out stiff and cold, his eyes open and round his mouth was a frozen white froth. I recognized it instantly.

'What's going on down there?' Bill's voice called out above me.

'Slim's been poisoned in the night,' I replied, as I looked up to see him hanging half-out of his bedroom window. 'The murderers have been back. You see, Bill, how necessary it is for someone to take over here from me? You may not find it so unadventurous after all.'   •

'Did they do anything else?' he asked grimly.

'Don't know yet, but I'll soon see,' I replied.

Quickly Umtumwa, Tickie, 'Mlangeni my second cook and I went over the house, outbuildings, and home garden. Except that one flower-bed had been trampled by human feet we found nothing amiss. But that decided me to give my servants the gravest of warnings, telling them I was certain this was only the second, but not the last, of a series of dangerous attacks. 'They', whoever they were, had obviously wanted to get rid of the dog so as to have every chance of getting at the house unobserved. I therefore ordered the servants, between them, to arrange a night watch on the house. Out of my anxiety I rather unnecessarily gave Bill the same warning, except that I added this qualification: 'I suspect it's really me they're after,

63

for fear of what the dead man may have told me before he died, and they may leave the house alone when they find I've gone. ... But do keep a good look-out, Bill, and please take good care of yourself.'

'Nothing bad's going to happen here if I can help it,' he answered with a flash in his eyes and a defiant note in his voice.

Just before eight the post came and with it a cable and a telegram that had been received in the night. I opened the cable first, thinking as the white knife slit the saffron envelope: 'This must be an answer to my message to Joan.' It was not, but it was from Joan. Sent off from Innsbruck at 21.00 hours the night before it read: 'Austrian prisoner returned Russia, given me certain proof Serge Bolenkov reached Western Russia from Harbin alive stop en route London now consult Foreign Office stop please come you must come help at once love Joan.'

'Look at that, Bill!' I said, handing him the cable without comment but my tension obvious from my tone.

Bill whistled between his teeth as a hunter does at a buck when he wants to lift its head for a certain kill. He asked at once: 'But do you think it right for your Joan to rush into the Foreign Office with such news just now? Won't that set off an almighty official hullaballoo? Would that be useful or necessary?'

'Certainly not,' I answered energetically. 'I've already warned her by letter. I'm convinced myself that it would be quite the wrong moment to start another official investigation into John's disappearance. If he was in the sort of situation where official interference could be helpful, I am certain, knowing him as I do, that he would have found a way of drawing official attention to his situation long since. No! Every instinct I've got warns me that we must go about this business as discreetly and unobtrusively as possible. I'm certain that's what John wants and needs, and I warned Joan accordingly again.'

'I quite agree,' Bill said. 'But, I say, it's grand news about Bolenkov, isn't it?' He paused. 'Has it occurred to you that the big game you're after might turn out to be not spotted lion or polar bear, but the Russian ursus major itself?'

'Of course it has: I can hardly think about any other possibility as it is. That's why I've not spoken of it, even to you,' I told him, 'for all my tracking has taught me never to allow my thoughts to run ahead of the spoor. Tracking demands a discipline of faith and humilty that would surprise you, and always the spoor in itself, and not what you would wish to think about it, can be the only leader.'

This I tried to explain to him as I started to open the telegram. It was from the Provincial Commissioner at Fort Herald and read: 'Le Roux wagons left five days ago stop have sent police jeep try catch him before crosses frontier stop with luck should have him on Friday's Southern Express stop delighted help don't hesitate demand assistance whenever required regards PC.'

Today was Tuesday. That meant that Oom Pieter could not get to me at the earliest for another eight days. It was disappointing, but it could have been worse and I was grateful to the Commissioner for responding with such prompt good grace.

To Joan I then cabled: 'Delighted your news but please await my letter airmailed yesterday stop on no repeat no account enlist official aid yet stop am off today on hot parallel clue of my own which maybe ruined thereby stop if that fails us will hasten to you forthwith love Pierre.' But as I drafted it I felt sick at heart wondering whether, after my post-war history, this, too, might not sound like a plausible excuse to postpone coming to her aid. I could only hope my letter was well-enough spoken to put that impression right.

At breakfast Bill gave me a letter he'd written in the night to the Captain in charge of Port Natal. 'You can rely on him as you can on me,' he told me. 'I knew him well when he was stationed here and we've been on many a cruise together up and down the coasts of Zululand and Mozambique. He's intelligent, efficient, and a rare good fellow. If I were you I'd go to him at once, confide in him as much as you can, and get his cooperation.'

In my anxiety to get away inconspicuously I did not go to the aerodrome by car but went down to the electric train station in the village, carrying a light suitcase, much to the chagrin of Tickie who thought it was beneath my dignity. I had, indeed, to be firm with them all over it, adding to my final: 'No, thank you' a 'don't forget to keep good watch and if anyone finds out I'm gone and wants to know where, tell them I've gone to Johannesburg for a few days on business.'

I was glad I did so, for as I walked across the road into the railway station entrance a Lindelbaum van came out of a side road behind me, swung left and drove off fast towards the harbour city.

At the main station, however, I saw no more of the van, though I'd no doubt that its driver would have got to a telephone soon enough to bring an observer from Lindelbaum's to meet my train. If that were so I could do nothing useful about it. With apparent unconcern I joined the crowd hurrying out of the station courtyard to the main street, turned smartly right and in a few minutes was at the Airways Centre. There I bought a return ticket to Johannesburg and an hour later was airborne over the Peninsula. In that lovely early morning light of winter, every detail of the landscape below me stood out with a disturbing valedictory intensity. Far away I saw Petit France standing guard over its vineyards on blue slopes by the edge of the sea, benign and unthreatened, as if it had never known the coming of the fear whose shadow darkened my heart.

Chapter 6

The *Star of Truth* Arrives in Port Natal

There was no one in the aeroplane who appeared unduly interested in me, but it did occur to me that Lindelbaum's by now might well be aware that I was in the aircraft and would telephone a description of me to some proxy in Johannesburg with instructions to pick me up the moment I arrived. As the flight lasted only just over three hours, however, I felt certain they couldn't do all that in time to get their agent out to the aerodrome at Palmietfontein to meet me. At the worst I had to reckon with the possibility that an observer would be posted at the air-centre in the heart of the town to screen all arrivals from the aerodrome. Accordingly, just in case Lindelbaum's agent telephoned to the aerodrome and asked for news of me, when the aeroplane landed at Palmietfontein I requested a seat in the official airways bus into town under my own name. That I hoped might both reassure and mislead him. I had no intention of going into town. Then I went over to the departure counter, bought a ticket for Port Natal under the name of Jensen of 359 Montpelier Road, Port Natal, both name and address being invented on the spur of the moment. I hadn't long to wait. The fashionable Port Natal season was nearing its annual climax and all sorts of extra aircraft had been put on the Rand route to meet the expanding demand of the people fleeing from the cold and shrinking High-veld to the sunny beaches of the Indian Ocean. Before my fellow passengers of the morning were packed into their bus I was on my way in one of the last aircraft of the day bound for Port Natal, having paused only at the last minute to slip a shilling in the bus conductor's hand and whisper: 'A friend in a car has unexpectedly called for me.' Once in the aircraft I felt free of immediate anxieties for the first time that day. Both reason and instinct told me only sheer indiscretion on my part, or extreme ill-fortune, could redirect any Lindelbaum associates to my new spoor. I didn't fear any indiscretion on my own part because the sense of urgency was too deeply entrenched in me. Neither somehow did I then fear ill-fortune. So I relaxed in my seat and prepared to enjoy the flight.

We travelled fast that evening in the aeroplane through the pink and blue of the cold, wintry twilight, high over the long Grey River, over the pouted lip of the Dragon Mountains, over long purple escarpments, angry gorges, and over a valley of a thousand hills and the green folded earth of the warm heart of Natal, racing the swift experienced wings of the night for light and safe harbour. Yet fast as we travelled, just before we reached Port Natal the night came up on us like a black ship flying a defiant skull and cross-bones of sunset at its mast. I looked out and there, ahead of us, on the edge of the dark stood Port Natal like a beauty brilliant in long silks, pearls at the throat, dark head crowned with tiara. Then we were high over the Bay, circling in the dark air over black water sequined with the light of an immense concourse of shipping. A glittering pile of buildings, strangely insubstantial and translucent with electricity, rose up underneath a long aluminium wing, fell away astern and quickly the pilot made a difficult landing with great skill. As the engines stopped in that brief hush that followed I heard the determined breakers of the Indian Ocean pounding on a beach hard by, like a tired traveller saying, 'Let me in, let me, I come from Malabar and Bombay and demand shelter and rest.'

From the aerodrome I took a taxi straight to the Port Natal Club. The Club is placed comfortably on a slight rise about half-way between two ends of the harbour, with the glittering waters of the wide bay at its feet, a lane of shipping almost passing its front door. This, together with the fact that I'd thought it easier to get the privacy I needed in a Club rather than in an hotel had decided me to put up there.

No sooner was I in my room than I telephoned to the Port Captain's Office in the harbour, told him I'd a letter for him from Bill, and arranged to see him at ten the following morning. After a bath and a change into cooler clothing, I went and sat on the verandah and ordered some tea from an Indian waiter.

The verandah was empty except for one table at which four men were drinking and talking. I could easily have overheard what they were saying but was not even tempted to try, for the Bay, its shipping, and the road below me held my attention until a fifth man arrived to join them, saying loudly: 'Sorry I'm late but I've had a hell of a day.' He then went on to explain that the night before his cook, who'd been with him on and off for years, had come to him begging in great agitation for permission to go home. He'd remonstrated but the old servant had just gone off leaving him flat.

At this one of the group exclaimed: 'Serves you right for employing a 'Takwena.'

'A 'Takwena? What an odd coincidence,' another member of the group remarked. 'I was just talking to George Hardbattle and his servant did exactly the same thing last night, and now I come to think of it he was a 'Takwena too.'

'Glad I'm not the only one,' muttered the first man, slightly appeased, as he sat down.

But I was far from glad. For my intuition told me that this was no coincidence. Zwong-Indaba clearly was not the only one on the long road to Umangoni for news of the dream.

Thereafter I could hardly contain myself in patience for Bill Wyndham's telephone call. Luckily he came through punctually at nine.

'What a day!' he began gaily. 'Did you have a good flight?'

'I did. But why that "what a day"?'

'Harkov,' he answered, with a grimmer note in his voice. 'I warned you he's no easy-going, fat fool. I had a nice, pretty meeting with him at lunch. D'you know one of the first things he said to me? "I didn't realize you lived out at St Joseph's, Mr Wyndham."' Bill imitated a high-pitched eunuch's voice with a Teutonic husk to it so well that I had to smile in spite of the disquiet the news caused in me. Bill then went on to describe how he'd stalled for time, thinking how best to spar with Harkov, but had soon realized that only a full confession of all verifiable details could lull the shipper's keen suspicions. For Harkov said that he'd passed Bill's car turning into the main road at the village station so early in the morning that he could only assume he'd suddenly changed lodgings. So thinking fast, Bill said: 'No, I don't live there.

69

But I had dinner and spent the night with an old friend of mine, Pierre de Beauvilliers.'

'I don't know him but I've heard of him,' Harkov had replied with the expression of a born *ingénu*: 'He wasn't by any chance the person who drove you past our offices at 12.30 p.m. yesterday?'

'That's him,' Bill answered. 'As a matter of fact he'd been called to town by the police. There'd been a murder at his place the night before.'

'What!' Harkov exclaimed with well-feigned surprise.

'A native, a black murder,' Bill went on casually. 'Just another of these week-end faction fights among black drunks. So the police called Pierre into town for a formal disposition, that's all.'

'Do they know who did it?' Harkov insisted.

'No idea,' Bill answered, dismissing the affair. 'Neither Pierre nor the police seem excessively interested in it.' But as he said this, Bill knew he was at a critical point in his relations with Harkov. Harkov obviously knew a lot so if he, Bill, now withheld news of my departure, he was certain Harkov's suspicions would be off again like a pack in full cry. Consequently he added: 'In fact, Pierre is so little concerned about the murder that he went off to the Transvaal today. That's why he wanted to see me. He wanted to ask me to look after Petit France for him until his return. He doesn't like leaving his servants in it alone.'

'I'm not surprised,' Harkov had replied. 'But will you be there for long?'

Bill saw through that but answered as truthfully as he could. 'Pierre didn't know himself how long his business would take him. You see,' he continued, using all his powers of imagination quickly to invent a mission in keeping with my known character, 'he's gone to look for horses salted against horse-sickness to take with him on a long safari somewhere north. He doesn't believe much in our southern inoculations against the tropical brand of the virus. But such horses are hard to come by – so I shall just sit out at Petit France until I next see him.'

'How lucky to be able to set off into the blue when you want to, instead of working in a dreary office,' Harkov had replied assuming a look of boyish whimsicality which sat oddly on his wide Mongolian face.

'Oh, Pierre's been planning this safari for a year to my knowledge,' Bill had answered with a laugh. 'His uncle's already up north collecting bearers and is soon due back here to report.'

With that Bill had felt the suspicion collapse in Harkov. They proceeded to have a rich, expensive luncheon, in the greatest amiability. Bill had even twitted Harkov over the *Star of Truth*'s sudden departure and the lunch he'd missed in consequence, and Harkov had promised Bill not luncheon but dinner in the very next ship in port, the *Star of the East*. They parted with expressions of great good will and esteem.

'But,' said Bill to me now, 'there was a sting in the tail of our parting. As he left me he said: "Well then, Mr Wyndham, I hope to see you again after I get back from Port Natal".'

'What!' I said, dismayed.

'Yes,' Bill affirmed. 'You'd better look out. He's due in Port Natal on Thursday noon. By accident or design he's not giving you any time alone with the *Star of Truth*; so now – over to you.'

Briefly I told Bill of my uneventful day, said I thought his handling of Harkov superb and finished by saying: 'Would you tell Umtumwa tomorrow to get out all my guns, go over them carefully, check the ammunition, and see that my hunting gear, clothes, boots, mosquito nets, groundsheets, bags, are all in order? And perhaps Bill, now that Harkov knows I'm gone you may all have peace – but please go on assuming the worst.'

'Don't you worry a bit, little old fellow,' he replied, and his gay voice was as clear as if he were in the room with me. 'I wish you could see Tickie now on his rounds outside with the largest knobkerrie I've ever seen. And you'll telephone me tomorow at nine? Fine. Well, good night then.'

'Good night, Bill,' I said, feeling so reluctant to let him go that I sat there ear to the telephone for some seconds after I'd heard the click of disengagement.

Then, hearing music in the street I crossed slowly over to the window and saw a Zulu walking easily under the palms by the road, dressed only in a long evening shirt so white that it

71

bobbed like a lamp against the dark water-front. A guitar slung from his shoulder like that of some medieval minstrel, he strummed as he went a little tune of his own invention, five urgent bars only, played over and over again, faint, soft, loud, louder, loudest, up down, down up. Long after the night had extinguished the wick of his shirt I heard his little tune go along deeper and deeper into the silence by the water like flicker and flare of fire in the dark, and I wished I had had but half such music in me then.

However I felt better in the morning. Probably knowing that I was sleeping not in a threatened house but in absolute security enabled me to have a really restful sleep. By nine I'd breakfasted and was walking slowly along the water-front so as to make the most of the busy harbour scene, as I was not due at the Port Captain's office till ten.

When I was finally shown into his office I understood at once why Bill had liked him so much. He had a fine head, large, steady grey eyes which looked very bright in the deep tan of his face and were well apart, and both his mouth and the skin of his face were even and firm. Everything about him suggested balance and proportion acquired by wide experience of vocation and life. As I watched him reading through my letter of introduction, I decided I'd do well to confide in him.

'Look, Mr de Beauvilliers,' he said, like one accustomed to making decisions quickly. 'I'll just leave word that we're not to be disturbed and then I'll be delighted to do all I can to help.'

I told him the whole story from the moment I came out on my stoep at Petit France to when I saw two black heads pop out of a strange ship. He listened with great concentration and growing interest. When I gave the *Star of Truth* her proper name, I saw the grey eyes come to a point of their own, as if somewhere unseen a great umpire had given the signal for the real game to begin.

'Oh! One of those!' he exclaimed.

'So you know about them too?' I asked.

'Let's just say I'm very interested,' he replied.

I continued, but when I mentioned Lindelbaum and then Harkov by name, I detected the same look in his eyes and said with a surprised laugh: 'Surely, Captain, not one of those again?'

He nodded his head, joined in my laugh in a way which suggested that I had gone up in his estimation for learning to read his face so promptly. Then he listened with silent interest to the end.

'I've no doubt you're on to something big,' he said at last with emphasis as I finished, 'though I've no idea as to what it can be. But listening to your story and filling it in with mine, I should say you couldn't possibly overrate the importance of the matter. . . . So much so that I'm forced to ask myself, and you, whether we shouldn't at once jump into an aeroplane and go straight to the Capital to the highest in the land with your story.' He paused. 'But first things first: the *Star of Truth*. Well, I'm naturally interested in all the ships and all that happens in my area. But this line has interested me particularly, though for a different reason from Bill's. What set me off – and I must say I'm surprised that Bill appears to have forgotten it – was something that happened last year when he and I sailed his ship up to Diaz Bay. The day Bill and I left this harbour, we were only a mile or two beyond the bar when this very *Star of Truth* came out after us, dropped her pilot smartly and stood out promptly north to sea, heading fast for Mozambique. There was hardly a bosun's capful of wind about that month. We came along in her wake doing a miserable four to five knots, but before we lost her I couldn't help noticing that she'd a remarkable turn of speed for a ship plying à freighter's trade. I know they're not much to look at outside but they've good heart and muscles in their engine-rooms. Imagine my amazement, therefore, when a week later, at sundown, a ship appeared almost hull down on the horizon and passed us on a parallel course going fast and at great range. The light was uncertain but I was sure as I fixed my glasses on her squat, ill-bred nose that she was the *Star of Truth.* What was she doing there then? She should have been in and out of Mozambique long since. Also she was well off the normal trade routes. I mentioned it to Bill and then forgot about it. Some months ago, however, I had to send one of my ocean-going tugs up to Mikandani to salve a Greek who'd piled himself up on a coral reef. When the tug came back the master said to me, "those Star boats are slower than I thought. D'you know I passed the *Star of the North* just standing in towards Mozambique after I myself had escorted her to sea four days before I left." Again I said nothing at the time.' He paused. 'You may think it peculiar that I did nothing about it. But what could I do? If fast ships like to go slow on the high seas that's their business. But now you come with a completely new angle to it and that makes it different.' He faced me. 'I think we should seriously consider the question of having the *Star of Truth* impounded and searched.'

'If you do that we may recover our black assassins, but the alarm bells will have been set ringing and my trail'll end just when the spoor is beginning to freshen,' I countered quickly. 'I've no doubt that time will come, but not yet. I've a hunch if I can only stick to the *Star of Truth* she'll lead me to the heart of this sinister matter. So help me as only you can, please,' I pressed. 'For instance, tell me, is it only between Port Natal and Mozambique that these ships are so slow! Is there a place anywhere in between where they could call or tie-up unseen?'

He did not reply at once. I knew everything I had said and all factors that appeared relevant to a man in his position, were being scrupulously weighed in the balance of his experienced sailor's mind. I knew that the decision when it came would be in the round. Yet I trembled strangely within, for the moment, of course, was vital and if he decided to act as he had suggested, then I despaired of ever unravelling this urgent mystery. The detail of the moment is still with me. I still see the light amber of the edges of his tidy mahogany desk, the anchors on his gold buttons burning in the midnight blue of his uniform. I still hear outside a sudden, sad outburst of gulls, hungry for food, hungrier for the open sea and the long sustained blast that went up in the harbour from the purple Royal Mail steamer's siren. Hardly had the blast faded when there flew up in the air a snappy tug's pert reply.

Suddenly he leaned forward and with a smile and a tone of voice that reflected, I thought, a tender but fierce pride in his vast organization ashore, asked: 'Did you hear that?'

I nodded and he said: 'The Royal Mail fussing out of fear that she will leave one minute late, but quite unnecessarily so,

74

as you would have gathered from the tug's reply if you knew these sounds as I do.' Then almost in the same breath he added slowly to my great relief: 'But I think you're right, Mr de Beauvilliers. Fate has clearly pointed a finger at you in this matter and we'd be foolish to ignore it. You were the first to take positive action and I for my part hand over to you willingly. This quest is your ship, you're the master, and I'll do all I can to help you sail it. As for your questions: Lourenco Marques is the only port worth mentioning between here, Sofala, and Mozambique, and when the Star ships sail in and out of there we're informed by radio. But I assure you that on the three occasions in question we were not informed. The explanation which leaps to mind instantly is that they have a sinister port of call on the way. But where? I know that coast well and there are no harbours or accommodating roadsteads for ships of any kind, let alone ones that size. . . . And your other question: what happens between Mozambique and the rest of the coast and the Baltic, heaven knows. But I could check for you as far as Suez, if you wish it.'

I thanked him warmly but said it wasn't necessary, as yet, to go beyond Mozambique in our inquiries.

'But Lindelbaum? What do you make of him?' I asked him. 'It really would help me greatly if you could tell me something about him.'

'I'm rather sorry for him,' he replied. 'Harkov's the only chap I dislike – though for no reason except the cut of his jib. His physical appearance just has that effect on me. But old Otto' – he shrugged his shoulders – 'I knew him quite a bit when I was Assistant Port Captain at the Cape. People say he's just a bitter, vindictive Prussian, but he had cause to be. He came here from somewhere in the Baltic as the result of some pogrom fifty years ago, an undernourished youngster with not a penny to his name. . . . He then got busy, made an immense fortune and out of gratitude to the land which gave him his wealth was generous to its charities and richly endowed its schools and universities. Then came the 1914–18 war and what do we do? Thinking "once a Prussian always a Prussian", in August 1914 we burn his business down here and in the Cape, and then intern him. When this war came we proceeded to break his heart a second time and burn him down and lock him up all over again. No wonder he's bitter, but I admire his guts. After each fire he comes out of the ashes like a phoenix and builds himself bigger and better businesses. You've seen his place in the Cape? He's got another as big here, and a large palace out on Beckett's Hill. You know, of course, that he's also the Trans-Uhlalingasonki Trading Corporation.'

'What!' I exclaimed in astonishment.

'You seem surprised?'

'No. It's just because I never imagined Lindelbaum's was such a vast concern,' I answered feebly, for how explain the complexity of emotion, memory and speculation which this one piece of news set off racing in me?

I knew the Uhlalingasonki Trading Corporation well. Who does not, who's been born and bred in the interior of Africa as I had? It's everywhere. In every native city, village, hamlet, along the rare highways, on the tracks, by the lakes and waterways, sometimes alone on a clearing in the bush where many footpaths meet, you find the Corporation's stores and representatives. And this is particularly true of Umangoni: hence Uhlalingasonki,* the great legendary river of the Amangtakwena, at the head of its title, for it was in Umangoni that Lindelbaum had first set up as an itinerant trader. In an instant, I remembered one evening nearly a quarter of a century before in our camp on the southern frontier of Umangoni. A great storm had been blowing up fast and it was nearly dark. The black acacia tops were crying like hungry puppies under the weight of air pregnant with wind and electricity. Then out of the bush came a European with two black servants and asked for shelter. His truck had broken down on a track two miles back, and he was casting round for a native settlement when he saw our smoke. In particular I remember the stranger's face. The handsome, dark face of a man about fifty, but with an expression showing deep, bitter, and permanent hurt; the face of a dreamer gone wrong, of a heart anchored and imprisoned in some unexplained nightmare moment of its own. It frightened me, but not my father. He had much of the same thing in him just then, and it drew him

---

* *Uhla:* Sindakwena for long; *linga* for twisting; and *sonki* the sound of fast water over stone.

strangely to the stranger. They talked together nearly until dawn, and when he left us the next morning my father remarked, 'There goes the commercial prince of Umangoni: The Trans-Uhlalingasonki Trading Corporation in person.' He then told us that when Lindelbaum had landed in Africa, penniless and alone, he'd at once seen little chance of making a career in the towns of Africa so had worked his way far inland, trying his hand at this and that and learning the native tongues and customs with all the facility of one who, because of his own past, understood well the oppressed and despised. Then one day, when a mere clerk behind a trader's counter in Umangoni, a great light had gone up in his mind. He'd seen his masters treating the vast black multitudes of Africa as if they were not individual races but merely one vast conglomeration of humanity; and he'd seen the opportunity presented by that fact. He'd left his job with a few pounds in his pocket, but was back within the year in Umangoni with the first sample shipments from England, calico printed in all the favourite 'Takwena colours – and how they vary from district to district – and blankets, too, woven in sub-tribal, tribal and national designs. That was the beginning of his fortune, and of more than that because, my father had concluded, 'he's right in the native mind. I've not met anybody who understands them as well as he unless' – he'd laid his hand on my head and given it a playful flick – 'unless it's this little bushman here.' I was not more than seven at the time and I'd not thought of the incident since, so casual and unconnected with our life did it appear at the time. But now, here today in the Port Captain's office, it walked alive into my mind with real meaning in the living sequence of things.

I stood up to go in a kind of trance, but at the door the Port Captain held my arm and asked: 'But what d'you want me to do?'

'Just find out what you can about the *Star of Truth* while she's in port this time. Perhaps you could arrange for someone to observe her night and day? I really can't decide what I'm going to do until the next spoor in the track shows up – but as soon as I do I'll get in touch with you. And promise to have a meal with me at the Club one day soon?'

He promised and I left him, but as I turned the corner in

77

that long corridor I saw him still in the doorway, deep in thought.

I spent the rest of the day at the Club writing another long letter to Joan and thinking over what I had learnt in the morning. My hopes rose steeply as I did so. I was more convinced than ever, after discovering this connexion between Lindelbaum's and The Uplands Trading Corporation, that I was on the right track and had but to stick to the watery wake of the *Star of Truth* to come upon the point where all these apparently disconnected threads joined. Already I saw at least two of the threads converging sharply. If Bill could tell me half as much news at nine o'clock I'd feel myself well launched on my journey.

Bill, however, had nothing important to communicate. The night had passed off quietly except that both Umtumwa and Mlangeni were convinced from various slight noises that some person, or persons, had kept them under observation all the time they were on watch.

'Then look out,' I stressed, 'with old Slim out of the way, they were probably doing a reconnaissance before attacking. Couldn't you borrow a dog or two to replace Slim?'

Bill said he'd try, and went on to say there had been no mail of any consequence for me. But when I told him of the Captain's account of the *Star of Truth* he was delighted. 'Of course, I remember now,' he said, 'but I was too busy sailing my ship that evening to look at her through glasses. Nor did the skipper mention her name, I think he just called her "that ugly Rooski", but I should have remembered all the same.'

'D'you agree with him, then, that there's no other natural harbour or port of call in those waters where she could have been lying up?' I asked.

'Of course I do,' he answered emphatically. 'I've been up and down the coast a score of times and I don't know of any such place. I admit I've always kept well clear of land for the last two hundred miles before you get to Diaz Bay because of the currents and the shoals –'

'Then what *is* the answer?' I demanded, as much of myself as of him.

I could almost see him shrug his shoulders. 'Can't pretend to know,' he replied.

'Well, let's hope the *Star of Truth* will give us a hint when she arrives here tomorrow!' I answered and we said good night.

I woke with the thought of the *Star of Truth* at once in my head and dressed with a feeling of quickening expectation. I breakfasted early and was about to leave the Club when the Port Captain telephoned to tell me the *Star of Truth* was expected in the roadstead at three; that he had arranged for a discreet but effective watch on her while she was in port, and then he asked if I'd like to go out in the pilot's tug to meet her.

I was sorely tempted to accept. However, I remembered Harkov was due at noon and might himself be hanging around somewhere to see his ship coming in, and that I could not run any risk of his seeing me. So I declined with regret, merely asking the Port Captain if he could borrow for me the uniform of a Junior Officer in the Harbour Service. It's characteristic of the man that all he asked was 'What size in hats d'you take?' I told him and he said: 'Call for it at my house at eleven.'

I spent the next two hours in a car making a quick reconnaissance of what might become points of great tactical value in the strategic plan of the next few days.

First I located Lindelbaum's. I found they had a large central office in Barton's Street and two shipping branches, one by the harbour entrance and the eastern quays; the other at the western end of the Bay. At the western end I looked at the *Star of Truth*'s berth, empty, cleared and ready for her. I was interested to see a man with first-class warrant-officership written all over him also inspecting the site. I then drove to Aliwal Street to inspect the twelve-storey building which houses the Trans-Uhlalingasonki Trading Corporation, anxious to get all this over before Harkov arrived. That done I drove to the Port Captain's house where his housekeeper gave me a suitcase containing the uniform he'd promised me. I returned at once to the Club to deposit it in my room. Stuck in the notice board of the Club was a telegram. 'Have arranged to telephone you at Club at one most urgent Bill.'

The telegram alarmed me, but as there was nothing I could do about it I drove out to Beckett's Hill to inspect Lindelbaum's 'palace' as the Port Captain had called it, from a distance. It was a big, squarish, two-storied house in the late 'nineties Port Natal style, a modern verandah running right round both ground and first floors. A pointed iron turret rose up incongruously from one corner of the building to hold up a sad, long flag-pole from which no flag flew. The house was without charm or character but the grounds were superb, full of dark, indigenous trees, flowers, and creepers, and in the centre a display of firework-flowers by some exalted spath-odias and outspread bohinneas. The house, set on the summit of the hill, had an incomparable view. The whole 'Valley of a Thousand Hills', blue this sunny morning with distance, lay at its feet, and the silver of a stream rushing to join the great Umgeni flashed in the centre of the view, and far away over towards Inanda the shadow of a cliff laid a clear blue-pencil-stress underneath the iridescent skyline of a knife-edge hill. Appropriately, too, I noticed he'd given his house the Sindakwena name: '*Dhlua'muti*', meaning 'that which is higher than trees'.

I then drove to town, left the car in the Club garage, and went to wait for Bill's call.

The tone of his opening 'Is that you, Pierre?' told me immediately that something was wrong. But, thank God, it wasn't another murder, only a burglary. Bill'd been kept late at the office. Coming back at eleven-thirty he was surprised not to see Tickie with his knobkerrie on watch. He was about to let himself into the house and ring for Umtumwa when he heard an odd banging noise coming from the back. Torch in hand he went towards it to find the noise came from Tickie, bound with his legs and body trussed over a stick, blindfolded, and tightly gagged. He'd been banging his head, which alone could move, against a wooden post for half an hour trying to attract attention. Bill was prepared to blame himself bitterly for all sorts of reasons, so I laughed him out of it, asking, 'But what did they burgle?'

'They took every scrap of paper out of your desk but not a thing else. Most odd . . .'

They're after John's envelope and the letter they imagined it contained, I thought to myself. Aloud I said to Bill, 'Afraid that means I'll have to start all over again on my book; for my manuscript was in one of the drawers. . . . I expect it was just Harkov being thorough before coming up here.'

80

'Expect so,' said Bill gloomily, though obviously relieved at my reception of the news. Then he added, 'Look, I'll call you again tomorrow evening, not tonight.'

I fell in readily with this suggestion because somehow I was convinced that, provided I wasn't there, the threat to Petit France was over.

The *Star of Truth* was an hour late in arrival and by four I was so impatient and worried that I nearly left my seat at my bedroom window to telephone to the Port Captain. But at that very moment I saw her odd, turned-up nose come round the angle in the long Point quayside, where the Bay opens out. Yes, there she came out from behind the hull of a black and yellow British Indiaman, edging slowly and carefully into full view, her timber once again gold and warm in the westering sun. She drew herself and her heavy load out clear and distinct from the huddle of masts and hulls, black crane-tops, and soaring smoke in the harbour mouth and rode straight into the clean, shining centre of the Bay, moving sedately on to her tidy berth as if she were just an honest sea-going woman on her way to bed to be delivered of legitimate cargo.

'You may not know it,' I said to myself in a whisper, looking hard at the ship, 'but you've come to keep a date with me.'

Chapter 7

'Higher-than-the-Trees' at Night

I have an instinct against planning far ahead. I expect it's due to my primitive upbringing in a land where God and nature tend to show a pointed disregard for human anticipation. Thus I had made no hard and fast plan for getting on board the *Star of Truth*. It's true I'd borrowed a harbour officer's uniform in the morning, but only on the general principle that nothing could make me more inconspicuous on a great waterfront. However as I watched the *Star of Truth* swinging casually towards her berth, I knew that the time to act and take risks had come. So I quickly got into my uniform, putting my officer's cap into a paper bag, buttoned my heavy winter coat over myself so that I should not excite even the polite curiosity of the members of the Club who now knew me by sight, and drove to the Port Captain's office. He'd already left word that I was to be admitted at once whenever I called.

I now asked him: 'D'you mind inviting your colleague on the *Star of Truth* for a drink with you?'

An ironic smile lighted the firm lines of his tanned face, as he quickly added: 'And you want to be the bearer of the invitation?'

I nodded and explained I only wanted it with me in case I had to explain my presence on board the *Star of Truth*. Without further ado, he pulled out a drawer in his desk, drew an official Port Captain's 'At Home' card out of it and proceeded to fill in the blanks between the printed words, holding the pen like a quill and writing a sloping curiously old-fashioned hand.

'There!' he said. 'I've invited master, mate, and purser.' He pronounced this last 'pussar'. 'And look, you'd better give yourself a real name: one William McWane, second officer of the tug *Sir William Hoy*. He goes on leave tonight – and if necessary I can verify that you're he! But please let me know as soon as you're safely ashore again.'

The *Star of Truth* had just docked and already had one gangway ashore when I arrived. I was just in time to see, from afar, the strange eunuch-like form of Harkov bringing up the rear of a row of white caps bobbing above the gangway's wooden sides as Port Natal's officialdom climbed busily on board. But Harkov or no Harkov I could not hesitate, though I admit my pulse quickened at the sight of him.

I had one advantage: I knew what I was looking for and where to look for it. So I quickened my step, went for the ship as if the Master himself had sent for me, elbowed my way through the crowd of idle sightseers on the quay, and ran up the gangway. A Junior Officer was just posting himself at the top of it but seeing my uniform waved me on and up, pointing and saying: 'Kapitan zere, and purrzur him zere!'

Thanking him I made for the purser's cabin because it took me straight past the portholes framed so vividly in my mind that Monday morning in Van Riebeeck's Bay. I walked deliberately towards them. I saw they were covered by thick curtains. I stopped as if to do up a shoe-lace. Stooping, I looked behind me. The officer on watch was busy turning back some sightseers who wanted to come on board. Clearly it was now or never. Righting myself quickly, I took my knife out of my pocket and rapped loudly on one of the portholes. At once the corner of the curtain flew up as if by reflex action, and I looked into a pair of surprised eyes in one of the leanest, grimmest 'Takwena faces I had ever seen. Almost at once the curtain whipped back again into position, but not before I'd had time to see that the skin over the high cheekbones of the black face bore the tattooed sign of 'Takwena royalty. That in itself was rewarding enough but there was more to come. When the curtain flew up I had at once resumed my forward stride past the porthole, meeting the astonished 'Takwena eyes with an expression of careful unconcern. I carried on thus to the corner of the deck-house. Another quick glance told me the officer on watch was still engaged with traffic from the shore. Reassured I rounded the corner and in the middle of the deck-house I came to an alleyway which divided into two. I ignored the companionway on one side, ducked underneath it and went straight into the heart of the deckhouse. I counted my paces and then stopped directly opposite a door I judged to be the right one, put my ear to the keyhole and heard a remonstrative 'Takwena voice saying distinctly in Sindakwena: 'That was a foolish thing to do, brother, when we have only ten more days to wait.'

I would have liked to go on listening, but an instinct which passed like a shiver of wintry air over the hair on the back of my head and which has saved my life many times before now, made me right myself. Quickly I took the Captain's envelope out of my pocket and with it in hand wandered vaguely towards the central alleyway. It was as well I did so, for at that very moment the mate of the *Star of Truth* came round the corner, saw me, stopped short, grunted as if he did not believe what he saw, then jumped forward, grabbed me by the arm and upbraided me in a foreign tongue, until the sight of my uniform and the cool way I took his arm and freed myself of it, put some caution into him.

'Who you? What you want?' he asked gruffly.

'And who are you? And where is your pussar: my business is with him,' I retorted coolly, looking him straight in the eyes.

'Then what you make here?' he demanded, less truculently.

'Looking for your pussar's cabin, of course,' I said, and continued with the stiff politeness of someone about to be annoyed: 'But I'm sorry if I've come to the wrong deck.'

'Pleeze to give me your name?' he responded much more politely, but still with suspicion in his arctic eye.

'Second-Officer William McWane of the tug *Sir William Hoy*,' I told him, asking as if I did not know, 'and who are you?'

'Ze firrst mate,' he replied, and was about to ask something else when I gave him a smile of feigned delight, exclaiming: 'You'll do even better than the pussar. Please give this to the Master with the Port Captain's compliments, an invitation for you all to drink at Port House tomorrow.' With that I put the invitation in his hand and the sight of the red harbour crest on the back of the envelope went a long way to reassure him.

Then, before he could think up a question for detaining me longer I was past him, out of the deck-house, down the gangway, walking fast back to my car, where I relaxed into my seat,

84

tingling with triumph and the release of tension accumulated in the last quarter of an hour.

I took care, however, not to indulge my moment of triumph. Glancing through the back window, I observed a brisk exchange of question and answer going on between the mate and officer of the watch. So I started the car and drove it quickly to an official car park a quarter of a mile away. Leaving it there I retraced my way to the long shed on the quay where the *Star of Truth* lay. The sun was just setting, but strolling about in my uniform I was clearly accepted as a normal part of the scene. When it was quite dark Harkov, still dressed as when I had first seen him, came down the gangway with that strange agility of his and walked extremely fast up the dock, like someone with urgent news on his mind. Going round the back of a shed, I struck out fast on a parallel course and picked up his gross, lumbering frame just ahead of me on the far side. Twenty paces on without a backward glance he opened the door of a large American car and I heard for the first time that high-pitched voice of his: 'Aliwal Street, George, but quick, I must be at Beckett's Hill at eight.'

That was all I needed to know. I hurried back to my car, drove to the Club, changed as fast as I could into my darkest clothes and pausing only to ask the Club's Indian operator to telephone to the Port Captain that I was back and would call on him in the morning, I went out to drive fast to Beckett's Hill.

About half-a-mile from the turning to 'Higher-than-the-Trees' there's a large roadhouse. I'd noticed that in the morning. I parked my car among at least fifty others, drew the oil indicator in and out of the sump a number of times, wiping it each time on some black cotton waste I'd found in the tool box until the cloth was almost dripping with oil. Then, cloth in hand, I set out on foot for 'Higher-than-the-Trees', feeling as if I were once more going on patrol in the jungles of Burma.

The night was without a moon, clear and very still, and the sky was as packed with great, flashing stars as the purple Umangoni shade with freesias in the spring. Here and there in the valley the night fires were lit, and as I got further away from the main road they spread on the clean air that lovely scent of burning African wood and coals of dry animal dung which I would not exchange for all the perfumes of Paris.

Now and then, round some point of ruby fire a dog barked, a cow mooed, or a lamb bleated with shrill desperation.

When the main road lay like a far stream of sound behind me, I took my waste and wiped dirt all over my face, neck, and hands. Near 'Higher-than-the-Trees' I took off my shoes, tied the laces together and slung them round my neck. I unstrapped my watch for it had a dial in luminous paint and put it in my pocket. It was just seven-four. Then, at a point which my eye had selected in the morning, I entered Otto Lindelbaum's grounds.

I'd already decided in my own mind that the part of the house such a man was most likely to favour would be the end with the best view of the valley. I pulled some creeper with thick leaves off a tree, wound it several times round my head, then silently, flat on my stomach like a mamba creeping out of its old skin into a bush of thorns, I worked my way towards the house through the indigenous undergrowth. Not a sound came from the house and so still was it that at one moment, lying on my back to rest (for crawling that patient, noiseless way is disciplined hard work) and watching the starlight spiking the heavy glutinous leaves above me, I believed I could hear them crackle. Then I went forward again with great caution. The distance from the boundary to the house was no more than a hundred and fifty yards but it took me nearly an hour to do it, during which time I saw the lights and heard the engines of a car drive fast in at the gates. It stopped at the front door with whining brakes, and after a brief interval drove away again. Harkov obviously had got there first, but I forbade the thought to quicken my chosen speed. Finally, I came close to an uncurtained window, crawled slowly towards it, rose carefully from the bushes on to my knees and looked in.

It was Otto Lindelbaum's study, curtained only against the front of the grounds but open to the side. He himself was alone in the room not a yard away from me at a long desk by the window. The room was lit only by a parchment reading lamp but I recognized him at once. He was stroking the head of a ridgeback so like Slim that it hurt me to see the dog. I crouched, intensely still, not even altering my angle of vision while Lindelbaum stroked and restroked the sandy head with

86

a desperation of affection which was most moving to observe. Of all man's inborn dispositions there is none more heroic than the love in him. Everything else accepts defeat and dies, but love will fight no-love every inch of the way. And if love be denied natural expression as it had been to this old man, then it will bind itself to an animal, or a bird, or to trees, flowers, a patch of earth or even the shaping of a stone. I myself in the darkness of my cell outside Harbin had loved a rat and shared my little rice with him. And I've seen no love so fierce as that which drove an illiterate, starving Australian prisoner-of-war to scrape a dead bone with a blunt knife into a ship with ivory sails. So, as long as Lindelbaum could stroke a dog like that, I knew there was some small island part of him still unclaimed by the sea of bitterness which broke in his face.

And his face? It was, of course, much older but it was essentially the same face I had seen beside our camp-fire twenty-five years before. It was older physically, but the look on it had not changed because time for him in its deepest meaning had stood still for ever in one bitter moment of rejection by the people to whom he had so confidingly attached himself. I stared at him like someone hypnotized, feeling I knew all that mattered about him, for was I not François de Beauvilliers's son born also in exile and bitterness?

I stared until suddenly the ridgeback growled and flew round so menacingly that his master had to restrain him while Harkov, changed and bathed, walked into the room. I kept so still under my wreath of creepers that an owl parked itself on a bush not five yards away. For two hours I knelt there. Sometimes I could catch a sentence, a word or two, sometimes nothing at all. But matching what I heard with what I saw, I gathered that Harkov was telling his master that the time of crisis had come. They couldn't carry on any longer, he was emphatic, without running the gravest danger of detection. In fact the *Star of Truth* must be the last consignment to – alas! I couldn't catch the name though it was on their lips often enough. Of one thing only I was certain; the word was not 'Mozambique'. Then I heard Harkov telling Lindelbaum of an unexpected visit to the *Star of Truth* by a ship's officer, which visit he'd proved genuine by telephoning the Port Captain, but he didn't like it. Public interest in the ships was gathering size and momentum and he wanted the *Star of Truth* out of port and away. Besides, there was something else to be considered, and to my amazement Harkov's podgy hand drew from his briefcase my manuscript on *The Mind and Myth of the Amangtakwena*. Opening it, he laid it before his master, who picked it up and held it to the light.

Then as he read my name old Lindelbaum exclaimed loudly: 'Not François de Beauvilliers's son?' As Harkov nodded his head, Lindelbaum added, 'A remarkable man, most remarkable; if the son is half the father we'll have to look out indeed!'

Yes, Harkov hastened to agree, thumping my manuscript, and look at this chapter on dreams! He was certain with knowledge like that I'd only need three or four weeks in Umangoni to know the whole story. Perhaps I knew something already, for who could tell what was in that mysterious letter those fools had failed to recover? No, there was no time to be lost, for he, Harkov, knew I was due to set off to the interior at any moment. At all costs he was going to prevent that. In fact, he had already arranged the appropriate reception for me the moment I returned to the Cape. But they must hurry. The only hope of success for the plan was to put it into operation forthwith, even if not quite fully mounted, and instruct Sydcup accordingly.

Through all this Lindelbaum had hardly spoken, but now he said in a quick, husky, resounding voice: 'All right. I'll draft the necessary instructions in the morning and the ship's wireless can send them off at sea. Put the stevedores on full night and day shifts, and get the ship out and away as fast as possible. And now to bed.'

Harkov's relief was immense. The ridgeback in an attitude of distrust and suspicion watched Harkov until the door closed behind him. But Otto Lindelbaum remained there for some long minutes peering intently into the night and the last thing I heard him say was: 'Yes, God knows it's long been time!' The way he said it saddened me as much as it revived all my fears.

When the light at long last went out in the room I sank back on the ground stiff and exhausted by my long and unnatural pose.

I lay there for half an hour slowly massaging new life into

my limbs before I began to crawl back in the way I'd come. I emerged to find the fires in the valley extinguished and the noise on the great road to Port Natal stilled, but somewhere close to a pool filled to the brim with amazing stars, the frogs had taken up their husky classic chorus, sounding indeed as if they were gathered there to give verisimilitude to the imitation of their music learnt for centuries by all the de Beauvilliers children in their nurseries:

> *Le Roi, le Roi, le Roi*
> *Est allé, est allé.*
> *Est ou, est ou, est ou?*
> *A cognac, a cognac.*

Oh! Time alone knew what kings, what queens too, for that matter, had already preceded us to some starry Cognac on nights just as this.

Chapter 8

Of our Meeting at Fort Herald

I was still deep in my short sleep when the telephone woke me
at seven-fifteen on Friday morning. It was Bill and the sound
of his voice sent a rush of alarm to my blood. But all was well.
He was ringing only to read me an urgent cable from Joan:
'Believe you may well be right but regard full exchange information between us so important propose flying out forthwith to join you unless you cable contrary I leave BOAC
Sunday Stop Grateful your letter much love Joan.'

I stared, I fear, at the words again and again, a brief glow of
hope going up in me that perhaps after all she'd understood
and forgiven the past. But with the spoor before me getting
faster and fresher every minute, could her coming do any
good? I couldn't even guarantee I'd be able to meet her. In
fact in view of the decisions I'd reached in the night it seemed
unlikely that I'd be able to return to Petit France for several
weeks if not months. In the end she might be no nearer to me
in Petit France than if she'd stayed at home. But if her instinct
told her to come I was not prepared to stop her. Besides there
was something in me that was tempted by her being my guest
in my own home even if I was absent. So aloud I said to Bill:
'Look, for reasons I'll explain later we must move fast today.
First I'll cable Joan to come next Sunday, but I fear I shan't
be there to meet her. You'll have to do that and take her to
Petit France and be her host and protector until I return. I'm
now going to telegraph to Oom Pieter by express wire telling
him I'm joining him today or tomorrow at Fort Herald. I'll
tell him also that Zwong-Indaba is due there today and ask
him to contact him. Secondly, and this is the immediate point,
I want you at once to charter an aircraft. Get it to meet you at
Wellington,* for I'm certain the Cape aerodrome is watched.

* About fifty miles from St Joseph's.

90

Pile yourself, Umtumwa, and Tickle, with all their and my safari belongings, guns, bags, and all – Umtumwa knows the drill – into your car and drive to Wellington. Transfer the servants, baggage, and all into the aircraft and send them streaking to the Rand Airport. I'll be sitting on the aerodrome waiting for them.'

I then went on to give him my reasons, telling him all that had happened the day before and saying I was certain there was nothing more of value to be learnt in Port Natal. What was vital was to discover why and how the *Star of Truth* took so long to get to Mozambique. Judging by what I'd overheard the 'Takwena say in the cabin, I'd perhaps only ten, no, only nine days left wherein to do it. Not only was that almost an impossibly small time for so complex and difficult a task, but it was our last chance, since Lindelbaum was cancelling the other shipments contemplated in his plan. I proposed therefore to set off at once for Mozambique by air, stopping only at Fort Herald to consult with Oom Pieter and to brief him. Mozambique, I felt certain, was the right direction to cast about for the next clue. I was, I fear, very matter of fact in my manner because of the fresh proof the night had given me of the extreme urgency of the matter, but I knew Bill understood.

When he rang off, I called the Club exchange to get me the Port Captain. Waiting for the reply I went to the window. The sun was about to rise on a tranquil Bay. The *Star of Truth* was looking her best in lovely light. But she was no longer alone, for in the night a vessel with the stamp of a Coaster's commuter character had come and berthed herself cheek to cheek with the *Star of Truth*. Before I could take in more detail the telephone rang and I was speaking to the Port Captain.

Quickly I gave him an account of what I'd learnt in the ship and to some extent at 'Higher-than-the-Trees'. I asked his advice and his opinion on the decisions I'd announced to Bill. His agreement was as heartening as it was immediate. He thought the vital clue must be found in or near Mozambique and the sooner we combed that coast the better. In fact, while Harkov was about, he thought it better for me not to do any more lone investigation. The great thing now, he thought, was for him to keep a methodical watch on these ships and to maintain good and constant contact by cablegram. So here and then we set about devising a simple code for the purpose.

'By the way, there's another ship by the *Star of Truth* this morning,' I remarked in the course of doing this. 'D'you know what it is?'

'Yes,' he said promptly. 'That's the *Kudu*, one of the Lindelbaum coasters. They're all named after animals. There used to be five of them but surely you'll remember how the *Inyati*, the newest and fastest of the whole fleet, disappeared in a cyclone off Madagascar, in July of last year, without leaving a trace behind her, not a lifebuoy, cork mat, or hatch cover. It caused a sensation almost as great as the disappearance of the *Waratah*.'

I told him I must have been away on safari at the time and missed the news. Shortly after, our code complete, I put down my telephone in the Club for the last time.

At ten I was in the Johannesburg aircraft climbing fast into the air over the lovely Bay and heading for the steep interior and reef four hundred miles away. By twelve I was at Palmietfontein, and at one o'clock on the Rand Airport reserved for chartered services. At two-thirty Bill's charter, a fast blue and silver machine, touched down. The first person I saw was Tickie, his face shining with undisguised excitement and delight at his first taste of air-travel. Behind him stood Umtumwa, in his rôle of a much travelled man of the world, with grave, sedate dignity. But they were both, I think, as pleased to see me as I them.

Half-an-hour later we took to the air again, but already the winter's sun was well on the decline. Obviously we could not make Fort Herald that night. I fretted keenly at the delay but agreed reluctantly with the pilot on an intermediate base for the night. As the sun went down in a sky red with the angry dust that is always in the air over the south-western desert of Africa, we landed on the aerodrome of a small gold mine in the Bush north of the Limpopo. The dawn next day met us six thousand feet up in the air and at ten o'clock we circled over the Boma at Fort Herald.

Oom Pieter was at the aerodrome to meet me, waiting patiently, dressed in familiar whip-cord bush shirt and slacks, once khaki but now bleached grey by the sun. He wore his favourite wide-brimmed green hat with band of puff-adder skin and subtle Abyssinian swift's feather in it. It threw a generous shadow over his keen blue eyes and lean, sun-lined face, of which only the tip of a neat Napoleon beard emerged in the sharp light. In his left hand, slung from his little finger, he carried a small bag of the Magaliesberg tobacco which he was never without. The other hand, thumb tucked well into a broad leather strap, held his gun, his seven millimetre Mauser, firmly to his shoulder. Ah! that gun: it was to Oom Pieter what a crutch is to a cripple. It was his all. He lived by it and killed with it only for life and in defence of living. It was to him what a spear was to a knight in a dark and unfamiliar wood: the quintessential symbol of a lost heroic age. As I saw him thus in the fresh shimmer of the tropical light, the many delicate and vivid memories associated with him crowded in on me fast.

Without waiting for the steps to be mounted to the aeroplane I jumped out and went to greet him. The metal sunlight and glittering sun-beetle sound was rising up everywhere in the bush around us like flame of virgin fire, a flickering, ecstatic Messianic insects' Hosannah, drunk with praise for this their far blue heaven. Taking his yellow curved calabash pipe out of his mouth, Oom Pieter met me half-way, held out a firm hand almost black with the sun, saying in Afrikaans to me: Dag ouboet: Good day, old brother.* And in Sindakwena to Umtumwa and Tickie who were standing by, 'Aye, I see you, Umtumwa; I see you, Tickie. Welcome to you one and all.' Then in that fearless, unclouded manner of his which pre-supposed a belief in facing up instantly to the worst, he added, 'Sorry but I've bad news for you. Zwong-Indaba is dead, I fear. Stabbed in the back some time early this morning between the railway station and the Trans-Uhlalingasonki Trading Corporation's store. We don't know by whom and have no idea why.'

But if they had no idea I had, and I hastened to tell Oom Pieter my whole story as soon as we were alone in the rest-

* *Dag* – literally 'day', idiomatically 'good day'. *Ou* – Old, used constantly in Afrikaans as adjective of endearment. *Boet* – Intimate form of brother. Oom Pieter called me thus and seldom Pierre ever since I could remember.

house that the Provincial Governor had placed at our disposal. I talked as fast as I could all the while the aeroplane refuelled, and Umtumwa and Tickie, silent and still with tragedy, went with a note from me to the police to pay their respects to their dead kinsman and recover what they could of his belongings. Long before I'd finished talking to Oom Pieter they were back, and had placed on the edge of the verandah two calico bundles and a pair of hunting sticks polished and smooth with age and long service. But of the letter I wrote there was no sign.

Oom Pieter, calmly smoking, listened to me without interruption or exclamation.

When I'd finished he didn't comment on what I'd said but merely announced: 'I agree, we've no time to lose. But now let me tell you something, ouboet. I too have been worried. Ever since I got back up here this time I've felt uncomfortable. I can't explain why, but Africa doesn't feel the same any more. There are a lot of people on the move, and if you doubt it go and sit and smoke a pipe as I did a few evenings back close by the river where the three frontiers meet close to the great north-south Bantu footpath. If one man went by me fifty did, all single and alone, plodding along, heads down, faces set with a determined and pre-occupied air. Odder still it was all one-way traffic: northbound. Strangest of all, they were not just the 'Takwena you'd normally expect to see there, for I swear I recognized Zulu, Matabele, Angoni, Amangwana, Amaqabe, Amafunze, Abatembu, Amahlubi, Abakwamacibisi, Amatuli, as well as Amaxosa from the far south amongst them.'

'My God, Oom Pieter!' I exclaimed in consternation that so great a variety and number of African races should travel the same, unfamiliar road north. 'Are you sure?'

Oom Pieter nodded his head. 'Yes, ouboet. Dead sure. I went back to camp that night with my uneasiness deeper than ever and without making head or tail of it all. But now after what you have told me I begin to see daylight.'

'You think then,' I asked slowly, 'that they too were all men who'd seen the feather and are hastening to Umangoni for news of the dream?' For I'd had to tell Oom Pieter all about the feather, knowing that my servants trusted him as they trusted me.

'Precisely,' he said with a vigorous nod of his white head.

'But what dream would bring out all these ill-assorted races on to the same road?'

'Only one,' I told him. 'The Dream 'Nkulixowe is rumoured to have promised his people on his dying day: the dream that forbodes great and terrible trouble; the dream which promises to bring together again all the far, scattered nations who have ever been Amangtakwena.' I jumped to my feet. 'But now, with Zwong-Indaba dead, I want to ask you just this as the most urgent of all our tasks. Please set off to Umangoni when I've gone and find out all you can about the dream for us. I can't, for you see I must cling on to the heels of the *Star of Truth.*'

With my movement Oom Pieter too got up from his chair, reached for his gun and hat and said: 'Look, ouboet, as you said; we've no time to lose. We can't sit here all day talking, and yet talk to you I must. So let's get into that devil's contraption of yours at once. Don't ask me why now. I'll explain presently. But just tell your pilot to fly, not to Mozambique, but to Diaz Bay, the little harbour a hundred miles south of it. It was once your father's base, and I was there last year again. I know all the officials and the District Governor, old Colonel de Fereira was a good friend of your father's. There's a landing ground on the flats behind the harbour. We won't lose time that way I promise you: my safari is not disbanded. I can fly back tomorrow if you wish it.'

So calling the servants, we all took off fast in our plane leaving a thick trail of red dust flying like a scarlet banner from the tall black bush, and headed, our engines full out, for Diaz Bay, while Oom Pieter talked long and earnestly to me.

Did I remember ever hearing my father speak of the Great Flamingo Water, he began. My father had heard of it first in 1905 when he was hunting deep in Mozambique. One evening he heard the headman of a small tribe isolated in this dense, unhealthy bush country telling his bearers about a Great Flamingo Water, saying that if they really wanted game to shoot they should go there. Asked how one reached it the man said he didn't know for he'd never been there himself, but everyone in his tribe knew the water existed in that direction, and he had pointed firmly E.S.E. My father was so impressed that he'd taken a compass bearing on the outstretched arm of the headman, but working the bearing out on his map later he was disappointed because it emerged on the coast at a point between Uhlalingasonki and the other great river of the East Coast, the Black Umpafuti, where the map clearly showed only flat mangrove marsh and swamp. My father never mentioned it again but when Oom Pieter was in Diaz Bay last year, to his amazement Colonel de Fereira asked him if he had ever heard that very rumour, begging that Oom Pieter should go and find this great water for him, and promising all assistance and facilities needed. Oom Pieter had been very tempted to say yes, but he was already committed to his safari with me. However, the moment I'd told him about the curious behaviour of the Star ships the thought of the Great Flamingo Water had rushed unbidden into his mind. There, he was certain, was my natural harbour of safe unknown anchorage. So why didn't I go to de Fereira, take up the proposition he'd made last year, and make for the country between the Uhlalingasonki and Umpafuti as fast as I could and find that water?

Of course, it was a shot in the dark: and if it didn't come off I might lose for ever the trail of the *Star of Truth*. Yet Oom Pieter's suggestion made strange sense to me. However, I didn't answer at once but called Umtumwa over to join us.

'Umtumwa, must it always be a flamingo feather that announces the dreaming of the dream?' I asked him. With Zwong now murdered and the evil that was associated with the matter so starkly and freshly illustrated I had no hesitation in asking him the question.

'It must, my Bwana, always be a flamingo feather,' Umtumwa said simply.

'D'you know why?'

'Yes, Bwana, because in Xilixowe's great dream a flamingo flew in front to lead him and all his people south, far on to the place where the Amangtakwena have not yet reached, to the great flamingo home on the water where once in their life-time all the flamingoes on earth come and go. But as I said at the beginning, it was always forbidden to speak of this except among ourselves.'

'There's your answer, Oom Pieter,' I said, thanking Umtumwa. 'The Great Flamingo Water it shall be.'

With that decision a peaceful stillness came over Oom

Pieter. He relaxed in his chair, filled his pipe and took out his Bible. It is, I believe, the only book he's ever read of his own free will. Now he opened the Bible on his knee in the middle of St John's last book, and began reading slowly, holding it far from his unspectacled eyes, his lips moving in sympathy with the unspoken word as they often do with people unaccustomed to much reading. After a while he saw me looking at him so he pointed at the text: 'Woe to the inhabitors of the earth and the sea; for the devil is come down unto you having great wrath because he knoweth he hath but a short time.' His fingers underlined the words 'short time' and he winked at me.

I do not propose to go into the details of how we persuaded Colonel de Fereira and the reluctant little harbour town of Diaz Bay, hiding out of the main stream of time there on the dazzled East Coast of Africa behind a pink and yellow coral reef and a mirage of palms, to hustle as they have never hustled before. Perhaps it was partly due to an ultimatum, tactfully conveyed to Colonel de Fereira that if we were not allowed to set off at once, and under guarantee of absolute secrecy, neither Oom Pieter nor I would ever consider the proposition again, and thus would perish his ardent dream of finding a fabulous new water.

However, so responsive was this proud but greathearted little Governor to all the considerations we put to him that, though we arrived at Diaz Bay only at four, we left his palace at sundown with his unqualified blessing and all the authority we needed. Our first problem was bearers. We raised nine that night in the convict dungeons in the old Portuguese fort. This was disappointing. But the trouble was that when the convicts heard the direction my safari proposed taking, except for those nine, they declined flatly to accompany me despite the promise of a full pardon.

After the prisons we tried the bazaars and rest houses, but it was soon evident that short of using force I would have to make do only with nine convict bearers. And I preferred nine willing to ninety sullenly driven men where I was going.

The rest of our task was simpler. Oom Pieter and I had done safaris of a similar kind so often that no details really had to be thought out. I'd already got all the guns, ammunition, and medicine that we needed. All we had to do was to buy

97

food of the simplest kind, borrowing from the Governor nine grey military shoulder packs, nine field flasks and nine mule ammunition boxes with tin linings for our provisions. On the other point I was adamant: one blanket, one mosquito-net for each bearer. The Portuguese gaolers thought me criminally indulgent but my safari was going to be difficult enough without sleepless nights and incessant mosquito bites for the bearers. So Government and Goanese stores between them were soon made to supply all these slight wants.

The choice of direction was even simpler. I was entirely in Oom Pieter's hands since he'd long since worked it all out. It was quite clear to him that the Great Flamingo Water, if it existed, could only lie between the two vast swamps created along the coast by the Umpafuti and the Uhlalingasonki. And as he'd so often taught me when stalking game, the long way round the rear was often the quickest way to the quarry. So, putting his finger on the map right on the remote police post of Fort Emmanuel on the Black Umpafuti, he said that that was the place to make for. If I crossed the river there and set out due east-south-east, he thought I might strike the Great Water within a hundred and twenty to a hundred and forty miles. And if the Star of Truth were to turn up there by Monday week as the 'Takwena conversation I'd overhead in the ship suggested, I'd have just on a week to do it in, which meant an average march of twenty miles a day. He was certain I could do it.

In emergencies, I've averaged forty miles a day with proved bearers before now, but everything would obviously depend on the nature of the country. I therefore suggested that, as we had our chartered plane, we might do a quick reconnaissance by air ourselves early the following morning. Oom Pieter was pessimistic about weather conditions, telling me how impossible that part of the coast was for aerial observation. However, I over-persuaded him and we were on the Diaz Bay landing ground at dawn the next morning and by eight o'clock three hundred miles south of it.

However Oom Pieter had been right. Over the mouth and swamp of the Uhlalingasonki the mist rolled heavily like the satined back of an avalanche between us and the coast. However, on our return a curious thing did happen. The mist,

98

though never dispersed, suddenly became agitated and torn apart and in the gaps in that fraction of a second before the rents closed again I thought I saw below me streak upon streak of brilliant fire. I instantly tapped our pilot on the shoulder and said: 'Pinpoint our position here and give me the bearing when we land.'

On return we once more went over Oom Pieter's plans. He was to take the plane to Mozambique and await the arrival of the *Star of Truth*. He'd watch her closely in and out of port and investigate her activities just in case I missed her. Then he'd hasten back to Fort Herald and get to Umangoni as fast as he could on the track of the dream itself. In particular, I urged him to concentrate on what 'Nkulixowe had said on his deathbed about the dream he was going to prepare. There was certain to be some old Induna alive who'd have this information. So great a man as 'Nkulixowe, with his father's disaster so vividly in his mind, surely wouldn't have died without leaving ample safeguards against the chance of another 'false' dream being spread among his people?

Poor Oom Pieter! He agreed to everything, but how he longed to come on my journey with me. It was, in fact, his journey, since he'd first thought of it, and I felt almost like a thief who had stolen it from him. That night on the way back to our rest-house, he did a thing I had never known him do before. Ardent Protestant as he was, he asked me to step aside into the little Roman Catholic Church, the only Christian one in Diaz Bay. It was midnight but the door was open and we went into it quietly and kneeling down Oom Pieter prayed silently for about a quarter of an hour. I know he felt better after that and as we walked to our beds under the stars he said, more to himself than to me: 'Yes, we must go on to fight the good fight to the end of our days, for though this Africa of ours, ouboet, is truly God's country, the devil is still largely in possession of it, and the battle for its soul must be long and bitter.'

For 'soul' he used the Afrikaans word 'seil' which I prefer because it sounds more forceful and less dreamy than its English equivalent.

At noon the same day I set off with Umtumwa, Tickie, and the nine bearers in the three military jeeps the Governor had provided. The last thing I did was to hand Oom Pieter a long letter for Joan, one for Bill and another for the Port Captain, saying: 'You'll cable to him as soon as you get to Mozambique, won't you?'

I left him standing by the steps of the rest-house staring after us, feeling rather mean again as I said like a kind of thief who had stolen his favourite safari from him, but an hour later his blue and silver plane came roaring over the trees behind us, did a valedictory dive over my jeeps and then sheered off north, streaking fast for Mozambique.

We travelled all through the night, the next morning, and early afternoon, for we had one hundred and fifty miles to do on the roughest of tracks through broken bushveld. But at three o'clock on Monday afternoon we woke up an astonished Portuguese lieutenant half-way through his siesta at Fort Emmanuel. When I told him that I wanted to cross the river by the ferry and go on safari deep on the other side, at first he didn't believe me. Slapping his chest, he said he wouldn't allow me to go to certain death, no, only over his dead body. Did I not know that on the other side of the river lay a dead land? Yes, *the* Dead Land. Not for fifty years had a living soul lived in it, and his own patrols darted in and out of it as quickly as possible, never spending a night there. Did I not realize it was the worst sleeping sickness area in Africa? Look! he commanded me, and took me to the window to point up and down the river, at a long empty lane, half-a-mile wide, cut between river bank and bush as far as the eye could see, dead tree trunks with a dull sheen of hot sun on them lying everywhere like bone in some fabulous graveyard of elephants. That was done, he emphasized, to keep out the terrible fly, the shade-loving tsetse menace. Look again, he said, on the far side at the black bush stepping heavily down to the very water's edge. The moment I set foot there, the fly would be on me. And beyond the Dead Land? Why nothing but the great forest of Duk-aduk-duk! Had I not heard of it? Dear Mother of God, was I as ignorant as I appeared fool-hardy? Did I not know this forest was so black and thick that in it the human heart went duk-aduk-duk. Yes, it was no smiling matter, for no one had ever penetrated it, and God alone knew what monsters infested it. 'Why, then, go to your death there, señor,' he concluded in despair, 'when there are plenty of other places to shoot game?'

In the end the Governor's written instructions left him no argument, though he still pleaded with me to desist: he turned out twelve convicts and a black corporal to man the precarious ferry. No sooner were we at the ferry-side than a sweating radio-operator came running down the glittering bank waving a signal. It was from Oom Pieter and read: 'Devils motor arrived Mozambique safely stop Zulu signals you he has good hopes persuading impatient lady prolong her stay forty-eight hours stop Godspeed ouboet.'

'Zulu' was my Port Captain's code name; the impatient lady needs no explanation. My heart warmed, for every hour the *Star of Truth* could be retarded might be decisive. The black-bush now looked less uninviting than before.

Chapter 9

I Enter the Dead Land

So an hour before sun-down Umtumwa, Tickie, nine convict
bearers, and I were landed on the edge of the Dead Land on
the far southern bank of the Black Umpafuti river, which coiled
and uncoiled its fat, anaconda current at our feet, the evening
sun showing up the glint of sulphur in its oily scales.

I watched the primitive ferry being pulled back to the far
side of the river as fast as twelve pairs of convicts' hands could
pull on the chains, and to the accompaniment of an improvised
tune sung in deep base voices:

> Aye, we have left him there, the red stranger,*
> Heave ha! heave, heave ha!
> We have left him by the dead land and Black Umpafuti water,
> Heave ha! heave, heave ha!
> We have left him to return to our food by the fire,
> Heave ha! heave, heave ha!

Near by a crocodile moved like an assassin's thrust from
underneath a cloak of evening shadow into a crimson flash
of sun, and the sound of human singing died. My own small
band seemed to look smaller, and my hope more forlorn.
Calling Umtumwa over I told him that I would break my
normal safari rule of pitching camp early, and on this occasion
push on for two or three hours so as to get as much bush as
possible between my untried bearers and even such slender
temptations as those of Fort Emmanuel. I put him at the head
of the line of loaded bearers. I ordered Tickie to be despatch
runner between head and tail because it was most important
to keep the line compact since none of us knew what lay ahead.
I put myself at the tail because experience has taught me that

* We are red to most Africans until we teach them to think of us as
white.

102

on single file in the bush that is where the trouble collects with untried people and *that* the place from which to lead. In fact I spoke the reason aloud to Umtumwa and as I did so noticed a tall bearer called Said listening to me with an odd humorous twist to the line of his mouth. I tested the loads of each bearer by lifting them myself. Umtumwa had done his work well: there was not a pound to choose between them. Then I gave the bearers the command: 'All set . . . Pelileh: Take up: And in the name of God, go.'

The underlying silence of the Dead Land broke like wave and ripple of a great dead sea over us. Down by the river a family of apes suddenly went hysterical with fear at the approaching dark. Then silence again, and in the silence a coil of greasy sound winding and unwinding as the swollen Black Umpafuti turned its back on us to swing its current to the north-east. Ahead of me, Umtumwa, gun on arm, disappeared down the narrow track, one grey box after another bobbing jauntily up and down, following him out of yellow sunset air into purple shadow. At the centre Tickie marched proudly, a gun on each shoulder and the medicine pack on his back. I fell into line in the rear five paces behind the last bearer, and as I listened to the pad pad of naked feet ahead of me on a track made also by naked though unremembered feet of vanished men, from far down in me my past in the interior took over and I was more content.

We marched thus in silence for two hours. Once away from the river the bush thinned and the trees arranged themselves in heavy clusters, ideal tsetse country indeed. But I hadn't long to study our surroundings. The sun went quickly down. I'd barely time to notice how the spreading acacia tops, the eternally autumnal mopani heads on their barley-sugar stems, the smooth ash-grey mukwa trunks and the flat pods that dangle so helplessly from their proud branches were lined with peacock light, before the night, like an eagle on the hover, was upon us. As it swooped, a moon two days old pointed itself like a jewelled Arabian dagger at the yellow throat of the dying day, and the gallant Southern Cross appeared like the riding lights of a homeward-bound ship.

At the end of two hours I came round a curve in a dry river bed to find a dark huddle of men waiting for me on fine dry gravel under a steep bank. 'It's two hours, Bwana, as you ordered. Shall we camp here?'

I looked up and down the river bed. 'No, we'll camp on top,' I answered.

I'd finished speaking before I realized we'd all instinctively spoken in whispers. It was a tribute to the majesty of the African night. But once we had a great fire lit, mosquito nets up, water drawn, a tin of tea and tin of mealie-meal porridge on the boil, the strangely assorted party quickly recovered their normal voices. Sitting apart on a boulder, I studied each face by the leaping fire-light. As I did so I remembered their gaoler's warning at Diaz Bay: 'Remember, señor, murderers all!' But all I could see was that they were as tired as they were undernourished, so I quickly put a stop to their talking and ordered them to bed.

I didn't sleep myself at once on this occasion, but lay there for long trying to picture what sort of country it was about us. And what sort of animals? Would we, for instance get enough meat to eke out our limited supplies to the end? Or would I, and could I, in decency, send bearers back alone to Fort Emmanuel as fast as we consumed their loads? The question was answered soon enough for hardly had I turned on my back to see the starlight in my net caught like hoar-frost on a cobweb when the first lion roared. The sound went through the silence on a tidal wave of passionate, uninhibited sound, and was so close that my white net seemed to flutter with it. Then all around me I saw the phantom shapes of ten mosquito nets heave with interest or alarm, but from the eleventh, a sleepy Umtumwa emerged to walk slowly over to the fire and throw more wood on it, sending a flight of ruby sparks up in the dark as he did so.

'We need not worry about *njama** now!' I called out softly to him.

'Aye, Bwana, njama plenty,' he replied.

Once more in the silence I heard the fire gathering flame briskly. A bush-buck barked over towards the river to keep up its courage, while a baboon whimpered like a child in its sleep with nightmare fright. Then a hyena howled, filling the air with cowardly regret: quick, a jackal answered it thrice,

* *Njama*: both meat and game.

104

as the Hottentots used to say, 'like a soul on its way out'. A night plover flew up wailing like a bosun's whistle in the dog-watch hour, and a long way off with a noise like a gun-shot an elephant tore a strip of bark from a favourite tree. The night indeed was well and truly found at last, and soon we were all asleep.

I was dreaming of Petit France when a sound burst upon me, waking me. I jumped up at once to secure mosquito nets, thinking it to be a great wind coming up fast, but one glance at the clear serene, starlight horizon showed me it was not wind but water, coming rapidly down along the dry river bed. My watch said it was five o'clock so I roused the camp to get breakfast of thick mealie-meal porridge and salt cooking and sweet black tea brewing, while I washed and shaved myself. Before I'd finished, the tired, travel-stained water threw itself with a rush and a flail-like swish upon the empty river bed below us. The bearers, who'd vacated it reluctantly on my orders the night before, now shook their heads and burst out laughing at themselves, making gestures of delight in my direction. Slight as it was the incident reassured me.

Sunrise found us stepping out smartly. It was a perfect tropical winter morning. The light was so clear that the silent land, still trees, unstirred bush and long, yellow upright grass looked almost like a coral-scape at the bottom of an Arabian gulf, and the startling blue sky the ceiling of a sunlit ocean above. Even the misanthropic hornbills darting low from tree to tree, the shining green and yellow water finches speeding towards water and the shivering, long-tailed streamlined mouse-birds, their spiked night-caps still on, seeking warm treetops in the sun, looked not as if flying in air but as if gliding like fish through crystal water.

But the illusion alas didn't last and hardly was the sun free of the trees than the day's being broke in with a texture and temperature all its own. First came the birds, the tinkling Tintinkies with the precise little peal of their music-box voices; cheeky Peter Bright-eyes, the urbane talkative Kokowiet, boring musical bass of the feathered club; then a fleet of magic-blue jays with their touch of peacock splendour; Jan Pierewiet end-lessly repeating his one bar of a Mozart minuet; golden aurioles, Dantjie Kiewiet pompous chest stuck out on strutting scarlet runners, busy bee-swift buttons of quail, gentle sad-eyed namaqua doves with the black ring of mourning round their Persian throats; well-to-do lories and bounding upstart tufted shrikes, while sparkling swarms of hungry weaver birds went up ahead of me to drift over the trees like the clouds of smoke of some vast fire. And every tree too seemed to have three or four love-sick, day-loving turtle doves cooing away at the top of their ardent voices, ceaselessly cooing their notes of fire, out of cool throats as if there were nothing else to do in life but to make music of praise for the day riding so high, wide and handsome in the sky. Then as the day advanced the sun-beetles joined in, overwhelming the music of doves. They sang as if the whole of the Dead Land were a beetles' heaven, row upon row of their seraphim singing to outdo mass upon mass of singing insect cherubim. They sang with such white, silver violence and hot metallic passion and at such a constant and unending pitch that the music seemed to become substance and texture of the light of the bold sun itself, and its rhythm to impart a slow, tranced mediumistic movement to the grass, the trees and all that stood upright in that land. As the determined sun rose quickly higher the shadows not merely shrank but were so dimmed by fierce reflection of fiery light around them that they lost their shadowy cast and became only paler forms of sunlight; as the trunks of mukwa and mopani, camel-thorn, tambootie and marula became almost translucent and the yellow fever-trees transparent with light, this rhythm of sun-beetle music implicit in the waves of air flickering like flame and quicksilver with heat, slowly but surely compelled the landscape to dance before our eyes. It began slowly but became shriller and faster until at the climax of the day I felt as if I were watching reflections of some cosmic *danse macabre* in a vast shining hall of glittering distorted mirrors. Even the odd secretary bird that came into view, neat quill behind the ear dressed in Ascot-grey topper and black swallow-tails, making up his daily ledger of snakes in the grass, intent and thoughtful as he was seemed to beat the rhythm's hypnotic tune with nodding head, while every now and then a male Khoran bird, suspicious aerobat of the animated troupe, hurled himself straight into the air to appear like a black puff of anti-aircraft fire above the trees, where he hung for a brief moment

106

in a tremble of fearful wings to make quite sure no prancing villain was stalking him. Higher still, each section of sky possessed a wheeling vulture also observing the shimmering, shaking, vibrating rhythm, wheeling, turning, sometimes fearfully dipping, up down, down up, as if it were a black hunter spider swinging on a pearly line. It all made me grateful that I walked this Dead Land not in summer but in the midst of its tropical winter.

Walking thus, I soon came to see why it was called the Dead Land. The track we were on at the beginning had been made by the feet of vanished men, and at first the sense of this gave me a feeling of tremendous companionship and continuity with the past; as if the footpath were not merely a pedestrian overt fact, but also a wise and proven instinct within. I was not surprised when we came across traces of ancient settlement: crumbling stone walls of huts, scattered pottery and broken urns lying in an unforgiving sun. But the deeper we went into the bush the fewer these tokens became until finally there was only the narrow footpath to bear witness to the life which had once invested this far, shining and trembling bushveld. Yet as long as that footpath lasted, I thought, I would have hope, for it suggested that the obstinate rumour of the Great Flamingo Water was, perhaps, not rumour at all but a surviving fragment of authentic racial memory.

My hope was increased at our first halt. After three hours I sent Tickie running down the line to tell Umtumwa to stop at the first convenient shade. There I took out my map and compass and took the bearing almost E.S.E. from Fort Emmanuel. I was delighted to find that the track bore down exactly on the point of the map where, from the 'plane, I'd seen brilliant ruby fire leaping through the satin mist.

I was about to tell Umtumwa and Tickie the good news when I felt insects alighting on the back of my neck. I slapped at them instantly with the flat of my hand and retrieved three dead flies, whose grey unimpressive appearance belied their deadliness. I looked about me and noticed the bearers every minute or two were gloomily slapping at some part of their bodies. For all the bright, dancing light of day around us, a deadly nightshade had risen up in our midst.

I walked over to Umtumwa. 'Put a tin of water to the boil

and give every man a mugful of hot, sweet tea and then come all and listen to me,' I told him.

When I had them around me, I said: 'We all know this is the worst fly country in Africa. I knew it before I started but still I came. D'you know why? Because I have powerful *'mhuti*, mighty medicine with me that will keep you all safe against Ngana!* Here!' At this, unashamed of my lie because I knew that, with luck, I should have us all back in a civilized hospital where we could be cured before the disease had a fatal grip on us, I took a bottle of Paludrine out of the pack on Tickie's back, went down the line and put a white pill in each hand saying: 'Swallow that with your tea. Each morning and each night I'll give you one of these and you need think no more of the tsetse fly.'

With that the crisis vanished, a brisk, spirited conversation, such as I had not heard before flared up in our midst, and Tickie gave me such a look of loyal admiration and transfigured gratitude that my conscience almost pricked me.

We marched on for another three hours, at the end of which I rested them once more and gave each man another mug of hot, sweet tea. Then, as we set off again, I heard a loud exclamation of dismay on the track in front of me, followed by a thud. I hastened forward. A bearer had stumbled and fallen and lay with the contents of his load scattered about him. When I came up to him, he cringed and covered his head with his arm as if he expected me to beat him for stumbling, and was amazed to see my hand stretched out to help him to his feet. However, what I'd seen on that emaciated face as it lay in the dust, decided me to change my plan. I sent Tickie to tell Umtumwa to pick the first good camp site, for clearly de Fereira's gaolers hadn't believed in overfeeding their charges.

Ten minutes later I came over the top of a fiery basalt bluff to find Umtumwa already hard at work pitching camp. He'd chosen his site well. Below us was a deep, wide *vlei*, lush and green-gold in the afternoon sun and every fifty yards or so a pool of sky-blue water. On the edge of the bluff stood an immense iron-wood tree with a trunk shining like smoked Javanese silver. Its massive column spun straight upwards for about seventy feet and there burst into a wide crown of

* Sindakwena for sleeping-sickness.

108

branches all aglitter like an amorous peacock's tail. The cooling air resounded with the homing song of many birds, guinea fowl, ducks and geese. Calling on Tickie to accompany me, I picked a game track covered with fresh spoor and went down it, my back to the sun, Tickie following gladly just behind me.

We'd not walked a quarter of a mile from our camp when suddenly Tickie's hand, pulling at my shirt, brought me to a quick stop. I turned round and saw him pointing at a great, lone elephant bull, a profound imperial purple in that light, standing not thirty yards away, sound asleep on his feet from the heat of the day. Although asleep, his great sensitive ears were never still but fanned his head so constantly and rhythmically that at one moment they seemed part of the breathing of some strange vast fish lying there, head upstream, in an amber current. His long broad brow was corrugated with furrows of age, his knees limp with his hunger for sleep, his eyes were shut in abandon, and the great arch of his shoulder was but the curve of the purple magnet of longing which clasped his supple legs so firmly to the warm African earth. His long trunk hung straight down in front of him with a heavy, sagging immobility until it began to curl over ever so faintly at the utmost tip and to glisten with a light rhododendron pinkness as it began to search the air in our direction. Both Tickie and I couldn't help smiling at the expression which then came over that monumental face as the heavy skin of his great trunk, with wonderful butterfly flutter puckered like the nose of a baby about to sneeze. Then our scent, faint as it was, won. One moment he was sound asleep, the next wide awake, eyes open, trunk out, ears still tense on the alert. Lone old elephant bulls are notoriously uncertain characters. As his trunk flew out searching the air strenuously in our direction, I slipped the safety catch of my gun. But that sound, slight as it was, added to the agitation already beginning to boil in him. He took one delicate step in our direction, curling up his trunk under his chin as if about to charge, then undoing it with a quick, heavy swish, to bring it once more to bear on us. At that moment, however, a new sound arose; the noise of animated bearers' conversation back in camp. That decided him. Head proudly up and ears daintily fanning, he slowly turned his back, like that of some fine old Patrician reduced by revolution to a pair of borrowed outsize trousers, and marched off with a long, nimble stride and immense disdainful Mandarin dignity into the eurythmic bush.

'Auck! Bwana! Surely he was a great chief,' Tickie, his young face brilliant with excitement, exclaimed behind me. As he said it I found myself ready to smile.

From there we walked on till my eye caught the glint of long water in the yellow *vlei* ahead, so I swung off the track and went carefully up a rise for a clearer view of the water. Close by, hundreds of animals were drinking or waiting to drink. Taking out my field-glasses I focused them on the water, my heart beating faster at what I saw, for all Africa was in that moment for me. Yes, the whole cast of the first natural, primordial, legitimate theatre of Africa seemed gathered there to make its final curtsy in the limelight of the sunset hour and receive twilight applause before the night dropped its final curtain. A noble water buck, accompanied by his women in purple furs, sank to his knees and drank deep of the blue water before he stood up and made his exit with great dignity into the wings of singing reeds. A *kudu* bull, his coat a Persian blue broken only by four bands of Chinese white, his head so proudly crowned with horn that he could scarcely hold it erect, walked easily through herds of lesser breeds to stand motionless, on the burning water's edge, narcissus-bound by the magic of the reflection at his shapely feet. I saw an *inyala* night-fighter standing where *vlei* met bush, astrakhaned already against the cooling air and regarding the scene with such a philosophic air that had he raised his pointed toe to stroke his Assyrian beard I wouldn't have been amazed. I saw a herd of impatient zebra charge down fast on the water, stop so short and hard that the transparent dust shot up to fly over the pool like a flag translucent in the sun. Then red and white *impala*, fearful of everything, drank with quick neurasthenic frenzy, throwing glances, sip after sip, over their elegant shoulders until satisfied at last, their soft impressionable hearts relieved, they bounded easily on light, elastic toes from off the stage. I watched a group of downcast gnu, sullen tails flicking ceaselessly, standing alone, heads lowered, blinking out from under bushy eyebrows their complex of inferiority, while behind them two elephants, wet skins shining darkly from their meticulous evening bathe,

110

walked clean and straight with long spartan strides into the level sun. I saw a woman of my beloved *tsessebe* tribe, the fastest antelope on earth, the wind of her speed flashing in her smooth fair hair, follow jealously after her master and two glittering concubines, like Atlanta resuming her race in the Hesperides. I observed some dark red hartebeest with evening tiara of curled mother-of-pearl horn, trip on ballet shoes into a vacancy in the crowded chorus, and a white ibis settle like a flake of Everest snow on the back of the leader. High on a tree-top in the vast backcloth of the wood a huge baboon, look-out for his flock, scratched his auburn head quickly with a long, purple finger. Then suddenly away on the far wing of singing green I saw the tight, yellow lines of grass begin to sway and move as if a catspaw of wind had clutched them. At the same instant a trio of earth-brown grouse flew swiftly up with frantic wings, a black ostrich guard gathered his Macedonian skirt under his chin exposing lean, yellow loins and suddenly took to Derby heels. And all the animals stopped drinking at the water – yes, all, with quick electric ears, narrowed eyes, their nostrils sniffing the motionless air between them and the patch of moving grass. Obviously it was the moment for the royal villain of this imperial piece to make his entry. Then down the track between us and the water came a lone sable-bull. He walked slowly, stopping every few yards to listen and to smell. He was old, obviously extremely wise, and, of course, unbearably lonely. His slow step was not merely caution but also reluctance to leave the goodly company in the bright-lit theatre by the water and face the night alone. But though his dark back was black and his long sharp horns sweeping back to his shoulders with a fine-spiked speed, were bravely militant, cleaving the air as he moved his aristocratic head like the pick of Jan Hoy's* swords, yet he was neither villain nor hero, but in the evening sun his long elegant face with white cheeks and striped nose wore the strange made-up pallor of a tragic clown I had once seen, his performance ended, going from the circus back to his dressing-room.

If I had to kill I could kill less cruelly by shooting this superb reject from the herd, I thought, so I waited until he paused, sideways on, at only fifty yards and then I shot him

* Jan Hoy: Amharic title of Emperor of Abyssinia and Lion of Judah.

through the heart. Slowly he went down on his knees, head desperately trying to keep erect, but finally like a destroyer holed in the bows sinking at sea, he glided steeply forward and vanished in the swell of grass. In an instant the bright company by the pool vanished.

'Quick, Tickie! Fetch four bearers,' I shouted while I ran towards the buck. Though he was dead when I reached him, remembering I had Mohammedans among my bearers, I quickly cut his throat and marvelled once more that, no matter how often one sees blood, it is always redder than one expects. Then I stood up, wiping knife and hands on the warm dry grass to find every tree-top round me obscene with vultures and the sky above a spinning vortex of scavenger wings, as if the going of this great sable antelope had made a maelstrom in the sea of evening which was sucking these hungry feathers after it.

That night, tired as my bearers were, they ate as I've seldom seen people eat and by nine, well content, they were all abed and asleep. But before I turned in I thought to renew a custom of Oom Pieter's which he never failed to observe in the bush because, in retrospect, it helps the memory. So I said to Umtumwa:

'Umtumwa, you've led us well. I ask you to name the camp for us.'

For a moment he stood still, looking deep in the fire, then, waving his hand at the sleeping bearers, he said with a sudden laugh, 'Master, you can call him Belly-full.' And so 'Belly-full camp' it was.

Promptly at six next morning we were back on our track, stepping out briskly, but I noticed the country was slowly changing. We were climbing out of the vast Black Umpafuti catchment country and the land was getting slowly drier and the bush darker with thorn-tree. The tsetse fly was worse than ever and as I hardly saw an animal all day, the land felt truly desolate and near to death. This feeling was heightened by the sight of the stumps of enormous trees, which stood up straight in the air towering over their surroundings, and looked from afar like broken Ionian columns, or uncared-for monuments in an immense graveyard. Often a vulture or maribou stork sat on top, bare-livered neck drawn deep into attentive shoulders, and never taking an eye full of sinister hope from my small line.

112

For all that I was accustomed to that sort of thing, I found the scene beginning to revive all my latent disquiet. Marching at the head of the column too, as I now was, I was the first to encounter the insects both great and small, little hunting spiders, red, silver, and gold like filigree Indian jewels in the sun, and red-bellied scorpions the size of lean, athletic young lobsters among the boulders, or again other spiders big as soup tureens, shaking like jellies on black, hairy legs, and blue-headed lizards with yellow throats and jade-bead eyes sparkling like powdered glass, drying off the cold dew on the sharp crest of loose iron-stone rock, and each reptile, as it stared unblinking into the sun, ceaselessly licking thin lips and lashing the stark light with the shadow of their flickering tongues.

Then there were the snakes, too. This morning, within an hour of sunrise, I saw their heads go up one after another as the first vibration of my feet reached them. At one moment there were so many glistening, swaying heads high above the grass in front of me on either side of the track that it looked almost as if I were about to be forced to run a ritualistic Maya gauntlet of lashing tongues playing like forked-lightning over their poisoned mouths. Many of the trees, too, had one or two serpents either draped like a limp lash of an ox-whip across their branches, or else alert and active, hanging by their tails from the branches, hissing and making quick, threatening passes below. One large tree near a water-hole was festooned with them and its dancing outline looked like the flaming silhouette of Medusa's hair. In the grass, black home-loving cobras predominated, sitting house-proud by the side of their holes, shining hood up at the first alarm, the ring of cream round their throat vivid in the sun and green poisoned spit at the ready on the tongue. Among the boulders the long copper hunting cobras, like newly-spun telephone wire stalked the rat, fieldmouse, and dassie warrens, but stood instantly on the tip of their tails to stare at the first sound of our approaching feet. And sometimes a hard, horny python head would drag across the track a body like a footballer's stocking filled for Christmas. I was tempted to shoot a twelve-foot mamba which just missed my head from his perch in a tree. That I did not do so was largely on account of Umtumwa and Tickie. The 'Takwena will kill snakes if attacked but otherwise leave them severely alone, for they regard snakes as privileged messengers from their dead ancestors, or even an ancestor himself and as such to be studied with attention and respect. Snakes figure vastly in their reading of the future and are used extensively in their most powerful medicines and charms, the rare, long, yellow cobra being considered most important of messengers – but more of that later.

We walked from six that morning until five in the afternoon, when my bearers were beginning to falter. Then suddenly we came out into the open on the edge of a shallow pan lying there in the midst of the dark bush like a wedding ring in the palm of a black hand. In the centre of it was a hole of thick green water and a lone, red hartebeest stood beside it with such a puzzled astonished look on his face that I knew he'd never seen a human being before. I gave him no time to study me, however, but shot him so that he fell over without a sound into his own sunset shadow so swiftly contracting to meet him.

While my bearers were preparing the meal I went to climb a solitary koppie behind the camp. On my way I noticed that all the spoor here were of dry land game, and told myself from now on we must ration ourselves strictly for water.

The koppie itself, fiery ruby boulders flickering in the white spear grass, looked like a tarnished ship's bell. On the summit, dark brown against a scarlet sky, stood a nimble klip-springer watching me with undisguised amazement. Not until I was twenty yards from it did it succeed in breaking through the hypnosis of so strange a sight. It bounded away high over a trembling broom-bush straight into the sinking sun.

I took its place about three hundred feet above the green-eyed pan and had a tremendous view of the Dead Land. To the north it fell away towards the Black Umpafuti in a series of sinking, shallow folds of bushveld, the long sunlight showing up the red flanks of many a bluff, the shadow between already running strong like water into a deep well, and rising swiftly up over sunlit columns and gleaming wall of red and purple rock and yellow sand. To the west, the same bush-covered land ran fast and easily up to the horizon which waited bravely, with bowed head, for the sword of the sun to fall. But to the south and south-east of me the land fell away swiftly. Clearly I stood on the watershed between the Umpafuti and

Uhlalingasonki catchment areas. My heart rejoiced at the thought, for that meant that nearly half my journey was accomplished. Only forty-eight hours in the Dead Land and already I reckoned sixty miles lay behind me. At this rate, if there were indeed a Great Flamingo Water, I should reach it long before even so impatient a lady as the *Star of Truth*.

But then I looked east-south-east again and immediately qualified my bright speculation. The sun was just touching the horizon behind me and its rays now level with the earth showed clearly, about nine miles away, a thick black line stretching right across my course for as far as I could see. For a moment I thought it was a range of hills, but then through my glasses I saw the broken bushveld country come to an abrupt, shuddering halt before the ranks of a sombre and mighty forest. It stood there armed and to attention, packed tightly shoulder to shoulder, like a line of invincible black rock along the edge of a sunlit sea.

It was my first glimpse of the great forest of Duk-aduk-duk and I remembered the warning of the N.C.O. at Fort Emmanuel. I studied it through my glasses like one obsessed, until it was too dark to see more, but already I'd noticed two things. In the extreme north-east both land and forest ran into a glint of vast water, the Umpafuti swamps I presumed: and in the extreme south-east into a long mane of cloud formations, which the Governor had claimed succeeded morning mist all along the Coast. Only then did I go fast down the hill to my fire while some hundreds of yards away a thirsty lion, baulked of his water by the camp, began to roar and roar for us to leave.

'Please, Bwana,' Tickie said shyly when I joined them by the fire, 'I would like to give the name of this camp.'

'Why certainly.'

'Please, Bwana, I would like to call it "Mabela'ghaudi," because of that.' Struggling to overcome a fit of girlish giggles which was already tickling Umtumwa's fancy, he waved his hand at the koppie.

'Mabela'ghaudi' is Sindakwena for a 'goat's tit' which certainly the koppie's outline resembled more than the ship's bell with which my *Star-of-Truth*-obsessed mind had compared it. So Goat's Tit Camp it became and so remains in my mind to this day.

To me the nights in camp are never dull, contrary to the expectation of many of my friends. To start with, comforted with the luxury of extreme physical fatigue, one's mind is unexacting and one's heart filled with a peace which sinks into it as lawfully and inevitably as the fulfilled day. In the second place there are many things to do, the wounds, scratches, and ailments of my company to attend to, cleaning of guns, and mending of clothes, for unless that is done as the damage arises the sharp thorns of the bush would soon reduce me to rags and tatters. And, lastly, in African company it is difficult to be dull, for in the bush there is not a stone, hill, shrub, tree, river, stagnant pool, up-silver fountain, insect, bird, or beast which is not full and overflowing with meaning and spirit for the Africans.

This evening in Goat's Tit Camp was no exception. While I cleaned my gun and watched my bearers I listened to Umtumwa and Tickie talking as they cooked liver, kidneys, and fillet of hartebeest steak.

'Yes, my boy,' Umtumwa was saying, 'it is a pity it was a hartebeest the master shot.'

'But, brother of my mother,' Tickie, loyally impetuous, rushed in to reject what he thought was criticism implied of me. 'How could he have shot another when there was no other? Would you have liked us to have another pot of porridge of this rotten Portuguese meal?'

'Do not be so foolish, my boy,' Umtumwa replied with mild superiority. 'Of course, the master could not help it. I say only that it is a pity since hartebeest as you will find presently is not tasteful eating.'

'That I know already, brother of my mother,' was Tickie's tart reply.

'But what you do not know is how lucky you are that a man is cooking it for you and not a woman!' Umtumwa said.

'My mother prepares it very well,' Tickie insisted.

'I agree she is better than most women,' Umtumwa stood his ground. 'But it needs a man to do it really well: women have not the patience. Ask any Keeper of our People's Memory and he will tell you that the best cooks in our nation have always been men. Now the secret of cooking hartebeest –' Umtumwa gave Tickie a long discourse concluding, 'And where

116

in all Africa will you find a woman at the end of a day's work in the field prepared to do all that?'

'Nandisipoh* would,' Tickie said shyly yet, as his nature was, without hesitation.

Umtumwa broke into an affectionately mocking laugh, having obviously hit the target of his roundabout approach, for Nandisipoh was a girl in Umangoni whom Tickie had once mentioned in an unguarded moment to my servants and had never been allowed to forget it since.

'Oh ho; ha; hé; hi; hi;' Umtumwa laughed at the bashful Tickie.

'There is a proverb, brother of my mother,' Tickie interrupted, summing up the desperate dignity of the young when faced with grown-up ridicule: 'There is a proverb of our people that scandal is unlike porridge: there is never a lack of it.'

Umtumwa only pretended to be more amused than ever and went on: 'Is it, son of my sister? But I grant you young Nandisipoh throws a shadow.' This is the greatest compliment the 'Takwena can pay a woman, meaning she has both beauty and personality. Then he broke off suddenly to exclaim, waving a burning branch in the direction of the roaring lion: 'In the name of Xilixowe how that animal roars: shall we have no peace tonight?'

'That lion is a fool,' Tickie said with immense scorn. 'If it wants water why does it not drink? I'll not prevent him.'

'Listen, son of my sister,' Umtumwa reproved him. 'Do not go walking boastfully through this bush thinking of lion as fools, for if you do you will never enjoy the shade of Nandisipoh again.'

He paused to let his words sink in and then said:

'Talking of women and lion, for it is clear to me you do not know enough of either, suppose there was a female with that roaring male now and the master gave you his gun and said: "Tickie, go and shoot those rude, impolite beasts for otherwise we shall not sleep tonight"; which would you shoot first?'

'The one that showed up the best, of course.'

'Even if that one should be the male?' Umtumwa asked.

* *Nandi* – a favourite 'Takwena woman's name; *Sipoh* – a gift. Hence *Nandi-sipoh* – a gift of a daughter to the husband of Nandi.

117

'Of course. How could that matter?' Tickie answered.

'It matters so much,' Umtumwa answered gravely, 'that if you did that you would not see Nandisipoh again. Listen, son of my sister, you must always shoot the female first, because if you shoot her man first she will be upon you before you have another bullet in your gun. But the male, if you shoot his woman first, will lose heart at once and creep away with many fearful looks over his shoulder, for such is the nature of the male beast.'

'Auck! Brother of my mother!' Tickie exclaimed surprised and deeply impressed, while Umtumwa pleased and encouraged went on to elaborate his theme.

So I leave them there by the fire in Goat's Tit Camp with the sparks flying straight up in the still air, the scent of proud hartebeest roasting on the wooden coals like incense of royal sacrifice to ancient gods rising up towards the crackling stars, the flames flickering red and yellow among the breathless acacia tops, the lion roaring, and the lightning, like flare of revolving lighthouse, flashing and reflashing from behind the great forest of Duk-aduk-duk.

In the morning I gave everyone as much tea as he could drink. I examined the battleship-grey field flasks each one carried on his back to make certain they were full of boiled water, and told them that no one was to draw on his flask until I gave him permission. Then I led them out of the clearing over the round shoulder of Mabela'ghaudi and down into the great Uhlalingasonki basin. The morning was hot, the air damp and close, the fly worse than ever, and the snakes, with the electricity of far-off thunder warm in their cold blood, more numerous and active than the day before. Yet my bearers, thanks to the diet of unlimited freshly-killed meat stepped out behind me with spirit and will. By eight o'clock we were within two miles of the forest and the nearer we came the less I liked the look of it. It was even darker by day than by twilight because of the contrast it presented to the glittering, shimmering dancing world about it. Indeed, as I strode quickly towards it, so dark, high, and dense did the trees rise up in the sky, so sullen and militant was their stance that I believed every drop of the thick black sap that ran in their ancient veins had long since rejected the advances of the day for ever. For a long time

118

I thought that the passion of the forest's rejection of the sunlit world might too have banished all animal life within it.

Then, just before nine, I stood in the black shadow of the forest itself to find the way aggressively blocked, for at its base the forest was defended by an intricate system of abominable thorns of all kinds, so hooked, barbed, harpooned, and closely interlocked that no way could be found through it. In vain did Umtumwa, Tickie, the bearers, and I try to break into it with our pangas in the hope that once inside among the huge trunks we would find clear ground and be able to resume our march to the sea on our original compass bearing. But each time the forest hurled us back.

'This damned thorn, Bwana,' Umtumwa sweating and bleeding from several deep scratches, exclaimed in one of his outbursts in Askhari English, 'he is shut with zip fasteners.'

'I know, Umtumwa,' I said. 'Don't do any more. It's no good. We've already wasted three precious hours so take up your loads and let's go.' The track on which we stood was forked, one prong going south-west and skirting the forest, the other going north-east. I turned to follow the latter, trying to follow our bearing as closely as I could when Tickle suddenly seized my arm, 'Quick, Bwana, look!'

I jumped round in some alarm to see a great black ape dropping with amazing agility on top of a boulder near by. He, too, had never seen man before. Nor had I ever seen his kind either. He was taller than a gorilla and though not so wide in the shoulder was much longer in the arm. His coat was a dusky purple, and his face so clear of hair and the skin so supple, that I distinctly saw the start of astonishment send the hair on his head flying back fast, and the long, narrow forehead break out in a dozen wrinkles. His strange midnight eyes blazed with the suspicion which lies at the core of that small seed of intelligence in the first man, and a long prehensile lip did an electric jibber of anger and dismay. His teeth were long, broad, and yellow, and as he bared them he uttered a deep booming cry that echoed and re-echoed in the stillness, before he jumped back again into the forest.

I found my hands trembling suddenly with release of a suppressed fear that I might have had to shoot him because of all beasts I most dislike shooting baboons and apes. Their cry of pain is almost more human than our own; it comes straight, without inhibition of mind or custom, from the heart of the trusting animal that dies rejected in civilized man and the sound is almost more than I can endure. As a result I spoke more roughly than I would normally have done to a tall Mohammedan bearer whom I noticed with his hand feeling for the flask of water at his hip. He was a tall Somali called Said and had before now attracted my attention with something vaguely military in his bearing for he had served once in the Somaliland frontier force:

'If you touch that water I'll shoot you,' I told him and turning to the others. 'That goes for all of you.'

'Ghaebre effendi,' Said answered so mildly in an Arabic patois of his own that I felt rebuked: 'I was but easing the flask on my hip.'

We marched from there until an hour before sunset. We made camp in a clearing in black thorn country. We were all tired, desperately thirsty, as well as somewhat discouraged by the day, having done, I reckoned, only seventeen miles, and only nine of them in the right direction. As the company came into camp one by one, they all instantly sank down to the ground to rest with their heads in their hands and elbows on their loads. Even Umtumwa and Tickie did the same as the bearers, which shows how deeply the resentful forest had perturbed their spirit.

I was about to go and talk encouragement to them when suddenly in the track on the edge of the clearing a saffron cobra, the most significant of all 'Takwena snakes, came gliding leisurely towards us. It shows how tired my company was that those who saw it made no move of any kind. When opposite Umtumwa it suddenly paused and threw its head swiftly, like a lasso uncoiling, five feet into the air. The wide hood flared and flashed full out and with head swaying in the grass like a strange somnolent yellow poppy among harvest corn, it regarded Umtumwa intently for some seconds. My heart stood still, for my servant and true old friend was looking at it like a frog hypnotized by the serpent's eye and I knew would not have defended himself. I had my rifle instantly trained on the swaying yellow head but at that moment the quick flame died down in the hood, the head collapsed in the dust and the cobra

120

glided out of view, making a chain of burnished 's' in the grass, each 's' strangely reproduced in my stomach as if the cord at my navel were a serpent unwinding coils of unremembered being underneath my heart. Dropping my rifle I went quickly to Umtumwa.

'Did you see that, my Bwana? Oh! Did you see it, Bwana?' Umtumwa asked in a strange new voice, black dismay in his eyes.

'Aye, Umtumwa, I saw it as I've seen a hundred others today, so what of it?' I said, trying to comfort him by making light of it.

'No! Bwana, no!' he answered with a sombre shake of his head. 'There are not a hundred others like it. There is not one single snake in the world like it. Did you not see the way it looked at me and only me? I wish I were at Amantazuma now to ask my father's doctor to tell me what it means, and give me the *'mhuti* I need.'

The agony of his concern was great, but on that note I was forced to leave the camp to look for game. Having been lucky enough to find and shoot a shining, fat duiker ram only a hundred yards from camp, I came running back for bearers to bring it in. But hardly had I entered the clearing when ten yards away from me the blackthorn bush began to crackle and sway, then the dark cheek of wood near me exploded and like a dreadnought shell a rhinoceros burst out of it. His short stumpy legs were going so fast that his round behind bounced like a runaway cart over boulders. His head stuck far out, eye red with typical piggish anger and liver full of burning adrenalin, his horn almost whistling in the wind and dust of his speed. Straight through the centre of the camp he charged but everyone, warned by the crackle, had already scattered – everyone save Tickie. He had just put his net and blanket out on top of a bush, unfortunately directly in the rhino's path. Alarmed by the glint of white and red the rhinoceros spiked blanket and net neatly in his horn and tossed them up backwards over his shoulder. The heavy blanket, however, hung on, falling over his head and shoulders and blotting out his view so suddenly that he stopped in a shower of dust on the edge of the clearing, legs wide apart, throwing his head about and pawing at ground and blanket snorting, huffing, puffing, and grunting with rage

121

and bewilderment. He looked so comic standing there, so truly and poetically judged and punished that the camp broke out in delighted almost hysterical laughter.

Tickie, however, his eyes blazing with indignation at the theft of his blanket ran quickly to the fire and before we knew his intention had snatched up a burning branch. Running back to the rhinoceros, he rammed the red-hot tip of the branch hard in the wrinkled rhinoceros behind, shouting, 'There you thing of evil, drop my things, you thief, drop them, I say, drop them!'

'My God, Tickie, you idiot!' I shouted. 'Look out and run!' For as the fire burnt him in so tender a spot, the rhinoceros whipped round fast and the blanket flew off. His inflamed eyes instantly saw Tickie. At once, down went his head and he charged with an unbelievable jump after the boy. Umtumwa and I both shot at once and to my relief the bad-tempered animal went over on his shoulders in the dust, where after a deep sigh he lay dead in the grass, presenting to us a profile that might have been that of some fabulous horned lizard dreaming before nightfall in the sun.

After a waterless dinner with only a mugful of tea each to wash it down, I gathered from Umtumwa's conversation that his mind was once more preoccupied with the yellow cobra, so, in an effort to cheer him up, I called out:

'Umtumwa, guess what I'm going to name this camp: Tickie's Reprieve.'

I was grateful for his laugh and Tickie's giggle that followed.

Chapter 10

In the Great Forest of Duk-aduk-duk

I shall always remember that dawn in the camp of Tickie's Reprieve. No part of Africa orders its morning crepuscule better than blackthorn veld. It is as if the millions of fine spikes of a hundred varieties of thorn, white, black, purple, green, and red blades, arrow heads, hooks, curves, and yeoman spikes of a steel-like quality, have a prismatic effect on the light, catching it and holding it up like a silk cloth. But this particular dawn was superb even by blackthorn veld standards. It was a true hunter's dawn, after Aurora's own fleet heart, coming up fast above the burning iridescent line of the bush, in scarlet Red Indian moccasins, with the day running like a supple red buck full out before it.

I was watching it, and listening to the apes booming, booming with relish at the coming of the day from everywhere in the dark, watchful forest when I saw Umtumwa without a gun get on a stone and gaze deeply into the running day. When the sun looked out of the corner of its eye over the edge of our horizon I saw Umtumwa spit in his right hand, raise it far above his head to give the sun the Royal 'Takwena salute, and hold it there until the cool feel of the morning air in the palm of his hand vanished. I found myself inexpressibly moved by the sight. I had not seen Umtumwa pray for years, for that was the ancient, mindless way of the Amangtakwena communing with their sense of God: at dawn the right hand, at sunset the left. I've often asked them what it means but all they say is: 'Try it, Bwana, and let the doing answer you,' and when I tried and felt a breath of cold air breathing in the moist palm of my hand, they used to say again and again with a tender smile: 'There now: don't you feel the great spirit touching the heart of your hand?'

This morning I am certain something profound touched Um-

tumwa's hand, for when he came off the stone the look of un-
fathomable concern that the cobra had planted in his eye was
gone. Instead he looked at peace, but graver than I've ever
known him.

'Umtumwa,' I told him, finding it difficult to keep emotion
out of my voice: 'since Tickie was brave enough to singe a
rhino's seat let's see if he is man enough to walk at the end of
the line and you come on at the head with me, for I shall need
your help and advice if we are to find the water we must
before the night.'

I didn't tell him, however, that, concerned as I was about
water, my real reason was to keep him company in the archaic
shadow that had so suddenly darkened his faithful soul.

'Aye, Bwana,' he answered gravely, 'but you need not fear,
we shall find water before the night. Look.' He pointed to a
pair of gleaming green-yellow water finches streaking fast over
our heads straight into the rising sun.

Much encouraged by the sight, we stepped out fast along
the track and would have had a comparatively carefree morning if it had not been for the resentful, watchfully waiting
forest which kept on throwing us out wherever we tried to
enter it. I'm not an unduly fanciful person but that forest
quickly acquired a human character for me. As the day pro-
gressed and the thorn bushes began their dance, I thought at
times I discerned a cynical half-smile of superior disdain on the
dark handsome forest face. I could almost believe that it was
perfectly aware of our presence and conscious of the need to
spy on our progress. I'd have soon felt downright hopeless, in
fact, if I hadn't noticed that the country was slowly changing
and the thorn very slowly diminishing, which made me think
that, if that happened to thorn without surely it must hold
good also for thorn within the forest. Yet when we camped
down that evening we still hadn't breached its defences, though
we'd walked and probed another twenty-five miles in the wrong
direction and used up another of my eight precious days, leaving me only four. Obviously I was going to need all the extra
hours my good Port Captain could gain for me by retarding
the impatient lady, and I realized with an emotion which was
like a sickness of the bowels that the odds were more and
more against my succeeding.

However, the sight of our camp cheered me, for at least we had a good pool of water. When Umtumwa and I saw it first, it had some 'chocolate wildebeest' drinking deep nose to nose with their own luminous reflections, and beyond the wildebeest, a great zebra-prince, looking as if he had walked straight out of a royal coat of arms, was making urgent love to a noble lady.

'There, Bwana!' Umtumwa said, the first laugh of the day bubbling up in him. 'There is a fine name for so good a camp,' and, pointing at the zebra, he used a good descriptive and homely Sindakwena phrase which can be translated euphemistically thus: 'The place of the Zebra's Delight.'

Next morning we took to the road much refreshed and eager for our battle with the forest. At the end of three hours both Umtumwa and I, though still repulsed, had rising hopes of making an entry before the day ended. The thorn was beginning to diminish along the grim margin of the forest while the trees appeared to be getting bigger and higher.

All day long the thinning process continued, while the fly, closeness of the air, and humidity constantly increased. By noon we crossed our first long blue and gold savannah lying tranquilly at an obtuse angle to our track and struck our first buffalo spoor. Five minutes later Umtumwa tugged at my coat and whispered, 'Inyati.'

Twelve yards away, his muzzle wet and shining with light and health, grey scimitar of powerful horn thrown back, expert nostrils searching the air, stood our first buffalo bull, the grass wherein he stood clasped close around his throat and lying like a cape of gold against his purple flanks. It is for me always a solemn moment when I first see buffalo again after a long time. The buffalo's powerful head darkening the yellow grass, like the lion's imperative roar and the elephant's long, somnambulistic stride, has more of the quintessential Africa in it for me than any other manifestation of all the scores of animals that I love and know. It's as if in the buffalo the very stones and earth of Africa, all its vast, ponderable, withdrawn and solidified matter have turned magically into a living design of life; as if all the tranced magnetic power of the land is released in their drumming hooves and in the easy lift of the weight of their head. In their passionate defence of themselves, in their

125

unpredictable reaction to intrusion, indifferent or benign, in their readiness to give way, their determination to avenge an injury with indefatigable cunning, in all these characteristics it's as if they're a living expression of the inarticulate character of the African earth. So with this powerful bull, carefully weighing up in his patient, mathematical senses what he should do about the virgin apparition of man standing there before him.

We stood for ten minutes and then I said: 'Umtumwa, we can't wait all day for him to make up his mind, take Tickie's place at the back. Close up the line as tightly as possible. Get Said to take the heavy rifle from Tickie and carry it for you. Send Tickie to me with the other and then let's go.' I picked on Said, the long Somali bearer who had already impressed me because if he had served in the Somaliland Frontier Force, he presumably knew how to shoot.

Keeping my eyes on the bull, I led off again and as we moved his head went down and quickly up again, while a snow-white ibis searching for ticks on his back, alarmed by the quickening current along the spine under its feet, shot like an arrow into the air. I took no notice of the warning but held on steadily: then slowly, the bull stepped backwards about twelve paces, turned his body sideways to us and with head thrown over his shoulder, nostrils sniffing incessantly and brown eyes burning with interest, he allowed us to pass. But in a few minutes we met a herd of about five hundred buffalo heads showing like large purple ticks in the yellow grass. On our approach it instantly contracted into a tight and flawless ring, as precisely as one of Chaka's well-drilled *impis*, children in the middle, mothers about them, and the great bulls alert on the perimeter watching us out of sight. Ah! there is no ballet master on earth who could recreate the precision and grace with which the vivid instinct of animal Africa puts its creatures great and small through their lovely intricate paces. All day until evening this sort of thing went on, my small company walking steadily further and further away from its true objective down a golden, shimmering lane between the watchful forest and the alert heads of great herds of buffalo. I don't know which of the two was the more impressive or made me the more uneasy. By nightfall the buffalo still stood their ground without going over to the attack, and the forest was still victorious.

We pitched our camp at sundown by a deep blue pool. Round its edges were finely-pointed starry blue and yellow lilies. Duck with bodies of speckled egg-tan were drifting like Chinese paper boats towards their bed among the reeds, and the water itself was so still and preoccupied with the twilight mood of this remote land that when Said came up to me and said in his Arabic patois, 'Surely, Effendi, you could call this place Bhir-Es-Salaam: the peaceful water,' I instantly agreed, pleased both at the aptness of the suggestion and also that he should feel free to come to me thus.

Taking Tickie with me, I went off in search of meat, and two hundred yards from the pond our track ended abruptly in a vast complex of decayed and crumbling stone walls. It was obvious that once a considerable city had stood here, and now it was a desolate and moving sight, filling me with a shadowy melancholy, made all the more poignant by the feeble scribble of dying sunlight on the green-grey tablets of broken stone and the feeling that an imponderable essence of the spirit of the perished people who'd built here still moved through the darkening air above us. As we stood there an owl went up on wings like a moth, mealy and dusted with butterfly pollen, and another hooted near by, while on a large rubble of stone which just managed to keep a desperate head above the paralysing thorn, a large grey giant bustard, the wild peacock of my people, sat watching us silently.

But then, as if to counteract my melancholy, my eye suddenly drew my attention to another track at right angles to the old, aimed like an arrow-head red with blood straight at the dark flank of the forest.

'There's our road for tomorrow, Tickie,' I said, pointing it out to him with relief, hoping that the new track through the forest would lead us back to the old road. But then I got no further with my thought for walking slowly down the track towards the dead city, we saw an elderly hippopotamus bull, like a retired, well-to-do and fat old Parsee merchant, enjoying the cool of the evening.

'How would you like some hippopotamus meat, Tickie?' I whispered to him.

'Auck, my master, that would be very good,' he answered, smacking his lips.

Slowly the doomed old gentleman came towards us with his lumbering rolling retired Admiral-of-the-Fleet's gait and my heart bled for him. He seemed too grotesque to kill. It seemed only fair to let him live and so have a further chance to redeem his shape with some inner loveliness, before I sent him so handicapped to join the lovely shades of beautiful life that had gone before him. For the hippo had a true ambivalence, and was a compound of two-way exaggeration, both negative and positive. His head was so big that he nearly toppled over with it, yet his ears were tiny and coral pink as a woman's. His jaw was like a lion trap and his tusks so powerful that he could have easily nipped the bottom out of a whaler, yet he was a mere vegetarian and so greedy of green and delicate things that I have known his kind walk ten miles from his water for a bite of lettuce. By day he would sleep with contentful ease in the water but by night he walked thus abroad. His chocolate skin was as thick and tough as any hide on earth, yet it carried a delicate goddess blush within. His legs were too small for his body and knock-kneed from his weight: his eyes were old from birth, being without lashes and lidded like a lizard's. He traded in many elements but was complete in none, and all day and night whether in water or on land he huffed, puffed, and grunted with the effort of feeding enough air to the prehistoric current of such vast transitional being.

'Forgive me, dear, rare, old antique,' I whispered, pressed the trigger and watched him sink down, gently, slowly, careful to the last as if not wishing to destroy anything with his great weight, sinking, chin on his hands, to his last rest in the warm shelter of the startled grass.

There was great rejoicing at Bhir-es-Salaam as a result. Hippopotamus lard, like the marrow of the long giraffe bone, is caviare to Africa's indigenous gourmets. Deftly the skinners peeled the huge beast like some vast custard apple and exposed the heavy layers of fat. In that light and against the chocolate skin, with the blush of goddess pink gone, it looked like foam on the edge of the deep sea of his ancient being. As they peeled him the bearers cut this lard in strips and handed it to their fellows to eat raw on the spot. I, too, joined in and felt better for it. But I didn't allow the bearers to linger long, for the dark cloud of mosquito wings over the swamps was rising steadily higher, and their music now was like the massed pipes of the raised Pathan clans coming fast down a gully in the Indian hills. It was urgent to get back to our fires before dark.

No sooner were we back in camp than the mosquitoes stormed the wall of trees around us and poured over the top like Tartar pirates over the side of a fat merchantman. I know of no insect more single-minded and fanatical in the pursuit of living man than the mosquito, a born pirate out for blood, and here at Bhir-es-Salaam they came in a mass of the heaviest Black Umpafuti battalions. The din was high, wild, and barbaric. I crept under my net as soon as possible and there cleaned my guns and ate my food. So did Tickie and Umtumwa, but the greedy bearers threw green leaves on the fire and sat roasting and grilling in thick cover of protective smoke for another two hours. Nonetheless it was a happy camp, or so I thought, until I heard Tickie say to Umtumwa:

'Brother of my mother, in that dead place I told you of, just before the master shot, a ghost owl flew up and another called "who is there" in the bush.'

'What!' exclaimed Umtumwa, obviously startled as well as amazed. 'Be careful how you speak, my boy, for the sun was not yet down and I have never known a ghost owl hoot by daylight.'

'Nor have I, head of Amantazuma. That is why I told you. But ask the master, he heard it too,' Tickie answered, insulted.

'Auck. Auck.' Convinced at last Umtumwa said gravely, 'Surely that cannot be good.'

The next morning, Sunday, and at best five days before the *Star of Truth's* arrival at the assumed Flamingo Water, we turned into our new track at dawn.

According to calculation from my map we had, at most, one hundred and thirty miles to do to the only place where the Great Flamingo Water could be. If this new track were to prove as good as the old and with the bearers getting stronger every day, I was convinced we could do the journey in from four to five days, so that even if I were not in time to meet the *Star of Truth,* which, of course, was what I most wanted to do, I still had a reserve of two or three days for catching her

129

at work – for I agreed with Oom Pieter that she'd have other business to do apart from putting her load of 'Takwena ashore.

I gave a last look at the dead city on the other edge of the Dead Land. With the great tide of light reversed and pouring in fast and brilliant over the thorny beaches, the ruin looked less melancholy than in the evening before and curiously un-African. Perhaps it had been built here by a people who came from the sea to guard their route between interior and ocean. The thought warmed me through and through and sent me leading off fast at the bush.

Though old, the track was good enough and like its predecessor had been kept open by game. It went straight for the darkest shadow in the lofty dark line of trees, cleared the darkness between two giants with not even a thorn to take toll of us. Dear God, the relief of it, the relief of seeing that brave spear-thrust of ancient human purpose strike deep into the heart of the arrogant and tyrannical forest! For one moment I turned to look at the bobbling line of grey boxes coming up fast behind me, saw the sunlit morning curling up over the trees like a Pacific comber coming over a submerged reef, and then I turned my back upon the Dead Land for good.

It was some time before my senses were adjusted to the sudden change. The contrast at first was so great that as I went deeper and deeper into the forest my eyes, so accustomed to the dancing shimmer without, felt strangely inadequate in this world of sombre leaves, trunks like the black columns in the temple of Karnack and damp leaf and moss-covered earth. Nor were my ears any better. They felt as if they'd been plugged. I could no longer hear the bearers padding behind me, nor even pick up the booming of masculine apes. So depressed did I become by this lack of companionable sound that I called out loud to Said who was leading the line. His answering 'Ghadre, Effendi' sounded so faint that I judged him to be far away, but in a few seconds his shape emerged from behind a tree and I knew he could only have been a few yards off.

I was perplexed to explain it all until at noon when the little light so firmly rejected in this deep forest dungeon was less feeble, I saw that the trees were covered thickly with a deep, springy moss, festooned with druid lichen and the earth

130

at their feet covered not only with moss and leaves but also a variety of ferns from the most delicate Chinese patterns with fine black stems and sensitive silk green tracery to trees with fountain-head of royal young palms. I understood then that the great forest of Duk-aduk-duk was deliberately padded with patient cunning and age-old experience against external and intruder sound, so that not one whisper or one gleam of the fierce corrupting light of the mad, feverishly dancing world without should disturb these great heads of leaves in their patient contemplation of a lost and vanished world. From that moment I began to see the forest differently and to notice many rare and precious things.

Tiny deer, not a foot high, with ears like the petals of saffron cinnas and eyes large and warm as a lover's came to peer out shyly at me from behind the leaves. White spotted wood-buck, moving like an agitation of shadow under the branches, waiting patiently for night to fall, appeared to watch me on my way. And, of course, inevitable in a natural world of infinite and classic compensation, there was fierceness and cunning to balance gentle inoffensiveness. The bark of many a great tree was ragged and torn, and hung in long cinnamon strips where leopards had sharpened their claws. At one place I saw the skeleton of an ape mother and her baby, and hard by, on a low branch hanging from a tree like the top of baroque manorial grating, lay a great, living leopard. He was so at one with his perch that he looked as if he'd grown out of the bark like the most imperial of orchids. In fact, at first I saw him only in motley patches through the leaves before my eyes were able to reconstruct the whole submerged mother-of-pearl glow of him.

Instinct made me stop short. I don't greatly fear leopard by night, for in darkness they are confident, but in the daylight, even such bottom-of-the-ocean daylight as this, they are uneasy, displaced, inclined to attack in a panic. Therefore as he snarled I shot and so near was I that I saw the shudder from the shock of a bullet in the brain go through him quickly like a wave from his jewelled throat to the last swish of the shining tassel in his tail. For a second he looked as if asleep, then slowly he turned over a yellow foaming belly and fell on his back into a deep bed of fern feathers. So cushioned against sound was the place that neither Umtumwa nor the bearers a hundred yards behind heard the shot.

I must confess I found the strain of marching underneath these silently watching and patiently absorbing trees far greater than anything I'd yet experienced. At times I felt as if I were drowning or nightmare dreaming in a deep sea of leaves: as if I were a character who had climbed out of the Nautilus of Jules Verne and was walking alone twenty thousand leagues beneath the sea. It was too dark even for the shade-loving tsetse fly, and when evening came not a member of my party had been bitten.

Of one anxiety, however, I was free: the forest was well watered and we crossed many a mysterious and secret stream noiselessly making for the Black Umpafuti catchment. Above these streams swooped an increasing variety of parrots, their colours as they darted swiftly from branch to branch making the shadows look less menacing, and at times it was impossible to tell flash of bird from sombre glow of massive orchids. I've never seen such flowers, reluctantly lighting up the shadows or caught reflected in the dark mirror of a smooth, black shining bark. Some looked like octopuses asleep in deep waters, others like the distended velvet mouths of puff-adders, dripping poison in a ghostly cup, and some were shaped like golden slippers which Diana might pick up with rosy fingers from her dawn bed. But over all brooded the great gods of this world, the trees themselves.

I draw a curtain over the detail of the next four days because they were all exactly like the first. From Lady Precious Stream, as we named our first camp in the forest, we did fifteen miles to Tickie's Kill, called thus because there Tickie shot his first game, a long-nosed bushpig with a collar of black and brown fur at his throat. From Tickie's Kill we did fifteen to Abu Hagar, 'the Father of a Stone,' christened thus by Said on account of a huge rock which raised itself up like an Easter Island monolith from the bed of a stream; from Abu Hagar we did fifteen miles to Apes Weeping. I myself called it so because that night for the first time the silence of the forest was utterly broken and scattered far and wide in tearful fragments by the clamour of apes about us. They congregated, these apes, in great numbers in the tree-tops around us, the

132

male apes booming, the females screaming, the youngsters crying and the babies whimpering heart-rendingly all night long for some unknown disaster that had overtaken them farther back in the dark.

From Apes Weeping, we did another fifteen miles, to Umtumwa's Rest, so named on account of a remark I heard him make to Tickie, as at last they relaxed by the fire. 'No! No! son of my sister,' I heard him saying wearily, 'I who have travelled far and visited many strange places with the master tell you that never will you ever see anything as good as the smoke at evening coming out of our round huts on the slopes of the valley of Amantazuma.'

I admit I myself also was nearly desperate, for we had another fifty-five miles to go, which at the very best would be a day too late to see the *Star of Truth*. It was a bitter thought, but I could not accept it as final. Although my native land, out of a sense of Olympian proportion, gives with one hand only to take away with the other, there are moments when she cups both hands together and pours into the lap of those who have not been discouraged from loving her something which is far greater than either giving or taking. So I took new heart from this reflection as well as from the stirring of light beyond darkness in the white moth wings of far-off thunder above the trees.

We left Umtumwa's Rest at dawn in a heavy mist which, though it made our going more difficult, did not add to my depression since it was perhaps a hint of change in country and climate. For two hours we struggled along, and then, when the mist cleared at about ten, I saw the forest had gone over into lovely park-like land with huge spreading trees, and in between the bush, the gold-green grass of sub-tropical winter and red poinsettias gay and reckless in the sun. And everywhere, heads purple, horns pearly with dew, noses glistening like silk, stood and grazed our monumental buffalo. Oh! what a weight fell from us all then! What a relief to see the blue of day again! On the faces of my bearers, I swear, the forest was so deeply photographed that their dark skins looked as green as black cloth bleached with age. They blinked amazed at the gay, leaping day, and I myself felt like someone released from long imprisonment.

Calling my company together I now explained to them how urgent speed was and demanded of them not to fail me but to step out like free men in a noble cause, walking as they'd never walked before. So without rest of any kind we walked from then until even the dusk, with a deep red gash in its side, was fast bleeding to death and the lightning ahead was so vivid that it threw strange shadows round us. Among the heavy trees by a round hole with some dark water at the bottom we threw ourselves down and made our camp, well content and proud for I reckoned we'd come thirty-two miles and had only thirteen more to go.

'What a hole,' I heard Tickie say with disgust as he tried to draw some water. 'It is hardly bigger than an old woman's porridge pot.'

'Yes, Tickie,' I agreed at once. 'And Porridge Pot shall be its name. But don't worry about water for it'll soon rain. Listen to that.'

A deep roll of thunder drummed on the flaming, flaring horizon and the dark trees already had their heads tucked well into their long overcoats of leaves. But tired as I was I lay awake for a while excited by the prospect of the day before me as well as by the incomparable electricity of African thunder charging in my blood with the assured promise of rain. No one who has not lived in Africa can ever know the sweet reprieve, the golden honeysweet reassurance, the instant and unfailing rekindling of spirit and refreshing of appetite for life that there is in the sound of thunder and at the coming of the rain. Not until the lightning all around me washed sheet-streaming earth purple and the spray of heavy drops crimson with its light, did I sleep. But at midnight I awoke wet and cold, to find the storm gone, a ship's poop of a moon riding a rare and purified sky, and a tremendous hymn of thanksgiving going up from the many complex insects and nightbirds of my native earth.

At dawn when we stood in the track, however, the mist was once more heavy upon us, but not far from Porridge Pot the track began to climb again, and every now and then I felt the crunch of stone underneath my feet. As the mist thinned, I noticed how the vegetation too was changing into low black sub-tropical bush. My heart beat faster at that since I recognized it immediately as the typical coastal covering of the earth in this part of the world. Then, after about two hours' marching, my ears picked up away in front and far to the left of me a sound as of a wind coming up fast and wide from horizon to horizon. I stopped and waited until my company one by one stood silent in the gloom about me, looking more like strange fish upright on their tails in shadowy water than precise outline of sweating men.

'Listen,' I told them. 'Listen well.'

We all listened and there it was ebbing and flowing, flowing and ebbing like the noise of air in a curled shell held to our ears.

'What is it, Bwana?' Tickie whispered. 'For though it is like wind, unlike wind it comes no nearer.'

'You ought to know it,' I told him, 'for you've heard it often enough at Petit France. It's the sea.'

'Ekenonya! Ekenonya!' Tickie shouted, leaping so high with joy into the mist that I thought he would vanish in the gloom above.

'Ie—yellah,' Said joined in with a Dervish call. 'In the name of Allah, let us go.'

'Quiet, you two, quiet,' I reprimanded them. 'From now on you must be very careful for this place by the sea may hold many evil men and I don't want to lose you for you've served me well and deserve generous reward.'

Unabashed but silent they took their places in the line and we walked stealthily on. The track continued to climb steeply until it suddenly levelled out, continued thus for about two hundred yards, and then began to drop. The mist at that moment was just clear of the trees, only a few entangled fragments flying like torn spiders' webs from the tips of branches, and as I took the first step down I saw the fire. Yes, suddenly far down below me, long streaks of vivid but unearthly fire.

I stopped short at once and passed whispered word down the line for Umtumwa.

'Go back with the bearers a hundred yards. Move another hundred to the right of the track and put the whole party under cover as if you were expecting air and ground attack. See that no one makes a sound and wait until I come to join you. I'm not going on until I can see what's ahead.'

Obviously in agreement with my decision, Umtumwa quickly

135

and silently vanished with the bearers and I was alone on the edge of a bluff of earth in a mauve margin of heavy mist. Dear Heaven, how dense it was, and how still the air with only the murmur and rustle of the sea, and occasionally the fall of a wet leaf, or drip of water from a tree to break it. Yet, most mysteriously, down below weaving and interweaving ceaselessly, flickering and trembling and shimmering like scarlet noon-day waves of light, there was fire in every rent and chink of the slowly rending mist. What could it be? Then suddenly I had it! Suppose I was glimpsing the early morning flame of African flamingo wings, and the Great Flamingo Water really was neither superstitious gossip nor idle Amangtakwena chatter?

Then on the tail of this astonishing thought a new sound from below broke the stillness, a sound I knew well and had listened to often in the war at dead of night on blacked-out quays. Somewhere below me in the mist a powerful ship's pulse was beating, and screws were thrashing. My heart went sick with despair for, unbearable as was the realization, clearly I'd arrived too late, since that sound was steadily going by me towards the sound of the sea. No, no, my heart protested to the sleeping land about me, you cannot inflict so cruel a blow upon me. But the silent mist merely swished its skirts disdainfully about its ankles and continued to drift by with its back turned, leaving me to the bitterness and irony of realizing to the dying tune of those engines that though we'd rightly and truly followed the first spoor, it was only to arrive too late. Over and over again I came back to the stinging conviction that, had I started working on Joan's intuition of John's survival several years before, I would not be standing there in the mist, a lonely failure. I've known many bitter moments in my life but none bitterer than those on the slopes of the bluff above the Flamingo Water, for so deeply rooted in my own character did the causes of my failure appear to me to be that I felt as if the hurt I suffered came from a self-inflicted wound.

Chapter 11

Setara Umtumwaensis

I sat there for fully an hour on the edge of the bluff with only the flame of flamingo fire to warm my spirit but at the end of that time the gloom suddenly began to lift quickly high above the trees and the beauty of the scene then revealed was hardly of this earth.

I looked down on a bay, almost a perfect oval, set between a ring of hills, with black smoking jungle coming right down to the gleaming water set like a pearl in the heart of deep seaweed wood. Only at the western end was the oval broken, for there a silver river, wide and swollen, cut a swift, clean cleft in the hills to hurl itself straight at the circle of hills in the east. How the river broke through those hills I could neither see nor imagine, yet break free it did and flowed out to sea so deeply and strongly that the ship I had heard was already on the Indian Ocean side of the bay. But what held my eyes was the flame of flamingo fire on the pearly water below, for if there was one bird there were millions, and, making a quick calculation, I reckoned this ardent congregation as seventy square miles of flamingoes. I wish I could describe the scene adequately, but words themselves are not enough. It needs the brush of Fragonard to reproduce the *salon* elegance of birds which fed themselves to their own flame, drawing the luminous stilts of their long mannequin legs like Venetian glass out of the crucible of that fire. It needs Stravinsky's music for the quick reds and fast intertwining classic pinks. And who could do justice to the supple curve of those long sea-foam necks and the greater grace of their heads? Above all, who could paint, what words describe, the sense of participation almost mystical in an innermost secret of life which made me feel that what I was seeing was not the birds themselves, but rather reflections thrown from behind the barrier of a supersensory dimension to the mirror of this tranquil water? So vivid was this impression that, when I looked up to the dark surround of black African jungle and the mist rising up from it like burning phœnix smoke, I was almost surprised to find that the land was not the mirrored walls of the inmost court in the Versailles of some vanished King of the Sun. Yet how like Africa all this was! How like the dark mother who so often seems to have no time for life which is not big and strong enough to suckle at the snowy breasts of Kilimanjaro, yet all the while is nursing apart and in secret these delicate, elegant and warming birds which once, nearly two thousand years before, drew a king and all his people towards them in a great dream.

With the memory of the dream my courage revived. 'No,' I thought, 'I'll be damned if I give up; I'll cast about here for fresh spoor and persevere until the matter is brought to a true end.' So I quickly went back to my company, organized a camp well off the track and cunningly camouflaged, and leaving Umtumwa in charge with orders to make no fires and maintain perfect quiet, then returned with Tickie to a bluff overlooking the Flamingo Water.

By this time the mist was transformed into cloud drifting darkly overhead and letting the sun through only in dull patches. Walking with utmost vigilance, making no noise and speaking only in whispers, for the track bore all the marks of recent and frequent usage by human feet, we reached the mouth of the bay in an hour. I saw at once then how well nature had

concealed and camouflaged this vast Flamingo Water. The river instead of breaking through the hills in one straight cut, had followed through at half a right angle to its course,* so that looking at the Bay from the sea one would never discern the opening at all but see merely a dark gash blocked at the back by a wall of hill. Nor could curious ships come close to observe the gash for, as far as we could see, the river had thrown up enormous shoals of sand in the ocean about a mile from the shore and long breakers were going white over them everywhere. Behind us the Bay was filled only with that lovely shimmer of flamingoes, and about a mile beyond the silver river entrance at our backs rose a column of blue smoke straight up into the air.

I was about to turn my glasses on it to investigate, when Tickie said: 'Look, Bwana, another smoke on the sea.'

I swung round and to my amazement there was another smoke column rising up fast from the south. My heart gave a bound.

Our excitement and suspense in the next hour was intense. The new smoke joined the first column, paused for a while, went ahead, and then followed by the old came fast up the coast towards us. My feelings over this development need no elaboration. I placed Tickie and myself in the best possible post of observation, deep in the shadows where we could see the ships pass a hundred feet below us without being seen. But long before they came abreast of us I recognized the turn-up nose of the *Star of Truth* going full-out. Behind her came a smaller vessel that I'd never seen before, but since the colour of her smoke showed that she burnt wood, I'd no doubt that she was a base ship, presumably the one I had heard going out in the morning! At about four in that afternoon when the first rumble of thunder at Flamingo Bay rolled like a large boulder down the hills both ships passed underneath us. I had to place a warning hand on Tickie's leg for he gave a startled gasp when he saw, strolling casually about the *Star of Truth's* deck, seventeen of his countrymen.

So close was the *Star of Truth* to us that I read with naked eyes her Baltic name in the bows: *Svensdy Pravdy* as well as that of her bulldog follower: *Inyati,* the Lindelbaum ship

* See diagram on opposite page.

presumed lost in a cyclone in the Mozambique channel the year before. Almost directly opposite to where I had stood in the mist in the morning the *Star of Truth* dropped her anchors with a rattle that resounded from hill to hill. Then, unperturbed, the thick-skinned *Inyati* came alongside and grappled herself feverishly to the *Star of Truth*. Such was the indecent hurry of the two of them that before the process of grappling was completed the derricks fore and aft on the *Star of Truth* were dropping the first bundles of cargo on the smaller ship's deck.

'Come, Tickie, let's go,' I said. 'At last we have real work to do.'

We went back to the camp as fast as we could but not as fast as I'd have liked, because there'd been a look-out in the *Star of Truth* fore-top and if her skipper was as careful as that in a storm at nightfall, I was certain we couldn't be too much on our guard.

When I told Umtumwa the news I was pleased to see how much it cheered him. Almost his old self again, he entered into a discussion of future plans and was eager with helpful suggestions. He agreed emphatically that the trail from now on would be much more exacting and that, if we were to pursue it undetected, we must reduce our numbers. So I gathered the bearers round about me, thanked them for what they'd done and told them that in the morning they could return to Fort Emmanuel and their homes. I appointed Said their leader since he'd served in the Somali frontier force and could shoot. I gave him a gun and fifty rounds and a letter to the Governor emphasizing how well they had all earned their pardon, asking him to pay each of them £20 and their fares to their homes on my behalf. Said to my astonishment accepted the mission reluctantly, saying he'd prefer to stay with us, but as he was the only reliable shot in the party I ordered him to go.

All this time it had been raining and thundering violently, but as on the evening before the storm passed after a few hours, leaving us an impeccable sky of yellow moon and emerald and ruby stars, the air purified and tenderly refreshed and so still that I was startled to hear far away, yet quite distinctly, the *Star of Truth's* loudspeakers broadcasting music to her crew. It felt unreal lying there in the bush, listening to radio, hearing a lion roar to a fast Tartar beat, and watching the moon-shadows making ballet macabre of the music whenever the shivering trees tried to shake water from their hair.

At dawn I had the bearers on parade for the last time and I must say I felt sad to see them go. Nothing brings men closer to one another than walking together in the African bush. Still, there it was, and with a stab of regret in my heart I had no option but to order them for the last time to take up their loads and to set them marching with 'Go in happiness,' the ancient African greeting I had from my father.

I was about to repeat my farewell in Arabic for Said, who was watching his charges step on to the wet, misty track, when he said with sly humour, placing himself at the end of the line: 'See, Effendi, I too walk where the trouble collects!'

'Good, Said,' I answered softly, feeling strangely moved by this spontaneous sparkle of spirit among men setting out on a hard journey at a gloomy hour. 'That is as it should be. But stop, look and listen often, and be ready always to scatter into the bush at the slightest warning. I don't think there's any danger if you go carefully, but I'd assume the bush ahead was full of evil men, until I was back at Apes Weeping in the forest of Duk-aduk-duk.'

'Ghadre, Effendi,' he responded at once gravely, 'I shall not fail to be careful, for I hope to serve with you again one day.'

'In the name of Allah, then, walk in peace,' I replied instantly, touched by his response.

'In the name of Allah, then, remain in peace!' he exclaimed, and whispering a determined, 'Ieh! – yellah: let us go then,' he turned about and followed the last of the bearers on to the track with a long swinging stride.

No sooner had the bearers gone than I set off alone to explore the other fork in the track leading west where I'd seen blue wood-smoke the evening before. I went alone because Umtumwa and Tickie had work to do, removing traces of our old camp, reorganizing our loads, and getting ready to move on my return.

'Whatever happens, Umtumwa,' were my last words, 'don't let anyone or anything surprise you into shooting. Don't if you can help it shoot at all, for one shot in this breathless country and we're as surely exposed as if we'd been seen.'

'Agreed, Bwana, agreed. I shall not be so foolish,' he answered with so much of the old firm spirit in his tone that again I was reassured.

Besides having beaten the *Star of Truth* to the Flamingo Water and having two such proved loyal hearts with me, I felt confident as never before and walked·off into the mist without a qualm.

Down by the water the air was already loud with the noise of the *Star of Truth's* winches busily discharging her mysterious and dishonourable cargo, but as I went fast up a broad track to the West this sound, too, faded. Well-used as the track obviously was, at this hour of the morning it was empty and silent. Nothing of interest caught my attention except that at one point, two miles from camp, a track equally broad had been newly made as if meant to be a short cut to the other path which had brought us to the Bay. I didn't like the look of that and determined to inspect it on my return.

An hour and a half later I suddenly heard the steady beat of a diesel engine ahead and the confused murmur of many people talking. I went on with redoubled caution until the smell of cooking warned me I was dangerously near a camp of sorts. At once I stepped out of the track, and crawled like a snake forward into the bush to the edge of a large man-made clearing on the banks of the silver river. The mist here was beginning to thin and visibility was helped by electric lights which burned by each of the many thatched shelters before me. The clearing was enormous but one thing struck me immediately: the order and cunning of the mind that had designed it. Its camouflage was perfect and no casual plane would ever have detected this clearing from above. I crawled on until I came opposite what appeared to be a hospital, for I observed an orderly with a bullet head and close-cropped hair, syringe in hand, standing at a table and quickly inoculating a long line of 'Takwena bearers. They had all obviously endured the experience before as none even bothered to turn their heads to look at bullet-head swabbing the pricks. Moreover they were magnificent men, tall, strong, and obviously all carefully picked. To the left other men were coming out of the mist from the direction of the water carrying long, heavy wooden boxes in hammocks slung between their broad

142

shoulders, and they were followed by more men carrying other boxes of other sizes and shapes also slung in hammocks. Somewhere out of sight the mist was loud with voices urging labour to greater despatch. In fact, the whole scene impressed me profoundly with its air of efficient, energetic, and sinister purposefulness. I lay there for a quarter of an hour, but in that short space of time I saw enough rifles, machine-guns, mortars, ammunition, and explosives go by to equip two companies of infantry. And that was really all I needed to see at Flamingo Bay: all I needed to know, for the moment, of the *Star of Truth's* business. The urgent thing left to discover was the destination of this sinister cargo. Surely I had only to follow the footsteps of those muscular 'Takwena who were being inoculated against a long journey there in front of me and they would lead me to it.

I was just about to crawl back into the mist-enfolded bush when a new sound fell on my ears – and so unusual a one that even the orderly paused, black arm in one hand and syringe in the other, to turn his head towards it. Deep from the heavy folds of the mist came a burst of well-controlled automatic rifle fire. It lasted about half a minute, ceased as abruptly as it had begun, to be followed by a few single shots at irregular intervals. Obviously automatic fire was finishing-off wounded targets with single shots. Then a resounding shout of command went up somewhere behind the hospital and out of the mist came eight white men with set square-jawed faces and Tartar eyes. They had on field-grey uniforms quite inappropriate to the locality and ran, rifles at the trail, with a strange lumbering gait as if their boots were too heavy for them and disappeared straight down the track along which I'd just come. So close were they to me that I could have tripped them up with the point of my rifle had I wished to do so.

Almost sick with dismay I crawled slowly into the bush and started back for my camp. The mist was slowly lifting. The track ahead was empty and so still that I could hear the water oozing back with a faint sigh into the hollows from which the jack-boots of the guard had just ejected it. Indeed, so innocent and so unrelated to human experience did the steaming bush appear, that were it not for what I'd just seen I might easily have believed it to be uninhabited. I got to the place where

143

the newly-cut track forked from the old in half the time it had taken on the way out at dawn, and began to feel confident I would get to camp long before any patrol. For it was now becoming obvious to me that whenever a ship was in port no chances were taken of anyone stumbling by accident on the vital secret, so patrols were arranged at all entrances and exits to this secluded water. I realized also what amazing good luck I'd had, for I must have reached the Flamingo Water just before the first routine patrols were posted and the first regular guards mounted. I just prayed that my poor homeward-bound bearers had been equally lucky and that the outburst of automatic fire had not meant that they'd run straight into an armed party of 'Takwena scouts. Somehow the memory of those redeemed criminal faces on the long, hard trail from Fort Emmanuel through the Dead Land and the dread forest was still so fresh in me that, at the thought of their peril, my spirit hardened against the *Star of Truth* and all her works as it had never hardened before.

However, of greater and more immediate concern even than the possible tragedy of the shooting would be the added danger of it. Said was carrying my letter to the Governor and I'd signed that letter with an unusually careful 'Pierre de Beauvilliers'. The Master of the *Star of Truth* at least would have been warned by Harkov of me and the danger I constituted to their enterprise. One glance at the contents of that letter and my name at the foot of it, therefore, and the biggest and most desperate man-hunt these waters had ever witnessed would instantly be let loose. This realization was a nightmare moment of near panic for me although, curiously enough, I felt not unequal to my task. With luck, perhaps, I could deal with a man-hunt in these woods and bush, for I'd be fighting on my own ground. But when the news of my presence here got through to Lindelbaum and Harkov what action might they not adopt as a result of it? I could see nothing but new and increasing peril arising out of it for all who were connected with me, for Joan and Bill at Petit France, for Ooom Pieter as well as for John: not to speak of the probable tragic precipitation of the whole 'Takwena plot, immature as it still was.

I'd soon become so obssessed with speculation of this kind that I wouldn't be here to tell this story if it were not for a bird, a nut-brown button quail, which came fast straight down the track with a clockwork whirring of wings, so pre-occupied with fear that it very nearly crashed into my shoulder before it saw me and only swerved at the last minute into the bush on the left.

An ancient reflex awoke in me, and I found myself standing silent and still behind a blackthorn bush at the side of the track, the sound of my heart beating loudly in my ears. I listened carefully. It was much too still. I was standing close to the anchorage of the *Star of Truth* where not long before the air had been loud with noise of donkey engines and winches raising cargo. Yet now not a sound came from across the water and I knew that could only mean that already the *Star of Truth* must have been warned. I'd hardly reached that con-clusion when far away I heard the sound of stealthy oars on the water followed soon after by the sugary crunch of a wooden keel on the sandy shore. Then came a splash or two in the water and once again a long silence. I hoped some whisper of human voices would come up to me from the water to give me an inkling of what was developing. None came. In fact, so unpleasant was the impression that this silence made on me, that utterly motionless I continued for long to crouch behind my screen of thorns. The only movement I allowed myself was to make sure that my long hunting-knife was loose in its sheath at my waist, for I'd not forgotten that the cause of my button quail's panic had not yet revealed itself.

How long I stood there I don't know precisely. It was so long that I was beginning to think it might be safe for me to go down on my stomach and crawl away in to the bush, when at that very moment I became aware that another human presence had moved into the mist near me, and was coming closer. There was no sound or rustle among the grass. But slowly I felt the silence sag until suddenly it gave way and the sound of the soft tread of a naked foot on the track ahead came through it. Then a shadow loomed quickly up and a 'Takwena scout came into view. He too, I think, must have been listening to the sound of the water, but now he walked fast and I noticed grimly that he was following my faint track of the morning with the eye of an expert. A wooden knobbed cudgel in his left hand, the long war spear of his nation held ready in front of him, he was coming up fast to the place where I'd abruptly left the track some minutes before. I could nourish no hope that he'd fail to pick up the fresh spoor and read its meaning correctly. Quietly, with a prayer in my heart, I drew my knife from its sheath within my right hand and sank, like a hurdler, into position, my eyes on a puddle where in the black water on the track was still a cloudy yellow from the mud my heel had raised in it. I silently reckoned the paces that now separated him from it: six, five, four, three, two more steps – I was keyed up and ready to jump when about half a mile away, on the new fork of the track behind me, came another burst of automatic rifle fire.

If the 'Takwena have one failing it is their lively and impetuous curiosity. This scout was no exception. He instantly assumed that the fire ahead could have only been directed at the man whose spoor he was following. Immediately he lost all interest in the track and sprang forward, the trance of expected battle in the burning glance of his eyes, and disappeared into the mist with a long-distance runner's stride. Realizing that this new outburst of shooting would claim everyone's attention for the moment, I didn't pause to try and account for it, but stepped quickly back into the track and went up it again but with far greater care than before. It was as well that I did for seven times I was forced to leave it and hide in the bush while 'Takwena scouts, their spears at the ready, and that far-away impersonal look in their eyes, strode purposefully by in intent silence. And if there were eight of them about in this one small sector of the bush, how many were there not in all?

By the time I reached the well-concealed site of our camp, the mist was hanging cobwebs on the trees, the flamingo fire on the pearly water was brightly lit and a moth-winged rain of diffuse light wooing the gloom of the bush. Not the faintest sound or light whiff of smoke came to meet me.

The clearing was empty and so well had Tickie and Umtumwa done their work that no sign of previous habitation was discernible. But where had they gone? I dared not call out to them since one of those silent-footed 'Takwena scouts might be lurking in the mist only a few yards away. So I went methodically under cover round the edge of the clearing, searching for the mark I was certain Umtumwa would have left behind for me. I found it soon enough but it was such a sign that my heart nearly stood still with the horror of it, for there by a large acacia tree were large clots of human blood so fresh that they flared in the ground at my feet like newly-fallen poinsettia leaves. All round them the bush was torn, the earth trampled and deeply marked with evidence of a terrible hand-to-hand struggle.

As I saw it a gasped whisper came up from the bush to my left: 'Ah, Bwana, my Bwana, Ekenonya! Ekenonya.'

I looked up and there was Tickie, camouflaged in the bush three yards away standing like a veteran jungle fighter with my favourite gun still trained on me. I stared straight into his eyes. They were no longer the eyes of a boy, but rather of a man who has accomplished the final transition into maturity in one painful and perilous encounter with death. All round those large brilliant black eyes, the heavy shadow of death still dark at the centre of them, were long ashen streaks of salt where many tears had flowed.

'What has happened, Tickie?' I asked in a desperate whisper, in a voice of a stranger newly come to my door.

'Prepare to string the beads, Bwana!' Tickie began and there was no need for him to say more. For centuries this is how the 'Takwena have introduced news of death among themselves, saying with the rich instinctive symbolism of their speech: 'Get ready to weep tears of sorrow as bright as the brightest beads, and like the bright beads you string to wear round your throat at the burial, gather your tears and string them on a thread of your memory to wear around your heart or its shattered fragments will never come whole again.'

'Where is he, Tickie?' I asked.

He rose from the ground and quickly took me fifty yards deeper into the bush, and there propped up against a tree, massive head on the chest, looking as if he was merely resting at the end of a long march, was Umtumwa. But his jungle-green bush-shirt all over the left breast and shoulder was dark with blood. Near by, flat on the ground, one arm stretched out just as Tickie had dropped it with distaste at the end of dragging the corpse from our camp, was the long body of another 'Takwena scout.

'When did it happen?' I asked, looking at Umtumwa, wishing that the ice which so quickly gripped my heart would crack and that I, too, could weep for him the tears his going merited.

Umtumwa had sent him to fetch some water, Tickie told me, and on his return, not fifty yards from the camp he'd heard a scuffling noise and one or two heavy, involuntary grunts. Putting down the water, he'd run for the camp to see Umtumwa and a tall 'Takwena scout fighting grimly hand to hand. Both were bleeding from wounds in the breast and shoulders but Umtumwa was bleeding most and his face was the colour of a burnt-out fire. Raising the gun above his head, Tickie had at once rushed at the 'Takwena scout and brought the butt down with all his force on his head. The man went limp at once but before he fell to the earth, Tickie said, he'd hit him again and broken his neck. Umtumwa meanwhile had fallen to the ground still alive and in full possession of his faculties. He'd ordered Tickie first to pull the dead man into the bush and then to help him up. He'd done so at once and brought Umtumwa to where I now saw him, but it was obvious to both of them that the brother of his mother was about to die.

Here Tickie nearly broke down again and before I could think of stopping him he kicked savagely at the 'Takwena corpse sobbing: 'Oh! What an evil man, Bwana; what an evil deed for 'Takwena to do to 'Takwena. He came to the edge of the camp where the brother of my mother had him covered with his rifle, stuck his spear in the earth as all the 'Takwena have always done when they come in peace and stepped forward hands up and out empty before him. At once Umtumwa, Bwana, seeing a peaceful man of our own people put his gun down too and stepped forward with his hands empty. But he had not walked a yard when 'this thing of evil', again Tickie kicked the corpse, 'flew round, pulled his spear out of the earth and threw it at Umtumwa hitting him as you see above the heart.'

Umtumwa had stumbled with the force of it but recovering quickly had pulled out the spear, and in a second, spear in hand, Umtumwa went for his attacker. He was, however, fatally wounded and would have lost the battle if Tickie had not arrived in time. His last words to Tickie were: 'Tell the

Master I could have picked up my rifle instead of the spear and shot but I promised I would not shoot. Tell him I thank him for having been a brother to me and say before nightfall I shall be with Xilixowe and speak with him of the evil his people are planning by his great Flamingo Water.' Then, Tickie said, Umtumwa had started to mumble about Amantazuma and, mumbling something about a lamb lost in the hills, he'd died.

When Tickie told me this I was nearly unmanned, for my first memory of Umtumwa was of a day twenty-seven years before, when our fathers brought us together to be friends and brothers. I could still see him, standing naked except for a soft, tanned buck-skin wrapped round his shoulders, leaning with his hands clasped round a long ivory stick in front of him and calling every now and then in a voice gentle as a girl's on his little flock of sheep to feed well. Like a view seen from a hill in a flash of lightning at dead of night all our long eventful years together stood before me from that first meeting onwards to the night of the coming of the feather far back at Petit France; to that first faint intimation of the tragic combination of chance and circumstance awaiting him, which made him break a spear by the fire, so on, on to the day a yellow cobra had looked him in the eyes with a summons from his ancestors and to the moment of that quick red hunter's dawn wherein the Great Spirit had breathed comfort into the palm of his uplifted hand.

I went with blurred eyes, knelt beside Umtumwa, and took his hand, saying, 'You may not see the smoke coming out of the hut-tops at evening in the valley of Amantazuma again, but you shall rest well because you died in a way which is more than death, trying to save us, your friends, from certain disaster.'

I called on Tickie to help me, and we lifted him up and buried him in an ant-bear hole dug deep in the red earth of Africa, at the foot of a young bao-bab tree which stood like a pillar of Biblical flame in the midst of the dark bush. In spite of Tickie's protest we also buried the 'Takwena in another hole near by. I had seen too much of the dark, impersonal forces that invade the hearts of simple trusting men to be able to hold the deed personally against him.

Before we left I stood, hat in hand, beside Umtumwa's blood-red grave and silently recited the only psalm I know by heart, 'The Lord is my Shepherd', adding to the 'my' also a 'thy', and then as we turned to leave, on an impulse I pulled up one of the tall unusually decorative grasses which grew round the hole, folded it carefully, and put it in my rucksack. As a result there is today a new species added to the list of known grasses in the world: Setara Umtumwaensis. I often take comfort from the thought that there is in Africa something alive, continually renewable and renewing, which bears his name as it adds its own individual note of music to the wind.

Chapter 12

One of the Three Ways

So there we were, Tickie and I alone in this silent, misty bush, presumably the only survivors of the party which had set out from Fort Emmanuel across the Black Umpafuti less than a fortnight before. And what to do next? The question was not difficult to answer.

If we wanted to survive, if we wanted to get to the end of the trail in Umangoni hundreds of miles away, we had somehow to prevent ourselves from being discovered between now and evening. The search, I knew only too well, had barely begun and was child's play to what would be let loose in those sombre woods once the mist lifted. If we could but evade detection until nightfall, or even until the rain came in the afternoon, we had a chance of getting away. But it was one thing to know what to do and quite another to do it. Nonetheless we tried as best we could to remove what traces were left of our brief occupation in the wood, working silently like persons caught in the rhythm of an agonizing dream, for I knew that an enemy as frightened and suspicious as ours, would look at the ground in a way which ultimately would see through all camouflage however skilful. Only time, the wind, and the rain could really wipe out our spoor.

We worked quickly and quietly, for we had no guarantee that some keen-eyed scout would not at any moment send a spear hissing out of the bush into our backs. All the while I watched the weather with misgiving, the mist slowly transforming itself into immense cumulus clouds which curled with a sullen reluctance over the land as if they had all eternity for completing the movement, while arrow after arrow of sunlight feathered with white of cloud struck a vital target of water or soft green hump of barbaric hill. Whenever I paused to look at the weather I wanted to call on the ancient gods of this

151

antique world to hasten and wrap us in their thickest blanket of rain and to protect us with their tallest thunder. When at last we'd finished, before we put ourselves under cover, I climbed a tree until I had a clear view of the fiery water on one side and on the other of the dark bush clinging with the passion of despair to the slopes of the hills as the land dipped sharply away towards the park-like plain. In the crow's nest of the *Star of Truth* I now saw not one but two look-outs watching the land through glasses. That I didn't mind at all. Where the dense line of coastal bush ended and the plains began the air was strangely agitated with birds in a manner far from normal. I watched for some moments and could not doubt that the birds marked out the movement of a long line of trackers coming through the bush, as surely as corks floating on blue sea water sketch the outline of the closing net deep underneath them. Our position appeared to be directly opposite the centre of the line and observation confirmed what I'd already suspected – we had no chance of getting past or through the line of trackers in daylight. Our only hope was to lie up near at hand so that the life of the bush around us could resume its usual rhythm before the trackers reached it. I scrambled down hastily to tell Tickie this, and though he disliked renouncing freedom of movement as much as I did, he agreed it was all we could do.

One of the characteristic features of the bush we were in was its colonies of a thorn tree that the 'Takwena call 'Hook, claw, and stab'. These trees prefer to form small, neat, tight clusters on mounds of earth with long yellow grasses round about them. They stand there so neatly, the grass coming up almost to the tip of their branches. The branches start about six to seven feet from the ground but fall so low that they sweep the ground bare beneath them. From without there is not a chink in their armour of thorn and leaves; but from beneath their skirts one finds the world outside glowing like a fire seen through a sieve. The trees are therefore, as leopard, cheetah, python, and weeping hyena well know, ideal shelter and have the incomparable advantage of being a normal feature of the landscape. Tickie and I, therefore, with all the skill we could command, concealed ourselves and our belongings beneath one of these trees determined to stay there if possible until dark.

We lay flat on our stomachs, Tickie facing one way, I the other, our bodies propped on our elbows, eyes level with the tops of the nearest grass, heads just clear of the first line of thorns, our guns cocked and ready, but knives unsheathed on the ground in front of us. We lay thus and waited. It was all we could do. But it was not easy and it lasted a long time. The cloud above got darker and darker. The sun shot its last yellow arrow deep into the glassy water. The sky began to moan far away with the burden of undelivered water and to shake with the thrust of thunder impatient to be born.

What went on in Tickie's heart I can only guess. What went on in mine was hard to endure. I lay there not so much as one person but as two irreconcilable fractions of a whole: one an automatic fellow of quick, mindless reflexes keeping expert watch on the bush; the other deaf and blind to the world about him, going deep below the surface of the moment into the irresolute past. There is nothing in the world which puts the individual as firmly in his place as does the wide earth of Africa waiting with bare, unbowed head for its equal, the sky, to strike at it with lightning. The whole of myself, undivided, just then would have seemed very little; how much less then with these warring factions within me? To this day I don't know how I got through those long hours under cover save that I had a memory which was for me as an anchorage in a roadstead where there is no shelter against storm but only a safe mooring on the firm sea-bed below. I speak of the moment of undivided resolution when my eyes first met Joan's in the Groote Kerk on the day of François de Beauvilliers's funeral. That memory most fiercely, yet how tenderly, protected me and kept me whole.

Thus slowly the minutes dragged by. We lay so still and silent that the birds came to collect yellow berries around our heads and picked unconcerned away among ferns at our feet. Then, about three in the afternoon, I noticed that the birds were increasing round about us with a tendency to mass in the bigger trees. This, at this hour of the day, was rare enough to make our nerves tingle. It could only mean that instinctive caution had made these prudent little creatures retreat warily in our direction.

'Bwana!' Tickie whispered softly and slowly in the manner

of his people when stalking game. 'People! Many people on your side, about half a mile away, searching the path you took th's morning.'

'I know, Tickie,' I answered in the same manner, wondering whether it would not have been better after all to have risked the patrols and made for the interior, and praying that it soon would rain. As if in answer to my prayer, a deep rumble of thunder rolled for the first time across the Flamingo Water. But it was still far off.

'Tickie,' I went on, so quickly that even the birds nearest us took no notice. 'Don't move or make one sound. We'll lie here until they find us – and they'll have to come close before they do so. Then we'll shoot to kill at every shape we see. I'll press you so when I want us to shoot ...' I dug my elbow in the calf next to me. 'We'll empty our magazines fast into them so they'll pause for a while and bunch somewhere at the back until someone comes to take them in command again. In that moment you and I'll slip out of cover. All you have to do then is to follow me. If I'm killed or wounded I don't want you to linger with me.' Here I felt such a tide of anxiety and protest welling up in the loyal body at my side that I hastened to add: 'No, I don't expect to be killed, but I speak to you now not as a boy but as one who's earned his right to be treated as a man. And as a man you must be prepared for the worst. If the worst happens, then I count on you to get back to Fort Emmanuel, for the lives of many people and the safety of Umangoni depend upon it. There you must get the N.C.O. to telegraph at once for Bwana 'Ndabaxosikas* to come to you so that you can tell him all.'

As I spoke I heard Tickie gulp and I wished it had been possible to turn round and look him straight in the eyes. But already fresh evidence of the progress of our enemies was coming into the scene about us. I'd hardly spoken when a tan-coloured duiker doe, the dove-grey train of her little tail clasped tightly behind, her sense of modesty so great that even flight from danger did not cause it to relax, dived to view over a bush in front of me and loped by fast without a backward glance. Hard behind, a steenbuck ram bounded lightly into an

* Literally SPEAK SHOOT SAME, idiomatically 'He who speaks as he shoots', Oom Pieter's name among Africans.

open patch, stopped short, turned about and with great eyes dark with amazement in his delicate head, ears moving in a stream of sound too fine for human senses, nostrils quivering and black little muzzle shining like satin, faced the direction from which he'd come. After the steenbuck, at intervals of a minute or so came three snakes; first a long and unbelievably fast whipsnake, as if it were the lash tied to its own name and a fire at its tail; then a dignified old copper cobra, obviously wise, experienced, and not over-perturbed, stopping to look and listen every so often in its forward glide over familiar ground, and, finally, on coils of sombre flame, a fast black mamba, ready to strike with sequin eyes and flashing tongue at everything in its way. Hardly was the mamba out of sight when three large turkey buzzards, a fat lump in their throats, yellow heads in that light glistening like sulphur ointment and fat-carrion bodies purple with blackness came flying low over the tree-tops. To my joy one alighted on the top of the tree next to ours as if to complete our camouflage.

I knew then that the climax of our day was close at hand.

The leaves were still going silver against the sombre glow of the sky when Tickie tapped a warning against my side and stiffened like a pointer whose nose was certain at last of invisible quarry in the grass. But he made no sound.

'What is it?' I asked in a whisper slower and lower than ever.

'I do not know, Bwana,' he replied, in a tone well under control, 'I do not know for certain but I think a man has just crawled on his stomach into the grass at the side of the track fifty paces in front of me.'

'Are you sure?' I asked, incredulous, for I was certain our trackers wouldn't be doing their urgent work crawling slowly through the bush until they'd spotted and marked us down.

'Aye, Bwana,' Tickie confirmed in the same even tone. 'It may have been a lion or a leopard, Bwana, but I think it was a man from the length of grass that moved.'

'And where is he now?' I asked, convinced and beginning to be alarmed as well as puzzled.

'I think he, too, has taken cover in that bush there, Bwana,' Tickie answered. 'The movement stopped by that blackthorn bush the moment the yellow-headed carrion came over the

155

tree-tops. I think they were a warning to him as they were to us. Eh'yo-Xabadathi!'*

'Then no matter what happens on my side,' I whispered, 'don't take your eyes off that place. If he moves again warn me.'

I'd barely finished the sentence when a sharp flash of light-ning cut through the sky and released a flare of mandarin yellow among the trees of the graphite bush. Automatically out of habit acquired in childhood I began counting the seconds between the flash and first note of thunder. On the eleventh a long roll of sound swept over us. That made it two miles away. I peered out at the clouds hopefully for the first blur of rain and to my dismay saw only the turkey-buzzard with head no longer tucked deeply into the shawl of his shoulders against the rising storm but on his toes, wings stretched full out and about to take off. Hard by, the bush on the edge of the grass burst open like a paper hoop, and five wart-hogs, their tusks curled like the moustaches of a Victorian villain, their tails erect, lips snarling and chins aggressively out came briskly past us to lay a black crinoline crinkle in the grass, before vanish-ing fast into the bush on the other side.

Dear God, they're coming up faster than I expected, I said to myself; and as I said it, from the site of our old camp, a whistle went up, loud, clear, and exultant. I knew the sound only too well for I had used it often as a boy to call the atten-tion of our dogs to quarry which had suddenly broken cover. The whistle was still ringing in my ears when far and wide on either side of us it was answered by a whole series of crisp, urgent whistles and then a trio of Francolin hissing with the hysteria of helpless fear, a bush khoran calling loudly for pro-tection, took to the air, a troop of guinea-fowl with evening jewels already at head and throat came by fast, clucking and dodging with expert elegance from cover to cover, and, finally, the whole bush broke out into the sound of men crashing through it fast without effort at disguise.

The sound was loudest on my side where a group of 'Tak-wena scouts were collecting and studying some sign of our recent occupation. They were all the while being joined by others. Judging by the volume of sound there were many of

* *Eh'yo-Xabadathi* – a 'Takwena term of surprise meaning, 'has a child of human mother ever seen such a thing before?'

them, the tone of their shouts suggesting that they felt the end of their task to be near at hand. I was certain they were waiting only to begin the final phase of their search. If this happened Tickie and I had little chance of escape, unless, of course, the rain broke almost at once. I looked at the sky but the rain seemed no nearer than before. I put my hand in my ammunition pocket and laid another five rounds on the soil in front of me. I was about to tell Tickie to do the same when the bush on his side, too, began to crash and reverberate with violent movement.

' 'Takwena. Many, *many*, MANY, MANY!' Tickie said, laying a warning hand on my leg.

Then I saw them, too, pouring past us, their backs to me, racing for the camp, silent, their long spears at the ready, bounding over the smaller bushes as easily as well-trained athletes over hurdles. They passed on either side of our cover so close that I could hear their long-distance breathing and smell the acid sweat on their glistening bodies. One of them put a foot down within a yard of the muzzle of Tickie's gun and vaulted over a tuft of bush so close to me that I heard it swish like water on a keel against his flank. Yet he didn't see us because, like the others his eyes and ears were distracted by that sharp, impetuous summons whistled from our old camp.

As the last of them went by, I was again about to speak to Tickie when his hand warned me to desist. Then I heard a different sound, following fast on their tracks, a sound I'd met for the first time in the early morning – the crunch, squelch and plod of jack-boots on African earth. The boots were going at the now familiar slouching double and soon out of cover broke my White Mongol guard of the early morning. I saw them this time, only in profile but I thought them a sullen, impassive and oxlike bunch, their field-grey uniforms ripped in a dozen places, their feet sore and blistered, their bodies sweating in their heavy, blousy tunics. Behind them came an officer and beside him, my lean, grim-faced 'Takwena of the *Star of Truth*, the mark of royalty upon his cheeks. They made an incongruous pair, but as they passed by I was struck not by their obvious differences but by an underlying similarity. They were moving not like free men but like persons obsessed, like mediums in a trance of deeply-compelled tribal being, like a

157

pair of sleepwalkers going to the end of a nightmare of sleep. When they reached the site of our old camp I was not surprised to hear an intense silence instantly fall. Then a drop of rain hit a twig beside me splintering so like a bubble of delicate glass that I was surprised not to hear it tinkle. I peered out and up, and saw that the solid outline of dark cloud was now blurred and dim with rain and drops of falling water were staining the air. Behind the silenced camp, the rain threw itself upon the Flamingo Water, driving fast towards us with a swish of its long, white-pleated skirts and the noise of a great wind. With it came searing flares and flashes of quick forked light-ning and thunder drumming an imperious march with great rolls on earth and hollow tomb-like echoes in deep caves of cloud above. I've mentioned before the general sense of re-assurance which rain brings to Africa's children, but never had it sounded sweeter than it did on this afternoon. I knew our immediate battle was over. Not only had the impetuous scouts just trampled over our faint traces but this storm would very soon remove for ever both their and our spoor from the bush. At the same moment, I believe, our enemies, too, came to the conclusion that it was too late to continue their search. A great shout of joy that all was over went up from our old camp; then the voices rose again in the oldest 'Takwena chant I know.

> Yes! Oh! Yes. Yes. Yes!
> We go one of the three ways:
> The three ways a man and his brothers go:
> The way to battle in the breaking morning
> The way from victory in the red of evening;
> The way of dust to the last sleep at nightfall,
> By the great Flamingo Water.
> Guess, Oh guess, guess, guess
> You who hear me,
> Which of the three ways do we go?

The reply that came was immediate, like fresh orchestration of the thunder overhead and a startling revelation of the num-bers of 'Takwena gathered in the bush. At the end of a long roll of thunder it came in deep waves, from far, far down in resonant throats, far down from the well of the past, straight from the source wherein the vital being of a great people springs, came the response:

158

Oh! How can you ask the way of our going,
How can you wonder at the measure of our feet,
When look the blood on our spears is warm
And the last of our enemies with the day is dead.
Aye, look! We go the way from victory,
Home in the evening:
We go to our cattle and our kraals and our women by the fire
In the blue of Umangoni.

I've heard this chant on many occasions. I've joined in it
myself more times than I care to remember at the end of a
day's hunting. I've sung it with my own troops not only in
Africa but in the jungles of Burma. Wherever the men of
Umangoni gather, sooner or later it is sung. The words may
vary, but the music is always the same and has not, I believe,
varied by a single note since far back an unremembered 'Takwena heart first experienced it. Even I, who after all am no
'Takwena, have only to hear it to feel a profound magnetic
pull backwards, a knowledge of the past recorded only in the
blood, a presence peering in like a magician at the window of
my contemporary senses. And if I can be thus affected, I wondered immediately, what about Tickie, whose emotions had
already been so cruelly exposed by general and particular
tragedy? True, when the song first rang out an involuntary
spasm had gone through the legs pressed against mine. I'd put
a steadying hand on his and stayed thus until the noise of falling rain, crackle of lightning and rumble of thunder overwhelmed the singing, and the break in the storm which followed was untroubled by human voices of any kind. Then, certain at last that our enemies had gone for good I turned round,
soaked through, to face Tickie, almost afraid of what I'd find.
However, one glance was enough to reassure me. He lay, his eyes
fixed on the bush, in the same position wherein I'd posted him,
and made no sign that he'd even noticed the change in my own.
   'Well, that's that, Tickie,' I said in my immense relief, trying
to speak quite normally. 'We can get ready to go now.'
   'Hush! Bwana!' He reproved me in a whisper just audible
above the sound of the rain. 'Hush, he is still there.'
   'What's that?' I asked, genuinely puzzled for the moment.
   'He is still there – he who crawled in the bush, just before
they came,' Tickie answered.

'Are you sure?' I asked, realizing that momentarily I'd forgotten the man I'd told Tickie to watch.

'How can I not be sure, when my eyes have never left the place as you ordered me?' he asked with a certain reproachful rhetoric.

Straining my eyes in the direction at which Tickie was looking, I was about to reply when he exclaimed: 'Look! quick, Bwana; there he is moving again, shall I shoot?' I put out my hand to restrain him. And through the silver streaks of rain I watched the yellow grass at the edge of a cluster move shivering apart. Something or someone was coming straight towards us.

Lips to Tickie's ear, I said: 'No. No shooting if we can help it. One shot if they hear it will fetch them all back. You keep it covered and if necessary I'll deal with it with my knife.'

The minutes that followed seemed unbearably long. Whatever it was in the grass, it was cautious to the point of genius. Until the last moment I was not certain whether it was animal or human. Then slowly, slowly, the movement came to within ten yards of us and stopped abruptly where the grass was longest and thickest. I waited so long for it to move and in such suspense that I despaired of it ever doing so. But then at last it moved again, only in a different way.

'Look, Bwana,' Tickie whispered, 'a man as I told you!'

He was right. A dark shadow was pulling itself slowly upright in the grass, rising up from flat stomach on to all fours, up to its knees, and so slowly up, to its full height. But long before it stood head and shoulders above the grass, looking anxiously about it with a gun at the ready in its hands, I knew who it was. I looked at Tickie for confirmation just as he turned his head to glance at me. We read the same unspoken question in each other's eyes, and nodded our heads simultaneously, exchanging the first smile of the day.

'Said,' I called out as loudly as I dared, 'Said! Salaam Aleikhum: look! Here!'

But on the first sound he vanished flat on his stomach into the grass, straight into the firing position.

'No, Said,' I called again more loudly so that he should recognize my voice. 'It is I, your Effendi, and Tickie who call you; have no fear, but come here.'

160

With an 'Allah be praised' that was more like a sigh of relief than a cry, the tall figure of Said shot upright again like an arrow out of the grass. At the same moment Tickie and I crept out of our cover and showed ourselves to him.

'Effendi! Effendi! Effendi! I came here to look for you without expecting to find you,' said Said simply, in a voice strangely young with the return of long discarded emotion, bowing with an air of grateful humility not so much to us as to the bush, the pleated rain, the burnished storm with its brandish of lightning and drums of thunder, and to the invisible totality of the blue heaven above it. 'Truly, Allah is great. But where is Umtumwa?'

'Where are your bearers?' I asked him obliquely, not liking to answer his question.

'Dead, all dead, Effendi,' he answered, his voice stark with the return of tragedy. 'Killed by the Kafir* you have just seen here. But Umtumwa?'

'Is it necessary to ask then? He, too, is dead; also killed by one of those,' I told him.

I wanted to add: 'Providence has spared you to take his place.' But at the mention of Umtumwa's name I was assailed by emotion as violent as it was unreasonable. Suddenly I felt unbearably resentful that the brave, loyal Umtumwa should have been killed and this ex-murderer spared. For a moment I hated Said for not being Umtumwa. I think something of what I felt must have shown in my eyes, for the glad expression on Said's thin face vanished and a pair of sombre brown eyes full of bewildered misery looked down into mine.

Instantly I was aware of the unfairness of my emotion and held out my hand to him, saying: 'I thank Allah for preserving you; he has obviously sent you to take Umtumwa's place. Come, let us find better shelter against the storm and you can tell us how you escaped.'

There was, he told us later, not much to tell. About an hour and a half after leaving us, walking along quite happily at the end of the line of bearers, his disquiet was first aroused by a flock of guinea-fowl going up with a nervy and unusually sustained clatter on the track ahead. Something must have alarmed the birds and at that hour, in that thick mist, the some-

* *Kafir* – unbeliever.

thing he feared could only be human. At once he'd hurried forward to pass word to halt for consultation, but coming round a bend in the track, he'd found a bearer in trouble with his load. He was helping the bearer to right the load when automatic fire broke out all along the track ahead. Realizing he was too late to save the others, he and the bearer quickly hid their loads in a thick thorn bush, left the track and began carefully to make a roundabout way towards our old camp, hoping to reach it before we left. But as the two of them went along Said realized plainly not only that they were being followed but also that their followers were fast catching up with them. He decided, therefore, they would do well to part company. Giving the man his direction to the camp, he crawled off into the bush the opposite way. He'd not gone far when another burst of automatic fire told him that he was now the only survivor of the party. From then on he made nightmare progress towards us. At times the 'Takwena trackers were so close to him that he could hear them discuss how his companions had been killed. He gathered that his trackers did not in the least know what to make of it all and their general feeling was that the real explanation was to be found not here in the bush but in the tracks to the forest of Duk-aduk-duk. A large party of European askaris and trackers, he learned, was already on the way there and this search in the bush was clearly more of a routine precaution than anything else. In view of this he was convinced that having found our camp empty they'd now waste no more time here. After that, there was nothing to do but conceal himself as best he could on the spot. The whistle and the storm had saved him.

'But my letter to the Governor, Said? What's become of that? Did you leave it with your baggage or carry it on you?'

'Here, Effendi. I have it safely here,' he replied, putting his hand on the breast pocket of his ancient tunic.

'Good, very good,' I said, profoundly thankful, the burden of one of my greatest anxieties falling from me as I realized that my presence here at the Flamingo Water was still hidden from my enemies. 'You've done more than well, Said. Now please give me back the letter.'

He gave it to me with a hand trembling with fatigue and the cold of the rain in his clothes evaporating against his skin.

Then I turned to Tickie, noticing that he, too, was shivering, his dark skin purple with cold and his young eyes gone strangely old with heavy and unfamiliar shadows underneath them.

Putting my hand on his shoulder I said with an effort at gaiety: 'Take Said, and collect the loads; Umtumwa's also. I'll start a fire to make some tea and cook some of the porridge you don't like while we have this storm to hide the flame and smoke of our cooking. When we've eaten we too shall go one of three ways. And guess, Oh, my brother, which of the three ways we'll go!'

Without waiting for an answer I turned him gently but firmly round and watched him walk towards our hiding-place with some of his old lift. Later by our fire as he tended the coals with the same dedicated air which had always sat upon Umtumwa I heard him softly singing 'One of the three ways' not to us or to himself, but, I suspect, to the man he'd discovered in himself that day.

Said, the warmth of our own fire like a drug in the cold and weariness of his blood, sat asleep between us, but at the first sound of Tickie's voice he opened a large brown eye like a mastiff who has just refound a long-lost master and glanced slowly from Tickie to me as if to reassure himself that he was not dreaming, before shutting it again with a sigh. Suddenly the darkness went black, and the night settled on the slender shoulders of our fire like the mantle of an Old Testament prophet. There was no glimmer about us now save what came from our fire or flew up from shattering flashes of the bright and battering hoofs of these black long-maned horses of the storm driving hard inland through the passes in the hills beyond the Flamingo Water. But already the rain was finer and so gentle that the heat of our fire kept it from us like a gold-poppy silk umbrella held over our heads. The thunder sounded more and more mellow and rolled solemnly over all the darkened land. When the light of the first great star came to walk the strands of cloud stretched above a shimmering mesh of thorn and leaves, like a pearly spider testing the silk of his night-spun cobweb, I roused Said and Tickie and told them to take up their loads and follow me.

Chapter 13

The March Up-Country

I had already given a good deal of thought to our line of action
should we still be alive by nightfall. In those long hours under
cover my instinct had been for breaking off contact with the
enemy at once and refusing any risks of further encounter for
some weeks to come. I thought I could do that best by doubling back on our tracks to where the path from Fort Emmanuel
forked into two against the flank of the impervious forest of
Duk-aduk-duk, one prong leading to the Black Umpafuti
swamp and the Flamingo Water, the other west-south-west into
the interior. If only I could get on this last track, I was certain
it would lead me back quickly into the basin of the great river
which fed the Flamingo Water and to the path which the
'Takwena bearers would have to follow to get to Umangoni
with their loads of forbidden cargo.

However, Said's account of what he'd overheard in the bush
and in particular his news that the heaviest patrols were
immediately being sent out in that very direction forced me
reluctantly to change my mind. There was only one track
through the forest of Duk-aduk-duk. I decided, therefore, to
go that way only far enough to reach a game-track which would
lead us into the interior and far behind the enemy's base camp
at the back of the Famingo Water. I'd no doubt I would find
suitable trails; the only difficulty was to find one in time, for
instinct urged me it was vital to do so before dawn. As long
as it was dark I knew we were reasonably safe. Africans don't
usually leave their fires and shelter after nightfall. They have a
long-established and effortless resistance against venture into
the bush by night. But at the first light of dawn I expected the
track to be alive with fleet 'Takwena runners sent out to keep
contact between the enemy's base and the spearhead of his
search, pushing ever deeper into the forest of Duk-aduk-duk.

Therefore, fast as we went in the dark the pace was not fast enough for my anxieties.

Past Porridge Pot, filled to the brim with water and brilliant with stars, we walked without stop for over seven hours, until a change in the emphasis of the noises in the bush warned me that the last hour of night was at hand. It was precisely 4.30 and I reasoned we must have come at least twenty miles from the Flamingo Water. I had now to find a place well away from this track where we could lie up for the day in sufficient security to give us all the rest we badly needed, for I knew from the state of my own nerves and sinews and the fantastic patterns forming unbidden in my mind that we were all fast nearing the end of endurance. So I went ahead, determined to turn into the first good game-track which crossed our path.

I found it within a few minutes on the side of a broad *vlei* wherein the rain-water was still a shining silver among long dark reeds and a couple of long-legged herons stood black and motionless and so like Japonaiserie on a lacquered screen that I was almost startled when one of them gave a melancholy croak as it stirred restlessly in its sleep. However, I didn't turn into the track where it crossed the path, for with dawn so near, I feared we might leave marks on the wet grass which would not escape the eyes of expert trackers. So I went down into the hollow of the *vlei* instead and found there a dark water channel between the reeds, full now and running slowly. Much to the disgust of the others I left our old track and led the way down the centre of this channel, walking up to our knees and sometimes even up to our armpits in water. It was difficult and unpleasant work, but so necessary that I continued thus as soundlessly as possible for about a mile to where the channel emerged on the edge of a long, deep pool of water. There I abandoned it for the well-defined game tracks and as I went down them I watched the morning mist curling like the smoke of discarded cigar-ends about our heads, soon to rise high above the trees, shutting out the moon and the stars and the great fire of the dawn which we saw briefly being rekindled far and wide behind us.

So I kept on in the game-track until eight in the morning, by which time I calculated we'd put from eight to ten miles between ourselves and the main track to the Flamingo Water. Even then the mist was so thick that I could safely have gone on longer, but Tickie and Said behind me were walking like men asleep on their feet, and my own mind was so immersed in sensations of fatigue that I didn't truly know whether the sounds of the day opening up far above this deep nether world of mist, the silky whistling, silvery tinkling, satiny swishing and flute-like calls of birds expressing their joy at having escaped from night darkness into the clear sun somewhere above, were not merely intimations of a first dream bubbling up like a fountain from the great world of sleep within me.

I turned off at right angles to our track and went into long tawny grass of a savannah, and was thrilled to hear all around us the snorting of buffalo and the swish of the yellow grass as invisibly and reluctantly they made way for us. Soon, however, the savannah yielded before a dark thrust of bush along the broad brow of the bluff between this *vlei* and the next. The bush came up at us like a blacker roll of the heavy mist and my smarting eyes gratefully picked out a buffalo track, faint with age, leading right into it. I followed it to where, under the crest, an ancient watercourse cut deep into purple earth, and on its banks my eye was attracted to a magnificent wild fig-tree which rose up in the centre of the bed of the watercourse like a giant toadstool. I made for it at once. At its feet, the water had long since spread a wide cloak of fine white drift sand beyond which lay an oval pool, black, smooth and filled with untroubled water. By the edge of the glassy water, like a bundle of Oriental silk, lay a young male cheetah, his ardent life glowing within him, lighting a flame to the shadowy water. When he heard me, he stood up quickly and over his long destroyer shoulder threw a glance of unafraid surprise which told me how quietly we'd come and how unfamiliar a sight we were. But as I came closer to him, he flashed his teeth, then uttered a curious birdlike sound and vanished with an ease and a speed which made magic in my leaden senses.

'Bas, Said, bas! Tickie,' I called out softly to the two shuffling up behind me while I began to slip my load. 'That's enough for today. To sleep with the pair of you. I'll take the first watch.'

Tickie looked as if he wanted to protest, but in his dark

face, ash-grey with weariness, sleep was tugging at the lids of his eyes like the long fingers of the final darkness fastening on the eyes of a wounded animal. He and Said seemed to have strength only to slip off their loads, prop them up beside their guns against the trunk of the tree and throw themselves flat on the sand.

While they slept I gathered wood, fetched water and started a fire close by them, as much to keep myself awake as to warm them and to dry our clothes.

That done, I quickly extinguished the fire before the smoke could show above the trees under the lifting mist and before waking Said gave them three hours' undisturbed rest. I meant to make it longer, but the sun was breaking fitfully through the vanishing mist and making the atmosphere in this airless watercourse so hot and close that I could no longer trust myself even to stay half-awake.

I was asleep at once and didn't wake until nearly six hours later to find Said's anxious face close to mine, saying in a loud whisper as he shook my shoulder gently: 'Effendi! Effendi! Wake up, Effendi!'

I was up at once, rifle in hand. Tickie was already on his feet, gun underneath his arm, head turned the way we'd come, listening carefully. The southern and eastern skies were packed with immense angry clouds and the distance between us and the Flamingo Water reverberated every now and then with a deep, prolonged growl of thunder. But just above us, north and west, the sky was a lovely, pure, transparent blue.

'What is it?' I asked, and my voice sounded small and forlorn in my ears.

'Voices, Effendi,' Said answered, still in a heavy whisper. 'Voices of people coming towards us from over there.' He pointed to the way we'd come.

Then, full of apprehension, I, too, heard human voices about a mile or so away.

'Yes, Bwana, there they are,' Tickie answered gravely. 'And coming this way. But . . .' He hesitated and listened again as another clear little ripple of sound reached us.

I knew then the qualification which had made him pause. Those were human voices, but they were voices raised without specific purpose for the sort of casual conversation which

167

Africans love to exchange over their shoulders, while walking in single file through the bush. I listened again, and distinctly heard a man's taunting laugh and the ringing tone of another's quick reply. Instinctively I turned to my companions and found two faces shining with relief, for those voices told us as nothing else could that we'd come through our cruel test by the Flamingo Water at last. Our track to this watercourse clearly had not been detected, for if our enemies were still on our spoor they wouldn't have allowed the owners of those casual voices to come wandering in between them and us.

When those happy 'Takwena voices, so innocent and unwarlike, had passed in the direction of the river, and the thunder and rain started coming towards us from the sea, I collected my own load and calling on the others to do the same I crawled out of cover.

'We're going to walk in the storm this evening,' I told Tickie and Said, 'and walk until there's no more rain to wash out our spoor behind us.'

The distance from Fig Tree Camp, as we called it, to the formidable Mountains of the Night which line the frontier of Umangoni with hardly a break in their ironclad flanks, was roughly three hundred miles on my map. I reckoned, however, that I'd have to add another hundred miles at least to that distance as we'd have to twist and turn in and out of the *vleis*, river-beds, valleys, and ravines of a land sweeping up to close on six thousand feet in the hills; not to mention the detours we'd probably have to make to avoid our enemies. Supposing, therefore, we maintained an average twenty miles a day we should be able to do the journey in twenty days.

Once we'd crossed the frontier into Umangoni, Heaven alone knew where the trail would yet lead us. It all was as urgent as it could possibly be. But I knew from what I had heard that night in the azalea bushes outside 'Higher-than-the-Trees', that nothing irrevocable would be done until this latest cargo and the fresh instructions carried by the *Star of Truth* had been delivered to Umangoni; and though the instructions the *Star of Truth* carried might already be on their way to Umangoni, her cargo was still far from discharged. In addition we were no longer casting about entirely in the dark. Nor was I following the spoor alone as in the beginning. By now Oom Pieter would be on the trail of the 'great dream' itself in Umangoni. That task in comparison with mine here may have sounded safe and prosaic enough, as I feared it had to Oom Pieter for all the grace with which he'd accepted it, but I'd never underrated it, for I knew it was the heart of the matter. I was dealing with the mere mechanics of the conspiracy: the dream was the living centre. I knew the Amangtakwena too well not to know that nothing formidable could gain a sure foothold in Umangoni unless it was believed to correspond to the necessities of a great dream.

It was exactly three weeks and a day since the Amangtakwena war-cry: 'Mattalahta Buka' had brought me rushing out of Petit France with Umtumwa in close support, and in the days that now followed there were many occasions when from second to second we expected to hear that very same cry ringing out in the bush about us with far fuller orchestration than before, charged with the same sense of that unexplained and desperate hunger to kill which still invades the human heart from generation to generation as if in response to some dark need of life for death.

I have no time for much detail of our long march up country, but I must stress that we'd escaped from a net only to run a continuous gauntlet with danger. If it had not been for the protective covering of those afternoon storms and the rain which nightly washed our tracks away, I doubt if we'd ever have got out of the coastal area alive. Though we kept well away from the river for as long as we could, walking on a different parallel course through the bush, to our dismay we found everywhere an elaborate network of well-used tracks fanning inland from the enemies' base to depots along the river. From early morning until late evening these tracks were crowded with busy 'Takwena traffic: large parties going out to hunt for food, bigger parties going out to collect dry wood for fuel, and long columns in single file coming back with loads of meat and timber piled high on their heads. Each party was organized so that every seventh man carried not a load but a rifle and at the head of every twenty-first man went two more, one armed with a light machine-gun and the other carrying ammunition and a sub-machine pistol. It was clear to me that these men were not ordinary, unskilled African porters but

169

were trained and organized into proper sections, platoons, companies, and no doubt battalions of light infantry. They'd only to shed their loads and collect their arms from among the huge supplies I saw going ashore by the Flamingo Water to be ready to fight as disciplined infantry. Nor did this discipline reveal itself purely in a military aspect. They'd clearly been forbidden to cut wood, so that they shouldn't mark this fatal land in such a way as to suggest to anyone flying over it that it was inhabited. Not once did we see a load that was not made up of dead timber. Not once did we hear them use a rifle on game lest the shot might fall on the ear of a casual hunter or chance wanderer. The only time we heard shots we had grim cause to know they were not fired at game. All the hunting was done with spear, bows and arrows, and snares set with matchless cunning for game of all sorts from frail Dik-Dik to peerless Kudu along the fine, tense animal tracks which lie in the hand of this dark land like the lines in an African palm. These snares had their attractions from our point of view. I'd always counted on being able to supplement the food supplies we carried by shooting game. But now, while the enemy did not shoot, I couldn't do so either without taking risks that would be fatal. So we raided these snares at the very first light of day and in that way had enough to eat, but I wished we'd not been obliged to, for every track and every spoor in the land about us was daily scrutinized by hundreds of expert trackers who, I was sure, would instantly detect the introduction of a new foot or heel mark in their midst. Finally, we never knew when we were going to stumble on one of those well-used, man-made tracks and find ourselves perhaps bumping into the end of some stragglers. Indeed, we had so many other escapes that there was not a second wherein our senses could relax. Fortunately, as I've indicated, we had our friends the evening storms to help us, and to this day the memory of the sound of thunder rapping out the first challenge in the wide silent land, the lash-like swish of the rain about our ears, and the purple flares of lightning going up in the dark make music in my mind. But the deeper we went inland, the later and the shorter the storms became until one night at the end of a week, we moved out of their protective covering for good and heard the thunder vanish behind us with a deep, reluctant growl. Slowly the lightning fires diminished to a delicate flutter and then finally they, too, went dark on us. By that time we were well out of the area so thickly populated by our enemy but about to find ourselves inevitably presented with a compensatory complication.

Up till now our friends the afternoon storms had enabled us to take our water for granted, but from henceforth it was a different story. For two days we were lucky enough, by careful observation of the birds, to strike water. For another four days we succeeded in finding holes of stagnant water after a not too great deviation from our original course. But from then on steadily, as if the land itself were taking sides against us with predetermined wilfulness, we found our search pressing us closer and closer to the river and to our enemy.

So we came to the evening of Monday, 18 August, exactly a fortnight after leaving Fig Tree Camp, a late, tranquil, infinitely impersonal moment, the sunset above the trees like the glow of the dying coals of an abandoned wayside fire. Already it was so late that I'd have thought the unsuspecting enemy snugly entrenched against the militant night in his well-established camps along the river. Nonetheless we came warily down a game-track in search of water knowing we might have to go right down to the river for the first time to refill our flasks which were nearly empty. A hot damp smell, a slobber of wet air was under my nose, and I was on the verge of quickening my pace when Tickie came up silently behind me, pulled gently at my tunic and putting his head close to mine whispered: 'Someone ahead, Bwana.'

I stopped dead in my tracks. The trees in front were thinning away into a round clearing in the centre of which was a ragged blot of shadow with an inky shine to it which I assumed to be water, and on the edge of the shadow, very still and hard to see, a man squatted on his heels.

Scarcely daring to breathe, so silent was the bush and so near the man, I studied him closely, but already my instinct warned me that it was too late; we'd been heard if not seen.

'It is no good, Bwana,' Tickie whispered again as if reading my thoughts: 'he knows someone is here. When I saw him first he was scooping up water to his mouth with his hand or

I would not have seen him at all, but as I saw him he heard us and stopped and listened thus.'

I heard all this with deepening dismay. The last thing we could afford was for the man ahead to dash back with the news that there were strangers about. Judging by his tense attitude I'd have to do something, and do it at once. The vital point to decide was whether he'd seen us as well as heard us. One quick glance behind me reassured me on this issue. The dying glow of the sun was well away over to the right of us. It could have been as little help to him as it was to us. We all three stood too deep in late twilight shadow to be visible. There was only one thing to do.

I gulped back the feeling of nausea which accompanied the recognition as I'd so often had to do in the war. A wordless prayer for forgiveness took wing in my heart and I whispered quietly to Tickie: 'Give me your gun and go out and talk to him as if you are one of his own countrymen and keep him talking – that's all.'

Tickie, his eyes unusually big and brilliant, silently unslung his gun and handed it to me. Hard by the water a night-jar came down with a clatter, a commando-bird wailed loud and long for his mate and far away a hyena howled. Then once again came that strange, tense, trembling silence of the bush. Tickie pushed gently by me, and going forward called out the politest of 'Takwena greetings like an honest person unafraid of scrutiny, just as if this meeting with a countryman were the most natural occurrence conceivable. Considering that the memory of Umtumwa's death must have been every bit as active in his mind as it was in mine, it was one of the coolest deeds I've ever seen, particularly since he didn't know that the moment he called out his greeting I'd covered the stranger with my gun determined that Tickie was not going to suffer his uncle's fate.

To my relief, with barely a change in his squatting attitude, the stranger replied in a polite tone as custom demanded, but so low that I could hardly hear him: 'I see you, brother, I see you. Do you too come for water and where are you going?'

'Aye, I too look for water and I am coming and I am going,' Tickie answered slowly walking forward as if reluctant out of well-bred 'Takwena sensibilities to thrust his company on the

172

stranger, telling nothing of himself, again in accordance with national convention which postpones these exchanges until the formal greetings are completed.

I listened no more but quietly putting my rifle by Tickie's on the ground and telling Said to keep the stranger covered all the while and to shoot at the first sign of treachery, I undid my knife, took it between my teeth, went gently down on my stomach and crawled into the bush as fast as I could, scarcely making a sound.

I crawled and wriggled thus deep in the shadows round the clearing, expecting at any moment a break in the flow of politenesses between Tickie and the stranger to announce that my presence there was discovered. But none came. However, when the sunset glow rose up between me and the stranger, I went with such slow care and restraint that it was almost more than my anxious heart could bear. Yet I persisted out of greater fear lest some of the red dust trampled to the delicacy of powdered Parisian rouge by the thousands of animals who had watered here for centuries might be sent flying up by my knees and elbows to warn him.

It seemed an hour or more to me before at last I found myself on the edge of the water and the thinning bush, immediately behind him. Actually it was barely five minutes, and even in that short time the night had deepened. I could just see that the stranger was no longer squatting but standing upright, his long war spear stuck deep in the mud beside him, talking easily to Tickie with no suspicion in his voice, but with a clear undertone of curiosity and bewilderment over Tickie's dress and presence there at that hour – a curiosity which sooner or later would demand enlightenment. Again Tickie's behaviour was that of an experienced and resourceful campaigner. He saw me at once and immediately took precautionary action on my behalf.

'Would you, brother, take some snuff with me?' he asked, undoing the button of the breast pocket of his bush shirt to get his pouch. The 'Takwena are great takers of snuff, preferring it as a rule to smoking. Every district in Umangoni has its own favoured varieties and that of Amantazuma is not among the least.

There was no mistaking the eagerness with which the stranger

173

accepted the offer. He moved slightly nearer to Tickie, who, his hand now in his pocket, was saying: 'I carry snuff with me, brought all the way from Amantazuma here, look.'

Tickie pulled out his pouch and the stranger peered forward. Quickly I slipped out of the bush. I had only two and a half paces to take and so absorbed were the stranger's faculties for the moment in the prospect of satisfying an habitual craving that he didn't hear my careful step behind him. At the last moment he half turned as if an intuition of my presence was coming awake in him, but it was then too late. I clasped him tightly round the neck with my left arm and jerked him sharply backwards. At the same moment Tickie fell forward and threw all his weight against him, gathering the stranger's legs and ankles in his arms. The stranger fell over against me as if shot, and, as he fell, I stabbed at his heart.

My knife was fine-pointed and razor-sharp. I struck with all the power I possessed and with some experience of this kind of killing. Nothing just then could prevent the death of the stranger, yet even so his skin protested. With a tight creak as of leather straining at the bit of a runaway horse, it alone in that abandoned moment proclaimed the reckoning unfair. Yes! for one sliver of a segment of time that skin rejected my knife. I felt the tremor of the heroic rejection in the steel between my tense fingers and the downward thrust of my knife halted for an imponderable fragment of time. But then that lonely outpost of a doomed spirit, too, was slain and the fortress fell. The skin snapped, and my thrust went easily home. I lightened my grip under his chin just in time to prevent the great wind of life that was gathering in his throat for the last time from escaping – and then he was dead.

For all the time it takes in the telling, it was over so quickly that he died without conscious pain and without even learning, I hope, that he had been tricked by one of his own race. Nor have I any doubt that the killing was stark unavoidable necessity. Yet I stood up to face Tickie filled with revolt against myself, the need and the manner of the deed. To this day, that moment of protest and rejection by a tender young skin lives with me and will do so, no doubt, to the end of my days.

Tickie and Said, however, I am glad to say for their sakes, had none of these reactions. As Said came running out to join us, Tickie got up, brushed the red dust from his bush shirt and khaki shorts and looked at me with eyes wide and more brilliant now in that light, to exclaim with a note full of deep, natural gratitude: 'Bwana, oh my Bwana, one for Umtumwa at last!'

'Quoish, Effendi,' Said remarked with grim Arab approval; 'Quoish Khitir: one for nine; it is a good beginning but the reckoning is still far from complete.'

That there was a rough justice in their reaction I could not deny. Recognizing it greatly helped me back to a sense of the proportions implicit in our situation, so much so that when Tickie with a gesture of disdain at the corpse asked: 'What do you wish us to do with it?' I'd dealt with my own private agitation sufficiently to command without hesitation: 'Strip off his war-beads and finery and take his spear. Fill your flasks and let us go.'

'But what if his friends find him here in the morning, Effendi?' Said remonstrated.

'They will not find him in the morning. Listen!'

They listened and once more, much nearer now than when I had heard him first a quarter of an hour before, again the hyena was howling a long, bleak, forsaken howl of woe. Farther away another replied and at once a troop of jackals near at hand began yapping with hysterical frenzy as if a vital competition between day carrion and night scavengers had just been announced. Clearly there was no shortage of natural under-takers in the land. I'd no fear that in the morning nothing but the bare bones of the dead man, scattered far and wide, would be left, and the fine dust about the pool so marked with the spoor of leopard and lion as to suggest an easy explanation of his going.

'We'll call this place,' I told them, getting ready to go: 'One-for-Umtumwa.'

'One-for-Umtumwa, Effendi,' Said exclaimed, grinning that long grin of his. 'But since Fig Tree Camp we have named no places. Are we to begin again then?'

'Yes, Said,' I told him. 'We begin again. We named no places after Fig Tree Camp because there were no names in our hearts to give. But here, as you and Tickie have just reminded me, we begin a new reckoning. So One-for-Umtumwa let it be.'

So it was and so it stays. And when I recall the march up from the sea between Fig Tree Camp and this pool in an amber space in the dark bush, I still think of it as a journey through a place for which there can be no name.

From One-for-Umtumwa we walked all night in order to put as great a distance as possible between ourselves and our killing. Just before dawn we crept under cover deep in a thicket of wild-raisin and peacock-gum thorn trees, underneath a ledge of rock in the side of the first little koppie we'd seen since we left the sea. We called it The Painted Rock because the walls behind us were covered with lively painting and engravings of the prancing animals of Africa and of some being, half animal, half human, never seen on land or sea. At Painted Rock the want of water drove us back to the river. In view of what had happened at One-for-Umtumwa I had made Tickie strip his bush-shirt and shorts and don the war-beads and finery of the dead 'Takwena scout, then he went a hundred yards or more ahead of us armed only with the long war-spear.

I hated having to put him in the position of greatest danger, only I couldn't help myself. Tickie took his new task as an honour, his eyes going wide and his face shining with excitement. When I judged the river to be a mile away I hastened forward to halt Tickie. Sharing out the last of our little water between Said and myself, I sent him down to fill all our empty flasks. He was away an hour that seemed ten to me, then came back grinning, the flasks full.

He'd had no trouble at all, he said almost scornfully. There was nobody about. From the river he saw not far away the watch fires of a large camp and heard men singing as his people sing after food at night to compose their hearts for sleep. He watched closely but was convinced no one crawled outside those unsuspecting shelters at night. The news clearly showed our coming had raised no alarm and was so reassuring that I changed my plan.

Next day, an hour after dawn, we found a hollow Cream of Tartar tree, a crack in its livid cheek, not fifty yards from the enemy's track. I saw Tickie safely into it and then went some hundred yards back, where I climbed a tall black-topped acacia which gave me a clear view of Tickie's Cream of Tartar as well as the area round the track. Then I waited and watched: Said remained at the camp site.

A lovely dawn spread into the sky. It was pure gold that morning, drifting into the still blue pool of the sky like a fabulous gold swan, long neck tucked well back with enchanted sleep between two arched wings of distant cloud. Even the birds and the animals seemed to feel there was magic in the moment and tried to break the spell by such an outbreak of singing, screaming, barking, yelping, roaring, and flute-like piping as I've rarely heard before.

Just before sunrise a new sound broke in on our ears. The sound of singing came over the tree-tops, the deep, measured singing of 'Takwena on the march, and soon a lovely gold-red dust went up like a swarm of bees newly-powdered with marigold pollen to hang above the trees and the top of Tickie's livid Cream of Tartar shelter. It was just after seven when the head of the column of dust reached him, but it was a full hour before the tail of it passed and the sound of that monotonous, hypnotic chant of heavily-laden men began to pass to the west of us. In that time I reckoned a thousand porters at least must have marched by the Cream of Tartar. After that there was a long silence. Then at noon when the sun was uncomfortably hot, I saw another quick, small cloud of dust on the track to the east. It was moving about twice as fast as the early morning one and had soon sped by Tickie's shelter and vanished in the west. Then another long, hot wait until an hour before sundown, when once again the sound of singing mingling with laughter, whistling, and light-hearted yells drew nearer, but this time it came not from the east but the west. A batch of porters, I thought, travelling light towards the sea and making for that camp near the river for the night.

And so Tickie confirmed it when I went to call him out of his shelter just after sundown. A thousand men with heavy loads on their heads, he said, went by him that morning, and a thousand men repassed him empty-handed in the evening – and not a white face anywhere among them. But had I seen that cloud of quick dust at noon, and had I any idea what caused that? Without waiting for an answer Tickie hastened to explain. Seventeen 'Takwena, the seventeen we'd seen on the deck of the ship, and him with the royal markings on his face among

177

them, had gone by him at a dog trot as if determined to make up for lost time. And three of them carried several fat letters in large white envelopes, like government envelopes, stuck in forked sticks, as is the 'Takwena custom.

The fatal instructions, I thought immediately, when I heard this. 'Look, Tickie,' I said aloud to him then, thinking there is no better way of turning fate into an ally than making virtue of necessities. 'We have to come here for water in any case and from what we learn of the enemy he's not likely to use this road except by day. I want to be in Umangoni as soon as those letters you saw this morning – but I won't be if we continue to fumble through the bush without a road. What about using this track at night?'

'I have been thinking that thought all day, Bwana,' he answered at once.

By nine o'clock we'd rejoined Said, by ten we were back on the track, Tickie in his rôle of a 'Takwena scout, war-spear at the ready, a hundred yards ahead. At two o'clock we found him waiting for us at a bend in the track and not a quarter of a mile away saw the low watch fires of a large camp throwing surly flashes on the dark. We turned away off into the bush and passed by the camp, found the track again and carried on until five, by which time we'd come a good twenty-five miles, and I was well content.

We laid up for the day in the shade of a blue krans,* along the edge of a narrow, dry tributary of the great river. We lay on a strip of fine white drift sand, between it and the dense forest of long, sensitive bronze reeds and tasselled rushes with which the watercourse itself was lined. All day long the reeds and rushes swayed under the slightest breath of air and far above our tired eyes made elegant, tasselled patterns in the blue-black sky, while insects and birds of all feathers and colours came to join the fitful sunny eddies. It was a lovely place, and though five times we stood to in alarm as the noise of a hot 'Takwena chase went by in the bush farther back, we loved it and called it Singing Reeds.

When I climbed on the top of the highest point on the krans

* Literally: a wreath, but also the Afrikaans and South African English for the cliffs of rocks that surround the summits of so many African hills like a wreath.

a few minutes later to have a careful look at the country before it was dark, I was gladder than ever that we had given it so musical a name, for the sun was just setting and for the first time since we'd left the Flamingo Water it was not going down behind a line of thinning trees. In the west, above the gleaming coils of the bush's head, a deep purple shadow rose like the silhouette of a giant to meet the sinking sunlight. At first I thought it was a bank of thunder-cloud but it was too solid, too steep, too regular and unbending a purple, without the silver satin linings, gold velvet cloak and foaming ostrich plumes which our African skies love to wear against the evening air. The air was colder, too, and then, with a great lift of my heart, I had it. No one who has not marched for nearly a month with his vision contained day after day in the flat, narrow unyielding contours of the bush, can possibly appreciate the joy with which I now grasped the meaning of that purple shadow, and saw the tyrant bush at last put in its place in the great African hinterland.

'Tickie! Said! Quick!' I called down below in the loudest whisper possible.

They dropped their loads and, rifles in hand, came scrambling up a crack in the krans as fast as they could, alarm in their faces.

'What is it, Effendi?' Said asked, never short of and always first with a question, while Tickie had a quick, wide-eyed look round the landscape.

'Look,' I told them both. 'Look!' And I pointed to the west.

They looked and then both, as if reluctant to believe good news too quickly lest it be proved untrue, asked together in awed voices: 'What is it?'

'The frontier,' I told them. 'The Mountains of the Night ... and the sun going down over Umangoni!'

'Allah be praised!' Said uttered with brief solemnity before putting the inevitable question: 'How far, Effendi?'

'Sixty miles as a bush pigeon flies,' I answered. 'Perhaps three to four days' walking. What d'you make it, Tickie?'

But he hadn't heard me. He'd just wet the palm of his right hand with spit and held it high above his head to the burning west.

That night we walked as we'd not walked before. The air was noticeably crisper and stimulated us to greater effort, and for half the night a yellow half-moon smoked like an ancient Etruscan lamp over our track. The bush itself was unusually noisy, filled with sound as of a hardly subdued and tense new inner excitement. Towards morning the earth beneath our feet seemed to rise to the first ripple of that tidal wave of distant mountains. Again we went safely round the fires of two large camps. I reckoned we'd come close on thirty-six miles by the time the morning star appeared. At dawn we found in the increasingly stormy earth another tributary between ridges of blazing red stone to shelter us. Then, gripped by this new excitement implicit in the new earth about us, I rested and slept with nothing but the ecstatic shimmer, the flickering, trembling voices of light-intoxicated beetles, the music of sun-stroke and hallucination of feverish insects with wings of burning glass to break like a Pacific swell on the expectant reaches of my dreaming mind.

Twilight came rather earlier than the day before and once on the march in the early hours of the morning our smoulder-ing Etruscan moon vanished. Then we got into difficulties, for the increasingly broken ground suddenly ended against a wall of rock some five hundred feet high. We felt our way all along its foot for an opening since none of us liked the idea of camp-ing down so close to the enemy in restricted space. But to my dismay the wall, far from becoming easier, rose higher, slowly drawing nearer to a river that flowed impetuous and passionate, among the boulders and cataracts in the dark around us. I therefore turned about and probed the wall in the other direc-tion, and at last it cracked and offered us the course of a dry hill stream by which to scale it.

We reached the top in the very first light of another swift red dawn. Behind us the river basin and track lay under a swirl of blue wood-smoke and grey morning vapour, but above us to the west the earth at last took to wings and swept and soared up to a long line of peaks, purple below and pink with cold above, barely six miles away. So high and steep were these peaks that they delivered the sky from the helpless, flat appear-ance that the bush had imposed upon it, and restored it to its native fullness.

'Look! Bwana! Inhlahaxoti,' Tickie exclaimed suddenly behind me, the dawn like a cardinal's cloak about him.

I followed the line of his pointing finger and there in the sky between us and the mountain, wings stretched out to remote feather tip, wheeling and rising like a note of music in an organ peal of a morning psalm, was one of the great legendary eagles of Umangoni which, as the name just used by Tickie implies, is 'eyes of the king and snatcher of sheep'. So high was the eagle that the raven-black wings, deep-sea foam breast, saffron beak, fawn riding breeches and purple talons, were all one dark colour, and that colour transformed by alchemy of the breaking day. For though we ourselves still stood in twilight, an effortless lift of the silver fountain of air whereon the bird soared now carried it out of the shadow of the night up into the light of the sun. For one moment it looked as if a fiery shaft had pierced the bird shattering it in a burst of flame, for the eagle seemed to vanish from our sight leaving behind only a gleaming fragmentary flicker, yet the flicker stayed; and then, with another wheel on seemingly motionless wings, it grew and re-established itself in the quick of the morning air as full eagle of flame in search of equal fire.

When at last I turned my back on it and the mountains and saw again the swell of dark bush out of the flaming east sweeping over the earth to break on the long slopes of green-gold grass below us, all that had recently happened there came back to me not in logical sequence but under a single focus, as if the multitude of experiences truly endured are all one and the same landscape, spread out like the far land stretched under the fiery feathers of Inhlahaxoti. Standing there I felt like someone already preserved by a miracle, moving forward, rather fearful of such privilege, into the presence of yet another.

Chapter 14

The Mountains of the Night

Lovely as both moment and place were, I couldn't allow myself to linger in either. Below us the river basin which all night long was as full of its own eager voice as a curved seashell is with the murmur of its parent ocean now produced a new sound – the grave, measured song of a thousand or more 'Takwena setting out on a long march: and thousands of others would be coming in at nightfall, might, indeed, already be on their way.

Already it was light enough to see the noble heads of a troop of about seventy eland watching us and listening to the far barbaric singing, with intense alertness. That finishes it, I thought, the hunters'll be up here and after that game in no time, and I was on the point of deciding we'd better get back into the abominable bush below before it was too late, when I noticed the spiral of a well-worn track coming out of the side of the watercourse up which we had climbed in the dark. So calling to the others I sped up and along it. The sun was spilling over the horizon in long waves of dazzling light when the trail at last led us over the crest of a deep fold into the dark belt of thick rain-forest, into a strange new world with a twilight being which provided us with well-nigh perfect cover.

I had an uneasy rest thinking I heard faint voices and bells and far strange sounds. At first I was too tired to be bothered by them but as the day wore on and my weariness decreased I became more and more restless, so I took my gun and glasses and told Said that I was going to follow the fold up to its highest point.

The climb through the tangled, pathless belt of rain-forest took me a good half-hour. There suddenly I heard again, very faint but unmistakable, those far-off voices and odd bells which had pursued me in my sleep since the day before. I climbed on up with redoubled caution and could not even hear myself move above the urgent whisper of a sun-born wind eddy which suddenly spun like a vortex of water over this lonely wreath of rock. I crossed over the skyline into the grass on my stomach, and continued so on to a circle of big grey boulders which topped the summit.

Coming up carefully behind the first loose boulder I saw a very old and very big baboon, sitting with his back to me in a toga of sunlight, his broad shoulders rounded, his head well tucked in and a long neurotic, oddly pedagogic finger, nervously scratching his head. He was obviously the look-out for some highland clan foraging for haggis of scorpions, stone-slugs, tubers, and hillside tulip bulbs among the loose rock but my mind, hungry for normal companionship, found his outline there in its cap and gown of sun so endearing that it made of him some natural professor of geology surveying material for an abstruse lecture on problematical stone.

'Hallo! Adonis,' I whispered across the empty space, using the name my trekker countrymen first gave his kind a century or more ago.

He whipped round obviously not believing his ears. For a full second he stared at me paralysed with this unbelief but long enough for me to look into the wisest and most experienced pair of hazel eyes I've ever seen in a baboon's face. At the back of his twilight pupils a long reminiscence of life presented itself for comparison with this surprising situation, light and shadow racing across his face in quick succession. Then the last memory condemned, and his long experience drained, the darkness of fear came up like night in his ancient eyes. He blinked them several times quickly, his brow became incredibly wrinkled, and his lips began to tremble with hysterical pressure. Blinking thus he came out of his trance, his hazel eyes went green with warning, and suddenly he turned a prodigious undignified somersault backwards, reveal- an unacademic behind so bare and naked that it looked as if he'd torn the seat of his mauve, silk suit in panic on the rock, and vanished into space below, uttering a deep, solar-plexus cry which sounded very like the Afrikaans: 'Oh! God! My God!' as he went.

Gratefully leaving my gun and hat in the grass, I took over

his eminent chair of study among the boulders, hoping that if distant eyes should be watching the summit I ought to be no more to them than their daily baboon in his pursuit of learning, and surveyed the scene at leisure.

I couldn't have had a better view, and as I searched the land barely two miles away I saw on the long slopes by the edge of the bush many cattle, sheep, and goats herded by young boys putting red, white, black, cream, and bright yellow stitches in jerks in the satin grass. The boys had their saffron-tanned blankets of skins tight about their shoulders and stood most of the time close by their charges, leaning, hands folded on their long ivory-white sticks, calling to their cattle or one another in clear, girl-like voices. I've never ceased to marvel how easily the human voice dominates all other sound in a natural setting and on this still, sub-tropical winter's day hundreds of miles from the nearest fever of traffic and the latest hysteria of industry, I marvelled anew at those young voices soaring in their natural right like small bright birds on quick little wings, or speeding like polished goldfish to the tinkle of crystal water towards the edge of a coral sea. Occasionally, too, voices were joined by a precise peal, a sparkle of ice-flake sound from bells hung round the sleek necks of some leading pagan goat or favourite hump-back cow.

Even at that distance the silhouettes of the young herds were so like Umtumwa's and the scene so like that in the valley of Amantazuma the day I first met him many years before, that the hurt of his going opened afresh in my mind. Then, beyond the cattle, two or three miles distant, tucked away under the crest of the mother-of-pearl wave of earth of which my own summit was a part, I saw the round huts, neat cattle kraals strangely black in the green grass, stockaded maize, millet, and pumpkin fields bleached a wintry yellow with stubborn little pig-tails of smoke over them all, and familiar blood-red foot-paths stretched out like the nerves of a human hand ready to take their naked traffic down into the dark bush or over the hump into the arrogant blue.

It was a full moment for me, seeing my own dark enigmatic native earth coming alive again in the care of man after those long weeks in the Dead Land and the sleeping-sickness bush. I thought that never had I seen Africa so lovely, so confident

184

and confiding, so continuous and passionately participant in the abiding rhythm of life. The feeling spread as a healing sense of communion which lasted until the memory of the mean traffic behind my back sneaking up the dark river basin into the interior suddenly came back to shock and disturb me.

I turned sharply and set my glasses on the way we'd come in the breaking morning. The view looked guileless enough. There were no dragon's wings, no vampire dactyllos or pre-historic apparitions of evil hanging over it to warn the trusting earth. The only sign of hidden activity was a long line of hunters and their bearers carrying loads on their heads, ponderously crossing the long fold to disappear one by one down the very crack in the wall we'd used in the morning.

Clearly with all this going on the cattle-owners on the far side could not possibly fail to be aware of the enemy's presence, but the fact that they kept themselves and their cattle separate and even well away from their greatest natural water did suggest they could not be deep in the enemy's confidence nor he close in their affections. I even found it significant that when the last of the hunters disappeared down the wall of the river basin there was one shape which did not disappear and looked as if he had been there all day: a burly 'Takwena sentinel, a black and white blanket wrapped closely round him, was left leaning there on his spear, motionless, staring out across the empty slope and heavy folds to the north. He was still there when I left.

But before going I studied with the greatest care the course of the river basin on its way down from the Mountains of the Night. The many-splendoured beauty of the view then was made almost unbearably poignant by the delicate and tender response of those rough mountain giants to the last moment of a dying day. The only element of discord was the river basin itself, and that because the hateful purpose for which the river was being used made it a rough, uninvited guest in that peaceful scene. However, with my glasses I repeatedly searched the jagged edges of this rude basin for evidence of a way out from it, natural or man-made, but I could find nothing.

On my return Tickie and Said had already started a careful fire, knowing that neither smoke nor glow would show up at that hour of the evening above our dense rain-forest cover.

While we ate I told them at length what I'd seen and of my conclusion that it'd be fatal for us to go back to the over-populated river, well as it had served us in the past. They listened to me in silence, with the air of Indunas long accustomed to concentration, only breaking it occasionally to utter a low: 'Agreed! Bwana! Agreed!' or 'Understood, Effendi, it is well understood.' When I came to the end of my account and posed the inevitable: 'So what are we to do?' both exclaimed simultaneously: 'Aye! what are we to do?' but made no suggestions of their own and I could see they were utterly perplexed.

'There is only one thing we can do,' I told them then after the long tense pause. 'And only you, Tickie, I fear can do it. You must put on your war refinery, take up that long spear again, and pretend to be one of the enemy. We'll take you down to the track we left this morning and once on it you must follow it alone to the nearest of those kraals of which I've just spoken. I want you to pose as a hunter who's been on the trail of a wounded eland all afternoon. You must explain that you didn't notice how far the day had gone until it was too late to get back to your camp by the river, so you made for the nearest light to ask for shelter and food. They cannot, if they are true 'Takwena, refuse you. Once inside I trust you to use all the wit for which your family is so renowned, and to find out what they know about the enemy without arousing suspicion. Above all, I want you to find out where the track in the river basin goes. What other ways are there from here to Umangoni? Which is the shortest in time? Which follows closest to the river basin? Which do they use themselves? Then, having done this, I want you to be awake the moment the morning star steps out of the bush and impatient to be on the way, like someone who fears punishment if he does not return to the river camp at once. If you're not back by morning. I'll know something has happened to you, and Said and I will set out to look for you.'

Poor Tickie. He was as brave as the bravest I've ever known, and had I given him any mission in the open bush he'd have gone out on it like a bridegroom to his wedding. But the prospect of shutting himself up for a whole night in the kraals of strange, possibly hostile people, and matching himself in
186

duplicity against the wide, experienced greyheads who, without any doubt, would be produced to cross-examine him since the safety of the community would depend on it, was as little to his liking as to mine. For one moment he looked at me, his wide, dark eyes dull with dismay and an unspoken plea to be excused. Then slowly he got up and walked out to fetch his spear.

It was a terribly long night for me. At first I lay awake by our little fire watching an oily glitter of the waxing moon on our dark roof of leaves and lichen, until the usual night sounds were suddenly interrupted by the faint noise of dogs barking a brisk alarm. For a full minute the barking went on, rose to a frantic pitch and then stopped abruptly as if by words of stern command. Tickie's arrived, I thought, and settled back to seek the sleep I badly needed.

At first I succeeded out of sheer exhaustion, but the more rested I became the longer it took me to recover my sleep. I heard the faint noise of a dry leaf secretly leaving the darkened attic of trees above me, the diamond water moving in the bottom of the fold like a trial of music through a bamboo flute, a red lynx with moonstone eyes hissing hard-by from far down in its burning throat. But I heard no sound from the kraals of my cattle-owners on the other side of the fold.

I told myself such silence was the best possible omen. I argued that it proved the kraals composed in peace and at sleep. Unfortunately my sense of what might have happened to Tickie remained terrifyingly neutral. In the end I could bear it no longer. I got up, made tea from all but the last of our supply, scattered the fire, and just before dawn, leaving Said behind, I climbed slowly back towards the summit. I scrambled up the crack in the first light and was back on my seat of ancient learning in time to see the whole Homeric wine-red sea of morning swell over the horizon. As the light spread I kept a careful watch on the land for sign of Tickie.

The kraals and stockaded fields were the first to detach themselves from the dark. They came out of it in a slow sleepy way, blue smoke seeping through the top of each round circle of light. That, I thought, looked normal enough. I'd have felt happier if I could have observed the movement of people about them, but the light was not good enough for that, so

187

I had to wait and watch the sunlight reluctantly creeping down the slopes like honey casually spilt and trickling irregularly along the folds. At last the light flickered into fire on a track which seemed to lead straight from the kraals to me. But it was empty and my spirits sank. Tickie should have been half-way along that track by now if all were well. Again I followed the track carefully, checking on every dark dip and line in its winding course, thinking every minute I must catch sight of him, and the greater my anxiety the more fiercely I stared. But the track remained empty.

I continued to stare out into the space, the fever of apprehension within me running as high as ever when I became aware that the light of day was creeping into the centre of my vision and that not a quarter of a mile from the edge of the fold was the shape of a person moving fast. I had my glasses on it at once and though I couldn't see any great detail, there was no doubt that it was Tickie. He was running, his war-spear trailing in his left hand, moving backwards in time with his forward stride, and in the other hand he swung a bundle. Though he ran fast, he ran in that long easy, swinging pace which is not fear-impelled; indeed, in that light, place, and time, his whole movement seemed so right and at one with instinct and occasion that I felt as if I were watching an illustration of Amangtakwena history coming alive, observing one of a long line of heralds who must, thus, have carried the news of many a Thermopylae from the threatened perimeters of Umangoni through the narrow passes in the Mountains of the Night to the capital. Light-headed with relief, I jumped from my boulder and soon Said and I were half-way down the fold to meet Tickie, too triumphant to feel tired, climbing up fast from the bottom.

Yes, Tickie said, when we were back in camp, undoing his bundle to hand us delicious sugar-sweet white 'Takwena maize cobs, roasted that morning in the coals for him by his hosts, it had all been very easy. He spoke in a boyishly boastful manner designed more to disguise his own relief than to display any pride in his achievement. Of course, he'd always known he could easily do what I'd sent him to do, but it was even easier than he'd thought. Once past the dogs his main troubles were over. The people, it is true, were hostile at first, but even more frightened than hostile, indeed, very, very, very frightened – Tickie emphasized the degree thrice.

Part of the fear on this occasion, he'd discovered, was fear that he'd been sent to make another exacting demand for food or cattle from them. He gathered that from time to time our enemies came out of the river basin, and requisitioned food in quantities which such a small remote community could ill-afford. It is true they were paid well in money, but asked Tickie with immense scorn, what good was money to anyone in so remote a place? When his hosts discovered that he truly demanded nothing more of them than a night's shelter, their relief was great. But fear, a real, permanent fear remained like night at the back of their eyes. Yes, fear, I gathered was his real host in the kraal. All night he was perplexed by it and noticed that even his own physical appearance inspired a superstitious dread among the people near him. They shrank away when he moved close to them. The oldest man in the kraals, with the thick metal ring of wisdom and badge of tribal duty done to honourable fulfilment on his head, was brought to speak to him. So old and wise did he look that Tickie himself felt full of awe and respect for him. Yet even he was afraid to ask questions and answered Tickie's own with a pitiful and frightened readiness. He'd had no idea what it all meant until late at night, pretending to be asleep, he'd heard the whispers of speculation and reminiscence which his visit had provoked going up in the kraal around him. He gathered that the whole of the river-basin wherein we lay had been placed under powerful ' 'Mwatagati'* and all the people down in the basin were under its protection.

'What, Tickie?' I exclaimed in amazement, wondering what witch-doctor could be powerful enough to inspire obedience to such an exacting 'Mwatagati, so far-reaching a tabu. 'Are you certain of what you are saying?'

'Sure, sure, sure, Bwana,' he answered. 'Two winters ago a messenger came to those people from the Umbombulimo.'

'The Umbombulimo!' I exclaimed, so perturbed by the terrible import of what he was saying that I wanted to reject it outright. For the Umbombulimo was the Chief witch-doctor of the Amangtakwena people; moreover, was on this occasion

* 'Mwatagati – a witch-doctor's tabu.

the Keeper of the King's Memory. He was, in fact, the spiritual leader of the 'Takwena, and the one source of authority which would never be suspected of foreign impurities or wilful corruption. If, and Tickie's evidence seemed to suggest it, the Umbombulimo was also a party to this conspiracy then the effect went beyond my imagination. 'Surely, Tickie,' I protested desperately, 'not the Umbombulimo?'

But again Tickie's head nodded an emphatic affirmative, his voice sagged with import and he said with unusual deliberation: 'I know it is true, Bwana. I heard those frightened people reminding themselves in the night of how this 'Mwatagati was announced to them two years ago by a messenger of the Umbombulimo himself.'

'How did they know he was from the Umbombulimo?' I asked, still preferring doubt to belief.

'Because here, here, Bwana,' Tickie answered, almost impatiently baring his left arm at the shoulder as he did so, 'here the mark of the Umbombulimo's serpent was carved on him and here' – his hands delicately hung an invisible collar round his neck – 'here he wore a collar of hyena teeth, and here –'

'Indeed, clearly it was a man from the Umbombulimo himself,' I conceded, conscious of a sudden increase of weariness. Bleakly I begged Tickie to go on.

Well, he said, this messenger came and administered to these people and not only to them but to all the many, many other people in the kraals near the river basin from there on right into the mountains, the most sacred of 'Takwena oaths. He made them swear in the name of Xilixowe that henceforth they would remove all their cattle from the river area and would keep themselves and their cattle north of this fold wherein we ourselves lay and never on any pretext whatsoever enter the forbidden area until told by the Umbombulimo that they were released from their oath. That done, the dread messenger sealed the oath by smearing their lips with a powerful medicine of the gall of the yellow cobra mixed with an extract of a baby prince's liver.

He paused, his bright young black face suddenly so solemn and sombre that I asked: 'And if not?' For I knew that such an oath couldn't be enforced without some terrible alternative.

'If they did not obey, Bwana,' Tickie went on, his low clear voice coming under the shadow of its first cloud of fear, 'they and their cattle would die of disease in one season. If most obeyed but some strayed by accident down to the river, then they would be instantly eaten by Ungungqu Kubantwana.*‎ And, Bwana' – here Tickie's voice had an involuntary tremble and a cold shiver seemed to go through him as if he realized that though he himself had sworn no oath, he'd been for some time a trespasser on magic and forbidden earth and feared now that that might have unforeseen consequences for him, 'already one leading-goat with a long beard and white behind, one snow-white heifer with purple stipples, one clever-clever umfaan and one curious intombizan† have been devoured, and that is not all, Bwana, there is something else . . .' He paused, looking from me to Said as if to take a deep breath before diving into the deepest of forbidden 'Takwena water, and added slowly, 'The feather, Bwana, it, too, has been shown to these people and already one wise old father has been told off to go for news of its meaning.'

'Is that so,' I remarked with deliberate casualness, then asked: 'And the roads? Did you remember to do what I told you?'

'Aye, but there was no need to ask since when they talked about the wise old father who was to go on the business of the feather, they said what a pity the road by the river was " 'Mwatagati" as it led straight to the ancient meeting-place of the Amangtakwena by the precipice below the cave of the Umbombulimo, whereas the road he now had to walk, though shorter –'

'Shorter?' I exclaimed.

Tickie nodded. 'Aye, shorter, but cold and difficult for an old father since it goes right over the top of the mountains.'

'D'you know where this track starts?' I asked quickly.

'Two thousand paces from the edge of this fold. I saw the place last night before I knew it,' he answered at once.

I was about to thank Tickie and leave him to have the rest he so richly deserved when he gave me a look full of meaning

* 'The all devourer', a supernatural female being in whom the Amangtakwena believe implicitly.
† A young woman of standing.

and went on, 'But that is not all, Bwana. ... The oath these people have taken commands them immediately to tell the men by the river when strangers appear in their district.'

'How can they do that if they're not allowed to come near the river?'

'By sending up a long arm and hand of smoke,' Tickie explained, holding his own hand high over his head, his ivory bangles rattling as he fluttered his long fingers to illustrate the smoke. 'Seeing that smoke, someone will come at once from the river to ask the meaning of it. And, Bwana, in the night I heard one old father say that he wanted to advise them to send up the sign of the smoke to report my visit to the river for he had never seen the Amangkubatwana* with one so young among them. But the others, when they heard that I spoke of the river as one who had been there, told him it was a waste of time to light the signal.'

'That's most important, Tickie,' I commented: 'I praise you and I thank you. Is that all?'

'That is all, Bwana,' he answered, a most touching flush of instantaneous pleasure warming his voice and showing in his tired eyes at the praise.

While Tickie slept, I sent Said up to my old seat on top of the krans to keep watch for us and in particular to look out for any sign of smoke such as Tickie'd described. If he saw such smoke, I ordered him to fetch me at once. Then I, too, lay down and slept until I found Said bending over me in the twilight, saying: 'All is well, Effendi; I saw nothing all day. No smoke rose up from the hills above the kraals of which you spoke.'

I was thankful to hear his news, for the atmosphere of ancient dread and the picture of the shadow of giant evil stalking the Amangtakwena, which Tickie had given me, had stayed so close by me in my sleep, that when Said woke me I looked fearfully about as if expecting every silent, dark, watching rain-forest tree to hide a vengeful African merlin with a host of bedaggered black magic minions coming up behind him.

The moon was only three days from full and wonderfully clear in that high mountain air. We stepped out fast that night

* Sindakwena – for 'bewitched men', the cattle owners' name for men in the river basin.

exploiting its help. But no speed could be fast enough to keep pace with my anxiety. Tickie's news that the spiritual ruler of the whole 'Takwena people too was a party to the schemes of Harkov and Lindelbaum was a terrible spur indeed. Soon we were achieving a night pace faster than any before. I'd have been well content if the dogs in the kraals above us had not now started barking loud and long. When the barking finally ceased, our new track had already curved so far away that the sound of the urgent river was only just audible before it too went silent. From midnight, though inevitably at a slower pace, we climbed steadily, till a yellow dawn caught us making our way along the trough between two waves of some of the stormiest mountains I've ever seen in Africa.

The track spared us those towers of cliff and implacable black chasms I'd seen through my glasses the day before, but already the waves of stone were whipped so high that we were well above the tree line, the black glistening, faintly-smoking rain-forest lying far below us. About us were only bare, steeply-rolling slopes covered with long, thick, proud grass bowing stiffly in the morning air. The grass cover was littered with huge boulders and great crystals of grey and speckled rock, and on all sides of us the crests contracted brows of ancient and incredibly wrinkled grey rocks. As the light of morning spread into the sky above us even the blue took on a mood of grey and turned down upon us a face forlorn and pale. The wind, too, at the first ochre intimation of the sun, began to move in unsteady persistence with a grey groaning sound over the grass and tone-deaf boulders, and travelled uneasily along the grey crests like a conscience visited by guilt in the night. Were it not for the evidence of our track the scene would have looked utterly rejected in the care and imagination of men.

As the day advanced we had to leave the track and find some cover among one of the numerous colonies of boulders, and I ordered Said and Tickie to keep well in the shadows and close to the rocks. I then climbed to the nearest crest and had a quick look round.

To the west I saw nothing but fold upon fold of mountain land rolling away under an empty sky, which here, well above the world of grey stone, came so close to me that I thought I saw some of the black of the permanent night without cast its shadow on the blue. North and south ran a quick sharp line of steep black peaks, their heads going purple in the sun. Behind in the east lay the glistening edge of the black sea of bush out of which we'd come only two mornings ago, a yellow dawn spray flying up over the beach of grass where the greatest combers of vegetation broke. And then – and my heart missed a beat as I saw it – between me and the bush some miles back, from the top of the hill, a long arm of smoke with hand out-stretched was lifting high into the sky.

I stared at it with the bitter satisfaction of one who sees what he's known all along he'd have to see, for that smoke meant that at least one colony of frightened cattle-owners, warned by the barking of their dogs, intended to present the people by the river with evidence that strangers had been passing along 'the forbidden road'.

I stayed long enough only to make sure that the track be-tween me and the smoke was empty, and then went quickly down with the intention of breaking the news to my com-panions. But when I saw how trustingly they slept on the stony ground, I had neither heart, nor for that matter, justification for it. By the time the enemy's messenger got to the kraals the day, I felt certain, would be largely over. It was possible that they could then still send a patrol after us, but from what I knew of African reluctance to take action in the dark, I couldn't see them fixing their zero hour before dawn the next day. Then, of course, they'd come after us fast and, having no need for concealment, would possess the great advantage of being able to travel by day.

Just for a moment I was tempted immediately to continue across this remote, seemingly empty mountain land. But I was restrained by the knowledge that vast and empty as Africa looks to the European, there is always by day some keen human eye on almost every part of it. All the enemy could learn now was that strangers had come out of the river area at night, and that the strangers, judging by Tickie's visit to the kraal, were Amangtakwena too. But should a mere rumour, let alone the actual news, reach him that a European had been seen snooping through his operation area the alarm would go up all along the line, and he'd come at us from every side. There was nothing to do but to compose myself in the shadow against the rock and, when my turn came, to take the rest which I needed for the night ahead.

I slept deeply but even in my sleep I heard a persistent tinkle of bells and a young voice calling for me, or so it sounded. So convincing was the sound, that I wrenched myself awake to find Tickie, finger on the lips, looking warningly at me. I knew why at once. The melancholy air of morning was dead now, the day, high, wide-awake and warm. In this exalted warm mountain stillness rose the persistent sound of cattle bells ringing oddly as hunger jerked the beasts from one good tuft of grass to another, and in their midst the voice of a young boy calling to someone far away and out of sight.

'Child of a black mother in the valley, do you hear me?

'Keeper of white goats on the far side of the hill, do you hear me?

'Say, oh say, do you hear me?'

Three times the cry was repeated, for some seconds there followed only the odd peal or two of cattle bells, but then, far away, there rose up another voice like the first, only smaller and rounder with distance, crying:

'Aye; son of a black father on the crest of a hill: I hear.

'Herder of red cattle on the steep slope: I hear you.

'Why, oh why! do you call me?'

At once the answer rose up near us:

'I call to ask the meaning of the smoke going up from the hills by the river.

'All along the crest of the hills beyond, the smoke stands high in the sky.

'Why! Oh, why? Please find out why.'

Here there came a pause, presumably while the far crier cried the request along a chain of herds back to the first smoke, but so long that I feared our unusual conversation-piece was ended. Then once more there came the distant voice, small, round, precise:

'Son of a black father on the crest of a hill: Do you hear me?

'Herder of red cattle on the steep slope: Do you hear me?

'Say, oh! say: do you hear me?'

The affirmative instantly soared up, to be followed by this answer:

'The people are all making smoke by the river.

'Because strangers are walking about the land by night.

'Strangers walking strangely about at night, are cause of the smoke.

'Since dawn the people have made smoke, to tell the men of the river so.

'But still the men of the river do not come.

'Say, oh say, do you hear me?'

'Tickie,' I whispered, smiling at the mischievous grin which came to his face at this last bit of news. 'If there is danger of that musical herd stumbling on us here you must go out once more as one of the river men, and head him off. Said and I mustn't be seen here.'

'Aye, Bwana, aye!' he answered, 'but it will not be necessary, for already the cattle are turning for their kraal.'

Glad I had not misread the situation I was asleep again almost before he'd finished speaking. When I woke to do the last watch of the day, the chorister and his tinkling red flock had gone from the hills. The only sound left was that of the air of evening taking up the grey note where the morning breeze had left it, while the sun strode with a long level stride towards the diamond peaks in the west, like the last of the ancient heroes going over the hump of the rainbow bridge to take his stand with the gods in Valhalla.

I waited only until it was truly dark, woke the others, and then quickly left our 'Groaning Valley'. We continued to climb fast until, by about eleven, it began to freeze. Our breath smoked over us, and a silver wisp of steam loafed around our armpits. The moonlight everywhere around us, even in the deepest hollows and the keenest gashes in the crests above, was brighter than the night before, and joined in a starlight which seemed to shine not only in its own glittering light but also in reflection from air turned to a dark mirror of ice by the frost. It gave us a sense of inter-planetary communion such as I'd never known. This feeling of all belonging was enhanced by the fact that we all, men, planets, stars, river of foaming nebulae and meteors bursting through the gateway to the earth, were going the same way, all travelling from east to west, for though our track twisted like a serpent yet its westward direction was as straight as the staff which supports the healing snake of Hippocrates. By midnight, this stormy, aspiring earth and air were so bright, the peaks and valleys so patterned, so given over to the moon, that I felt we were walking among the moonstone mountains themselves, under their own moon-snow light, and I seeing in the sky above us not a fated satellite, but the reflection of a magic mirror of our own bright earth. Yet in the midst of this overwhelming cosmic vision, there was always some reminder that this high land was linked also to the life of a humble and imperilled earthbound people, for we seldom walked a mile without coming to lesser footpaths tracking out of our own.

In this manner, just before morning, we reached the roof of this remote African world. Our track didn't change dramatically all at once, yet all three of us knew simultaneously that we'd faced the climax of our road over the tumbled mountains of the night, and that music of the earth and the high night sky were playing out their final crescendo. It was confirmation enough for me that the setting moon was no longer white but flushed and ripe in a warmer atmosphere as a harvest is ripe for the sickle in the late summer air on the south side of the mountains.

We cast about us for cover and happily found something better than boulders, and found it soon. We came to the edge, a false summit covered with wonderful redwoods and beyond a long slope of earth slowly rising to the crest of shining stone which crowned the sun-royal head of the valley a mile or more away. Of smoke, cattle, kraals, tilled fields, or other sign of man, however, there was no sign and I realized that, although we'd crossed the roof of this ancient world we were still deep in the mountains, perhaps further from the permanent habitations of Umangoni than we had been since we climbed out of the bush, for the Amangtakwena have no love of the cold and keep to the shelter of the valleys.

Confident now of being able to evade the enemy I prepared to settle ourselves in for the day. Lying down beside Tickie, who was already fast asleep, I dozed off, but hardly was I asleep when, just as if a postman had knocked at the end of some long corridor in my mind, rifle shots rang out sharply. It is a sound that I've never liked since the war, so I was on my feet, rifle in hand almost before I was awake. Listening

197

intently, I heard nothing at first but the sound of Tickie breathing deeply at my feet, his young face drugged with innocent sleep like a black Chinese poppy drooping with opium in the summer sun. Then once more a volley of shots rang out so far away, and so much less loud than they'd sounded in my sleep, that I wondered how I could have heard them at all. Hard on the shots I heard Said's careful step coming fast towards me.

'You have heard them, Effendi?' he exclaimed, relieved to see me standing there, while another faint volley followed on his words.

'Yes,' I answered, grateful to this good old murderer for his prompt vigilance: 'How long has it been going on?'

'It has only just begun, Effendi,' he said, with an anxious note in his voice, 'and I think it comes from the other side of the valley. But what can it be?'

Again there came a long roll of rifle fire, then a silence, then more shots, and so on.

'Look, Said,' I told him, after this had gone on for some time, 'I'll come with you to your post, and see if the shooting makes more sense to us from there.'

I led the way to the fringe of trees, and for an hour stayed with him at his post there, listening to the shooting going on unabated, trying to make out its meaning. Had my grim-faced 'Takwena royalty, last seen dog-trotting up the track by the river really beaten me to it, delivered his orders, and joined the supreme conspirators in launching forthwith the revolution, whose opening performance we were now hearing? The noise, it is true, was voluminous enough for a small battle, but equally, too static and regular for real war. No, there had to be some other explanation and in the end with a calmer heart and patient searching I felt I had it.

'Said, you were a soldier once?' I said. 'D'you remember when you were a recruit at the training depot?'

'Aye! Clearly, Effendi.'

'Then doesn't that shooting over there remind you of something?'

He listened again, head on one side for some moments, and then looked at me, a rush of understanding rising in him. 'By Allah, Effendi! you are right. Firing training, shooting practice.' And I knew the picture of a busy military field range had been painted as clearly in his thought by the pattern of that sound of shooting as in my own.

'Yes, Said, I'm certain it means something of that kind,' I agreed. 'It means also that we've nothing immediate to fear from the shooting but are once more so close to armed people that I ask you to watch these slopes and the valley below you as well as you've ever watched before.'

Soon I was back with Tickie, and the day proceeded as it usually did for us on these occasions, until just after six. By then I was already half-awake, exploring in a rhythmical semi-conscious way a memory tugging for recognition in my sleepy thought. The memory was connected with the name of some-one called 'Sydcup', and the only Sydcup I could think of, was Regimental Sergeant-Major George Henry Sydcup, once of the Durham Light Infantry, but seconded for service with us in Burma. ... I remembered the day he'd joined us (looking every bit a Kitchener man, right from his toes up to the hon-groisc-pomaded tip of his red moustache) as clearly as the day he died a gallant death when with John and me in the jungle. ... Yet I knew this was not the association this odd subsconscious memory demanded. Somewhere there was an-other Sydcup or sound of Sydcup in my past. ... That 'sound of Sydcup' did it and instantly I saw again the expression of Lindelbaum's face at 'Higher-than-the-Trees', as he listened to Harkov imploring him to put their plan forthwith into opera-tion and 'to instruct someone called Sydcup' accordingly.

How strange that I should think of it now, I speculated, when I'd hardly spared it a thought since I first heard it. Per-haps the shooting was responsible? Perhaps this is where Mr Sydcup has his headquarters? Perhaps here is another instance of my little general's 'great togetherness', and I ought to climb the crown on the head of this royal valley, and inspect it. Perhaps – ....

With that 'perhaps' I opened my eyes, and saw the huge red-wood trees around me shining in all the finery of a great Um-angoni sunset, solemn and attentive like ancient princes sur-veying their final reflection in a mirror before obeying a summons to court, bands of copper and gold around their scarlet ankles, garters of peacock velvet above dimpled knees, silver and opal bangles on saffron wrists, and all the most precious and delicate stones of evening light set intricately and clasped in burning brooches to their heraldic collars of sparkling and finely-pointed electric leaves.

As always when I see something truly beautiful, all other processes of thinking abandoned me instantly and my mind turned on its central thought of Joan, while my heart wondered whether she would ever know how far and wide I'd travelled with my particular vision of her in a great church, and through what strange places, from a Mongolian dungeon to this moment dressed in Arabian Nights' jewels and silks and flushed with the red wine of this high sunset air, I'd carried undiminished the general thought of her.

Almost simultaneously a dark shadow loomed up in the midst of my thinking. It was Tickie, moving as swiftly as he could, beckoning and calling urgently in as loud a whisper as he dared. 'Quick! Bwana, more 'Takwena!'

'Coming this way?' I asked, snatching up my gun and glasses.

'No, but quick, or they and their horses will disappear over the hill,' he answered over a shoulder already turned to run back.

I followed him at once to his post. A mile away the bare head of the valley lay in a tender afterthought of the sun that had been denied to us. Riding one after the other up to the crest went seven 'Takwena on the tough, sure-footed mountain ponies with long manes and slim Tartar ankles for which the highlands of Umangoni are justly famous. Already their blood-red tribal blankets, edged with a border of black wool, were clasped tightly across the chest and shoulders of the men against the rapidly cooling air. Their fiery silhouettes were those of weary, sagging warriors, legs dangling without a will in a long, natural stirrup, giving the ponies their head at the end of a long day in the saddle. The sight would have looked innocent enough were it not that the barrels of seven rifles stuck out clearly above each rounded red shoulder. And I happened to know that it's one of the clauses of Umangoni's treaty with Britain that only princes, chiefs, and headmen are allowed to own guns; I was not tempted to think that seven chiefs would suddenly come riding altogether across the cold remote height on a winter's evening. Besides, from what I had seen in the Dead Land below, the number seven had lost its innocence for me.

'Tickie,' I said grimly, as the red on the last of the seven riders burst into apocalyptic flame under that glow from the west and then disappeared over the crest, 'we'll go back and cook ourselves a hot meal, and drink the last of our tea, and then you, Said, and I are going to find out what goes on behind that noble valley head.'

'Auck! Bwana, Auck!' Tickie exclaimed, and began to giggle with excitement, and giggling and shaking his head every so often he uttered another, 'Auck! Bwana, Auck!' and followed me back to camp.

But Said, with his touch of the Arab and his Oriental respect for caution, was not at all keen, demanding rhetorically: 'Why seek to know more, Effendi, when we already know enough? Why risk another alarm of smoke here now when already we fear the enemy is on our heels? Why not push on to the capital as fast as we can, and get there the help we need before returning here?'

But I was tired of argument and told him rather sharply: 'Because I want to be on top, Said, so eat up your porridge and swallow your tea.'

So there we were, soon after eight, crawling through long grass towards the crown of our valley barely a hundred paces away, solemn under the unbelievable moon. It's a moment I'll always remember, both because of its own inner beauty, and for the change in my spirit which accompanied it. Ever since Flamingo Water, I'd been forced to do many negative things: to run from the enemy, to hide from him, to evade him, to talk always in whispers, to try and sleep by day, and to slink past him at night. Were it not for the reminder I constantly gave myself that all my actions were directed to a positive end, these things might well have had a destructive effect on me.

Now, however, I felt as if I were come to the end of negation. I was setting out to do the first of a series of positive things to the enemy. The thought stirred my blood like a call on a trumpet and sent it ringing to my ears. For a moment I stopped crawling and turned on my back, looking straight up into the face of the moon riding high above the main valley flooded with her light. Tickie and Said, close on my heels, stopped to do likewise, and in that co-ordinated and silent movement they seemed to come closer to me than ever before, as if indeed they were not, one a murderer and the other little more than a black 'Takwena boy, but rather natural continuations of myself made full in response to a difficult challenge from life.

I lay for one lovely second staring up at her, seemingly so close in that moment of trumpet call on this far peak in the mountains of Umangoni, until Tickie touched me on the shoulder whispering with an odd tremble in his throat: 'Oh! do you hear Bwana? My Bwana, do you hear?'

And indeed I heard. From behind the crest came the sound of manly Amangtakwena singing the songs men sing when they are only men together, and out on some mission far away from their full-breasted women and their beloved cattle. There was no magic in the sound, no gaiety. It was just full of ever-lasting nostalgia for that other half of ourselves from which we are all separated, of the nostalgia which the moon on the eve of her own rounded fulfilment provokes in all living matter, not excluding the most dimly-lit animal heart.

I'd have liked to prolong that moment listening to the singing under the moon indefinitely, but I felt a fierce tug at my tunic and heard Tickie imploring: 'Please, Bwana, let us do what we came to do. I'm getting very cold.'

I complied at once, and resumed my crawling to the crest, but if Tickie thought it was really the cold and not the feelings called forth by that deep distant singing of men of his own people which gave him the courage to urge his master on, he fooled only himself.

Soon we all three lay on the far edge on the other side of the valley's head. We'd all, of course, expected to see something unusual from there, but none of us had imagined anything on the scale of what we now saw. We looked straight down on an immense but shallow basin under some of the highest mountains in Umangoni. The Basin was an almost perfect circle, perhaps four or five miles in diameter, a sheet of burnished water in the centre of the basin showing up dramatically a bare two miles away. Towards the south, a yellow serpent river detached itself from the livid sheet, and wriggled quickly away into the east where it disappeared into a dark gash in the side of this mountain-basin. Could this be the source and head of the river we'd followed so long from the Flamingo Water? I could hardly doubt it, particularly as I now saw a very large military camp pitched with text-book precision between us and the river. Indeed, the first lines of tents at that distance, shining like the peaked white caps of innumerable gnomes, seemed drawn-up on the banks of the river itself. The last of the lines ended not a mile from where we stood. Each set of tents appeared to have its own open space, and in the centre of each space leaped a Gothic spire of fire. Round each fire, a chorus of deep 'Takwena voices made the music we'd heard.

What with the moon, the general beauty of the night, the singing and all the memories and parallels of experience it evoked, I found the scene profoundly moving. It looked so strangely predestined and tragically fated, as if by a conspiracy of the gods themselves. I could imagine another great encampment drawn up between the black ships and the shining fore-shore on the edge of the great Plain of Troy looking just like this, and some Odysseus watching it and wondering if he were really to be one of the few destined to reach home. Though the men down there were our enemies, I couldn't hate them, despite all the hatred I felt for the purpose which was using them. I even found myself envious of their company, and filled with an inconsistent longing to go down and join them by their Promethean fires.

However, something now happened quickly to rob me of the idle luxury of such a longing. There was something moving in the track which lay like a trickle of congealed blood on the grass just below us. At first I thought it was a bush stirring in the breeze. Then I realized it was slowly coming nearer to us, and every moment becoming more and more like the shape of a man.

'Look! you two,' I whispered, 'if that's a man, and alone, we'll take him as he passes under this crest below us. You go for his feet, Tickie, I'll go for his throat, and you come down on top of him, Said. But, I want him alive. If there's to be any killing, I'll do it after he's spoken to us and not before.'

Slowly, very slowly, the blur of darkness in the silver light drew near. Often it paused, turned round as if about to change its mind and go back to the fires. At such moments I was tempted to pursue it, but soon realized the figure was hesitating almost as might an admirer of the moonlit scene – but that surely no 'Takwena ever would do? Then, as the figure came near indistinct as it was an odd feeling that I knew it without knowing it began pounding madly in my heart. Finally, now very close, it suddenly started to whistle the music of the first tune taught to me as a child:

> *Au clair de la lune*
> *Mon ami Pierrot.*

and a sense of bewildered knowing began to rage in me like a madness which drove me into action with unintended desperation.

At last the figure stood beneath us, I gave Tickie and Said the prearranged sign, and the three of us descended upon him. I first at his head and throat, Tickie at his legs, and thirdly, our long Arab at his middle. He went down like a stone without a sound or struggle and lay so still between us there on his stomach in the moonlight, that I feared we'd been too rough with him. However, I made him feel the point of my knife at the side of his throat and whispered loudly in Sindakwena: 'One sound and I'll kill you; one cry and I cut your throat at once.'

As he uttered a muffled 'I understand', I signed to Tickie and Said to let him go, stood up myself, and ordered him to his feet saying, 'Who are you? What are you doing here? Are there more coming? . . . Answer me softly, but at once.'

He was so slow complying that I felt compelled to grab him fiercely by the collar and start helping him to his feet saying, 'Get up, damn you! and speak up. Who the hell are you?'

He got up then, without loss of dignity while we made a ring round him, our knives shining in our hands, ready to go for his throat at the first sign of treachery. Just for a moment he remained bent, his back turned to me while he brushed a neatly-pressed tunic and freshly-creased slacks. Again the gesture seemed infuriatingly familiar. That done, he turned slowly towards me, saying as he did so, with the slow, almost choking deliberation of a stress of emotion: 'John Edmund Cornwallis Sandysse to the world in general, but to you in particular, Pierre François de Beauvilliers, just John; John at your service, dear boy.'

'My God, John!' I cried. 'It can't be true! it can't be you; dear God, it can't be you.'

'It's me all right –'

'Are you all right – we didn't hurt you?' Without pausing for an answer I turned towards the others. 'Tickie! Said! See . . . the Bwana I've come to find!'

'Bless you, Pierre –'

'You're sure you're not hurt?'

'No. I heard you coming and fell with you before you hit me,' he said, grinning at me as if slightly guilty at having raised so great a storm of feeling in me. 'Bless you, I'm all right; alone at the moment, too, and –' He paused, then added quickly: 'It's odd, but I've been thinking of you all day.'

However, his reassurance that he was unhurt had already sent me off on another tack. 'Then quick,' I whispered urgently, 'let's go now before they discover below that you've gone.'

I signed to Tickie and Said to collect our guns, and turned about assuming he would follow, but he caught me by the arm and held me back saying gently, 'Hush, Pierre, hush, not so fast, I can't come with you, at least, not far.'

'What!' I whipped round, hardly believing my ears.

'I can't come with you.' He spoke in a low and apologetic whisper. 'You see, I'm in command of all that down there!' And now I could hear bitterness in his voice.

'What?' I exclaimed again, while another wave of undiminished singing in a thousand throats from below mounted to a breaking crescendo with what seemed to me suddenly a triumph of irony of the deadliest kind.

'Yes, I'm in command down there,' he repeated, holding me firmly by the arm, as if he feared the news might send me running from him. 'But it's not as bad as it sounds. Only it's a long story. Look, let's find a place where we can talk in comfort without whispering, and I'll tell you all.'

'But won't someone come and look for you if you are gone long?' I asked, still dazed by the shock that it should be he who was commanding one end of the long line of evil traffic between the great Flamingo Water and the heart of Umangoni.

'No, no one will come,' he assured me, the chill of a bleak

reminiscence in his voice: 'You see, for eighteen months now, every night when it's been fine, I've come up here to be alone and to think.' He made a face of distaste. 'They're used to my being away for hours at a time. But first tell me what news of my mother. Of Joan? How are you? And what have you done with Kawabuzayo? Why isn't he with you?'

'Kawabuzayo?' I asked, utterly bewildered.

'Yes, Kawabuzayo, the man I sent to bring you here.' Puzzled at my reaction, he peered hard at Tickie as if hoping to see the missing man in him. Finding it all impossible of explanation in that place I took him by the arm and led him quickly back to our camp among the great redwood princes. There we lit a fire of our own, and there I told him, and he told me.

Chapter 15

We Talk among the Redwood Princes

Tickie and Said were already asleep up at one end of the fire,
though every so often Tickie would open a pair of black eyes
to look from me to John, who seemed to have captured his
imagination from the start. I was not surprised for I too could
hardly keep my eyes from the face on the other side of the fire.
Strictly speaking, I suppose, it was not a handsome face and
yet for me it was something much more. John was as fair as
his sister was dark, and his hair had an unusually fine and
illuminated texture. So neat and elegant in other respects, he
wore it long and rather untidy, and in the army, I'd had, at
times, to remind him that it needed cutting. A fine grey mist
of grey now creeping into it made it even more of a shining
platinum than before. The effect there in the ancient light of our
Gothic fire was startling. Above a face and brow burnt black
by the high mountain sun, it appeared to be not hair but an
emanation of clear fire from within him, a halo of Da Vinci
light around a noble head. By contrast, the brow beneath was
unexpectedly broad and firm, the eyes set wide apart and of a
singularly warm and shining brown. His nose was high, his
mouth generous and at one with a chin, and jaw, firm, steady,
and clean. Though he stood five feet eleven inches in bare feet
he had the slender knack of looking a full six feet if not more.
At the same time he was immensely strong, and I'd have found
it difficult to say which was the greater of his capacities for
endurance: that of body or the spirit. Had it not been for that
fine tide of grey rising in his hair, I'd have thought him no
older than when I first met him riding with Joan on that shining morning along the dawn-pink foreshore of the great False
Bay. Then, I saw something new which went to my heart as
my dagger had gone into a 'Takwena heart not many days
ago, for there, printed on the familiar features, like a swift

master-sketch straight from the atelier of time itself, was the design of a trial and a bitterness of experience beyond the understanding of those who have not shared it. Those devils have tortured him into doing this, I told myself, angered and dismayed. But even that was not the answer. The story was not so simple. In any case, I should have known better. But the beginning of it?

It began, of course, in December 1944, he said, his fine hands spread out against the warmth of the fire, it began on the night of the new moon, when he and Serge Bolenkov fled from our prison outside Harbin, not knowing whether I was alive or dead. But since the story was so long, he'd leave the account of this escape until later and go straight for the point which was most relevant to our immediate predicament, and begin where they were picked up by a Russian patrol on the outer Mongolian frontier exactly a fortnight after the Japanese surrender.

'Yes, you would readily have appreciated the irony of it, Pierre,' he stressed, 'for there we were, more dead than alive in the promised land at last – only to find that not only might we have spared ourselves all that terrible experience but also might have been free a fortnight earlier if we'd not budged from gaol at all! . . . Great as the irony was, there was greater to come.'

He paused for an almost imperceptible moment, then quickly resumed his story.

He was alone, utterly exhausted, starved almost to death, and he suspected gravely ill, waiting in the August heat for Serge's return to their hiding-place in a tamarisk clump on the Mongolian frontier, and asking himself over and over again what could account for Serge's delayed return. He'd only gone out at dawn to investigate some smoke they'd seen going up in the distance, and he couldn't have lost his way on such a still hot day with no wind to erase his tracks. Dear God, how hot it was! Then suddenly he, John, had seen a monstrous black shape speeding towards him, its head high in the glycerine sky, and a red-brown dust at its seven-league heels. An armoured truck was bearing down fast on his lonely tamarisk clump. It pulled up sharply, only a few feet away, a crew of untidy soldiers with the pointed star of Russia in their caps

tumbling smartly out of it. Behind them descended an alarm-
ingly despondent Serge who at once looked a warning at John.
Pointing to John, Serge told the soldiers in Russian that there,
as they could see for themselves, was the companion of whom
he had spoken, obviously in need of the help he had truthfully
requested. Then he broke into English at a speed which even
John could hardly follow, warning him that he was not
believed, was under grave suspicion and had thought it wise to
tell the soldiery that John knew no Russian except the little he'd
learned from Serge in prison out of sheer love and admiration
for a great and gallant country. 'And out of that small
deception of Serge's,' John said, giving me a teasing smile, 'grew
the great deception which you find me practising here, so much
to your distress.' He then plunged quickly deeper into his tale.

He was helped into the truck and deposited on the bottom
with Serge in the midst of a group of unsmiling, phlegmatic,
slant-eyed faces and suet-pudding heads. Immediately the truck
drove off fast, not in the way it had come, but round and round
the tamarisk camp in ever widening circles, like a hound casting
around for a lost scent.

'What on earth are they doing?' John wondered of Serge.

'Looking for parachutes,' Serge promptly told him.

Yes, he and John were suspected of being American spies
dropped there by parachute. They refused to believe anyone
could have escaped from Harbin and lived to tell the tale.

But, John protested at once, weren't the Americans as much
allies of Russia as was Britain? Serge merely shook his head
and told John that the war had finished only a fortnight before.
Russia no longer had either need or desire of allies. But,
anyway, wouldn't they take his word as an officer and a gentleman that he and Bolenkov weren't spies? John insisted. This
merely stung Serge into saying with bitterness that, though
there might still be officers left in Russia, he feared there were
no gentlemen. In fact, from what he had seen and heard that
day at the big base camp further back, he thought it'd be far
better if John did not disclose himself as an officer or a gentleman, but pretended to be a man of the common down-trodden
people – that was why he'd told them John spoke no Russian.
He believed John would have a far better chance of getting
back to England that way, for make no mistake about it, they

were in the soup. He was convinced that if they knew John was an officer, they'd separate him from Serge, the volunteer private he'd already described himself to be. And *that*, Serge stressed, would not be good for John, and possibly disastrous for him, Serge. The Commandant back there in camp had given him a very Siberian-salt-mine look when he'd confessed he was a White Russian, come back freely to fight for his country in the war.

'No, my Colonel,' Serge told John, with a vigorous shake of his great head, 'believe me, it'll be best for you and me if you enter that Siberian wolf-pack's den ahead in the pose of a man of the ordinary British people, a common man with passionate Left-wing sympathies.'

Serge had wanted to go on, but a look on the face of their escort warned him that already they'd talked too much. The elaboration of the first slight deception had begun, another strand drawn for the tangled web we human deceivers weave for the busy shuttle of fate. Before they arrived at the Camp, John had ceased to be Colonel John Edmund Cornwallis Sandysse, D.S.O., M.C., of His Majesty's Fifty-second African Commando, and become No. 360928 Regimental Sergeant-Major George Henry Sydcup of the same unit.

'What!' I exclaimed before I could stop myself.

'Yes, R.S.M. George Henry Sydcup,' John repeated. 'Don't tell me you've already forgotten our gallant R.S.M.?'

He'd chosen the name of Sydcup, he went on to explain, because he wanted the name of someone real whom the War Office knew, and who might be alive, in case the Russians started checking up on him.

For days, John said, he hated himself, feeling himself to be a coward and a cheat, and deprived of the self-respect which was his only armour. But one look at Serge to whom he owed his life, and then at the tight Tartar faces always around them with their unyielding expression of closed minds and barred hearts, was enough to convince him that the deception was necessary. And as their interrogation became more and more skilful, and the pressure on them steadily greater, the last of his doubts vanished, though his regret remained. They were not physically ill-treated. From the start they were given promptly the expert medical attention and food they needed.

But it was the sleepless, unending suspicion of the West rising and falling ceaselessly like a black sea at the back of their minds, which made it impossible for them to accept the account which John and Serge gave of themselves. The minds of those men were permanently in a focus of distrust, created by a generation of isolation and one-sided propaganda. They couldn't help themselves. They were people without belief of any positive kind, belief having been cut so short at its instinctive roots by their coldly materialistic and intellectually willed Marxist dogma, that it left only a wretched negative shoot of a belief: a belief only in the dubiousness of all belief. How, therefore, could they recognize truth in others? Besides, these slant-eyed men with their Arctic-grey eyes, high cheekbones, and close-cropped heads had not respect for individuals. They thought and moved only in masses, and valued only in numbers. It was not that they despised the individual; they just had no awareness of what an individual could mean. It would have been enough that Serge and John puzzled their captors for them to pack the pair off to a forced labour camp before Moscow even knew of their existence. They themselves would have forgotten the incident before the order for their removal was dry on paper, as they'd done with millions of German, Austrian, Polish, Ukranian, Japanese, and, indeed, Russians. Two things only saved them, John said quickly touching a stump of rainbow wood beside him, two things only stood between them and a labour camp.

The first was his pose as an ardent admirer of Communist doctrine in general, and Russia in particular. That flattered them, and excited their interest sufficiently to make them report it to their political superiors. The other, closely linked to it, was John's claim to have served with an African Regiment. He still remembered vividly the green light that went up in the eye of the political Kommissar, and the looks he exchanged with a deputy-marshal of the Forces come straight from Moscow on a tour of inspection, when they cross-examined him about his African Unit. Hard on this came a hurried visit from a bespectacled specialist flown from Moscow, with an incredibly detailed knowledge of Africa, who cross-examined him at great length in fluent Swahili and in Sindakwena, better than his own, and almost as good as mine.

'Yes, little old fellow,' John remarked with a gay lift to his deep voice as he observed my astonishment: 'That strange bespectacled little bureaucrat nearly knocked me flat, too, with astonishment, but I convinced him so thoroughly that I was what I pretended, that he offered to send me to school. He did so by asking me if I'd ever heard of the School of Revolution at Tashkent? When I said no, he explained that for years there had been a school at Tashkent where people like myself, who believed in the Communist gospel and Russia, came to learn how to disseminate it in other parts of the world. Would I like to go there and join the one hundred and fifty Africans already studying there? he asked.'

'A hundred and fifty, John?' I interrupted out of unbelief.

'There were close on three hundred when I left, but more of that later,' he assured me, then went on to say that his bespectacled bureaucrat had promised him that if he did well at school, mastered his Russian and the other interesting subjects taught at it, he would be given a rôle with a splendid future in the great plan the Soviet International had for the suffering black millions in Africa.

'This, then, is part of that great plan,' I interrupted again, waving my hand in the direction of the valley.

John nodded vigorously, but begged me not to go too fast. Of course, he liked the proposition in more ways than he cared to tell that clever bureaucrat, for here was something far greater than a possible line of escape, here was an imperative duty to find out what that plan was, and to get intelligence of it out to the world before it was too late. So he told his intellectual Marxist spider that nothing would please him more, since the exploitation of the long-suffering millions in Africa had long been a cause dear to his heart. He asked only that Serge should be allowed to go with him. Unfortunately the bureaucrat didn't like that: once a White Russian always a White Russian, he said. How could John expect them to believe he was a friend of the revolution when he insisted on being shackled to one who was forever an enemy of the régime? With that the bureaucrat went off in a cold-intellectual huff and fresh spurt of suspicion against John. Once more a salt-mine seemed just round the corner.

Yet there was nothing John and Serge could do except

remonstrate whenever possible, and wait and pray. The answer came quite soon, and came dramatically enough and, of course, ironically. Consider what had happened. At two in the morning he and Serge were sent for by no less a person than the Chief of Staff, already sitting at his desk, a 'most immediate' telegram from Moscow before him. He looked up at their entrance and asked immediately: Did they know a Colonel Sandysse, J. E. C. Sandysse of the Fifty-second African Commando in the prison from which they claimed to have escaped?

John couldn't honestly say that he and Serge were not astonished at the bald question, but they were prepared for it. They answered promptly that of course they knew the Colonel well. He was the man who broke from prison with them, the man they'd left weak after sickness, to recover with a Mongol prince way back on the edge of the Gobi, for they had already agreed to tell the story that way. By now it was far too late to disown his identity with 'George Henry Sydcup', because doing so would inevitably have prevented him from going after the African conspiracy. No, necessity forged for him by his inscrutable fate, decreed that he should play out No. 360928 R.S.M. George Henry Sydcup to his appointed end. That, however, was not the whole of the irony. The lie about the Mongol prince coming on top of this unsolicited evidence from the outside world finally convinced the Russians that the story of the escape and journey was true! Soon after he was sent to Tashkent.

'Did they let Serge go with you?' I asked.

'No,' John said, 'they took Serge away from me almost at once. They separated us without warning, but promised to let him go back to Manchuria only if I gave them satisfaction.' There was no mistaking the sadness in his voice as he spoke the word 'satisfaction'.

So there he was at last in the school of Revolution at Tashkent, learning Russian, Marxist clap-trap and all the cheap, slick, cunning tricks of the modern saboteur in all dimensions of life: of the marionette agitator and begetter of industrial unrest, the ventriloquist inciting lesser puppets to class and racial strife, the chauvinistic exploiter of the real grievances of millions of backward and impoverished peoples and the complex hurt we inflict everywhere with our daily racial and social arrogances. How he wished, in one way, I could have been with him. His bureaucrat had called it a school, but it was really a university with close on two thousand students, all carefully picked for the wounds and injuries inflicted on them by the world outside. There were scores of Africans among them; not one part of Africa, from Ras Hafun to the Green Cape, or Suez to Good Hope, was not represented. There was not one country in the world which was not amply, actively catered for in this militant establishment. Skilfully chosen, these instruments of a Tartar inquisition came in hundreds from all over the world with hurt, hang-dog, or starry eyes, to learn the latest dirty method of spreading chaos and unrest in the mind and machinery of man. Anyway, his personal progress at the school was the sensation of the year. His knowledge of sabotage in the physical world was as complete as theirs since he'd learnt it in five years of war. He already knew Swahili and Sindakwena, and could talk Marx, Engels, and Lenin with the best of them. Besides, he had one great advantage: they badly needed someone like him, and had no other immediate human alternative.

Then, exactly two years ago, John went on quietly, he found himself once more face to face with his bespectacled bureaucrat from the Kremlin. Was he still prepared to work for the cause in Africa? John said he was, subject to the usual condition: Serge must be freed and sent back to Manchuria. This time there was no impatience. The man from the Kremlin gazed at him steadily like an ardent entomologist believing that he has truly discovered a new species of butterfly. Then he gave John the word of the highest in the Kremlin that, if he accomplished this mission *successfully*, Serge would be released and helped to return. That, for what it was worth, John had to accept. At once a dispatch case was produced, a map taken out, opened and a sallow finger began stabbing at the east coast of Africa and the Great Flamingo Water. Only John didn't call it that, he gave it the name it had on the secret Russian map: Otto's Bluff.

'Otto Lindelbaum's bluff! And a bluff in more ways than one,' I couldn't help remarking.

'Who is Lindelbaum?' John asked, clearly perplexed.

'D'you mean to say you do not know?' I exclaimed.

'I certainly don't,' he said.

'D'you know Harkov?'

'Ah! Harkov, that . . .' No further comment was necessary. 'Lindelbaum's Harkov's boss,' I told him, 'but go on, I'll explain later.'

John's mission was quickly explained to him. It had a simplicity which somehow he couldn't associate with the suspicious, devious, semi-Oriental mind of the man who explained it to him. This bureaucrat knew his Africa and its languages, but he'd never given John the impression that he had any real understanding of the continent and its peoples. The imaginative understanding which had realized that the Amangtakwena were the one nation sufficiently complex, supple, and disciplined to launch an organized revolution in Africa, was astonishing: let alone the foresight which had known that they could be won over to the cause of revolution. How this one-sided Russian mind could have seen so far and so truly in this matter remained incomprehensible to him.

'But, John, you're right: the means may be Russian but the inspiration's not. It was all Otto Lindelbaum's,' I told him.

'But, Pierre, that still does not explain to me how the 'Takwena were won over,' he protested.

'Have you in all this heard any talk of a dream?' I asked – beginning to realize how skilfully the mind of the master-conspirator worked; how careful it was not to give its pawns more knowledge than they needed for their own limited move.

'No, I don't think so.' John appeared clearly set back by the apparent irrelevance of my question, and then said slowly: 'But wait a moment! That's what Kawabuzayo and the others had a row about at Tashkent – a dream. I was going to tell you, only it all seemed so silly.'

'I'm afraid it's far from silly and probably explains how the 'Takwena were what you call "won over",' I told him, begging him to continue.

He hesitated no longer then and told me how his bureaucrat, holding his sallow finger on Otto's Bluff, explained that it was a secret harbour known only to Russia. Already it was organized as a first-class base of supply and prepared to accept its first big shipment of arms and other war stores. That shipment was due to leave in two months, and he ordered John to

215

accompany it to a destination inland where he was to take over and organize a self-contained military base and training depot for the 'Takwena army which was going to liberate Southern Africa on the great day of the final disintegration of its white capitalist and debased bourgeois world. That was all he needed to know at the moment. Detailed orders would come later. Now was he still so keen to go?

John hastened to reassure him that he was keener than ever, and a week later five Amangtakwena men, all with the marks of royalty on them, arrived at Tashkent for the usual tuition, and with orders to be put in John's charge. He'd bother me only with details of two of them, John said; one was the Kawabuzayo whom he had already mentioned, the other was Ghinza. Kawabuzayo was a most attractive character, in spirit a 'Takwena of the old school, tall, broad, massively good-looking with a manly bearing. He was one of Nature's country gentlemen, generous and open as an Umangoni spring day. He was soon filled with natural distaste of all he saw and heard at Tashkent. John liked him from the start, and they became such friends that John had to discipline himself not to show him favours at the expense of others.

As he finished his description of Kawabuzayo, I had no need even to ask a question for confirmation, so clearly was there re-established in my memory the picture of the dying man in the kitchen at Petit France opening his patrician eyes to smile at me and exclaim 'Ekenonya'.

Ghinza, on the other hand, I heard John continue, was as unattractive as Kawabuzayo was attractive. He was a tall, gaunt, grim, leathery fellow, vain and excessively ambitious, and embittered beyond reason by two things: he had never forgiven fate for depriving him of the throne by making him the son of a second instead of a first son; and he smarted for ever under the injuries mental and physical received from a bullying white overseer during a spell in a copper mine.

Again, as John spoke, I instantly recognized the grim face of the 'Takwena at the porthole in the *Star of Truth* and said:

'If I'm not mistaken, he's on his way here now with Lindelbaum's final instructions. Tickie saw him some days ago back there in the bush, dog-trotting fast this way.'

'Arrived already,' John remarked with a certain grim amusement. 'Arrived this morning with what you call Lindelbaum's instructions, but what I call my marching orders from Moscow.'

Then John was back again at Tashkent, telling me how neither Kawabuzayo nor Ghinza could stomach the other. They were Cassius and Brutus to each other, quarrelling fatally though, more to the point, before and not after the great conspiracy. The first row John overheard through the half-open door of his room. It was over something which appeared trivial to him at the time but he realized now, of course, it might not have been so trivial as it sounded. It was all about a dream, and some story of a feather.

'John,' I interrupted gravely, 'I assure you this is terribly, terribly important. Try and remember everything, however small that was said, every detail could be vital.'

The 'all' was not much. Ghinza, in that bitter sarcastic voice of his, was reproaching Kawabuzayo for not telling him what he knew about the dream of 'Nkulixowe, the late and great 'Takwena king. Apparently Ghinza knew half of it, and Kawabuzayo the other, and Ghinza wanted to swop information. But Kawabuzayo refused absolutely. What is more, he slated Ghinza roundly for making what he called a 'treasonable' request, saying they had both inherited this knowledge from their fathers, and both knew they could speak of it to others only at one time, and at one place, when properly summoned to do so. Kawabuzayo had gone on to say with rising indignation, that Ghinza had better look out. He was already far too lax in his talk of dreams, for he, Kawabuzayo, had overheard him discussing Amangtakwena dreams with Harkov when his ship was in Cape Town recently. Ghinza had given a shriek of rage, saying Harkov was a true friend of the 'Takwena, and threatened Kawabuzayo that he'd kill him unless he told what he knew before they returned to Umangoni, which they'd soon have to do in order to show the people something – John thought it was a feather, but he was not sure. As Ghinza uttered this threat, even John's room became so charged with the electricity of the quarrel that he feared violence, and went out to calm them. Not knowing Harkov, or anything about 'Takwena dreams at the time, the incident concerned John only as evidence of the deadly incompatibility of the two men.

I told him he'd helped me more than he knew, for clearly

217

his story could only mean that 'Nkulixowe had indeed created, as Oom Pieter and I had suspected, a machinery for checking the authenticity of any great dreams that might be foisted in his name on his people in the troubled future. What John had just told me could only mean that Kawabuzayo held one half, and Ghinza the other, of the key to the dream test. I could hardly restrain my estimate of the probabilities of the solution from rushing out there and then. Only the knowledge that John was nearing the climax of his story restrained me. Also I had in my imagination a picture of Oom Pieter already in the capital, patiently puffing his calabash pipe while he waited for me to join him, and every second would now drag heavily until I could do that.

Six weeks after the quarrel, John went on, the bureaucrat was back in Tashkent. He told John to pack and be ready to leave in a week. Asked what he thought of his 'Takwena pupils, John gave them all a good professional report except Kawabuzayo, and urged that this man should be allowed to return with him to Umangoni. He argued that though Kawabuzayo was a failure in school, he was convinced he'd be excellent in the field. He also spoke of the danger of keeping him in the same place with Ghinza. On reflection, and after inquiries among the staff, the bureaucrat thought there was something to be said for John's idea. A day before John left, a telegram came from the Kremlin ordering Kawabuzayo, to his undisguised delight and to Ghinza's disgust, to accompany John.

From there, John said, he'd spare me all details until a more leisurely day, for nothing of importance occurred on his journey from Tashkent to Vladivostock.

'Vladivostock?' I queried. 'You came from Vladivostock and not from the Gulf of Finland?'

'Yes,' John affirmed. The first and heaviest shipments came from Vladivostock, but they had to be severely rationed since there was no obvious reason for trade between Siberia and Africa, and too many ships rounding the Cape in ballast would have soon provoked unhealthy curiosity. So the majority of ships came from the Gulf of Finland carrying at least two-thirds legitimate cargo. But he and Kawabuzayo came from the Far East via Singapore and Colombo. In harbour they were kept locked under cover, and the slender hope John had

had of communicating with me or his family on the way quickly vanished. Then twenty months ago they arrived at the Flamingo Water, where he was met by Harkov. He could see from the look on my face we had the same impression of the fellow, so he'd say nothing about him except that I mustn't underrate him. Harkov's thorough Prussian mind with its indefatigable love of detailed organization had worked out all the arrangements down to the minutest item of John's training plan. He'd met John, briefed him arrogantly, sent him off like a privileged slave into the interior before boarding the *Star of the East* for the Cape. Eighteen months ago John had arrived to establish himself in the near-by base, to find tents already up, four thousand recruits waiting, and a score or more picked 'Takwena who'd seen service in the last war to help with the training.

Already he'd trained twenty thousand men and in two months he'd have another four thousand ready. In the beginning the plan had been to train enough men to maintain a disciplined army of thousands in the field as well as numerous saboteur and guerrilla auxiliaries. But that, he had gathered with dismay from the latest dispatches received that morning was no longer to be so. Checking the question he saw rising to my lips, he continued rapidly to the end of his story. He had all the rifles, machine-guns, sub-machine-guns, pistols, ammunition, explosives, and saboteurs' gadgets for a protracted campaign, a landing-ground capable of taking the heaviest aircraft, not to mention a sinister new weapon which had come in with the first bearers that evening. How he would love to show me over his ordnance and quarter-masters' stores in the great system of caves which lined the deep rain-forest filled gorge where the river left the basin to leap down on to the bushveldt, and hack its way through to the sea. He'd fear no inspection of his light infantry battalions by no matter what adjutant-general; as for his mounted infantry, his storm troops as he called them, they were as good, he believed, as any commando the Boer War or even the last War produced. Since he had no choice but to do this sinister work, he'd done it well, he said with an air of forlorn pride, because, when he first arrived, he had felt reasonably sure that he'd soon be able to get out word to me to join him, and once together he had felt certain we'd be able to deal with the situation as it had to be dealt with. But as the days went by and no opportunity came, he became more and more despondent. Somehow at all costs the plan had to be defeated, and if he failed in that he failed not only Serge, but something far greater than the fate of Serge. In vain he cast about for a way to get word out to me. But his orders forbade him even to show his face outside the basin and there was no one, literally no one, he could trust, except, in a measure, Kawabuzayo, who he knew shared his own uneasiness over what was happening. But Kawabuzayo, like himself, was a prisoner in this high basin. And though he couldn't understand it, no stranger, no shepherd even, had ever come wandering in summer over those silky grass slopes above the tree-line. I could have told him here that the area was all tabu, ''Mwatagati' by the supreme witch-doctor's command and spell, but I didn't like to interrupt the flow of his story and held my peace.

So desperate did John become that one day he thought of teaching his recruits some of the sabotage they had to learn by drilling holes in his ordnance and supply caves for mines and high explosives, and elaborately laying live charges in them, on the excuse that this was an elementary and accepted precaution in the general defence of a military base. That done, he felt happier, since if the worst came inevitably to the worst he could now blow the whole lot up rather than let them be used for the purposes for which they were intended. At that very moment he could take me to his caves, and, by lighting one fuse, send all those elaborate supplies of war hurtling for ever into the gorge below.

However, three months ago, something happened to give him hope. Word came mysteriously for Kawabuzayo. John saw, quite by chance, someone strange showing him something that looked like a feather, before whispering at length in his ear. What was it? John had no idea. All Kawabuzayo had said sadly afterwards was that he had to go down south to Van Riebeeck's Bay where he was to meet Ghinza and come back with him by ship to the Flamingo Water. As he said it, Kawabuzayo shook his massive head and exclaimed, 'I am not I,' which, as I knew better than John, was an ancient 'Takwena expression of acute dismay. He couldn't get more out of Kawa-

220

buzayo. Yet that one expression of distress encouraged him to extract a promise from Kawabuzayo that he'd try to go to me, secretly, and direct me up here. He couldn't trust his information to a letter, for if such a letter was found on Kawabuzayo, that would be the end of both him and John and all chances of frustrating the conspiracy. All he could do was to ask Kawabuzayo to give me a verbal message, in the full assurance that I, too, was one of the right side.

To his amazement Kawabuzayo's hesitation had vanished the moment he heard my name. He said he knew of me, had once seen me as a boy, and he even called me 'Son of the white chief without a country of his own' which is what all the 'Takwena who knew me called me as a child. At the first sound on John's lips of a name I'd not heard for years, all the good in the great African past seemed to walk like a friend out of the darkness to sit beside us in legitimate place by our fire. Instinctively I turned to look at Tickie, his face swollen with heavy sleep. John caught my glance. I said, 'Yes, I know. Thousands of young chaps like that with this menace hanging over them. We've got to stop it – and we've no time to lose.'

So John hastened to say that all he'd had to do then was to write my name and address on an envelope in case Kawabuzayo forgot it. If the envelope was found, all he feared was unpleasantness for me out of the discovery, but it was a risk he had to take.

That now brought him to the morning of this very day. Until then his hope that Kawabuzayo had found me and that I was on my way, remained undimmed. But since morning he'd had the blackest time yet. Ghinza had arrived early, more arrogant than ever, with orders for John. He was to finish training within a month, and be prepared at the end of that period, by 26 September to be precise, to equip on a full fighting scale the army he'd trained. How serious it all was I could gather from the fact that already seven senior officers of the light infantry horse had ridden into camp for their orders that very evening. Once mobilization was truly launched, he was to hand over command to Ghinza and return to the Flamingo Water, where a ship, the last apparently, would call for him on 26 October. Before sailing, he was to see that the whole of the base at the Flamingo Water was utterly destroyed, and it was suggested by his superiors that setting fire to the whole dense bush would be the most natural way, and the one least likely to attract outside attention. Since he was expressly commanded not to disclose this most secret part of his orders to Ghinza or the others, he realized his masters were sending the 'Takwena into it all even more cynically than he'd imagined, with a promise of support they'd no intention of giving.

Bad, however, as all that was, it was not the worst. He was receiving a shipment – and the first had come in that morning – of thousands of glittering cigarette-lighters such as sophisticated Africans can afford and love buying. Yes, John assured me sombrely, it was a deadly fact that cigarette-lighters were arriving already filled, not with benzine, but with Russia's latest organic poison. This poison, according to the instruction which he was ordered to translate into good simple 'Takwena, was odourless, colourless, and tasteless, but one drop of it placed in liquid of any kind was enough to kill the drinker in five days, leaving no appearance of poisoning, but rather of a strange new plague in the blood. As fast as these new cigarette-lighters came in he was ordered to produce bearers for Ghinza to send them to their proper destinations whenever told to do so. What that destination was, he had no idea.

For a moment after he'd told me this, John paused as if the horror of the thought made it impossible for him to continue, then he turned to me rather desperately and said surely he needn't remind me what drinkers of teas, coffees, and other liquids all Europeans in southern Africa were – and all prepared and served by black hands. The opportunities for such a novel weapon in the sacred cause of the final disintegration of the white world in Africa were immense. In fact, he'd no doubt we'd find that the general administration of poison in the ample European teacup was timed perfectly to precede the invasion, of the native armed forces. Unless he and I could prevent it, history might have its most compelling illustration there in Africa of the foolhardiness of the overlord trusting all that is dear to him to the care of subjects whose inner dignty he constantly flouts and whose needs of special being he daily rejects. ... Yes, on Ghinza's instructions, the first bearers with loads of deadly lighters were already selected and standing by to move off whenever the word came from the arrogant fellow who'd left soon after mid-day for the west without disclosing his destination, but merely saying to John over his shoulder that he'd soon be back to relieve him of his command.

'Did you ask him about Kawabuzayo?' I wondered.

No, he hadn't, for he'd felt, in view of the history of the case, it was better to appear to have forgotten Kawabuzayo. Therefore, as Ghinza hadn't mentioned him he himself had kept silent. But all day long he'd been thinking both of him and of me. I, in particular, had been very close to him with a nearness for which even his desperation could not entirely account.

He checked himself and then asked what did I think of it all, and what were we to do? Whatever it was, it had to be lightning quick, for we had twenty-eight days at the most wherein to do it.

I gave John a quick summary of my story from the death of Kawabuzayo in my kitchen and the first coming of the feather into my life. Above all, I stressed repeatedly my conviction that the 'Takwena were not yet committed fatally to this plot cooked in a foreign pot; not yet 'won over' as he'd put it a moment before. Ghinza and his buddies might be; the Umbombulimo we knew was; and there might be others, even more powerful. But they were not the whole nation. What of all the peoples stealing through the African bush from far and wide for news of a new great dream, whom Oom Pieter had seen on that ancient track by the ford where the three frontiers meet? And what of the King? Had John forgotten the King, a not unworthy successor to a great father who'd stood by and helped us generously in the war? I couldn't imagine him being automatically on Ghinza's side. No, the King and all his complex and contradictory people could be united for revolution only if they were all convinced it was at the dictates of the dream promised them by 'Nkulixowe. With the lesson of the disaster caused by a false dream only a century ago they'd not be enticed into another desperate course by anything but the real thing. Those experienced, wise old Royal Indunas, with the thick round rings of honour on their grey heads, would test the metal of this dream for purity, as no suspect gold coin has ever been rung for counterfeit by a miser's hand. And the one thing we knew for certain was that there was some way of checking the interpretation of the dream's authenticity. We knew for a certainty that the great King before he died had seen to that. How it was to be done we didn't know yet, but Kawabuzayo had known and so did Ghinza. If they knew there must be others who knew, for it was inconceivable to me that the great King in a world full of accident and disaster would have entrusted so vital a knowledge only to two mortal men. No, he must have made certain that it was known by enough trusted persons to ensure continuity for this all-important safety device in the social and spiritual machinery of the Umangoni. I felt sure that when I met Oom Pieter again he would tell me of others who knew the secret that had died locked in Kawabuzayo's heart. For I was sure that that was the one reason why Ghinza had killed him: Kawabuzayo had refused to give Ghinza his knowledge out of fear that Ghinza would tell Harkov, who would then go and tell the Umbombulimo how to dress up the spurious dream in full stolen authenticity in order to pass the test to which it would be put on the day of announcement to the people. I saw hope for us in that. Ghinza had failed with Kawabuzayo and had arrived on the scene perhaps too late to discover a substitute for him. These ancient tabus in the minds of the 'Takwena went deep and were not to be uprooted merely for Ghinza's arrogant asking. If I were not mistaken, too, there'd be more men going the way of Kawabuzayo before the dream was unravelled, for Ghinza I suspected would kill other loyal custodians of the knowledge he hadn't got and invent a second plausible check of his own, rather than run the risk of having the dream exposed by them on the great day. We had some slight advantage over him there, since Oom Pieter had already been on the track of the dream for weeks. I was sure that what I had to do now was to set off at once as fast as I could to find Oom Pieter.

I think when I first began to talk to John of the rôle of dreams in 'Takwena life he'd listened with a certain scepticism. I couldn't help suspecting it from the way he took out his pipe and played with it between his fingers without ever lighting it. I didn't blame him, for I knew I was talking of something as much out of the range of his experience as his life at Tashkent was beyond mine. Nonetheless, I was relieved to see that the closely-reasoned case I put to him soon carried conviction. He didn't interrupt once until I came to this point, when he exclaimed: 'Extraordinary – but, of course, I accept implicitly what you tell me. But has it ever occurred to you that perhaps this dream you and I fear may have been a genuine dream. What then?'

I told him it had occurred to me, but I'd dismissed the possibility at once for two reasons. Firstly, we had overwhelming evidence of outside complicity and instigation in this matter; secondly, 'Nkulixowe, loving both his country and his people as he did, could never have inspired a dream such as we suspected this one to be. Still, even supposing the worst and that the dream was genuine, or again even supposing the dream was not genuine but we couldn't find anybody to expose it – then there'd still be time to send Oom Pieter out fast to warn Umangoni's neighbours, while I hastened back here to help John blow up his caves. I concluded that I had only one immediate major worry, and then I told him of the smoke, that long arm of warning smoke informing the river patrols of our presence.

'I'll take care of that, old fellow,' he promised, adding that none of the river patrols were allowed to go by without reporting to him first. But it was wise to have warned him, since he had no doubt that the smoke signals would have set the always alert and nervous river camps swarming like anxious bees.

At that he came quickly to his feet like a man about to go into action, that timeless look of coming battle in his eyes, a look which belongs not to the individual, but is a dispensation of ancient gods. I stood up with him. He took a swift look at the watch on his arm and the light of our fire made it a signet of gold, a badge of Hermes fastened to his wrist. I remember it was one o'clock in the morning of 29 August, and then I heard him say slowly as we looked at the fire: 'Yes, dear boy, I believe you're right. Go after Oom Pieter as fast as you can and please give him my love. I'll hold the fort as before – and expect to see you here with news good or bad, sometime between now and 26 September. No, you're not to walk one step with me, it's late enough as it is. ... Goodbye, and God bless you.'

He made no effort to shake hands. All that was necessary was in the tone of his voice and the look on his face. He just turned about with that easy, elegant nonchalance of his that

I'd always envied and walked away out from among my red-wood princes and on to the moon-white head of the valley like someone going home and not to a place where at any moment he might be asked to keep his final appointment with his fate.

'Here, you two,' I said, shaking Tickie and Said perhaps more roughly than I intended: 'Wake up! Come on! Wake up!'

Tickie sat up, vaguely looking about for John, and said sleepily, 'What a pity the Bwana has gone, I wanted to ask him to lend us some sugar.'

'And I for some salt,' remarked my practical old murderer, yawning and stretching himself, 'for of that, too, we have none.'

'Never mind,' I told them from the surface of my mind, thinking underneath, only twenty-eight days to go, only twenty-eight precious days, only from moon to moon, wherein to prevent the salt of the earth from losing its savour. 'Never mind! . . . Salt or sugar: we've five hours' walking to do before daylight and with all the extra sleep you've had I count on you two to walk fast.'

I gave one look at the high redwood heads above us, and the surf of moonlight foaming and hissing among the leaves. I remembered how the bright shining moon-face had looked down upon us in the grass, and took heart from it. Down in the main valley a lion roared, a royal roar. 'All right, Your Majesty,' my heart called out to him. 'We're coming.' And with that I kicked out the fire.

Chapter 16

Oom Pieter Fights the Good Fight

At five o'clock on the afternoon of 31 August 1948, we rode into the capital on horses I'd hired from friendly farmers in the fertile valleys on the western side of the Mountains of the Night, where there had been as yet no need for 'Mwatagati. I say 'friendly' but I must be careful not to give the impression that they were also cheerful, for the first thing that struck me, as I travelled towards the capital openly in the guise of a hunter back from his hunting in the depths of the interior, was how the country appeared to have changed since I'd last seen it. The change was difficult to define yet it was real, and everywhere there was something different in the way the people looked, greeted and talked to me. The whole of Umangoni seemed to have a black thinking-cap on its mind, a sombre cover, an intense inner preoccupation which it could share with no one except other 'Takwena. Secrecy in one is enough to blur the amber of truth for two, but what a blurring of light when more than a million people have gone secret and started moving secretly to a secret fulfilment.

I believe that for the 'Takwena getting up from where he was resting in the saffron sun to raise his hand high above his head in the Roman salute of the greeting of his people, the peasant resting on the arms of his wooden plough behind his great gentle purple-eyed black oxen, the warrior, well-rubbed-in with lion fat trotting past us impatient for his courting, or the women in single file like figures on a Greek vase crossing a yellow evening skyline with urns of water on their heads, I believe it was enough for them merely to see a red stranger to start thinking automatically, 'there goes one who does not know, and who must never know'.

The irony of it was, of course, that I did know, and this, somehow, opened up another dimension for the secrecy automatically stirring in the hearts of those who saw me. I'd no doubt it was that restriction in the natural movement of their warm uninhibited hearts, that tabu on their spontaneous natures which were daily moving with acceleration into the awesome presence of another imperial dream, which created this dark electricity trembling on the air, belying the light of spring welling up over the Mountains of the Night. When I spoke to these people, of course, they greeted me gravely with all the natural dignity and courtesy which is theirs, and bargained with me over the hire of a string of horses as shrewdly and patiently as ever. But the innocence, the appetite, the lusty, wholesome spontaneous zest for things seemed, for the moment, to have abandoned them. I had to wait until noon of my first day in the open to hear a laugh. Two years ago, I couldn't have gone a mile without laughter bubbling up from somewhere around me. When evening came, and the darkness rolled down the valleys over the round beehive huts, the sense of something missing was heavy within me. Hours later when I heard singing round a fire which grew, like a scarlet tulip on the black hump of the rich land, I realized that two years ago every one of those flowers of fire on the slopes around us would have been surrounded with natural minstrels, voices shining in a glitter of song.

After that, as we rode on half-asleep in our saddles, there was no sound except that which is the heart-beat of the Umangoni night: a calf calling uneasily for its mother, a ewe waking suddenly to bleat with unnecessary panic for its lamb, jackals yapping sadly, dogs on a hill quelling a hyena's laughter with an outburst of barking, and sometimes far away, a lion roaring or a faint drumming of hoofs of stampeding mountain zebra, while over all lay an incense of wood-smoke burning in the fires of a thousand kraals, entrances fastened securely with ipi-hamba* thorn against the dark. The whole land about me, indeed, was calm before the storm.

All the way to the capital, along the bright-red bridle tracks winding through the long fertile valleys, the feeling accompanied me, right up to the hill where the British Mission stood. There, for a moment, the feeling left me so suddenly that my mind felt like a spectator without a ticket tumbled out of a

* 'Where are you going' thorn.

Grand Guignol Theatre before the climax into some neat suburban street.

In among the tall blue gum trees, among scarlet poinsettia bushes, pink and purple bougainvillea, behind neat square lawns, a touch of the brown of winter in their green spread out carefully before ample verandahs with purple cummerbunds of shadow wrapped tightly about spreading middles, rose the flashing white walls and shining quicksilver rooftops of a score or so of official houses. They were all designed by the same neat office-of-works mind, adequately to fit their function, and completely lacked grace or character. Moreover, in that setting of high, barbaric hills and thatched huts and kraals, the dutiful faces of these official houses could not restrain an expression of polite surprise at finding themselves in so untoward a situation.

We rode through the gate, and down the middle of the road dividing the houses and gardens in this small English island, between gum trees dripping with evening light and flashing white-washed stones on the sides of open gullies. The houses were silent. The blood-red road was empty except for five ridge-back puppies briskly skirmishing and two 'Takwena nurses in blue calico dresses and white aprons walking slowly with effortless patience behind their perambulators. Two little chalk-white faces sent their startled colour up at us like ghost moths out of the dark of their prams as we rode by. Then away on the right, almost as high as the feathers of tall evening smoke, we saw a fiery Union Jack bowed over the day like a plumed sentry beside a royal bier, and below it the gleaming crest of the Mission's offices. In an instant a vivid memory of Umtumwa somewhere in a golden glow of the untroubled past returned to me: Umtumwa pointing at that very flag and saying simply: 'You know, Bwana, that is the only flag I know.'

Unfortunately, the Mission offices were already shut on the business of the day. Only a serious Basuto radio-telegraphist and a bespectacled Nyasa clerk were there on night-duty. Both were new to me, and that, I reflected, was much of the trouble with Africa since the war. Before, people in the administration stayed happily a lifetime in one country. Officials knew their districts, their people and their tangled needs, like the palms of their own hands. But nowadays the restless authorities seemed to be unable to change their staffs fast enough for their uneasy liking. For instance, the head of the Mission himself, so I'd heard, had only recently come from Gambia, and I asked myself with bitter rhetoric, would he have any idea of the change in the atmosphere in Umangoni?

'Where,' I asked the bespectacled clerk in English since I unfortunately knew no Chin-yanja, 'would I most likely be able to find the head of the Mission?'

'At his residence, sir,' he told me in excellent pedantic English, 'His Honour is having an entertainment of games of tennis at his residence.'

Staying long enough to give Said and Tickie a note to the Mission storekeeper, I went in search of the entertainment of games of tennis.

Even if I'd not known the Residency from its size, I'd have known it from the noise which came from it, the sound of tennis balls being well hit and smartly returned. Dismounting at an iron gate with a pepper-tree bowed over it, I walked quickly towards the distant noise.

'Oh, good shot,' one player was crying.

'Absolute fluke,' came the modest answer. 'Couldn't do it again if I tried.'

'Oh, well played, sir.'

'Jolly bad luck.'

'Best game we've had for years.'

Despite my admiration for the chivalry and love of proportion which lives in the games the English have created and play, I confess these voices made me rather impatient because of the sense of unreality and unrelatedness which they gave me. Impatiently I quickened my pace round the dense shrubbery of the garden, and there in an island of sunlight in a water of shadow, I came upon a 'Takwena nurse sitting, between me and the tennis, her back to a thick bougainvillea hedge, her white apron pulled down, dark eyes black with sudden fear. A child with a snow-white face, tears not yet dry on its cheek, eyes shut, little fist of putty tightly clenched, was tugging like a puppy at her full breast, a fabulous aubergine in the sun. Jerking her breast out of the child's mouth, she slipped it back into her clothes with the deftness of dismay which didn't surprise me, since I could well imagine how her white lady or master would have reacted to such a vision.

'How good of you, oh mother, to share the milk of your own child with one who is not,' I called out to her in Sindakwena. 'I see and praise you.'

A light of relief and sensitive pleasure went unbelievably warm in her face and at once a shy hand went back to her breast, while she mumbled a modest disclaimer of the praise too low for me to hear. Then I, too, joined the entertainment of tennis.

For a moment I thought I was not going to recognize any of the faces or figures among the people who, all cream and white, were grouped under a vast flamboyant tree, the first glow of its inner fire forming little coals of pink bud at the tips of its spreading branches. There were four women (one no doubt the mother of the child happy on illicit milk) and four men talking together with animation; two other men, their backs to the company and apart at a table glittering with cut-glass, seemed to be using the opportunity for a quick exchange of serious confidences.

Again the feeling of almost insane dissociation from the reality of Umangoni came over me. This, I told myself, was no brave camouflage, no Elizabethan company finishing a game of bowls before tackling the business of an Armada. This was a company simply unaware of the dark invasion striding down on them. Although I told myself that I wasn't being fair, that these people marooned far from the life into which they had been born were entitled to this kind of thing to help them do their lonely work in the upright and conscientious manner in which it is normally done, I resented it. In my mind I saw this same scene being enacted all over the vast continent of Africa. I saw the correct, lovable island British forming islands, not in single sparkling units but in hundreds. And, as I've said, I resented it; I resented it deeply, because of the manifest unawareness that the original island foundations were inadequate and needed widening if the resurgent tide of neglected, hurt and dishonoured African darkness was not to overwhelm them.

However, I didn't get very far with my resentment; for, as the sound of my step fell on the conversation of the players, they all stopped talking to turn and stare at me with the uninhibited concentration automatic in people for whom the sight of a stranger is a rare event. The two at the table also turned round, decanters in hands, one tall, slight, fair, oldish, the other dark, broad, and short with the figure of someone born and bred in the high mountains. This latter not only turned at me with wide-open mouth but after a gasp exclaimed: 'This is truly uncanny, sir. There he is, Pierre de Beauvilliers himself!'

With that, decanter still in hand, he came quickly to greet me say: 'I can't tell you how glad I am to see you again, mon cher Pierre, but where on earth have you been?' He hesitated, his warm Latin eyes looking me over keenly but unable to hide a sense of shock at my appearance. 'You look like someone who's seen a ghost, no, a lot of ghosts.' Again he hesitated before adding with concern: 'Obviously you need a drink, and you'll have one just as soon as you've been introduced.'

Aramis, to give him his school nickname, because he was one of a trio of friends always known to masters and boys as the 'Three Musketeers', turned impulsively to lead me to his host, but I restrained him. 'You can't be half as glad to see me as I to see you,' I said. 'But help me to get these formalities over as soon as possible, and then let's talk alone. I have been in an underworld as you so truly guessed – and I must return there almost at once.'

To my surprise he didn't answer my request but observed in dismay: 'What's happened to your voice, Pierre? It's gone!'

The concern in his eyes was so great that I broke into a laugh at myself, realizing I was still talking in the whispers of the Dead Land. So in my normal voice I answered, 'Sorry, it's a bad habit contracted in this world I've just come from, where whispering was always necessary. But quick, I see the others are beginning to move. Tell me, is Oom Pieter le Roux here? I was hoping to meet him here.'

His look told me he'd not failed to observe the note of urgent anxiety which compelled my question. 'No; but he was here ten days ago. His Honour has a letter in his office from him to you.' He then explained that he himself had only got back from a three weeks' tour in Southern Umangoni at noon that day, and so to his deep chagrin had missed the old hunter.

How I longed to make him turn about with me there and then and fetch the letter. But already I'd appeared rude enough. So all I could do was to reiterate, 'Try and get us away at once. This letter makes it all the more essential.'

He reassured me, but said it wouldn't be easy. His Honour was a stickler for precedence and formality, with an atavistic appetite for ritual and ceremonial. He would certainly not take kindly to any effort aimed at relieving him of so precious a windfall as a new face – particularly so distinguished a one. Nonetheless he'd try and might succeed, since fate had been generous with its visitors lately and I was, he understood, the third in ten days.

However, it took us a good hour of my grimly rationed time before we were able to leave. Even then, H.H.'s goodbye to me was charged with polite reproach at my reiterated decision not to spend the night at his house but with Aramis.

At last, however, there came the moment when Aramis put me in an easy chair by the fire in his bachelor home, gave me a glass of hot milk and rum, for I was shivering so much from cold, fatigue, and reaction that I could hardly speak, and said in a voice of warm concern: 'Drink it up, Pierre, while I go and see to your servants and fetch your precious letter.'

Slowly sipping my drink, I thought of Aramis and my incredible luck in running into him here. I'd known him since our schooldays. The youngest son of one of the most remarkable missionaries France has given to Southern Africa, he was born and bred a British subject in Umangoni. After school and college at the Cape, he joined the British Mission Extraordinary to Umangoni. He'd not served anywhere else until the war, and should have been head of the Mission long ago. However, because he hadn't been to an English University, I doubt whether he'd ever been considered for the post. The fact that he had qualified many times over in the university of Amangtakwena life counted apparently only enough to raise him to a chief secretaryship. There he had stuck until the war came to yank him out of his groove. I'd last heard of him serving in our Occupation Administration in North Africa and had no idea he was back.

At that moment Aramis came back into the room a letter in his hand, which I saw was marked *'Urgent. Personal. Strictly*

'Confidential', and addressed to me in Oom Pieter's open, steady hand.

As I took it Aramis remarked: 'For a letter so marked our gallant hunter has not sealed well. Look, the flap of the envelope appears quite loose.'

I edged my knife into the envelope sideways, and at once the flap flew open. 'Odd,' I replied, taking out the letter and giving him the envelope. 'Because once it was properly stuck down, as you can see from the fluff still sticking to the gum.'

'Odder still,' Aramis frowned, 'when one remembers that someone wanted H.H. to open that letter this very morning.' As I looked up quickly he added: 'But read your letter first, and I'll tell it you all soon enough.'

The letter was dated 21 August 1948 and written in characteristic Afrikaans; it read:

My dear Ouboet: I hope you are as well as I am and have found what you wanted in Mozambique. I am glad to tell you that the spoor I am following is daily getting hotter. At first it was faint and my heart went black for a while, but with God's help I found the right spoor at last. I fear in casting around like a dog for a lost scent I may have aroused the suspicions of some of the trading corporation's brethren who kept on coming to my camps at nightfall, asking and receiving hospitality. But I pray daily to God to help me not only with the gentleness of the dove, but also with the cunning of the serpent which the Book commands. With His help, I shall not fail. Only I would ask you to come to me as fast and as soon as you can. We have no time to lose. The day of the dream is set for sunrise on the morning of 16 September, at the People's usual place at Kwadiabosigo. I do not know yet what it is to be, but I leave tomorrow to go to the kraal of the oldest royal induna, the youngest and last surviving brother of the late King. He knows what we need to know. I have Mlangeni with me. I had to send for him because all my new 'Takwena servants have, no doubt at the instigation of the Brethren of whom I have spoken, suddenly become bewitched. Mlangeni says you have a beautiful Intombizan* living in your room at Petit France, and daily asks me how much cattle and money you paid her father for her. Pray for me as I pray for you, and though I beg you to put your trust in God, do not neglect to keep your guns bright and clean, and their action slightly oiled, for we shall, I fear, need them yet. I bid you farewell and God speed, Ouboet. Always, Your loving Oom Pieter.

* Sindakwena for a girl of standing.

234

For a moment I forgot about the open envelope, forgot about my anxieties and was filled with grateful emotion to that gallant, true old man. I could read between his faithful, reverent, joking lines and see weeks of frustration and toil with unwilling, superstitious bearers, and the ever-present danger of suspicious and unscrupulous agents discovering what he was really after. But he hadn't, I was certain, failed. Above all I was touched once more by the delicacy of his understanding of my own personal inner needs, which prompted him in the midst of so much anxiety to include that sentence of Mlangeni with that miniature of Joan safe at Petit France.

'I'll keep what's in here to myself for the moment,' I told Aramis, trying to pull myself together, 'but tell me what you meant about this letter.'

At the moment of my appearance at the tennis party, Aramis said, H.H. had been telling him about a visitor he'd received that morning. The old man had arrived at his office to find someone waiting for him, someone who in these remote mountain areas fell in the category of a 'V.I.P.' a Trans-Uhlalingasonki Trading Corporation representative called Harkov.

'Oh God!' I cried, my eyes staring with dismay at the open envelope still in Aramis's hand.

Aramis instantly read my look and hastened to say that Harkov, after paying his oily respects to H.H., asked specifically for news of Oom Pieter and me. He said he'd come all the way from the Cape with an urgent business proposition for the two of us. H.H. thereupon had replied quite naturally that my hunter uncle had indeed been there but had left for an unknown destination. As for me, H.H. went on, he'd really no idea where I might be, and doubted even if Oom Pieter knew, since he'd entrusted a letter addressed to me to H.H.'s care.

'A letter,' Harkov had exclaimed with an interest which even H.H. had thought tense. Then, Harkov had pressed, since his business with Oom Pieter was so very urgent and so much in Oom Pieter's own interest, and since Oom Pieter no doubt had left an address of sorts for me in the letter, would not His Honour perhaps feel justified in opening the letter and disclosing the knowledge of Oom Pieter's whereabouts?

But at the suggestion that the Head of His Britannic

Majesty's Mission Extraordinary to Umangoni should open a letter marked 'Personal and Strictly Confidential', entrusted to his care, on the request, as he saw it, of the first commercial traveller in an African truck that came along, the blood in His Honour's veins began to boil. Harkov saw at once that he'd made a bad mistake for his future relations with the Mission, so he quickly condemned out of his own mouth the request he'd just made, declaring that on second thoughts there was nothing to be done but wait until I turned up. He then asked with flattering, diffident deference whether, when that happened, H.H. would perhaps be good enough to tell me how anxious he, Harkov, was to see me. But it was odd, Aramis concluded, that only this morning, Harkov was asking for the letter to be opened and here it was this evening, opened.

'But aren't all important letters locked up in your office?' I asked him.

He shrugged his shoulders. Surely I knew as well as he that the 'Takwena were neither snoopers nor thieves. In all the years the Mission had been in Umangoni there'd been not one case of theft or burglary, and not one house was locked, year in year out. In the Mission Offices it was little better. True, they locked money and dispatches in safes against inquisitive clerks, but letters like this one were all frankly pigeon-holed in the open rack kept for the purpose in the public office of the Mission.

'Then that settles it, Harkov opened it,' I told him, 'and I fear I shan't be able to spend the night with you after all, but will have to leave at once after we've talked.'

'No, Pierre,' he protested vehemently, 'you're dead-beat. You need a fortnight's sleep. As for these servants of yours, you've nearly killed them. I tell you, my old brave, it will finish badly if you continue this way. In any case what the devil's it all about? Why does it matter if Harkov read that precious letter of your uncle's? And how can you be sure he did? If he wanted the letter why bother to put it back again? Why this insane haste?' He spoke with the rising emotion of an inexplicable anxiety and for a moment revived my original resentment.

Before I knew what I was saying I interrupted him impatiently, 'You're wrong to doubt either my conclusions or need for haste. I tell you that while you all sit sipping iced whiskies and sodas at tennis parties, the biggest disaster Africa has ever seen is bearing down on you. I can understand your correct ceremonious boss not knowing it. But you, surely, Aramis, of all people, must be aware of it!'

Instantly his expression changed and his eyes went bright with spirit as he said tensely: 'Of course, I know something is wrong, Pierre. But d'you realize that we're all so chained to our desks these days by the insensate paper work Whitehall sets us that it's difficult really to keep in touch with the African people? Besides, I was not doubting you so much as trying to protect you against yourself: there is not much more left to protect, my old!'

He then went straight on to say that of course he knew the 'climate' in Umangoni had changed. He'd known something terrible was going on from the moment he'd clapped eyes on me, for the look in my eyes had confirmed the feeling in his own blood and bones which had started from the moment he'd met Kawabuzayo on the road.

'Kawabuzayo! You saw him here? He told you something?' I exclaimed.

Yes, Aramis had seen him some months back and had noticed the general change of 'Takwena climate in Kawabuzayo's simple bearing. But Kawabuzayo had told him nothing. Though they were old friends, Kawabuzayo had refused to tarry and talk. He'd exchanged only a grave, polite, preoccupied greeting and then pressed on south with something of the same look on his face I had on mine. He, Aramis, had noticed other signs, too. For instance, that strange ebb and flow of men between the interior and the capital was something quite new to him. There was a general decline in laughter and song, too, and his tour increased his uneasiness. Then, when he'd returned that very day to learn that the King and all his indunas had left for the Summer Capital of the High Place in the Mountains two months earlier than usual, he was really rather alarmed. Now, of course, I'd thoroughly frightened him, so would I please be good enough to tell him what it was all about?

On a pledge of secrecy I told him of the plot, adding that the tribes would not be committed to it until 16 September and that the zero hour for the uprising could not come before

26 September at the earliest, and in view of the distance it would probably take several more days before the tidal wave of destruction reached the capital, and some weeks before it swept across the frontiers. But when it did come, it would be on a scale such as Africa had never seen. This was to be a revolution with a difference: involving poison for every white home, and a well-trained, well-equipped army with modern fire-arms following fast behind! Fifteen million Black incited to fall on what was left of a bare two million White. Again I couldn't go into the detail of it; the only thing to do was not to let it happen. And that would still be possible until the morning of 16 September. It was no good taking precautionary measures before then, for any such move would only precipitate the whole monstrous conspiracy. That was Harkov's share in it. Give him or his agents even an inkling of extraordinary activity and they were liable to set off the whole conspiracy at once for to them any trouble was better than no trouble. It was precisely because Harkov suspected that Oom Pieter and I were trying to prevent this dirty work that he wanted to do away with us as he had done away with the Kawabuzayo who died in my kitchen at Petit France. And that was why I had to go to Oom Pieter at once. Oom Pieter and I knew how the whole ghastly plot could be peacefully foiled by the 'Takwena themselves, without a drop of innocent blood being shed. And as long as that chance existed we had to take it. But I could say no more of that then. He, Aramis, had asked why, if Harkov took the letter, he put it back? Obviously so that I'd know where to go to join Oom Pieter and then Harkov could kill two dangerous birds with one stone. Already I was certain he and his agents were after Oom Pieter, and in a moment or two I'd have to be off to warn and protect my uncle. Meanwhile I begged him to speak of this to no one except H.H., so that the two of them, should I fail, could quietly make preparations to evacuate the Mission. I'd send word either way to him on 16 September. Supposing it took three days to reach him, it would still give them a week, till 26 September, wherein to evacuate the Mission. And how would they set about that? I asked.

Again Aramis shrugged his shoulders to ask what I expected of so colonial a step-country as Umangoni? There were no roads, so the only way was as of old: by horse for those who could ride and by litter for those who couldn't, up to the frontier; by jeep thereafter. I asked, what about aircraft? Another shrug, and a statement that though they'd pleaded for air communications many times, Whitehall still denied them those. As he spoke, I saw again our privately-chartered two-seater aeroplane sitting like a silver swallow on the edge of the aerodrome at Fort Herald on the day Oom Pieter and I flew in it. I suggested, therefore, that he telegraph Fort Herald to charter the light aircraft he needed for evacuation and to hold them there at his disposal from 19 September onwards. At this Aramis interrupted, saying H.H. would never agree to take so expensive a step on his own initiative without higher sanction; particularly, he added, since he doubted whether the cautious civil-service soul of H.H. would believe so melo-dramatic a story as mine, even with Aramis's backing. His Honour was terrified of ridicule or exaggeration and a story like mine, so outside his own ordered experience, would seem to him too far-fetched. Before he acted at all he'd most likely institute a ponderous and exacting inquiry – in fact, might even send his Chief Secretary hastening to the native provinces to ask the King – which, of course, would be disastrous.

In that case I told him to charter the aircraft at my expense, but I counted on him to see that H.H. did nothing to precipitate the conspiracy. If no word had reached him from me by 19 September, then he must assume the worst, and after that, the sooner the outside world was warned the better. And now, would he tell me who and where was Oom Pieter's Royal Induna?

Aramis answered without hesitation that it must be Kawabuzayo's father, now very old, but a fine and true 'Takwena country gentlemen, living three days away in the south-west.

With that I thanked him, and concluded I'd better get back on my horse. But as I stood up, the music of fatigue in my ears and the macabre dance of shadow before my eyes told me I just couldn't go on without rest.

Aramis, of course, spotted the look of physical defeat at once. Taking me gently by the arm, he said: 'There now, Pierre, my old brave; I'm glad you see the sense of it, too.

You've seven hours to dawn. Sleep them out with a clear conscience for I swear you've earned them a thousand times over. I'll call you myself at sunrise and with the best horses and saddles under you you'll soon make up the lost hours. You'll not regret it, I promise you!'

But he was wrong; to this day I regret it. To this day I cannot forgive my body for its failure. I can still see Aramis standing by the window of his guest-room drawing the curtains on my bright bridal-moon's swift decline, saying as he did so: 'You know, Pierre, after what you've told me, I wouldn't have been surprised to find the earth quaking, and the sky flashing with comets and shooting stars at one another. Yet it's an ordinary Umangoni night, if one can use the word ordinary for so perfect a thing, so sleep well, my old, sleep well.'

And whenever I think of Aramis thus, I feel an unfair reproach against him for aiding and abetting the rebellion of my physical being against a purpose that could not afford to wait.

Aramis was better even than his words. He worked throughout the night on our behalf with his own personal staff rounded up for the emergency, and when another great uplands dawn was leaping in flames along the crackling crests of the purple mountains, there we were sitting outside the Mission's offices, on fresh horses, with saddle-bags and spares charged with good Boer Commando rusks, biltong, sugar, salt, and coffee; and also armed with the latest intelligence.

A red-eyed Aramis, as grave now as I'd ever seen him, was telling me he had studied the matter closely in the night, and given it considerable thought.

Harkov, he'd ascertained, had left the capital at 2.30 p.m. the previous day with an armed escort of five, ostensibly on a tour of the outlying trading posts of his vast Corporation. Aramis declared the hour was significant because it coincided with the Mission's immemorial siesta and he could no longer doubt that the extraction of the fatal letter was made at Harkov's behest between twelve and three, when the Mission was at food or asleep. He then pointed out on a map the route Harkov had taken to the Royal Induna's kraal, but suggested, his finger tracing out another track for me, that this was the route we should take. It was more difficult because it followed a dark pass higher and steeper through the mountains, but in fine weather it was nearly half a day shorter than the other. Above all it had the incomparable advantage of having no trading posts along it; nor did it join any other track before reaching the kraal which was my destination.

Then he stood beside my horse, deftly rolled up the map and handed it to me, looking up to say, 'Pierre, *mon cher,* I've no words, but I salute you. I cannot believe that the good God who sent you will let you fail. Good-bye, good luck and *à bientôt mon brave.*'

We left him standing there by the Mission's standard, a quick catspaw of morning air flicking at the flag above us. At the corner I turned to encourage him with a wave of my hand, which I made as confident as I could. Then we were riding down the road, through the iron gate on the far side, and so out of the neat sleeping office-of-works enclosure, down the slope of the hill to the waters of the authentic stream of Africa which flowed round the feet of that unknowing British island. When I turned in my saddle for a last look at the Mission gleaming on the hill, the smoke, standing tip-toe on the chimney pots, suddenly collapsed and came tumbling down like the offering of Cain rejected by Heaven. After that I looked no more, but put my horse into its best long-distance canter and kept my eyes on our red-track leading up and out of the valley to where it skimmed the steep, pearly crest like a burning arrow whizzing at the blue of the morning.

We rode steadily until evening, and as we rode, I realized more and more the terrible justification of Aramis's warning to take care of ourselves. Until Aramis the night before had drawn my attention to our extreme physical exhaustion, I'd truly never given the matter a conscious thought. I'd travelled as someone obsessed by unconscious purpose and without that would have collapsed before now. But since he'd made me aware of it I was agonizingly conscious of the terrible weariness of my body, and I blamed Aramis bitterly for having put the idea into my head, as if the idea, and that alone, was responsible for my condition. But I had Tickie and Said riding with me now to remind me continually how desperately real our fatigue was. Soon I, who'd had hopes in the early morning of travelling by night as well, realized I'd be lucky if we could keep it up until dark. To this day I cannot remember the detail

241

of that journey between the capital and the friendly kraal where, after a good meal of goat's flesh and thick, sour milk forced down our throats in the twilight hour, we slept until dawn. Yet that night did us good. Though I was still so tired when I woke that I felt the fatigue like a sickness of the bowels, once on my horse and the cool, upland air sparkling like Moselle in a blue Venetian goblet at our lips, I realized the healing good the rest had done us. I realized it with a wonderful glow of gratitude and hoped Tickie and Said felt likewise. Yet Tickie, whose maturity was only just won, was the least benefited, and in the afternoon he again went that terrible grey from sheer weariness.

Once more we had to find a hospitable kraal at dusk, and while we ate I was told by generous, though grave and reserved, hosts that the kraal of Kawabuzayo's father was only six hours away. There and then I longed to set out and make it that very night, only the vision of my companions and the ebb-tide of blood from my head foaming in my ears instantly banished such presumption. So I stayed with my hosts by the fire only to ask for news of Oom Pieter and Harkov, giving them the names of Indabaxosikas* and Mompara,† by which the Africans knew them.

At once I had fresh evidence of how quick a service of intelligence the African has in the chain of lonely herds, travellers, hunters, the roadside hut-wives and washerwomen by the fords who naturally sing news to one another all day long from one valley to the other. Oom Pieter, they said, had done an odd thing: Suddenly before sunset, just when the food in the pots was ready and waiting to be eaten, he had left the kraal of Kawabuzayo's father with the Royal Induna and a man from Amantazuma. My hopes soared at the news for I thought at once that meant that Oom Pieter had heard of Harkov's coming and was not sitting still to wait to be overwhelmed by him in a narrow basin.

As for Mompara, the other, the Bull Frog, my black hosts told me, unable to spare a mischievous laugh and a sideways glance at me now they knew I shared the secret of their derisive name – as for him, he rode into the big trading post in the broad valley on the other side of the hills seven miles away

* He who speaks as he shoots.   † Bull frog.

when the sun was half-way down the sky. He, too, was doing a strange thing never done before. He was riding with seven armed men.

So he's collecting reinforcements from his trading posts as he goes, I thought grimly, as I thanked them and crawled into my blankets to sleep.

At twelve o'clock the following day on 3 September, we crossed a characteristic hump to draw up our horses in the shadows of the grey rock which fringed it, and to look down on the kraal and ample huts of the Royal Induna's hamlet. It looked natural and peaceful enough until Tickie called out: 'Look, Bwana! the cattle are still standing in their kraals. Listen how hoarse they call for food and water. What a lazy place! Eh'yo–Xabadathi.'

He was right. Through my glasses I saw the colourful herds packed tight in their stockades and in the centre of the settlement a dark cluster of men gathered under their Indaba tree.* They were all sitting on their haunches except one in the centre who was addressing them, while the women and children stood apart at the entrances of their huts anxiously watching their men.

'Tickie, give me your gun,' I told him. 'There's been trouble down there if I'm not mistaken. Ride down and find out what's happened, and if it's all right for us to join you, wave your blanket about your head. But quick – we'll keep you covered.'

So Tickie descended on the kraal as if he were a herald of kings, the vivid blanket Aramis had given him streaming out behind like the cloak of a red knight. Before he reached them, however, alarmed at this clatter of hoofs from above, the men under the tree scattered, ran into their huts and reappeared almost at once with their war-shields and spears, their points diamond in the sun. But when they saw after all it was only an unarmed horseman of their own kind riding towards them, they stuck their weapons into the ground and with arms folded leaned on their tough, oxhide shields and waited peacefully for Tickie to join them. Something's wrong, I thought, it's unlike the Amangtakwena to be so nervous.

I was not kept wondering long. Tickie was not many minutes in the centre of the crowd, swollen and swelling every minute

* Here it means: council tree.

with women, children, dogs, and puppies speeding towards it like dark iron filings drawn to a magnet, in fact he'd not even dismounted, when he'd learnt enough to undo his scarlet blanket and wave it energetically about his head.

I thought there was more than just a note of relief in the bright, deep voices that rose up from those anxious faces to greet me: 'Son of a chief without a country, we see you, aye, we see you.'

'Old fathers, mothers, and children, one and all, I see you and I greet you,' I called out warmly to them. 'I greet you, yet it troubles me to see you thus. What keeps you talking while your cattle stand hungry in the sun?'

Then they all started telling me at once, pouring out the facts inextricably mixed up with the emotions provoked in the simple hearts of the kraal.

It had been bad enough when the wise old Father of them all, and Indabaxosikas and that pleasant man from Amantazuma had left them suddenly the night before because of gossip shouted up at them from the other side of the valley. But it was not so bad as what had happened that morning, for at dawn when the girls began blowing new life in the misty coals of the fires and the boys and men went out to milk and tend their cattle, who should ride abruptly into their midst but Mompara and twelve armed men. Yes, twelve armed men, and a Mompara not friendly as when bargaining with them years before at a trading post, but angry and threatening, asking this, ordering that, one minute lashing out at a dog with his whip and the next threatening to shoot a mother if she could not stop her child from crying. Never had they seen such behaviour in any man, not even a red man. What had the son of a chief without a country to say about it? And the anger had all started just because their wise old Father and Indabaxosikas were not there; and because they could not tell Mompara where they had gone. But how could they tell what they themselves did not know? All they knew was that the three men had left suddenly without explanation and ridden out of the valley on that track which led to the sparse country and higher mountains – a dozen quivering fingers pointed it out to me. They were decent friendly people. What had they done to deserve such treatment? Who was Mompara to ride there into their midst without even waiting at the outer entrance of a kraal to be invited as I, and Indabaxosikas, and all men of breeding always did? Mompara gone, their ancient, primitive dignity bruised and dishonoured, their elders had gathered under the Indaba tree to consider sending a messenger, with a report of Mompara's behaviour, and a protest to the King in the capital of the High Place. What did I think of that?

I assured them at great length that never, never, never had I heard of such behaviour. But I begged them at the end of it not to let the matter trouble them any longer. I myself was looking for Mompara and for their wise old Father. I myself would take Mompara to the Head of the Mission of the King of their King over the water, and see that he was never again allowed to come back to Umangoni. I was grateful for the light of joy that went up in the attentive, listening faces of the women and children and the great shout of 'Agreed!' was one of the most rewarding sounds I've ever heard.

Well then, I said, would they please tell me, how long was it since Mompara left? How many horses did he have? Were they good horses? What was the track like? What sort of country lay ahead?

They promptly answered in corresponding order. As the sun rose; twenty-six horses, all fresh and good as my own if not better than my own and certainly better than those of the wise old Father, for his had fed on nothing but grass all winter. As for the track, it was a summer track that led to the high pastures vacated every winter and it wound in and out among the mountain tops right to the people's Meeting Place at Kwadiabosigo. Kwadiabosigo? I asked, beginning to see the light and anxious to be sure. Yes, they nodded their massive heads vigorously, Kwadiabosigo, seven if not eight days' journey away on horseback. Now would I not please stay and have some sour milk or beer of millet freshly made?

I thanked them, and said no, but promised to come back with their old Father to visit them. Just for the moment I was tempted to get half a dozen of the liveliest men to accompany me. However, I rejected the idea almost at once when I realized the time we'd lose by getting them organized. Already it was after one. Harkov was seven hours ahead of us. Moreover, he had no weeks of fatigue in his bones to retard him,

245

and as his progress from the capital clearly showed, he travelled fast by day as well as night when necessary. No, the sooner we turned our backs on the settlement, the better. Its cry of farewell travelled far with us up that track at the back of the dark brown kraals and mushroom huts, up and out of that select and secluded valley.

We rode on until dusk, my thought constantly repeating: 'Seven if not eight days to the place of the dream at Kwadiabosigo.' That would bring us to 11 September – to within five days of the dream itself. A safety margin of five days was depressingly small when dealing with so ruthless and cunning an enemy.

So five more days from dawn to dusk we rode over high country very like the roof of the Mountains of the Night. Here and there a lonely hunter or odd traveller crossed our path with news of Oom Pieter and Harkov. From what they told us we all appeared to be keeping our distance the one from the other. I wished, of course, that I'd been gaining on Harkov, and Oom Pieter increasing his lead on us both, but had to console myself with the fact that our course, anyway, was steadily bringing us nearer to Kwadiabosigo.

Then, on the morning of 8 September, when we were within three or four days at most from Kwadiabosigo, suddenly the even rhythm of our stubborn progress was broken. On top of an immense skyline just after sunrise as I carefully pulled up in shadow just below the crest to survey the immense view through my glasses, I saw two things. First, on my track was a 'Takwena in a red blanket about a mile ahead, dog-trotting towards us. Then far away on a minor track well down the slope, a group of men on horses were climbing out of the heavy shadows into the sun on a bearing which looked as if it'd bring them back on our track six or seven miles behind us. I watched them until they disappeared but they were too far away for me to tell who they were: all I could see was that there were nine of them in all and that they were hurrying. The number appeared to conform neither to Harkov's nor Oom Pieter's party. Yet the sight was so unusual that it made me uneasy.

By the time I'd watched them out of sight the man I'd seen trotting towards us was almost upon us. To my amazement, when I rode out of the shadow of the rock to greet him, he looked as if he were seeing the devil, and would have turned to run if it hadn't been too late. However, a few friendly sentences from Tickie and me soon calmed him enough for him to explain himself.

He was on a peaceful mission from one distant kraal to the other, he said, but there was no peace in these mountains, so he had decided to give up his mission and go home. For, would we believe it, the previous evening for one whole hour he had listened to men shooting at one another. He'd known it only this morning when, fully a mile from where he slept, he'd seen vultures busy near the track, and found, within a circle of only a few hundred paces, five dead men. And that was enough ... so if we would excuse him he wanted to be back in his own kraal, with his own people before dark ... No, none of the dead men were red, all were black, but please would I excuse him now. And off he went.

So, too, did we, and at the gallop, for my imagination had immediately turned the sight of those men on the track below us into a gloating, successful Harkov, his sinister mission concluded, returning with his followers. For the first time hope died in me and I was certain that when I came to search the ground black with vultures ahead, I would find not only the remains of Mlangeni, Kawabuzayo's father, and four of Harkov's minions, but also of Oom Pieter.

I was wrong. We found Mlangeni and four of Harkov's dead 'Takwena fellow-travellers. Of Oom Pieter and the Royal Induna there was no sign. Then at last I understood the meaning of what I had seen that morning. Oom Pieter, wise, good, old serpent, with his deadly gun had held Harkov there where the dead men lay until it was dark. Then in the night he'd doubled back like a hare, with the precious old man, Kawabuzayo's father. He was trying to throw Harkov off his spoor, and who was I, who knew his resourceful, experienced old heart so well, to doubt that he might have succeeded?

'Come, Tickie,' I said, taking the stricken boy gently away from the half-eaten body of his kinsman, realizing that now he was the only survivor of four of the best friends and servants a man could ever have had. 'Come, Said! We are turning back. I'll tell you why as we ride along. But use your eyes as

247

you have never used them before unless you want us also to feed ourselves to birds like these.'

'Auck, Bwana, Auck,' Tickie cried as he threw himself fiercely into his saddle: 'will this evil never end?'

For three more days we twisted and turned in and out, up and down these empty remote mountain pastures. Every morning we woke to find the spoor had changed direction. From that I knew Oom Pieter was going one way by day, and another by night, presumably determined that whatever happened, he was not going to be driven far away from Kwadiabosigo. Each day, as fearfully we searched the ash-blue morning distances, the neutral noon-day deeps, and many-splendoured evening views for clusters of vultures, we saw none, but only their hungry patrols suspended far above us. And the hopes I had of Oom Pieter's resourcefulness rose higher. I would, perhaps, have been utterly confident of his success against Harkov were it not for the fear of what this constant riding day and night must inevitably be doing to his strength. He was old. True, he'd lived a hard, clean life and was tough, but he was old and I knew from the state of my own body how great the strain on his must be. Moreover, he had that very, very old Induna with him who must be limp with feebleness after such unending and unprepared journeying. Oom Pieter must almost certainly be carrying him as a helpless passenger.

Then, on the morning of the fourth day, at 10 a.m. on 12 September, with only four more days to go till the day of the dream and Kwadiabosigo we met a hardy, burly hunter with news. Just after sunrise he had seen in the distance two men on horses, riding away to the north-east, and they looked, horses and men, like things moving in their sleep. Then, a while back, he was stopped by a red stranger and eight armed men, also on horses, who questioned him roughly and to whom he told what he had just told us. Auck, they were strange, wild men, for no sooner had he told them this than they set off riding fast without a thank you into the north-east. I fear his opinion of us could hardly have been any better, for when he told me this, I threw him a brief 'Thank you', and whirled about to set off in the same direction as fast as my horse could go.

We rode thus, north-east all morning, stopping only to change horses every hour. Said protested, warning me the horses would be worn out on the morrow. I told him I didn't care about tomorrow: today was the decisive day. Unless we joined forces with Oom Pieter before dark, it would be too late. So we rode our horses without mercy, and never was I more grateful to the British love of horses than on this day. For not only were these Mission mounts well chosen, but also they'd been well cared for. They responded superbly. The way they climbed towards the closing afternoon up a long steep valley, the foam sea-green around their bits, coats fiery with sweat, nodding their willing heads deeper and lower to help their weary hind-quarters up the steep slope, was moving evidence both of their tough uplands spirit and devoted training.

Then, as we approached the top of the valley I thought I heard the sound of shooting. I halted listening, my head on one side, my eyes on my horse's saffron ears. How still it was, the faint wind of evening stroking the tired head of the pass and the swish of our horses' tails fanning their steaming buttocks. There it was again! I even saw the sound tremble in my horse's delicate ears as they pricked quickly towards the noise.

'There it is,' I told my companions, speaking with the odd deliberation that comes when the need for haste threatens confusion to one's thinking: 'There it is! Now listen carefully. Check the action of your guns: push one in the barrel. Set your safety catches. We're going to ride fast up to the head of the valley. No, Said, don't interrupt – Mompara just now is too busy to bother about look-outs. ... Listen to that sound for yourself. In any case, it's a risk we must take; so ready – steady, go!'

It took us only ten minutes to reach the neck of the valley that led into the pass beyond, but need I stress how long they were for me? They were not ordinary minutes but the master moments themselves, kept in God's great bureau of standards where an infinity of minutes are measured not for speed, but for meaning. For barely had we set off when the sound of heavy indiscriminate shooting broke out again. Somewhere in the centre of it was the sharp, precise bark of Oom Pieter's mathematical Mauser. I knew it far too well to be mistaken. Every time a volley rang out, that purposeful, calculating shot of Oom Pieter's broke it up – and so deliberately that it made all the other shooting sound hysterical. He was alive!

I slipped fast from my horse, pulled the bridle over its glistening bowed head to leave it trailing on the gravel praying silently: 'Dear God, stand by him just long enough for me to join him, and I'll do the rest. Give me just ten minutes of Infinity and I'll not grudge you ten years of the little that is mine.'

Knowing our horses, Commando-wise would never budge with their bridles hanging thus, I turned my back on them without hesitation, left the track and scrambled up towards the head above the neck of the pass. Within three minutes I was crawling carefully over the edge into the long grass on top. Again how still it was, no unnatural sound about us, only a nostalgic air of evening trembling on the strings of lean gold winter grass. Carefully we crawled to the edge on the far side, and looked down on about half a mile of pass, curving with a still majestic slowness away into the north-east. The bottom of the pass was filled with thick blue-green bush and heavy shadow, but the tops of the flanks of the pass were a limpid yellow in the sinking sun. On our right, however, the south-western side was black with shadow and not a sound came from below us.

But if there were no sound, surely there would be some tell-tale movement? For a while I sought that, too, in vain, finding my eyes in the process instinctively returning over and over again to a large black shadow on our right about three hundred yards away. The shadow appeared to be made by a deep ledge under a vast overhanging rock about halfway up the slope. Obviously it had the maximum view both ways of the pass and judging by the boulders and bushes growing around would provide excellent cover and a wide field of fire. Moreover, situated with its back to the sinking sun whoever attacked it would have to attack it with the sun in their eyes. 'I wouldn't be surprised,' I thought, 'if that's where we'll find Oom Pieter.' But though I looked and looked, I saw no sign to confirm the thought. Indeed, I saw and heard so little that I became impatient, feeling if the enemy does not reveal his whereabouts of his own accord soon, I will have to force him to do so. Then a brief glint of something on top of the highest point on our side of the pass, a bare hundred and thirty paces away caught my eye. Quickly I trained my glasses on to it and there was a large white man crawling in between two rocks overlooking the ledge of which I've spoken. He vanished between them, leaving only his boots exposed but brief as that glimpse was I could not be mistaken.

It could only be Harkov. That I concluded not only from the shape and size of the man but also from the cunning of his position. It looked well down into whatever was underneath that overhanging rock. Somehow that explained all I'd heard: a series of fierce volleys to keep Oom Pieter busy below, while Harkov made his way to this well-chosen position on top. And he could only just have got there for a shot from that exalted height would have rung out above all others in our ears. No, he couldn't have been there long, and if I had any say he wouldn't remain there long. For clever as he'd been, he'd made one mistake. In his anxiety to settle this matter before another fall of darkness gave Oom Pieter one more chance to escape, it had not occurred to him to guard against anyone coming to Oom Pieter's help. So there he was, lying between his rocks on the edge of the crest, protected and covered from almost every point of the compass, but perfectly exposed to us; or, rather, would be in a moment or two. I had only to crawl a score or more paces to my left to look straight up the passage between the rocks. At once I dropped the glasses which had been focused on Harkov, and whispered to Tickie and Said: 'You two concentrate on the pass below. At the first sign of movement anywhere except on that ledge of shadow on our right, shoot as hard and fast as you can.'

Then as fast as I possibly could I crawled the short distance to an ideal position behind loose rock, where I could get a clear sight of Harkov with no grass between to deflect my shot – for I wasn't going to risk a miss. All that, I swear, amounted to no more than a minute. But it was a minute too long. I was still crawling into position on this bare patch, when another ragged, hysterical volley rang out below us to be broken up by Oom Pieter's calculus shot.

'Thank God! He's still alive!' I cried out involuntarily with grateful hope. But hard on that, the first shot, one single shot of alarming authority rang out from Harkov's position. Then Tickie and Said opened up. I was looking straight at the back of Harkov propped up on his elbows and could not, therefore, have seen the expression on his face, even if I had not been so far away, but the startled jerk upwards of his body at that sound of fire into his followers was unmistakable and good to see; good, too, because it made him an even better target. I pulled the trigger almost casually so easy was it all. He collapsed on to his face without a tremor. Then to make absolutely certain, I shot him again. The dust flew up from the coat on his back where the bullet found him, but the body lay still. Yet I believe I may well have shot him once more if Tickie had not called out to me, his eyes shining with the ancient light of triumph in battle, as he recharged his magazine: 'Oh, Bwana, this is better than shooting buck! Look how they run. Help us or some will get away.'

Below us, desperate in the panic caused by this totally unexpected attack in their rear, five black men had broken from cover, thrown their rifles away, and were bounding like deer over the boulders and the sparkling electric broom-bushes, running, jumping, sliding, no doubt to where their horses stood in the thick bush below. Somehow that sight saddened me beyond words. For me it was all over; no more was necessary. I ordered Tickie and Said curtly to desist. 'Mompara is dead; they'll never again harm a soul. Let them go.'

I hardly noticed the curious, astonished disappointment in their faces at the order, for I was wondering, my eyes on that dark ledge: Why doesn't he make a sign? Surely he must know now that his help is here?

Climbing on to a grey boulder, the last red ray of sun warm on me, I heard the sudden clatter of hoofs flying desperately up the pass. When the sound died quickly behind a purple curve of royal mountain earth, I shouted again and again a loud 'Hullo there! Oom Pieter, Hullo!' But no answer came.

'Said, fetch the horses up as fast as you can. Tickie, come with me,' I said, refusing to accept the worst, refusing to believe that the timing of chance and fate could be of so exacting a precision. 'I fear our Indabaxosikas must be wounded.'

252

But for all that, for all my prayers, for all our laborious yesterdays, I was wrong. When we arrived he was lying among the grey boulders on the edge of the ledge, his head down between his arms, hands still on the rifle pointing at the crest of burning ruby red opposite him, looking so natural that he might have been a sentry fallen asleep after days of effort. On his left lay his khaki hat with its snake-skin band and swift's feather; on his right, a yard away, in the shelter of another boulder was his bag of Magaliesberg tobacco, calabash-pipe and matches, all oddly expectant, as if waiting to be smoked at any minute.

I turned him gently over, half hoping even then that some slight feather of life might still stir in him. Then I could no longer hope. There was the hole on the top of his forehead where Harkov's bullet had found him when he raised himself into a firing position to deal with the men manoeuvring in the pass below. His Napoleon beard was trim and pointed as ever. The top of his head and the skin at the temples and halfway around the forehead were still the same startling white against the rest of his sun-blackened features, which had fascinated me right from the moment when Oom Pieter had first emerged from the rainbow mist and star-sounds of my vanished childhood to become distinct and individual by the light of one of my father's far safari fires.

Despite that dark hole in his head, his features were composed and at the mouth there was the merest, most subtle suggestion of a smile, as if in the moment of dying he might have heard our answering fire and was certain of our coming. I felt this last was more than a mere consoling fantasy when beside him I read, traced with his finger on the sandstone dust, 'Look well inside my hat.'

Behind the band of his hat, neatly folded and carefully tucked out of sight, I found this letter written in Afrikaans on some pages torn out of one of the elementary school exercise books Oom Pieter always used for his simple records and calculations on trek. It was dated Sunset, 11 September 1948 and read:

My dear Ouboet: If you ever read this it will mean I shall have gone to join your mother and father. I shall not grudge God my going. I have had a long life and I have tried to live it in a way

253

that makes me unafraid of meeting my Maker. Almost I could go gladly, because for years now I have felt a stranger in this new world growing in this beloved African earth of ours. Yes, gladly, did it not mean that I would not see you again, and could never explain that if I failed you and the good fight it was through no fault of my own. Oh, Ouboet, my spirit is willing but my flesh is weak. I am tired; dead, dead tired. Mlangeni is dead: died four nights ago when Mompara and twelve others surrounded us and charged my camp just before sundown. He will never do it again, we taught him such a lesson. But he is still after me. I have travelled one way by day, struck obvious camp at nightfall, and after dark upped camp and away in another direction. Only to find at the end of the next day that Mompara was again close behind on our spoor; and I can't last much longer. This old Induna can hardly stay on his horse any longer. Our horses are beat. We have only three left; Mompara shot as much at them as at us. So I have decided that tomorrow I shall put the old Induna on the main track to the place of which you know. I still feel in my bones you will come in time to catch up with him, if not me; but if you do not, he knows what to do. He will do his best on the day if he gets there in time. That's the devil of it, Ouboet; without someone to help him, he may be too feeble to get there in time. But it is the only thing left. I myself shall lay a false scent for Mompara and lead him away from the Induna. I hope that it will be too late when he discovers the trick. Please do not think I write this because I despair. I write it only because I fear I shall not have the strength or time to write for many days. I put my trust in God and His Will must be done. If it is His Will that I am to go, I promise you I shall be pleading with Him in person to make it His Will that you do not fail. I go now to pray that, if I am too busy to remember Him in the hours to come, the Almighty will nonetheless not forget me. Totsiens Ouboet: your loving Oom Pieter. P.S. Read Revelation, 21 to 22.

That very evening I read the chapters from his favourite Revelation in his own Bible. I read them sitting beside our the mountain tops and in the sky above us one by one the night sounds and the abiding patterns of darkness and light, the baboons whimpering in their sleep among the kranses, the plover calling to the homeless wind humming to itself in the electric broom-bushes, proclaimed that that universe was carrying on business as usual – part of that business now being to maintain and repair forever that greatcoat of the earth of all

254

Africa which Oom Pieter had put on that day against time's bitterest changes. This place where Oom Pieter wears it is marked on the latest maps as 'Le Roux's Post'. However, for the 'Takwena it is, and I expect will always be: 'The place where he who spoke as he shot, speaks and shoots no more.'

Chapter 17

The Day at Featherfall

Though it was cold and dark and only five in the morning, we were already all four of us awake and eating hot porridge beside the fire. Two days before we had caught up with the royal Induna hanging on, exhausted, to the neck of his horse, but thanks to a short cut known only to him we had camped the evening before, at sunset on 15 September, under suitable cover within sight and earshot of our final destination. I didn't feel at all like food. I hadn't slept much, but had sat up late writing essential letters to Joan, to John, to Bill, and to Aramis. I was not despairing, but I had to face the fact; the odds against my surviving the day which lay in front of me were considerable. What I wrote in the circumstances can readily be imagined and needs no detailed recapitulation from me. I would like to mention only specifically these things contained in my letter to Aramis:

1. A request to see that both Tickie and Said were sent to hospital as soon as possible for observation and, if necessary, for treatment against sleeping-sickness.

2. A command to fly one of the aircraft chartered at Fort Herald with my letter to John at his depot in the basin above Redwood Princes. I said that with Harkov dead, the pilot could pose without fear of detection as a carrier of urgent dispatches from Lindelbaum. He could land on the landing-strip of which John had spoken to me with such a strange pride, wait just long enough for him to set the time fuses for blowing up his caves, and then fly him out to safety.

3. What lawyers would call my last Will and Testament, witnessed by Said in a hesitant Arabic scrawl and Tickie with a black thumb mark against a bold cross. Apart from an ample legacy to Said, a generous one to Tickie and provision for the families of my murdered servants, I left Petit France and all I had possessed, outwardly so richly, inwardly so poorly, to Joan.

That done, I had tried to sleep like the others, but the bee-sound, the swarming urgent droning noise rising up to the twitching stars from the massed Amangtakwena Clans gathered on the other side of the neck below which we slept, kept me perturbed and restless. As a result of it all I ate now as a duty, just as I'd eaten and made my men eat before going into action in the war. Tickie and Said, I suspected, felt about it much as I did, but Kawabuzayo's father, the Royal Induna, 'Nkulixowe's only surviving brother, ate with the slow, controlled relish of a wise, experienced old soul long since lifted out of reach of such ignoble fevers as excitement and unrest.

His dark eyes so dim with age that they were almost purple, a red and black woollen blanket about him, and the thick metal ring of his office in that bright firelight like the halo of an Apostle around his head, he slowly dipped his long fingers without a tremor into our common dish of dry mealie porridge. Once more I marvelled, as I had ever since we caught up with him, at this immense calm dignity which did not sit upon him so much as rise in a steady glow from within, to shine naturally in the measured tone of his speech, the expression on his face, his general bearing, and the movement of his hands from fingertips to curiously unblack palms. It had impressed me from the start and at once made me realize how well Oom Pieter had chosen. The feeling of respect had steadily grown as we rode together towards Kwadiabosigo.* No Roman stoic could have borne that terrible journey, enough to unman someone half his years, nor endured discussion of the death of Kawabuzayo, his only son by his favourite wife, as he did. When I gave him my detailed account of Lindelbaum's, Ghinza's and the Umbombulimo's Tashkent-aided plot he reacted as a great patrician might have done when told of a conspiracy against his imperial city. Oom Pieter had already told him enough to convince him it was his duty to go to Kwadiabosigo to see that the Dream was properly and not falsely presented. What I told him turned duty into a crusade. Not for a moment did I doubt his will for the task which lay only an hour and a half ahead; it was his capacity that I feared.

First there was this humiliating question of physical strength.

* *Kwadiabosigo* – spear of morning, the sacred mountain of the Amangtakwena.

After taking his short cut we had helped him from his horse, on whose neck he lay, made him as comfortable as possible, and after a hot meal made him sleep for nine hours. It had done him good. But as he confessed to me now with a shake of his head and a smile of self-reproach he doubted whether he could go on unaided. Then there was the matter of the protection which I felt convinced he would need. I knew Ghinza only had to set eyes on the father of the man he'd murdered for his vital knowledge of the Dream cipher first to become suspicious, and then to take drastic steps to silence him. Thirdly, there was an even more subtle and a deadlier possibility. Much as I respected this wise old country gentleman of nature, was it fair to expect him, alone and unaided, to remain an individual firmly maintaining an individual purpose, when all around him were fifty thousand of his countrymen, united and darkly harmonious in the undifferentiated mass of a mindless, timeless indentity with their barbaric past? After the war I knew only too well how easily civilized people are sucked down in a maelstrom of their own blood into this netherworld, this common underworld of man's despised and rejected self. And I knew that the 'Takwena and their like show a greater susceptibility to the common disease than we. To start with they are closer to it in time than we, and when the call starts its hypnotic drumming in their blood the individual is all the more easily forced to sink his identity and compelled, as a corpuscle, to conform to this tide in the collective blood. Even if our old Induna got there unhindered by Ghinza, I couldn't be certain that wise, enlightened and ready to crusade as he was, he'd be able to keep his head and not become hypnotized like the rest. Perhaps my fears now sound fanciful, yet the wild sound going up around us as we ate with an effort by our fire in the dark on that morning of 16 September made them very real.

All night long this music of mass excitement of tribal hypnotism, and heard magnetism, had throbbed in the air around us like a far-off beating of war drums mobilizing the black nations from the stormy Outeniquas and Maluttis to Ruwenzori and the Great Lakes. It rose from beyond the head of the pass not half a mile from us on the other side of the slender neck, its outline precise even in that darkness because of the grand tiara of stars sparkling on the head above it. At times it flamed into fiery, abandoned singing or died down into a glowering, watchful hush. But mostly it was a deep, persistent, excited, busy droning as if all the black honey-bees of Africa were swarming. I am certain that of the fifty thousand Amangtakwena and the carefully selected representatives of their affiliated and related tribes not one slept. All night long they sat beside their fires, talking, singing, and feeling only one stinging emotion, provoked by the first great national Dream for a century, already in being, and about to be delivered.

Listening to this hypnotic sound and pondering the considerations mentioned, I knew I could not let our wise old Father go alone into that excited swarm of beings to which, after all, he belonged. For the same reason I could not let Tickie go. Once Tickie and our wise old Father were face to face with the Umbombulimo, considering their implicit belief in his powers and unbounded respect for his exalted position, how could they be relied on to maintain a separate identity if he willed it otherwise? What certainty could there be that Tickie or my royal Father would be able to stand firm against what was the equivalent of an Old Testament High Priest? I knew that even at this very moment, as he sat solemnly uneasy by the fire, Tickie was experiencing an excitement and enduring a pull of magnetism he couldn't understand, but which, nonetheless, was urging him to go over the neck and join the rest of his people. Young, susceptible and impressionable as Tickie was, I was convinced that, if I sent him with the old man, he would, in a most terrible sense of the phrase, 'melt into the crowd'. Afterwards he'd never come out of it again the same bright crystal, but would be reassembled in a pattern with a flaw, a crack made by hatred of his deed of betrayal, and of me for puting him in the way of betrayal. Indeed, so concerned was I about Tickie on this morning that I determined to leave him tending the horses, with orders not to come one pace nearer Kwadiabosigo.

So there remained only Said or me, and Said was obviously no alternative. Clearly it had to be me. Only I could give some protection to the Induna. Only I could hope to hold out against fifty thousand passionate, willing hypnotists and help him to do likewise. Should my old Induna fail, only I had the knowledge and command of language to try and talk them all out of believing the false Dream. But would I be allowed to? Perhaps, nodded my old Induna, if he vouched for me, for was he not the King's uncle, and was I not known to them all of old?

I am afraid I didn't share even his modest confidence. On a day such as this the Amangtakwena would not have a mind free to recognize surface contacts with a white man. On the contrary they could know only a past long before the white man came to trouble them. In such a moment and such a mood they would tend fiercely to reject, probably to destroy, anyone or anything which jarred the harmony of their archaic uniformity. And what could do this more dramatically and provocatively than the white face of one white man among fifty thousand black?

No, I had no illusion as to the danger I was running and I was not open to easy reassurances. I could only put my trust blindly in the truth of the purpose which had brought me there. Somehow I felt that if I became as deeply identified with that purpose as the fifty thousand were in the anticipation of the Dream, if I allowed no thought of fear or disaster to come between it and me, my white face might be the slight chemical ingredient designed to prevent the coagulation and precipitation of that dangerous inter-racial solution preparing in the deep bowl there on the other side of the neck below the rim of Kwadiabosigo. If I could stand fast, I believed, the truth somehow might get through. If I truly had no accident and disaster within, neither perhaps could attack me from without. Yet it was easier said than done. As I stood up, one of Tickie's blankets about me, in order to go over these orders with my companions, I suddenly felt sick in my stomach, and my knees weak under me.

'Now let's get this clear,' I said firmly to Tickie and Said. 'In twenty minutes the Old Father and I are going to ride out on to the meeting-place of all the people. You, Said, will accompany us to the top of the neck. There you will put yourself and your horse in cover among the big boulders. You will take my glasses and through them watch the meeting, never taking your eyes for one minute off me and this old Father. I do not expect anything to go wrong, but if it does, if you see us killed or captured you must not hesitate to jump on your horse, ride back here, collect Tickie, and hasten back to the Mission in the capital where you will go straight to the Chief Secretary with the letters I'll give you presently. He will reward you and send you back to your home as a man who has honourably rehabilitated his character. You, Tickie, will take all our spare horses down to the ford. I noticed last night there's a deep clear pool with a long reach of fine white sand. I want you to swim, and bathe the horses in that pool, and let them roll in the sand to their heart's content. It will refresh them – and small a thing as it is, it may make the difference between life and death today. You need not be afraid that anyone will come to interfere with you there. Not until the meeting is over will you see any faces except our own around here. That done, you will load and resaddle the horses leaving their bridles off so that, loaded though they be, you can put them to the best grazing hereabouts. I want you to be careful to choose a place where you can keep your eyes on Said's position on the crest. The moment he moves towards you, you must slip the bridles on the mounts who possess them, and be sitting on your horse ready to gallop off when he reaches you. I have asked the Chief Secretary to look after you should I not come back, and to give you more than enough cattle and sheep and goats to buy Nandisipoh from her father, and to live in comfort for the rest of your life. Above all, Tickie, I want you to remember, attractive and exciting as that which is going on in the basin on the other side of the neck sounds to you, it is all part of the evil which killed first Kawabuzayo, then Zwong-Indaba, then Umtumwa, then Mlangeni and finally Indabaxosikas. For the rest I can only thank you and praise you. Now is that understood? Any questions?'

For once even Said had no questions, but just shook his head miserably, saying: 'Ghadre, Effendi, Ghadre.'

Tickie gulped back something in his throat and without looking at me answered in a dazed way: 'No, Bwana, nothing, nothing.'

'Well then, here are the letters to the Chief Secretary, and look after them well,' I told them, handing Said the letters I'd written in the night. He buttoned them with an unsteady hand into the same tunic pocket wherein once at the Flamingo Water he had so jauntily deposited a letter from me to a Portuguese Governor.

'Very well then. Begin collecting the horses, Tickie. We'll be off.'

With that we lifted our royal old Induna on to his horse. Though he made no sound his black stoic face went grey with pain as his crutch found the saddle. Said and I, too, mounted. Tickie gave us the long, high Roman salute of his people, turned about abruptly, kicked fiercely at a shrub in his path, and marched off with a long disconsolate stride, but he went only a pace or two when he stopped abruptly, listening, head bowed towards the ground.

Instantly we all were aware that something had happened. What could it be? We listened and listened but heard nothing. Then I realized what it was. That 'nothing' was new. There was no longer any sound to be heard. The droning, disturbing, bee-swarming noise had suddenly vanished, and the pass, neck, and basin had gone as still as the air at midnight inside a coffin in its grave. I don't know which was the more sinister, that mindless, mass-droning of the night, or this silence which had now fallen like a black cloak over the head and shoulders of the flaming young body of the upsurging dawn. All I knew was that this was merely the hush which descends upon a crowded theatre when the curtain is being raised on the first act.

'Son of a chief without a country,' the wise old Father spoke, 'we must be careful not to be too late. The sun will soon be up.'

Now I'd already discussed with the old Induna in great detail how best to time our entry on the scene. We had agreed that it was important not to arrive too early. We both feared that if we came too soon we'd find the gathering still loose and flexible enough to permit people like Ghinza time and opportunity for individual action against us. The moment for our entry, we'd decided, should be when the whole gathering was complete, united, and under one central authority. That could only be when the King and his Indunas took their seats on the high ground at the head of the gathering below the cave from which the Umbombulimo would issue at sunrise to proclaim the Dream. When that moment came the Induna and I, with one of Tickie's blankets about me so as to keep the presence

262

of a red-stranger hidden for as long as possible, would ride down fast on the gathering. From that moment the gathering would come to a focus and express itself only through the King and his Councillors. Now, judging by the sudden silence, that moment had come.

'Thank you for reminding me, old Father,' I answered, and promptly pulled my horse into a fast gallop.

We rode straight for the neck of the pass, making such a clatter in the profound silence that I fully expected a black *impi* to come pouring over the gleaming crest to arrest us. However, we made the neck easily without interference, left Said among the boulders, and then, winding carefully down a corridor of pearly rock, came to a halt in the shelter of the cliff on the rim of the basin.

It was the first time I had seen Kwadiabosigo. I had always had too much respect for the instinctive scruples of the Amángtakwena about showing the most sacred meeting ground of the nation to strangers to try to overcome them. Yet I knew it so well from their stories and legends that my first reaction now was a feeling of surprise at finding it so like its description. There it was spread out in the brilliant, upsurgent, fountain light of the early morning of 16 September, like the legendary chart conserved in the colourful archives of my childhood. First, there was the summit of Kwadiabosigo half left of us, 'Spear of the Morning' as its Sindakwena name implies, soaring two thousand feet sheer above the rim of the basin, the sun just beginning to strike sparks out of the glowing peak's point. Below it, as if cracking in the effort of trying to hold the Spear from flying forever away into the sky, there was a deep rent in the steely rock surface. There, above a fringe of African myrrh, reviving asphodel and many-armed euphorbia, was the sacred cave of the nation. Opposite Kwadiabosigo to the east, the rim of the basin was curiously regular, its crest a wreath of cliffs high round it, but behind the cliffs a gently-rolling plateau, where three miles away stood the King's summer kraal, the Capital of the High Place. The rim ran level for about a hundred paces or more, and then soared swiftly with a dramatic turning movement to join the shining shaft of Kwadiabosigo. Right below us was the heart of the grass-covered bowl itself, in the shape of an earthenware vessel

263

of old, and about a mile from where we sat was the crack, the sudden cleft, the deep volcanic rift in the northern half of the basin which figured so often in the final act of the country's most tragic legends and episodes. This crack opened with startling abruptness almost in the centre of the enamel of the basin. Beginning nearly opposite the cave, it cut quickly in a sharp, jigsaw fashion through the bottom as well as the face of the mountains in front of me.

I knew the crack was deep and frightening. I knew it not merely from the legends of countless 'Takwena condemned to throw themselves over its edge by the High Court of the nation, which has met there ever since Xilixowe first came to be alone in the cave for contemplation in times of trouble. I knew it also from the peculiar, tense, trembling, coal-fern glitter which pricked at my eyes from the centre of the crack, and from the curious underworld mist which curled in a surly wisp or two over some of the toothsaw edges. There, where the crack broke from the basin for good and its blackness was not only deep but also raised a giant shadow between two high peaks, the air of morning had collected the smoke of thousands of night-fires, and was driving it, like the flock of sheep of a one-eyed giant, to graze out of sight of the fabulous cave.

I don't know whether it was my awareness of the sinister potential of the day before me that did it or not, but even from where I stood the sight of that cataclysmic cleft in the earth made my senses reel. Quickly I looked away. Then I saw something which was not in the legendary chart of my childhood at all. I saw fifty thousand clansmen, each clan with its own blanket, specific design of texture and pattern of colour, silently converging from all sides on the open ground below the cave. Oh, Lindelbaum, the inspired African merchant, had served the tribal tastes well! Below us were the fifty thousand of a thousand different tribes, each group in its own blanket, and each blanket woven and dyed deep in the colour which the heart of Africa takes straight from the palette of the land's mythological sunsets and its high, barbaric dawns. Clasped round fifty thousand throats these blankets had the light of many-coloured candles tied by flame against the moving air to long black wicks; or, perhaps, considering the breeze of morning, they were like ardent leaves wrenched from the princely redwood of some autumnal dawn, swept, gathered and now steadily drifting towards the mouth of the cave. For that was the curious thing about this scene. The crowd below did not appear to move of its own volition, it appeared to be sucked helplessly towards the great hole of the cave. But just below the cave the fiery movement was abruptly halted, was damned against the rim of the basin like burning lava against a fall of rock, and like lava it quickly formed a lake.

Already the yellow sun was beginning to sink down the purple shaft of Kwadiabosigo and I heard my wise old Father, urging me softly with an odd huskiness in his voice: 'When the sun reaches the mouth of the cave, the Umbombulimo will emerge and the Dream will be told. We must go now if we are not to be too late.'

'You're right, old Father,' I agreed, and with a prayer unspoken, I rode out of the protection of rock on the neck, and fast down the easy gradient of the track.

Fortunately for us the blasphemous clatter of the hoofs of horses on that intense, expectant, dedicated silence was drowned in a deafening outbreak of a new sound. It was one of the most exciting sounds I know: the sound of jubilation and praise the 'Takwena women make at the top of their throats and against their palates – a wonderful trilling, trembling, silvery sound, tinkling and ringing out in clear waves on the pure metal of firm, uninhibited voices. Often in the past, when sent up to welcome me into some village, it had made the hair on my head stand on end. But coming as it did on this September morning, suddenly, spontaneously from a hundred thousand women and girls lining the top of the eastern rim of the basin, it was overwhelming. I looked up sideways from my straining horse to the eastern crest now full in the sun. I saw the burnished skyline dark with the shapes of dancing, waving, clapping figures. I saw a gold hem of morning, and an electric needle of the sun darting black stitches of living 'Takwena being in and out of the silky skyline. I felt stunned by the deafening jubilation which seemed to say: We are not allowed by custom to attend this meeting but our voices unite us and keep us at one with you. Here, as throughout the ages, are your women and children watching and waiting for you.' On any other day I would have found it as beautiful and exciting as the 'Takwena themselves. Today, however, it raised the old, old mist of fear again.

Dear God, I wondered, what hope for reason with so much emotion already about?

Then my fear was rebuked by the realization that thanks to this very sound on the crest I had already come unobserved to within three hundred paces of the flickering edge of the gathering, sitting with its back turned to me, ears attuned only to the acclamation of the clear female voices on the shining Eastern rim.

So I continued galloping, my heart beating in my ears. Then abruptly the sound vanished, vanished as quickly as a light switched off in a room at dead of night, and in the dark silence that followed, the sound of our horses' hoofs rang out like the noise of some Siegfried bursting through the fiery entrances of a sleeping Niebelungen palace.

At once the squatting gathering was on its feet, turned about, and staring with amazement at us. As far as I could see not one person, even from the King to his circle of Indunas sitting on their mats of leopard skins just below the entrance of the cave, had not instantly whirled about. What *one* did, all fifty thousand had to do. And how was I to break that up?

Instinctively I sharply pulled up my horse and beckoned the old royal Induna to pass me and take the lead. Slowly at walking pace he came round, put his horse between me and the crowd, and halted. Still no sound came. The people just stood there staring and staring at us in a strange seeing-unseeing, unbelieving way. On the crest, a hundred thousand women and children, too, remained silent. I felt as if the light of all those thousands of eyes were collecting in the fire-glass of a central emotion of resentment, like the heat rays of the sun in a glass focused on the top of my burning head.

Quickly I looked about me as if it might be my last taste of that lovely day, my last drink of that deep, unfailing goblet of the sky, so serene and impervious to all this brusquely suspended frenzy about us. How close the gathering was to the edge of the gorge. I heard the water moaning like a wind far down in it. A black crow came over us with a melancholy croak. In the mouth of the cave, something appeared to move abruptly into a watchful, waiting position. What it was I couldn't tell for I was too far away, but I realized the sun was beginning to shift along the ledge just three feet above the mouth of the cave, stalking the shadow like a lion *a sable*, the reflection of its tawny coat making a milky purple of the black.

How tightly the crowd was packed in curving lines about the rim, like bees swarmed or locust hoppers clustered against the cold! How tautly staring! Would they never relax and speak! I don't expect it lasted as long as it felt, but it seemed hours to me before there was a movement at the head of the crowd on the slope below the cave where the King and his Indunas stood. Apparently the King had found his voice and a chain of loud voices roared this question at us: 'Who comes here so rudely at this late moment?'

"Nkulixowe's brother, great-uncle of the King and oldest of his Indunas; and the nature of his business with the Dream must excuse the rudeness and lateness of his coming,' my old Father replied, without budging from position. Unfortunately his old voice did not carry well, and some more shouting back and forth went on before his answer was clear to the King. Instantly there was a violent reaction among some of the people closest to the King. Again it was too far for me to see the detail but I had no doubt a furious protest was being lodged against the royal Induna's admission to the gathering. On any normal occasion, I would not have questioned the King's ability to deal with such a protest, but on this day I feared for it, and believing that any action is better than none in dealing with crowds, I dug my heels into my horse, rode up to the old Induna, smacked his horse on the behind and said: 'Ride on, old Father, you know they have no right to keep you from the meeting.'

We had not gone fifty paces, the crowd once more silent and gaping at this new move, when another shout went up from the King's end of the gathering: 'Halt!' it said. 'Halt! and await the King's decision in the matter.'

The old Father halted his horse, but only for a moment. Encouraged by me, he replied with indignant spirit so that all could hear: 'Since when has the oldest Induna in the land had to wait on a decision to attend a gathering of the people which it is his duty and his right to attend? What strange new custom is this, you men of Umangoni? I refuse to wait!'

'Well done, old Father, well done,' I urged, listening to the reluctant murmur of approval wrung by his words from the crowd whose only law is an unwritten law of tribal custom. 'No, wait no more, but ride hard at them.'

I didn't pause for his consent, but lashed his horse so smartly that it went off again at full gallop straight for the crowd, with me, head well down, following close behind. The tribesmen seeing the horses coming at them with such determination opened up. How they did it in their packed condition I don't know, but they opened up a narrow lane for us, split open as the waters of the Red Sea once parted before Moses's command.

Up to that moment in that light, thanks to Tickie's blanket, and to the blackness of much sun on my white face, they had remained miraculously unaware that the Induna's companion was a red stranger. On any other occasion when their sharp senses were not imprisoned in archaic concentration they would have spotted me by any number of things, from my mount and its trappings, to my seat in the saddle, and grip on the reins. Now at last when they did see my face among them, so unexpected and unimaginable was it in their scheme of probability that at first they doubted their senses, doubted them just long enough to let us get to where the King and his Indunas stood. But as I jumped from my mount to lift my old Induna from his horse, awareness of my presence was running like grass-fire through the gathering, and an instinctive angry murmur swarming over it at the outrage of my appearance.

The King when he saw me needed no prompting either from that sound or from the lean, gaunt Ghinza and other Indunas who stood by him. His eyes brilliant with anger he looked past me, ignoring the smart military salute I gave him, and with the coldness of the kettle just before it boils, said to his uncle, who, as custom demanded, was kissing the ground at his feet: 'You may have the right to attend, Uncle, but you know it is treachery to bring a stranger, above all, a red stranger to a gathering like this.'

He did not speak loudly but with such biting precision that I believe his voice carried in that still air from end to end of the gathering. A growl of angry approval greeted his words and, tightly as the gathering was packed, it produced a convulsive

268

heave which sent a ripple of people higher up the slope towards us.

The willing heart of my old Induna seemed to miss a beat at all this hostility, and I could be the last to blame him. I don't know what it is that a crowd emanates, nor how it is transmitted, but I do know that it is as definite and real as reinforced concrete. I myself felt as if I were about to choke in whatever was issuing out of the hearts and minds of those about me. I don't know what I would have done, if far down in me, beyond my conscious reason or volition, the history of centuries in my own blood had not taken charge of me.

I looked at the old Induna, speechless at the feet of an angry King. The King's full, handsome face shone with indignation, his royal purple and gold blanket was flung back and the leopard skins of his royal tartan flared round his middle. I discovered my voice.

Speaking quickly in Sindakwena as authentic as the King's own, with a ring of authority I never knew I possessed, I said in loud words: 'You go too fast, King of the High Place; since when does a descendant of Xilixowe judge before he has heard the cause? If this is treachery, it is a small misdeed compared with the great betrayal in your midst which provoked it.' And here I looked hard at Ghinza who was looking at me with a complex expression of anger and bewilderment in his eyes before I added: 'Besides, I may be red but I am not a stranger! Have you forgotten me and the days when you hunted elephant with my father, the chief without a country?'

At once a new clamour went up from the crowd which, after the astonishment of a red stranger speaking Sindakwena as if he were one of themselves, found it easier to express itself in curiosity than anger. Everywhere those who knew me or of me hastened to explain who and what I was to the thousands of others who did not know. In the midst of the clamour I saw Ghinza beckon to someone at the back of the Indunas, whisper in his ear, and I watched the man out of the corner of my eyes making his way swiftly out of the royal circle to disappear behind the fringe of euphorbias below the cave where now the sunlight like a sea was lapping the black entrance.

Then the King, all anger gone, spoke to me with an air of tragic decisiveness. 'Your presence is hearing enough: and your knowledge of us, son of a chief without a country, is all the more cause why you should have known better than come to a meeting which is only for the Amangtakwena. I may know you, but the occasion certainly knows you not."

'No,' I said without flinching, 'all the more cause why I had to come. Could I, knowing you as I know you all, stand by indifferently while others prepared disaster for your people? Look, King, ask your uncle, this wise old Father; I am only here because without me he could not have come and without him in a few minutes another dream, not the dream your grandfather promised you, but a dream even more false than the dream which nearly wiped out the Amangtakwena a hundred years ago would have been forced on you.'

But I got no further. This was too much for Ghinza. He jumped to the side of the King and pointing at the royal Induna still respectfully waiting for permission to rise, cried out at the top of his voice: 'Have you not heard enough? What further proof of this old man's treachery do you want, cousin? See, he has told this red stranger of the Dream. There is only one answer to that: throw them over the cliff!'

A wordless howl of approval rose from most of the crowd like the wail of a hungry flock of hyenas, but not from all the crowd. Also I saw something in the King's eyes as he listened which suggested that Ghinza's voice was not his favourite sound.

So I spoke back as fast as I could saying loudly: 'Ghinza!' His start at the sound of his name was good to see. 'Ghinza, look at me!' Reluctantly he turned to face me. 'Yes, look at me, because you have seen this face before.' At that everything but bewilderment left that tight, cold, dissatisfied, and superhumanly ambitious face. 'Yes, you saw it some weeks ago. You saw it from behind a curtain on the deck of the *Star of Truth*, the Svensky Pravdi to you, in Port Natal. Yes, I see you recognize it now! I know all; all about you and your Tashkent treachery!' Ghinza was grey now, not with fear, for I don't believe he knew the meaning of the word, but with a demonic rage at the risk of exposure. I turned disdainfully sideways to him and spoke direct to the King: 'This cousin of yours who speaks of this wise old Induna's treachery with the Dream, has betrayed the Dream not to one but to thou-

270

sands of red strangers. I have followed him for weeks from the night he murdered this old Father's son, Kawabuzayo.'

'A lie! All lies! Over the cliff with them,' Ghinza cried out. But this time the crowd was silent.

'If it is lies then,' I challenged him, 'where is Kawabuzayo who went to meet you and who had a connexion with the dream as important as yours, Ghinza? Why is he not here?'

'Because he sent a substitute,' Ghinza shouted, his eyes fixed desperately on the mouth of the cave.

'This old Father will soon show you how false a substitute,' I answered, bending down impulsively and without the King's permission raising the old Induna to his feet and showing him to the crowd, many of whom knew him by sight and all by reputation. 'He knows Kawabuzayo is dead. He knows his son was murdered by Ghinza and died in my house because he would not agree to betray the secret of 'Nkulixowe's dream –'

The sight of that dignified old head, its round metal ring flashing in the light, nodding agreement as I spoke, raised the first serious conscious doubt in the mindless mood of the crowd.

An Induna, a cousin of Kawabuzayo, suddenly stepped forward and said quietly: 'Please let the red stranger speak to the end.'

'Cousin, I swear to you in 'Nkulixowe's name it is all lies,' Ghinza interrupted to plead with angry intensity before the King. 'Do you think the Umbombulimo would betray the people's memory, since that is what it means if this red stranger is believed? Ask the Umbombulimo!'

The thrust went home. The deep murmur of agreement from the crowd and the new shadow in the King's eyes clearly showed how truly it had gone home.

'In the name of Xilixowe I tell you it is true,' I countered quickly using the most sacred of the 'Takwena oaths. 'And the truth of it can be very simply proved, oh King, not by what I or this traitor Ghinza, this servant of red strangers' money and seeker after your office says, but by the secret test 'Nkulixowe provided. That is the only reason I brought the oldest of your Indunas here: to see that 'Nkulixowe's measure of the dream was truly applied. Put it to the test, I say, O King! If the dream is false you know what to do. If it is true – well, I have come here today not as a red stranger but as one of you, and, if it is true, I will take this old Father by the hand and walk with him over the cliff, as the custom demands. As proof of my good word, I give you this.' With that I unslung my gun and put it on the ground in front of the King.

Yet the crowd was still silent; so still indeed that I, who had staked all on their psychological and intuitive predisposition to respond to the true word when married to the appropriate dramatic gesture, went black with misgiving. I looked quickly at the blue and the sunlight pouring like wine into the basin, at a vulture on a lone patrol, and then at the mouth of the cave, translucent yellow and red and mauve. Yes, the decisive moment had come and I was not sorry. I would be glad to end the terrible suspense. For the Umbombulimo was appearing, with his skirt of tails of baboons around him, headdress of jackal fur and eagles' feathers, a collar of lion's delicate V-bones, and a long forked stick with a newly-killed yellow cobra stuck in it and held in front, while Ghinza's messenger followed in close support. Slowly the Umbombulimo emerged from the purple cave with a strange mediumistic walk.

All this I took in in one brief second, yet long enough to feel that I had failed. But as the crowd set eyes for the first time on the Umbombulimo and Keeper of the People's Memory, it recovered its breath and an enormous shout broke from it like a storm. 'He speaks well, the son of a chief without country! Agreed. Let the right people test the dream!'

'Aye, let the right people test the dream,' the Umbombulimo boomed from above, for the first time now in full view of the crowd which at once went silent as it looked up, startled. 'But let the wrong people be removed first. Over the cliff with this treacherous old Induna and the red stranger who has no right here.'

I expect the priests of any religion which is foreign to one tend to possess an element of exaggeration bordering on caricature. I believe many a person watching the scene from a safe distance and in cold blood would have found the Umbombulimo rather funny as he stood there in his archaic trappings. I fear I did not. If there was anything ludicrous about him or the occasion it was merely the touch of mockery in his fantastic appearance which classic fate subtly uses to add an extra dimension to its favourite tragedy. As I watched him standing there with extraordinary satyr's dignity, a strange crepuscular compromise of man and beast, and the light of an uncompromising spring morning upon him, I became aware of the extraordinary silence his words and appearance had imposed upon the gathering and I feared greatly the power of the people's associations from childhood with him and his craft, and its effect on the aboriginal quicksilver element in the massed African tribal mood.

Fiercely I urged the royal Induna: 'Quick, old Father, answer him and do not fear. Remember he is a traitor like the rest and no spirit of your ancestors will help him. In the name of Xilixowe, speak up like the man you are!'

'Keeper of the People's Memory,' my gallant old companion then said with impressive dignity. 'You, too, are a servant of the dream and not above it. You, too, are subject to the test. It is not for you to say who are the right and who the wrong people. Listen, you men of the Amangtakwena, listen, all you we call brothers ...' And the wise old Father, truly launched, sailed out with a strong tide to the sea of an inspired eloquence that even this ancient meeting-place could not have heard. He told them in burning words how 'Nkulixowe had sent for him on his death-bed, told of the dream he was going to prepare by the Great Flamingo Water and how the people would be able to make sure one day when the dream was proclaimed that it was not false. Yes, 'Nkulixowe had confided in him the entire tests for a series of dreams, and asked him to divide the secret between the male members of two families, his own, and that of the father of Ghinza. No one else – above all, not the Keeper of the King's Memory who had failed before – was to share the secret. But, on the day of the dream, the senior members of the two families would test the credentials of the dreamer before the dream was delivered. Yes, he emphasized, shaking his long finger at the crowd, the test was to be before, not after the dream was delivered. Since he himself was so old, he had deputed Kawabuzayo to carry out his part of the test for him. But Kawabuzayo was dead, and he had only just heard of it. That was why he came so late. But late and rude as it was, he had had to come. True, Ghinza had said Kawabuzayo had sent a substitute. Well then, let Ghinza and the substitute step forward and ask the Umbombulimo the questions the test demanded. To show how sincere he, the royal Induna, was, he would take the King and three Indunas on one side and confide to them the questions set by 'Nkulixowe. But until then let the Umbombulimo be silent, remembering that he, too, was a servant of the dream and not its master.

From start to finish, the old Induna had the gathering in the palm of his elegant old hand, not because he spoke so well, but because he spoke the truth. Such a shout of agreement went up at the end of his speech that Ghinza and the Umbombulimo had to pretend a grace of acceptance they were far from feeling.

Ghinza, to give him his due, never feared responsibility of decision and was the first to act. He beckoned imperiously to someone at the back. A solid, sulky, obstinate, aggressive 'Takwena came forward, another cousin of the King, and therefore a likely substitute for Kawabuzayo, but also a graduate of Tashkent and, therefore, suitably indoctrinated, for I remembered him strolling on the deck of the *Star of Truth* with Ghinza that thundery evening in another age when she steamed so jauntily into the Great Flamingo Water.

'Here,' Ghinza said to the King, going so far in his arrogant spirit of bravado that what was intended to be indifference came perilously near to rude disdain. 'Here is Kawabuzayo's substitute and here am I. Shall we begin?'

'Aye,' replied the King, eyeing him keenly, 'aye, let the test begin and you, cousin, begin it.'

Whereupon Ghinza swung arrogantly about and walked up the slope with that tense, long nervous stride of his, under such tight control that his back, straight as an assegai, seemed to be trembling like the haft before a throw. In full view of the tribe he climbed twenty paces, halted one pace in front of the Umbombulimo, raised his hand in the royal salute and shouted out these words in his ringing, high-pitched metallic voice: 'Umbombulimo and Keeper of the People's Memory, I greet you to ask you three questions about the dream which you say 'Nkulixowe has given you for the people: What did 'Nkulixowe wear on his head in the dream? Why did he not carry a feather in his hand as always? In which hand did he hold his spear?'

'You ask me questions in the manner of a jackal, doubling back to hide the intention of going forward,' the Umbombulimo instantly boomed back: 'I'll answer them in the way of a king. 'Nkulixowe wore nothing on his head because his hair was white with wisdom, and wisdom its only covering. His left hand was not empty, but, as always, open, and Xilixowe's first flamingo feather in the palm of it, 'Nkulixowe had no spear, but in his right hand a book of learning with a name yet to come. Do I, or do I not speak truthfully, brother of the King?'

'You speak the truth as I was commanded by my father and by his father before him. In the name of Xilixowe I say it.'

'Perhaps that grey old traitor beside you, cousin, will say whether my words are or are not so?' the Umbombulimo persisted.

'Indeed, it is as 'Nkulixowe commanded,' my wise old Father replied, unperturbed by the taunt, and the deep hum of approval and expectation which broke from the gathering rose in such a wave of sound that it rolled across the valley and broke over the crest lined with their women and children catching excited breath.

Another stir in the crowd: Kawabuzayo's substitute moved forward and fear assailed me anew. What if this solid fellow has been truly prompted? What if someone else has cheated and he has been told the true test? The end, Pierre François de Beauvilliers, for you. But I could not help looking at the jagged edge of the abyss beyond and I carried the thought no further. A 'but' had preserved my courage so far; indeed, but for a profound 'but' in the core of my shrinking and transitory being I would not have been there that day. I was content to leave it at that.

Instinctively I folded my arms to watch this surly, solid 'Takwena prince climb up to the Umbombulimo and to hear him roar like one of the bulls for which his country is famous: 'Keeper of the People's Memory, I, too, ask three things. Why did 'Nkulixowe not come to you in the dream alone? What was the skin he wore round his middle? Was it copper, or gold, or ivory, or black steel in the ring around his neck?'

'Your words are as sly as the footfall of the hyena,' the Umbombulimo beamed confidently, 'but I'll answer them openly as the lion roars. 'Nkulixowe came alone; he wore no skin round his middle but stood leaning on his great shield of war in front of him. The ring round his neck like his head was white and made of ivory. Do I or do I not speak truthfully?'

'In the name of Xilixowe I swear you speak the truth,' the stolid 'Takwena cried, and turned about expectantly.

But this time no sound broke from the gathering. There was only an uneasy murmur among the Indunas close to the King, and then the King himself stepped forward. It was obvious from the way he walked, as if carrying the world on his shoulders, that something tremendous was about to happen. But what? Approval of the test? Order to proclaim the dream? It was impossible to tell from his bearing, and fifty thousand tribesmen, with the faces of children waiting for the denouement of one of Grimm's grimmer fairy tales, turned silently upwards to watch him, while from the hills above once more came that drawing in of the long-suspended breath of thousands of women and children.

'Is there not a question he has failed to ask you?' the King called out to the Umbombulimo in the voice of a judge to a vital witness, as he brushed purposefully past the surly 'Takwena. 'Is there not something forgotten here?'

'As you can see, O King,' the Umbombulimo, warned by the tone of his question to be on guard, answered with cautious ambiguity, 'I am still waiting.'

'Then say what colour was 'Nkulixowe in the dream, and say at once,' the King cried out, sternly.

'As always, 'Nkulixowe was black, black and shining like the bull elephant when he comes out of the waters of the Uhlalingasonki after his bathe in the heat of summer, black –'

'Enough!' The King stopped him in a voice bitter with undisguised distaste, his hand flung out in front of him. 'Enough!'

Slowly he turned round and stood a foot or two below the Umbombulimo who was standing behind his yellow cobra standard still with a remarkable semblance of confident dignity. But if he could have seen the King's face as I saw it then, he might have faltered. For fully half a minute the King stood there in a silence so great that I could hear the sound of the crowd's deep fearful breathing, mixing with the impersonal rustle of the fitful wind of the morning, heard the blood sing-

276

ing in my ears and Ghinza swallowing something in his throat near me. What passed through the King's mind I could not possibly tell, but that look in his eyes was of a bitter forlorn disillusionment and I could only guess that his heart just then was not of that time or place.

At the end of fully a minute he beckoned to his Indunas to join him. All went quickly, including Ghinza, but long before that one got there, the King waved him back. When the other Indunas reached him the King addressed them briefly in a low voice. I could not hear his words, but from the way their ringed heads nodded, and the way they all promptly sat down in a semi-circle around him, I knew they were unanimously agreed, and the decision, for good or ill, taken.

'People of the Amangtakwena and you, our brothers,' – the King spoke in the poignant voice of irrevocable resolution – 'There is no dream to proclaim. There has been no dream. The test shows that Prince Ghinza and the Umbombulimo are false, and have tried to betray you. The first half of the test entrusted to Prince Ghinza was truly answered by the Um-bombulimo. In the second test not entrusted to Prince Ghinza, the Umbombulimo failed. There were never three questions in this second half as the substitute produced by Prince Ghinza told you. There was only one – the one you heard me ask: "What colour was the great 'Nkulixowe in the dream?' The answer to that is not black. Listen carefully, O you people of Umangoni, and all you we call brothers: On the day of his dying, 'Nkulixowe told this wise old Father, his brother, that he was going to prepare a dream for all by the Great Flamingo Water because no people could live for long without dreams. If there were no true dreams, false dreams would be made up and sent to take their place. In order, therefore, that the people should be able to tell the true from the many false, he con-fided in this old Father signs by which the one could be told from the many. The most important of these signs was the colour wherein he, 'Nkulixowe, would appear in the dream. Never again, 'Nkulixowe said, could a dream be either all black or all white. No true dream, he said, could ever be possible for his people until the thing that made white and black so dan-gerous to one another vanished. So in the great dream to come he declared he would be neither black nor white but yellow, as

277

yellow as the sacred snake in the work of this stick of the traitor behind me. .... Clearly there has been no dream and all there is left for you to do here is to say what is to be done with those who have betrayed the dream.'

The King finished and waited, his eyes looking at his fifty thousand people but seeing only, I believe, another era of dreamlessness for them all, wondering bitterly perhaps how and when it would end, and thinking with anguish how good it would have been, how wonderful a day if only there had been another true great dream to proclaim.

The gathering, I am certain, without thinking it, felt the same, for a heavy sigh, a poignant, pitiful 'Ah!' fell like lead from fifty thousand pairs of lips, to be followed by a curious, prolonged whimper rippling along the gleaming morning crest from one vivid woman to a hundred thousand others.

I looked at Ghinza but he did not look back. Individual and apart from his people in his pride, ambition, and will, now in the final defeat of all three, he was left exposed to the very emotion he had sought to use; was a prisoner of the situation he had helped so elaborately to create. In his guilt, like the Umbombulimo and his initiates, he looked more bound to his people than he had ever been in his innocence. He stood there hypnotized by his share of guilt as surely as any frog by the dead cobra on the Umbombulimo's stick.

When the King now called out 'Ghinza! Ghinza!' he started like someone disturbed in his sleep, looked wildly up but did not speak.

'Ghinza,' the King told him, 'sixteen came with you, where are the others? Call them to you.'

Even then, Ghinza did not answer. He turned to the crowd with the slow dignity of a somnambulist or of a blind man feeling his way along his own darkness amid the bright day, and merely beckoned to the people. At once fifteen 'Takwena came, the blanketed crowd silently making way for them. Silently they joined him and stood there, like a huddle of sheep waiting for courage to round a dangerous corner.

'People of the Amangtakwena,' the King called, when the huddle was complete, 'here are eighteen sons of black mothers. Do you see them or do you see them not?'

There was no hesitation in the response. I myself, now it

was all over, was so assailed by the pity of it that I found myself wishing there could be some slight hesitation, some faint
brushing of the wings of the infinite compassion which our
frail flesh and blood so constantly need to shield them against
the harsh glare of the unforgiving consequences of our im-
perfect actions, some softening of fellow-feeling to console,
even though it could not cure the going the eighteen had to
endure. But there was none. King, Indunas, fifty thousand and
all, immediately turned their backs resolutely on the eighteen
and stood or sat silent and still waiting, waiting, while that
strange pitiful whimper once more rippled among the crags
lined with women and children.

Ghinza gave those flickering blanket backs one long, long
glance, looked up and stared straight into the sun just swinging clear of the last purple peak, then proudly turned his back
on the averted gathering, waved to the others to follow, and
slowly, without a tremor, walked steadily looking neither to
right nor left, towards that cataclysmic rift in the basin.

The others followed obediently with bowed heads, all except the Umbombulimo who first laid down his forked stick,
took off his trappings one by one until all his discarded finery
lay like dead animal shapes upon the ground. Then naked as
he had entered the world he proceeded behind the others to
walk out of it.

When they came near to the edge of the abyss, I found my
eyes moist so that I could hardly distinguish one shape from
the other. All I know is that Ghinza without hesitation led his
party over the edge and the Umbombulimo bringing up the
rear followed without a whimper. Silently they went and still
as it was, so deep is that crack in the basin below Kwadiabosigo
that no sound of these proud assegais of flesh and blood,
swiftly splintering on the rock below, came up at me. I heard
only the undisturbed swish and rustle of water churning far
below us, the air of morning stirring in the grass and the black
crows in the distance croaking sardonically.

I cleared my eyes, looked up and felt surprised and almost
shocked to see that though eighteen lamps had just been extinguished, the day was no darker, the basin and the hills around
us no different. I turned about and found the gathering doing
the same. It was all over, yet I found myself looking at an un-

spoken request for confirmation in the glance of the King. I nodded my head. Slowly he walked out alone to the edge of the abyss, stood there silently for some while before he came back to address the crowd in the voice of final authority as if turning over a page in the book of life: 'Amangtakwena, brothers from far and near, we thank the eighteen for going in such a way that we need not be ashamed of them. We thank them for going in a way that brings them back to us and once more makes us all one. All there is now left for us to do is to send the herdsmen to bring in the slaughter oxen, and the women and children to fetch beer, milk, and honey to celebrate our deliverance from a dream of disaster before we all go our different ways to our distant kraals. I have spoken.'

And when Tickie, Said, and I set out for the capital at nightfall, the festival fires in the basin, along the crests and all over the plateau of the Kraal of the High Place were piled to the stars and ruby-lit. The sound of dancing and singing once more rang out far and wide, while the smell of tender ox-meat roasting drifted with the darkness over Kwadiabosigo, that ancient spear-point of morning, like the incense of sacrifice rising to the oldest of gods. Yet through and upon it all, I felt a subtle element of regret trembling in the brightness of the rejoicing, like the shadow of the midnight which is born at noon and goes black in the blue of the brightest African day, and which I myself shared; regret that that day there had not been a true dream to be truly delivered to a dreamless people.

Chapter 18

The End of Three Ways

Early in the morning of 19 September, back in the Mission, I
was able to keep awake in Aramis's presence just long enough
to tell him, without much detail, that the crisis was over, to
ask him to telegraph to Fort Herald immediately for an aircraft, and to send this telegram to Bill Wyndham at Petit
France: 'Tell Joan but no one else John safe well all immediate danger past stop charter aircraft fly her Fort Herald soon
as possible stop grateful if you accompany her stop love you
both Pierre.'

Aramis, after reading through the draft of the telegram exclaimed: 'Good! I confess I've been wondering for some time
why you didn't put the lady out of her suspense before, and
tell her last time you were here that her brother was alive.'

But I was too tired to answer that I'd deliberately forced
myself not to communicate with Joan because the chances of
John's and my survival had appeared so slight that I thought
it far better to leave her in a suspense to which she was accustomed than to try to give her definite news of us, anyway until
we were out of danger. However, indifferent to Aramis's
opinion with the indifference of profound exhaustion, I had
said nothing, but crept into bed and slept.

I slept for two nights and two days, but Aramis told me
that for a whole day and night the sounds I made in my sleep
were so pitiful and violent that he seldom left my side for
long, and had the Mission's Director of Medical Services along
thrice to inject me with sedatives.

When I looked my unbelief at this, he laughed, took me by
the arm and pushed up the sleeve of the pyjama coat of his I
wore and showed me the marks of the hypodermic pricks on
my arm and said, 'There! Now my unbelieving Thomas, there.
And what's more, d'you remember eating anything recently?'

I shook my head smiling. 'No, Aramis, I don't.' But as I said it a wonderful realization of having well and truly come through flared up in me like a draught of wine in an empty stomach.

'Well, *mon cher*,' Aramis told me, 'the egg-flips in milk you've drunk these past few days are impossible to believe!' He sobered. 'Truly, you were in a bad way. However, the point is, are you better? Are you rested enough for some slight business?'

As I nodded my head emphatically he told me there were many things to attend to, starting with an imperious summons from His Honour. Then the aircraft I had chartered from Fort Herald had arrived the evening before and was standing by on his landing strip. And this radio telegram had just been relayed to him from Fort Herald.

I took the telegram first, but it was not from Bill as I'd expected. It read: 'Pierre I knew you would not fail us stop Bill and I flying north 22 September due Fort Herald 23 stop most grateful love Joan.'

'Aramis, old friend,' I said as I heaved myself out of bed the moment I finished Joan's telegram, 'you must forgive me but His Honour must wait. I'm sorry but I have a live situation here which *cannot* wait. There's John sitting at his illicit depot not knowing what's happened. If he hasn't heard by nightfall he'll assume all is lost and prepare to do his worst. You shouldn't have let me sleep so long; I meant to be there yesterday at the latest, so I'm off.'

Aramis made no attempt to dissuade me, willingly made notes of appropriate messages for Joan and Bill, also Tickie and Said who, he said, were sleeping and eating, eating and sleeping their reeling heads off in his own servants' quarters, and altogether helped me with such a will that I was in the aircraft at noon circling the capital of Umangoni for the first time in my life, before heading in the milk-blue sky north-east straight for the Ranges of the Night.

We located the basin above Redwood Princes without difficulty, first finding the black gorge where the flashing Oriental sword of the river cuts its way out through the ranks of the giant hills. Flying at thirteen thousand feet, which was all our two-seater loaded with spirit and oil could do, we picked the gorge out sixty miles away because, though there were many other gorges, there were none comparable. The flash of water in the centre of the basin flew up like a burning phoenix and was later confirmed by the lines of mushroom tents beyond. A column of smoke, too, suddenly flared close by the flashing water.

Just before reaching it, we saw the St Andrew's Cross of a strip cut and levelled in the grass, and what looked like a company of soldiers formally drawn-up. At one-thirty precisely we landed. Though I knew all was over behind me I found my heart beating faster as I unstrapped myself and waited for the roaring, revving engine to stop. What if something had gone wrong in my absence? What if some deputy of Ghinza's had heard of the happenings at Kwadiabosigo and plunged into desperate action to try and retrieve it all? But I need not have worried. As I jumped down and came out from underneath the wing of the aeroplane there was John in person, as if on parade outside Wellington Barracks, ordering a company of 'Takwena infantry to present arms, and the company promptly doing it in a manner the Brigade of Guards couldn't have bettered.

'Well!' John whispered to me too low for the pilot to hear as he greeted me and started to conduct me down the precise lines of his taut 'Takwena soldiery.

'All's well,' I answered, grateful to have this framework of a formal public duty to contain us both just then.

'Thank God!' he exclaimed, stopping at the end of the first line, staring briefly with a swift upward glance out of burning brown eyes at the high-sea line of the hills with the powdered light of afternoon tumbling down thickly over them, and added generously, 'and thank you, Pierre.'

Soon we were sitting alone in John's tent, talking, explaining, planning, and I pleading not a little. For in John had now emerged, in full stature, a definite and irrevocable resolve. He had hinted at it in our first meeting at Redwood Princes, but I had not understood. He was not coming back home with me. This was the logical and honourable end of the journey for me; but it was far from that for him. His course was plain. He had to go back to the Great Flamingo Water, carry out his instructions to the letter, destroy the base and all evidence of it, and then on the appointed day in October take the last ship once more for Russia. Yes, he had to do that for two reasons. One, because only part of his work was done. He was sure after what he'd told me that I couldn't think of Umangoni as the only corner of Africa, the only part of the world threatened in this and similar ways. There were the Lindelbaums, Harkovs, and Ghinzas of life past numbering, who still had to be defeated, and perhaps he could help. No! I needn't fear that he'd be blamed for the failure of this particular plot. He had carried out his part of the orders to the letter. If I played my hand well and prevented a public hue and cry he feared no consequences from his diligent spider-spinner in the basement underneath the Kremlin. On the contrary, he believed he could give them such an account of his stewardship, such a constructive and devastating analysis of the folly of excessive reliance on gifted amateurs like Harkov, that he would earn promotion spectacular enough to prevent the next diabolic turn of their revolutionary screw.

I'd have liked to be able to indicate agreement, but I was too moved to be able to do so. I tried to say something appropriate but the words wouldn't come. So after a pause wherein his brown eyes never left me, he went on, as if I'd disappointed him, to speak rather flatly of the second reason for going back. Of course it was Serge. Were it not for Serge, he wouldn't be alive today. The whole of Umangoni and the greater part of Southern Africa would have been committed to massacre had it not been for Serge. So he was returning to see that Serge was freed, to claim fulfilment of the promise made to him that Serge would be released to go back to Manchuria. From Manchuria he hoped Serge could make his way by devious degrees to Petit France and start a new life in Africa. Yes, he would ask of me only these services: to help Serge get from Manchuria to Africa; to give him, John, some assistance in blowing the caves after he'd gone; and then to go to Joan and his mother and explain it all.

Here, however, I put my foot firmly down. I told him flatly that if he wanted any help from me he could get it in only one way: he could climb into that aeroplane with my pilot first thing in the morning, fly straight to Fort Herald and spend some days with Joan explaining it all himself. I was only sorry the time was too short for him to fly to England, or I'd make that a condition as well. But to Fort Herald and Joan he was going without a doubt.

I say that I was downright, but it was necessary, for I was amazed at the wealth of argument John put up to excuse himself from going to meet Joan. A superficial observer might have thought he didn't care whether he saw his sister and mother again or not. Puzzled at first, however, I was not deceived, and finally came to recognize it all as a deep fear of the effect on his resolution of seeing someone he loved as much as Joan.

He asked me if my insistence on his seeing Joan was not perhaps a cruel and pointless indulgence of sentiment? I would have none of it. I told him that I was certain if he went without seeing Joan he'd never forgive himself for the knowledge that he'd failed to give legitimate explanation to someone he loved. Indeed, I asked myself, only a few days before, at sunrise below Kwadiabosigo, had not my own heart confronted me with an image of Joan in precisely that accusing way? I then went on to remind him that even if he succeeded in satisfying his own conviction in the matter, neither Joan nor his mother would ever understand. What he proposed doing was hard enough for them without being denied the chance fully to understand him. I told him frankly that shirking giving the real explanation to Joan would subtly weaken his spirit in days to come; but that not shirking it would strengthen him.

That, thank heaven, did it. He gave in with a laugh, raising his hands in mock surrender above his head and saying: 'You win! I'll go to Fort Herald in the morning, spend three days there with Joan, return here on the 26th, while you, I hope, prepare the base for dissolution so that I can set off for the coast at once after my return. I've not been left much time margin as you know.'

I then told him what I had already agreed with the King at Kwadiabosigo before my departure. He would ferret out Ghinza's and Lindelbaum's agents and quietly settle with them for good. As soon as the celebrations were over, his own messengers were going to cancel the Umbombulimo's call for mobilization. Meanwhile John and I had his permission and blessing to disband the men already under arms at the depot.

285

Furthermore, we had agreed on terms of an address John or I would deliver at a mass parade before disbandment, for I'd already understood from John that the 'Takwena officers, N.C.O.'s, and trainees had never been told the truth about the purpose of their training. So I could easily address them, therefore, on behalf of the Government from overseas, tell them the good news that all danger of war, which had occasioned their training, was averted; thank them in the name of the King over the Water for their readiness to serve, and send them back to their homes with the assurance that if war threatened again, they would be the first to be called upon.

To all this John agreed. Nonetheless, to guard against any future suspicions of their conduct which gossip and after-thought might fester in the impressionable 'Takwena soul, and to prevent their primitive integrity from being damaged by national innuendo that they had been guilty of disloyalty, he looked to me to persuade H.H. and Whitehall to issue all his soldiers with a special emergency medal. Nothing, he assured me with that rare, delighted grin of his, would rob Tashkent and the Kremlin more effectively of whatever potential of thunder they might have left in the affair.

I had very little to add, save that in the morning John should introduce me as a special envoy from the King over the Water, and hand over command to me at a parade of all ranks. I'd address them accordingly, and while John was away at Fort Herald would dismantle the depot, store all equipment and arms in the ordnance caves, and then disband the last of his army. That done, I would see that all the charges in the caves were suitably primed. When he came back, there would be nothing for him to do but a quick march to the coast, winding up each intermediate camp on the way. Once he was safely gone, I'd blow the caves.

The three days that followed passed only too quickly for me. The aeroplane was hardly off the ground skimming over the water in the basin like a blue dragonfly, when company by company the soldiery, happy as schoolboys given an unexpected holiday, began striking their tents and depositing their arms with the grave bespectacled storekeepers at the entrances of the caves in the gorge. All day long and the next, the operation went on, pioneers, signallers, engineers, light infantry,

286

mounted infantry smoothly fitting into their appointed places in the pattern of dissolution. By the evening of the second day the last of the fighting troops, paid off and provisioned, were disappearing over the crest where I had once seen seven red-blanketed horsemen take an apocalyptic glow upon themselves, and I was left with only a couple of tents, some cooks and quartermasters, standing in the fiery twilight, listening to the departing soldiery singing 'The Three Ways':

Aye, look, we go the way from victory, home in the evening;
We go to our cattle and kraals and women by the fire in the
    blue of Umangoni.

On the morning of the third day, we struck the last of the tents and I sent the remnants of what was to have been a great and all-conquering army, headquarters personnel, bottle-washers, cooks, and colour-sergeants, quietly to their kraals. I spent the day until noon priming the detonators in the caves. I put the links in the safety gaps in the chain of explosives and connected them to the master switch. That done I ate a hurried lunch and climbed to the top of the crest where we had ambushed John and there waited for his aeroplane.

How still, peaceful, unchanged, and totally unimpressed the great scene in this remote heart of the mountains had been by all the frenzied military activity which had just ebbed from it. How profoundly uninvolved and indifferent it appeared. Were it not for the St Andrew's Cross of the landing-ground and the bare circles, rings, and squares where the depot tents and marquees had stood, one couldn't have told that the basin had even known anything of humanity except the casual, friendly nomad herds and their tinkling flocks brought along in the warm months of summer. I sat there in the September sun thinking and reviewing it all with a paradoxical nostalgia, until I began to fear John was not coming back that day. But an hour before sundown, in unbelievable stillness, I heard the drone of the machine very far away like the buzzing of a blue-bottle in summer and I had to run fast down the slope to get to the landing-ground just as John and the pilot climbed out of the machine.

'No need to ask how you've got on, Pierre! We hardly recognized the place!' John called out, waving a greeting to me.

His manner, his tone were obviously intended to be gay, and he stood there with his convincing pose of innate, elegant, nonchalant ease but I knew him too well to be deceived. I couldn't be mistaken, he was desperately preoccupied underneath. Somehow my heart sank at the prospect of the evening ahead.

After a meal by the fire in the open, all business discussed and concluded, I walked with him over the crest down to Redwood Princes under a sky of polished moonlight as bright as on the night we'd first met up there. The night, indeed, was very much the same, moon, stars, air, trees, even the roaring of the lion at a forbidden gate in the main valley below as before. We alone had changed and our immediate rôles were ended. Our lives had merely come to one of those lesser deaths which prepare us in due time for the greater to come: one of those black Umpafuti tributaries which conduct the waters of the clearest life to the final river. That dark, submerged value rose like a stupendous night-bird to cast a gloomy wing on the air, changing what a month before had been an heroic salutation of moon and stars into an urgent gesture of final valediction.

'How did you find Joan, and how did you leave her?' I asked him at last when no one could overhear us.

He lit his pipe and his face and hair were lit briefly in the light of the match into a portrait in medieval oils. Then he puffed hard at the pipe, saying:

'She was wonderful; older, of course, but more beautiful than ever. I forget when you last saw her?'

'In the mail ship, the day she sailed from Van Riebeeck's Bay for England,' I told him promptly.

'Of course. But it's a long time ago. I don't think you'll find her changed in any essential way. Sent you her love, of course.'

I interrupted him roughly, that diabolic impediment within me of which I have spoken before preventing me from taking his last sentence at its face value. Quickly I asked, 'But did she understand?'

'Yes, dear boy.' He spoke rather abruptly. 'She understood. There's nothing, I believe, she doesn't or couldn't understand, given a chance.' He paused, looked pointedly at me as if waiting for the full meaning to sink in before continuing: 'She gave me her unqualified support and blessing. I'm so glad I went – but it wasn't easy for either of us, as you can well imagine.'

In an effort to lighten the moment I asked: 'But tell me, how was she at Petit France? Did she like it? Did Bill look after her well? What did you think of him?'

He answered my questions backwards. He liked Bill a lot. He'd been wonderfully good, considerate, and helpful; a tower of strength in a nerve-wracking time. He and Joan had become the closest of friends. It was a joy to see them together, and a comfort to know she was still in Bill's keeping.

John answered my questions, I am sure, objectively enough, but my reactions suddenly became painfully subjective and I found myself exposed to a humiliating emotion. I was instantly jealous of Bill and his time with Joan at Petit France; jealous of the opportunity and leisure they must have had there for all the complex delicacy of feeling, fore-thought and imaginative application that the growth of a lasting personal relationship needs, while I had been walking the Dead Land and places innumerable without name. Angry with myself I again interrupted John half-way through his eulogy to ask, 'But what's Joan going to do now?'

'Leaving in the morning with Bill by aeroplane for the Rand Airport,' John said, 'and from there in the first available aircraft for England to go to my mother.'

At that the humiliating emotion abandoned me, and I felt utterly grey within, thinking, So there it is, Pierre, you're never to see her again.

Despite the darkness I believe John was aware of the change in me. However, he said nothing. All I know is that his face turned towards me, and that for a long while after he spoke he stood there staring at me thus in that fading light, rather as a prophet about to return to the desert might look at his chosen apprentice.

And so to this day I see him. That attitude of his remains as one of the terminal paintings of what is unforgettable in the totality of the experience. For it is curious that, though my recollection of our last night up there is one of the longest I've ever known, I have no specific memories other than these to bear me out. Once we'd spoken and skirmished round our emotions, there was nothing left but the dominant and certain knowledge that in the morning he was to leave, probably for ever. I have no recollection of detail, of our walk back for the last time from Redwood Princes, except that we went arm in arm like schoolboys returning fearfully to school. I remember nothing but this general distress between that moment and the other at sunrise when I stood on the edge of the track below the caves watching him walking down into the dark gorge leading to the black bush and the far Flamingo Water. I sat there watching him sinking like a diver into the deep sea shadow of the gorge, while high above us the purple ranges rolled like waves on the surface of the first sunlit morning after a storm.

I stood there thinking how like him it was to go alone, refusing to take even one bearer with him, refusing to expose one more simple 'Takwena soul to guile and deception. At the last twist of the fast-sinking track he turned round in order to find me on the rock where I stood in the sun. Already the undergrowth around him was so dark that I couldn't see the gun on his shoulder nor the pack on his back. He raised his hat, waved it gaily, almost triumphantly, at me and in the same movement swung about to stride nonchalantly round the final bend.

Turning I climbed on up into the caves. I set the gadget of the master fuse timed to blow in three hours' time, thinking John ought to be clear of the gorge then. I returned to our burnt-out fire in camp. I packed up. I took the pilot down to the plane. I waited until a quarter of an hour before the explosion was due, for I wanted to be near enough to know the fuse had not failed and yet far enough away for the pilot not to realize precisely what had happened. We were still climbing towards our blue ceiling when a violent wave of air lifted the little aircraft like a blown leaf sideways and fluttered it violently.

If I felt it, then John must have heard it. I imagined the great reverberation drowning the noise of the passionate river below the gorge and ringing out in his ears like a salute of guns royally ordered for a commander who had persevered to the true end of a long campaign, though from the start all the odds had been against him. The thought comforted me as I hoped the sound cheered him.

We landed on Aramis's pre-war landing strip close by the

Mission soon after noon and there and then began some of the most disillusioning weeks of my life. Unduly naïve, perhaps, until this moment I had never doubted that it would be easy for authority to draw what was the obvious moral of the history and evolution of the plot we had both discovered and defeated. For weeks I had lived so close to the horror and the danger of it, that I still hesitated often in my stride on the brightest of days out of retarded fright over how near to disaster we had all been. I had no misgivings whatsoever of being able to convince everyone of the vital importance of preventing a recurrence of so dangerous a state of affairs, a recurrence of events which seemed to me inevitable and which could easily be disastrous unless we all changed our ways. All that was necessary, I believed, was to tell my tale to those in authority, stress the obvious and simple conclusions, and at once a fresh and tremendously invigorating start would be made in Africa. Over and over again on my journey I had said to myself: You only have to come through alive, tell your story, and all will be well, and the thought had sustained me. I had even gone so far as to envisage His Honour urgently summoning a conference with the Secretary of State, Governors, Prime Ministers, and leaders of elected European members of Advisory Councils of the neighbouring territories. At this conference, I could tell them the whole story from beginning to end and propose a few common fundamentals for a new policy in Southern Africa. Indeed, amid all the many circumstances and factors that had brought me near to despair on my journey, ironically this was the one prospect I had never questioned nor feared. But I was soon to know better.

I got the first warning on the aerodrome from Aramis, who insisted on rushing me straight to His Honour, saying he feared that already I might be too late. Apparently His Honour, so grateful at first but now somewhat huffed by my departure, had begun in the past few days to have second thoughts. There was no public issue, however grave, Aramis affirmed, that was debarred from serving the egotistical grievances and vanities of those in command, and H.H., though he would rather die than admit it, felt I'd not taken him seriously enough, and therefore was pretending to himself that it was I who was not worth taking seriously. He was slowly swinging back to his initial attitude that the story relayed to him by his Chief Secretary must be grossly exaggerated and finding a lifetime of cautious training and service ready to aid and abet his conclusions. Perhaps, Aramis shrugged his shoulders, perhaps I could put it right, but he had to warn me.

How grateful I was for that warning afterwards. Frankly, at first I didn't accept it at its face value. Yet I took it just seriously enough to extract from His Honour a reluctant but explicit undertaking that not a word of my story, which I had not as yet told in full to anyone, would ever be made public without my consent. I then spent a whole afternoon and evening with him and Aramis, talking with all the skill and clarity I could command and answering questions that were so beside the point and framed with such incomprehension of the issues involved that time and again I was nearly driven to protest and exclaim: 'For God's sake, if you want the right answers, learn to prepare and ask the right questions.' Just before midnight we broke up without any decision being taken, except that in the morning I was to prepare a confidential memorandum for H.H. which he would study carefully, 'with a view' (those were his final words) 'to formulating a definite recommendation to accompany it to the Secretary of State.'

I spent all the next day and most of the following night doing this, a sense of the desperate urgency of the issue persisting in me, and presented myself with Aramis at H.H.'s door the moment the offices opened the next morning. This time we were not admitted at once but left waiting for half an hour. When at last we entered, H.H. took my report, thanked me politely and then without another glance threw it on top of a file of papers in his tray and began talking polite generalities to me. Though I pressed him to let me know his intentions, he sidestepped the question with expert formality, saying they would depend on the result of his study of the contents of my report as well as the evidence presented by a commission of inquiry which he, on further reflection, was setting up to investigate the whole affair. When that was done, he would gladly let me know his decision. In that connexion, perhaps I would be good enough to leave my address with his Chief Secretary? And now, if I would forgive him and not think him ungrateful, he had an awful lot of work to do.

'Sacred blood of the wood, *mon dieu, mon dieu, mon dieu*!'
Aramis exploded as we got back to his office, an expression of
dismay on his face so profound and undisguised that it was
almost comic, and I might have tried to laugh it off if my mind
had not been driven back instantly to the day I had found His
Honour having an 'entertainment of tennis at his residence'
and to the sense of unreality it had provoked. Kwadiabosigo
and all that might not have happened for all the difference it
made to him, and I could not help telling Aramis now with
some bitterness that his precious Service was rapidly becoming
a kind of museum, artificially preserving dead values and
stuffed attitudes, while the real, contemporary, urgent Africa
of which I had just brought in some slight awareness sailed
unheeded over its head like a thundercloud over the heads of
a nest of twittering sparrows.

He found it impossible to answer me and said so, and I may
say here almost all that ever came of my report was an expan-
sion of the Mission's staff, since its ignorance of the plot was
put down to pressure of work. Also there was a prolonged visit
by an anthropologist sent by the Secretary of State to
Umangoni to report on the ritual and function of native witch-
doctors. After that His Honour's imaginative apprehensions
were satisfied with regard to the whole affair.

Meanwhile, still hopeful of a better outcome elsewhere, I
moved on to the adjacent territories, talking, pleading, arguing,
explaining to all in authority, and I'm glad to say that the
response was not without hope. The minds of some of the
leading men, born and bred in Africa as I was, were not closed
to the dangers of a determined policy of negation on the Dark
Continent, and not afraid of the sustained and thankless effort
needed to change it. However, in the areas which had done
most to provoke the plot, in my father's country south of the
Limpopo, my words fell on wide-open ears but shut and barred
hearts. I might have expected these people, most of them
ardent nationalists, to give me some credit as François de
Beauvilliers's son, but I found the fact that I had fought in the
War nearly cancelled out the effect of his name. It counted
only just enough to make them listen to me.

It was a heart-breaking experience. Ironically, with them,
I had no difficulty in getting my story believed. They accepted

293

it with such ardour that in the end I was made to realize that they believed it in a sense in which it should not have been believed. It fitted in so neatly with their own political theories, they were so ready to put down the causes of the great unrest in Africa to Communism and what they called the innate and ineradicable barbarism and primitive incapacity of the black man, that everything I told them was clasped to their bosom as living, irrefutable confirmation of their narrow prejudices. Over and over again, I wished the plot could have been abetted by some country other than Russia, since that aspect of it seemed to me personally so unimportant as almost to be irrelevant, but they would not allow me or themselves to forget it.

In vain I argued that none of these things would have been possible had we not closed our hearts and minds to the black people in Africa, that they would all recur again with fuller, more desperate orchestration unless we changed, not Russia, but ourselves. Everything that had happened in Umangoni, I said, the sudden increase in ritual murder and eating of human flesh, which I'd encountered all over Africa since the War, were merely the symptoms of our terrible failure to integrate the displaced, de-tribalized, the bewildered African into our community; our criminal unwillingness to give him the shelter of our firmest values against the militant darkness which forever threatens any being shut out from the light of honourable communion with the rest of mankind. I told them how terrible a reflection I found it that, after all these years of contact with us, the 'Takwena and others now tended to turn for reassurance and inspiration, not to us, but to their once discarded and discredited past. I said I was old enough to remember some of the feeling of wonder and hope that the coming of the European had brought to many parts of Africa. The white man had been almost a kind of god to the African and, alas, subtly and fatally tempted as a result to exceed his common humanity. For generations the African had been happy to live in the hope of something better coming to him from the white man. But that hope was now running rapidly dry through our persistence in denying him his dignity and his own special capacity and honour as a human being.

The people to whom I spoke, both official and otherwise,

smiled a superior, tolerant smile at this and called me 'broad' and 'liberal', so often that I became angry. I asked them to read history and learn that, invisible and imponderable as these things were to our physical senses, they were nonetheless vital; no human being could live indefinitely without honour and dignity. They could deny it temporarily to the African, but not indefinitely, no matter how much they bribed him by better wages and the like. The history of what was happening to the white man in the East was a terrifying illustration of the futility of so one-sided and materialistic an approach.

'How strange that you should be so concerned about the honour and dignity of these people, Meneer de Beauvilliers,' one of the ministers exclaimed, 'after what you have told us of their disloyalty, their cruel superstitious practices and degrading belief in witchcraft.'

'No stranger, sir,' I told him, 'than that you should be concerned about the honour and dignity of a people who were responsible for most of the horrors of two world wars: for Belsen, and lampshades made out of the skins of coldly-murdered Jewish victims. If your sympathy is understandable for a people who did all this out of a sense of power, then is not mine justified for a people who acted out of a sense of fear, out of profound and real insecurity?'

I went on to maintain that in everything that happened to humanity we all, positively and negatively, shared not only in the effects, but also in the responsibility. We all, actively or by omission, were party to the plot, accessories before or after the criminal fact. What was important, and doubly so in the case of the white man in Africa, since he was in command, was to get clear our own contribution to the unrest that was driving the black man mad individually as well as collectively, for the process was going on ceaselessly night and day, weaving in and out like the woof and shuttle of the ancient, tragic Fates, manufacturing the Lindelbaums, Harkovs, Ghinzas, and Umbombulimos of life. As I said that I'd looked up as if expecting to see some slight crack in their sub-human determined front. But all I saw was an expression on their self-indulgent faces as unhumble and set as any I had ever seen on the faces of Ghinza or Harkov. I argued no more, for they, on their side of the fence, were what Harkov had been on his;

what was needed was someone, something big enough to straddle both.

I rose sadly to say good-bye, and suddenly I saw in my mind's eye my father, Oom Pieter, my mother, and the long succession of Afrikaner pioneering faces and figures I had known in my boyhood, spare, generous, upright, fearing God but no man, always venturing courageously on and on into Africa's dark interior. Is this how the Great Trek for a better life is to end? I asked myself passionately. Is there no one great enough to take over the adventure and carry it on in some other dimension, to carry it on from world without to world within? Close to despair, I left them and their ostentatious offices in their capital looking as un-African on that grey old koppie as a top hat on a Zulu.

I had failed utterly for the moment, and in the days that followed the evidence of the extent of my failure multiplied. In my despair I wanted to write the story as I've written it here, telling of the nobility of mountain, plain, lake, and forest, of the vivid animal, and the black African life as I'd found it on my journey, and to contrast it with the sordid conclusions of our coward way of living. But I was barred from doing that by the knowledge that publication might mean death to Serge, John, and his future enterprise. I have only been able to write this story at this late hour because of something which has just happened to make it possible. Immediately that moment arrived, poorly-equipped as I am, I've hastened to pursue hunterwise this unfamiliar spoor in the dark continent of meaning, until it now remains only for me to close my personal and private pages in the tale.

After this defeat in the capital of my father's country, I returned to Port Natal. One of the conditions of my telling my story had been that Lindelbaum, if I revealed his name, should not be prosecuted. I had persuaded everyone that he, an old and very sick man now, could not be held responsible for his actions. Accordingly, no sooner had I arrived than I went out to see him, for I had something to tell him that I felt was important.

At 'Higher-than-the-Trees' I was conducted by a Zulu butler through the house into a garden beginning to flame with spring, and there found Lindelbaum in a bath-chair, a uniformed nurse and his ridgeback beside him, the latter bristling as I approached. One look at Lindelbaum, however, was enough to show me that whatever sentence was necessary had already been passed on him by life. He had had a severe stroke and was in his chair immovable, staring out of his diminishing self at the tender re-beginning of light and life in the garden around him. On his face was an expression I'd first seen that night at the window when he had exclaimed: 'God knows, it's long been time.'

'His doctor, sir,' the nurse whispered to me, 'says he'll never speak or move again, but he does hear and understand quite a bit.'

I went and knelt by his chair, and, looking into his eyes, asked: 'Mr. Lindelbaum, can you hear me?'

He didn't move, but I thought the light in his dark eyes signalled understanding.

'I'm François de Beauvilliers's son, I am Pierre de Beauvilliers.' I paused to let that sink in and again something in his eyes told me that we were both far back in time, joined in a memory of his first appearance in my father's camp with the storm rising fast over the bush, and the acacia tops crying like hurt puppies over our heads. So I went on: 'I've come to tell you that nothing bad happened in Umangoni. You can face what is left of life with that comfort. Harkov is dead. He died because his ways were evil, but I, and others better than I, will try as long as we live to put right the injustices which you suffered so cruelly and hated so much.' At that he closed his eyes as if tired and wanting to sleep, but suddenly I saw the tears coming from underneath the closed lids and running down his cheeks.

'There, you've gone and upset him,' the nurse reproached me sternly.

'I hope not,' I countered. 'Perhaps I've just taken a load off his mind.'

I turned to find the ridgeback licking my hand and rubbing his head against my knee. Somehow I took that as a sign and left in a lighter mood than I'd come.

From 'Higher-than-the-Trees', I went back to Umangoni, not to the capital but to Amantazuma. Ostensibly I went to provide for the families of my murdered servants and to see

297

Tickie and Said, whom I'd sent there on leave. In reality I went because somehow my return to Petit France had been spoiled for me by the stubborn quarrels I'd had with the leaders of my own countrymen in recent weeks. I felt isolated and perturbed by the glimpse that my failure gave me of the giant shadow of back-door barbarism which our one-sided culture inevitably begets, and in need of rejuvenation in the spring of a more natural and spontaneous way of living.

But I quickly discovered it was no good blaming the world for my restlessness, nor even for the anguish which haunted me over the death of Umtumwa, Oom Pieter, and the others. The truth was beyond all that. I was profoundly ill at ease within myself and suspected more and more I was failing in some vital but unexplained issue of my own.

So I stayed only a week in Amantazuma. I engaged new servants to take the place of the old. I tried in vain to persuade Said to return to his own people but he rose in open rebellion at the first mention of the idea, characteristically bombarded me with rhetorical questions, and announced firmly at the end: 'Effendi, where you go, I go. Allah brought us together, and in the name of Allah, let us go on together to the end.' So I had to leave it at that, and I accepted it gladly because he and Tickie had become such firm friends. They walked about Amantazuma everywhere like heroes back from a Trojan beachhead, their little fingers linked together.

I arranged for Said and Tickie to follow me to Petit France with the other servants in a month's time, and prepared to make my return there at once. The evening before I left I was glad to observe one of the most comely 'Takwena girls, a soft cream blanket wrapped gracefully around her so that one black marble shoulder and one firm shining breast was exposed, one bangled arm holding the blanket to her middle and the other occasionally going to feel the grass mat on her head on which a crimson jar of beer was balanced, walking with sure-footed, effortless grace down the slope to where Said and Tickie were sitting talking and smoking outside a hut. She sank down on her knees behind them without a word, took the jar from her head and placed it on the ground in front of her. Then, with her long hands in her long lap, she sat waiting, eyes demurely fixed on the ground, without saying a word. I could tell that

298

Tickie, though he hadn't turned his head, knew that she was there, for his manner and speech suddenly became charged with electric self-importance. With an enormous effort of will he ignored her for some moments, then at last, without turning his head, made a lordly gesture for her to come forward and present her gift.

'I congratulate you, O Tickie,' I said to him afterwards, watching his hands come up to hide the inevitable smile. 'Nandisipoh indeed throws a shadow.' But as I said it, I realized I was almost envious of him and I left, all the more restless for having seen the incident.

At four in the afternoon of the last Saturday in November, I returned to Petit France. It was two days earlier than I'd expected, because an appointment I'd made to have another talk in the capital of the Union with a Minister was cancelled at the last moment. Rather than spend a week-end alone with my devastated recollections I just had time, on the spur of the moment, to jump into an aeroplane bound for the Cape. But I had no time to telegraph Bill that I was coming.

I was not surprised, therefore, as I climbed up the steps of my stoep to find the house silent and empty. The doors and windows were all shut in accordance with the routine I had always observed in the warm weather, the wings of green shutters tightly folded hiding the soap bubble gleam of light I loved in the seventeenth-century glass of the broad panes. But the front door, though shut, was not locked. Trying the handle, I noticed my cluster of Masai spears neatly re-arranged, my mind not failing to draw my attention to the fact that one was missing.

I opened the door and went in. How cool and how dark it was after the heat and light outside, and how still! The only sound was a swish of sea on the shining beaches outside, and the ceiling creaking above me, like the deck of a ship taking a swell at the harbour bar.

Peering down the long passageway I called first in Sindakwena, then Afrikaans, and finally in English: 'Is there anyone in?' No answer came. Still, I wasn't surprised. Saturday was one of Bill's busiest days. Thinking I'd telephone him presently at his office, I put my light suitcase down and went through to the kitchen. It, too, was empty. The blinds were

299

drawn, and behind them some flies trapped between darkness and light buzzed feverishly against the burning glass. There was no fire in the open hearth, but the kettle was humming and the rare soup-sweet smell of fluffy Boer buns baking in the oven hung in the air. 'Looks as if Bill's coming back for tea,' I thought, oppressed by the emptiness and darkness of Petit France rushing in so readily to join the loneliness and sense of meaningless within.

I strode quickly to the back door and threw it open to let in the light, and the alert brilliant afternoon pounced on my eyes like a lion on a buck. I stood there blinking helplessly for a moment, seeing and feeling the light like a tumble in the boiling, foaming surf of an angry sea.

'Anyone there?' I called again, blinking in the sunshine. But no reply came. I walked across the courtyard. The rooms were shut and empty. I decided I'd go over and see Diamond.

But Diamond's loose-box in the stables, too, was empty, the half-doors wide open. 'So Bill's out riding,' I told myself, yet for all that feeling more and more depressed, even resentful that my own favourite horse should not be there to welcome me and that the whole place had too readily found another way of life and all too soon cast out all memory and expectation of me.

I turned and went back fast into the house, a fugitive from the greater emptiness and indifference without.

I went first into my study, where a lovely scent of freesias, in delicacy and tender innocence as truly and unexpectedly African as the flamingo-flame, or Kilimanjaro's giant strength, came out of the room to meet me. Quickly I drew the curtains, opened the windows, and threw wide the shutters. The room was starry with flowers, skilfully arranged. But even freesias and their beloved scent could not anchor my attention to the room for long. Soon I was back at a window looking hungrily over the shining blue waters of the great False Bay, to the overhanging Cape and the blue line of the Hottentots–Holland Mountains, beginning the great music of the ancient mythological theme of the greater Africa beyond, from which I'd come, and looking very much as they did that morning when I saw them over the head of the frightened *Star of Truth* sneaking out of the Bay. Only there was this difference: the angle of their shadow then showed them bound for the day, whereas now they were heading for the night. Between them and me big South Atlantic gulls flashed in and out of the afternoon light like the sun on glass. Sometimes they wheeled swiftly inshore and wailed urgently overhead like plovers at night in the Dead Land or else cried with nostalgic longing to my senses bound so irrevocably to this marooned ship, Petit France, cried as if pleading with them to free themselves and to resume their journey and return to that great ocean of land which had borne me and from which I had just come. So agonizing did that call of gulls, the restless switch of the siren-singing sea flicking the tense summer silence into ripples of sound about me become, that I turned my back sharply on it and went to my writing-table. There were no letters on it for me, only a stack of telegrams, from Aramis, from Fort Herald, from Government House, Salisbury, from Lusaka, Livingstone, Entebbe, Zomba, Diaz Bay, and Colonel de Fereira, all asking: 'Where do you wish your mail sent?' 'When are you returning this way?' 'What has happened to you?'

Almost automatically I sat down at the table, and my eyes fell on the photograph of Joan and me sitting on our horses in the surf of the shining African sea of that very Bay at which I had just been looking. That finished it. All my conscious resistances collapsed and the cause of my own private and personal unrest flashed like the lightning of a long threatened storm at the windows of my mind. I was tired of myself. I was tired of a life wherein I was only an odd half, for ever condemned to repeat only its incomplete self. I remembered how complete and whole had been those short weeks, years back in the schoolgirl Joan's company, and I realized how much I had counted on meeting her at the end of my journey. Not all the arguments and impediments of a carefully-conditioned reason had been able to dispose of that profound and secret hope.

Seeing thus darkly in the glass of my own heart, I heard far away in another dimension of my senses the noise of a horse's shoe remotely striking a flint in the stable-yard, to be followed a while later by a murmur of voices in the kitchen. However, so bitter and profound was my concentration, that I was incapable of drawing any conclusions from the sound. I went on staring at the photograph in front of me, emotion in me

301

crying out: you might have written, left word, a crumb of something for me, seeing all I did for you.

Then I heard a gasp somewhere close at hand, but so low I couldn't tell exactly where the sound came from. I lifted my eyes from the photograph to the round French mirror over the great fireplace, and looked straight into the cool reflection of the door wide open to the main passage. In its centre was the vision, not so much changed as fulfilled, of the face of Joan as I had seen it first in church. For a moment I thought I must be mad, and then all the scattered elements of my lonely, bereaved, and incomplete being seemed to come together and into focus on the lovely face in the mirror.

I stared for one brief second then jumped up, the chair falling over as I swung violently about. The door stood wide open, and there was Joan.

'Forgive me,' I said to excuse my rough, startled self as I started towards her, 'I thought you were in England . . . I'd no idea. I thought you were gone for good.'

'I've been and just come back,' she answered, her eyes never leaving my face and her voice trembling. 'Didn't you get my letters? Didn't you know I couldn't go until . . .'

She stopped short for, as I came near to greet her, the light from the window for the first time falling full on my face, her voice suddenly seemed to fail her. I believe we both saw each other at that moment through a blur, but what she saw was enough to make her cry out: 'Oh Pierre, my darling Pierre, what have they done to you all these years?'

Then quickly, like someone long convinced of the limitation of words, she came to meet me, clasped her hands behind my neck and holding me thus, lifted up her face as she had done once eleven years before. I took her in my arms and the grim, inarticulate years between us instantly vanished.

And there I must leave it. In most lives, and particularly in a life such as mine, points of departure inevitably are arbitrary, so are ends; are ends, indeed, only of other beginnings. This end, too, which comes down like a curtain upon us is the end only of that search which brings a man to the threshold of his private and personal task, the task that life demands of him day and night in his blood: to live with love out of love; to live the vision beyond reason or time which draws him from

302

the centre of his being as the vision of Joan drew me in spite of my fearful, conscious self. To serve this vision, to protect it against all plausible substitutes, reasonable approximations and coward compromises is still, I believe, the knightly duty of contemporary man. If he shirks it I believe he shall never know inner peace. If a man accepts the challenge, however, even if his vision is never confirmed, as mine was, in flesh and blood, but forever beckons him in a quicksilver reflection of a cause beyond himself, then he has only to remain steadfast in pursuit of it and his life will achieve, as John's has done, something which is greater than happiness and unhappiness: and that is meaning.